IRISH FIRE

"Will you have me bend a knee and ask for your hand?" Taggart asked, amusement twinkling in his eyes.

"I would never ask you to grovel at my feet, Taggart, for it is a husband you would be, never a servant," Millicent answered, her love for him shining in her eyes. "Is it not customary to shake hands during these negotiations, sir?" she added impishly. When he did not answer, Millicent began to turn away to get a parchment and quill. However, a muffled cry of surprise escaped her lips when he hauled her back against his hard body.

"English hellion," he muttered, only half in jest. "We Irish seal our bargains with more directness than stuffy English fops." He pressed his lips to hers, firmly, then more forcefully, and it delighted him when he felt her fiery response to him. Perhaps, he mused, marrying Lady Millicent Fitzroy would not be such a sacrifice after all, for this first kiss between them did, indeed, hold many possibilities. . . .

ZEBRA'S GOT THE ROMANCE
TO SET YOUR HEART AFIRE!

RAGING DESIRE (2242, $3.75)
by Colleen Faulkner

A wealthy gentleman and officer in General Washington's army, Devon Marsh wasn't meant for the likes of Cassie O'Flynn, an immigrant bond servant. But from the moment their lips first met, Cassie knew she could love no other . . . even if it meant marching into the flames of war to make him hers!

TEXAS TWILIGHT (2241, $3.75)
by Vivian Vaughan

When handsome Trace Garrett stepped onto the porch of the Santa Clara ranch, he wove a rapturous spell around Clara Ehler's heart. Though Clara planned to sell the spread and move back East, Trace was determined to keep her on the wild Western frontier where she belonged — to share with him the glory and the splendor of the passion-filled TEXAS TWILIGHT.

RENEGADE HEART (2244, $3.75)
by Marjorie Price

Strong-willed Hannah Hatch resented her imprisonment by Captain Jake Farnsworth, even after the daring Yankee had rescued her from bloodthirsty marauders. And though Jake's rock-hard physique made Hannah tremble with desire, the spirited beauty was nevertheless resolved to exploit her femininity to the fullest and gain her independence from the virile bluecoat.

LOVING CHALLENGE (2243, $3.75)
by Carol King

When the notorious Captain Dominic Warbrooke burst into Laurette Harker's eighteenth birthday ball, the accomplished beauty challenged the arrogant scoundrel to a duel. But when the captain named her innocence as his stakes, Laurette was terrified she'd not only lose the fight, but her heart as well!

Forbidden Hearts

MARY BURKHARDT

ZEBRA BOOKS
KENSINGTON PUBLISHING CORP.

ZEBRA BOOKS

are published by

Kensington Publishing Corp.
475 Park Avenue South
New York, NY 10016

First printing: December, 1988

Printed in the United States of America

To the memory of my father, Francis Michael Donovan of Oswego, New York. His gentle ways showed me the quiet honor in dedicated hard work.

Chapter 1

Kinsale, Ireland, July 1740

Sixteen-year-old Taggart O'Rahilly stood watching the tranquil beauty of the water once more. It might only be the estuary of the River Bandon, but he loved this picturesque little harbor.

Thin and tall, Taggart had never owned a suit of clothes that were new. His unruly black hair whipped around his rawboned face. He was dressed in work breeches, gray stockings, and an old coat given to him by Squire Nolan. The Irishman squared his shoulders, realizing it was time to go back.

He winced. His ill-fitting clothes reminded him of the healing welts across his back, which still pulled. Geoffrey Fitzroy, the Earl of Holingbrook could whip a man's back with vigor, Taggart thought bitterly. The other day Fitzroy had beaten him for merely pointing out that the older horse the earl wished to ride could not carry his lordship's increasing girth. His dark eyes scanned the rocky shore of the wide and sheltered harbor, then looked higher to take in the green hills, with their light and dark stones. But Ireland was no more than a prison to him now. The English had seen to that. How he wished for the sea. To sail away—away from Fitzroy Hall forever. But who would take care of Edna?

With a sigh of bitter resignation, Taggart trudged back up the hill toward the Fitzroy stables.

*   *   *

Lady Millicent Fitzroy clung shakily to the narrow branch. When she ventured a look down at her younger friend, the twelve-year-old felt worse. "It's all your fault," she murmured at the small bit of fluff cradled against her right arm.

"Is Mittens all right?" Edna O'Rahilly asked anxiously. The cat meant everything to the petite child. Without toys and now that her brother was kept busier by the earl and his constant faultfinding, Edna found Taggart had little time to play with her anymore.

"Yes . . . ah, Mittens is fine," Millicent shouted down. "But. . . ." Her words were cut off as the old branch started to crack ominously. Instantly Millicent scampered back to the thicker part of the gnarled limb. Still holding her friend's precious pet, she used her free hand to push back a few strands of her straight auburn hair, which had escaped from under her white ruffled pinner. Feeling protective of her smaller friend, she'd insisted on being the one to do the daring rescue. Only she hadn't realized until now just how far the branch was from the ground. As she watched the earth below, she almost wished she hadn't kept her glasses on. Most ladies only used their round wire frames for reading, the housekeeper, Mrs. Halsey pointed out constantly. However, Millicent was never one for fashion beyond reason. After she found they helped her see better all the time, she kept them on.

"Oh . . . be careful. Millie!" Edna screeched, her black curls bobbing up and down as she wrung her hands, completely forgetting to address her ladyship properly. "Ya best be wantin' me ta go for help." Emotion made her brogue thicker.

Relieved that Edna had been the one to bring it up, Millicent nodded from her precarious perch. "My brother should have returned by now," she offered.

Edna delighted in the opportunity. English he might be, but she liked Dunstan Fitzroy very much. At fifteen, he was five years older than herself, tall like his sister, with reddish-brown hair and the kindest gray eyes she'd ever seen. The plainly dressed Irish girl wasted no time racing toward the brick mansion.

"Stay calm," whispered Millicent to her charge. The sleeping kitten seemed oblivious to their plight. "Dignity," she

8

mouthed Mrs. Halsey's often repeated words. However, when she looked down at herself she couldn't hold back a wince. Her striped frock had smudges of dirt across it, and there was a large tear near the bottom, where a piece of once white lace trailed below her skirt. The severe Mrs. Halsey would be furious. Proper English ladies did not climb trees, nor did they "consort" with "dirty Irish peasants," the Engligh housekeeper was fond of saying. Mrs. Halsey and her somber husband, Benton, virtually ran the house and grounds. Why not? Millicent asked herself as she sat down uncomfortably on the tree limb. Her father took little interest in anything but drinking, gambling, racing his horses, and what she overheard their cook call "bits of muslin."

Another glance downward brought a frown to Millicent's fine-boned features. She moved her wire frames farther up on the narrow bridge of her nose. Edna was coming back alone.

"Oh, it's sorrier than I can say," wailed the distraught Edna. "Dunstan . . . I mean the Viscount Fitzroy isn't back from the Somersets' yet. What shall we do? I . . . Oh!" shouted the child mid-sentence. "I'll get Taggart. He's in the stable yard with the new foal."

Before Millicent could protest, Edna was making a dash down the meadow toward the stables. Since coming here from London two years ago after the death of her mother, Millicent had taken to the two O'Rahillys instantly. But in truth, she dreaded having her hero see her in such an undignified position.

The corners of her mouth turned upward as she thought of Taggart. At sixteen Taggart O'Rahilly was a magnificent god to her—black wavy hair, brown eyes that sparkled when he laughed, fine strong features even if he was a little underweight, and that wonderful deep dimple in the center of his chin. Oh, she thought dreamily, he was her knight in armor, coming to rescue the beauti—That word dashed her romantic musings. It was an adjective no one but her mother had ever used in referring to her. How she missed her mother. Catching herself, she forced her thoughts away from these sad musings. Today should be a happy day. It was her thirteenth birthday, and there would be a party this afternoon.

In minutes Edna returned, dragging her brother with her. "Come on, Taggart. Hurry."

Despite her efforts, Millicent felt her heart flutter and her face grow warm when she looked down to see Edna's brother.

Hands on either side of his waist, Taggart O'Rahilly shook his head as he eyed his employer's daughter in the large oak tree. "Now is it a bird ya are, Lady Millicent?" he asked with a chuckle.

Returning his good-natured teasing, the lady in question eyed the toes of her yellow satin slippers. "I dare say," she replied pertly. "Will you kindly ask Benton to have my tea brought up here?" Then she studied him for a moment.

He was dressed in gray knee breeches, worn boots, and hip-length coat with short, unpleated side vents. The uncuffed sleeves of his plain coat only reached halfway down his arms. He'd grown so fast these last few years, his meager two suits of clothes hadn't kept up with him. The one time she'd offered to purchase a new suit of clothes for him, that cool look entered his dark eyes and he'd promptly thanked her but refused the donation. Yes, he was proud, she thought. Any future kindnesses to the O'Rahillys would have to be done more discreetly. Gingerly, she stood up once more.

"Is it tea you'd be wantin', then?" Taggart's eyes danced with suppressed laughter. He glanced down affectionately at his little sister. "And it's herself comes racin' after me, cryin' loud enough to wake the saints. Her friend's stuck in a tree says she." He paused, enjoying the expressions of the two girls.

"Well," he continued, "I've got work to do and can't be playin' games." He made a move as if to leave.

"Oh, wait!" Millicent cried, truly afraid he was going to abandon her. "Please, Taggart, will you help me down?"

"Indeed," added Edna, her green eyes flashing fire. "That a brother of mine would leave the Lady herself standin' up there," scolded the little girl. "And after she'd rescued me cat. 'Tis ashamed of ya I am."

A bark of laughter escaped the young man's sensuous lips. He reached down and tousled Edna's curls. "Now, did ya really think I'd leave her up there?" he asked gently.

Edna's shrewd eyes stayed with her older brother when he

tossed off his coat. "Well," she added softly, as she accepted his coat and folded it over her arm. "With you I can't always be sure. I know how you dislike the English, and you've made no secret ta Colleen and me how much ya despise his lordship." She looked up, her eyes pleading. "But Millie's not like the others. She's kind and—"

"Is she so different?"

But before Edna could defend her friend, Taggart was climbing up the tree.

When he reached Millicent, he knew she was nervous and trying hard to hide it. "'Tis a fine day for a climb," he said, then smiled up at the English girl.

She returned his smile shyly. "Yes, but I . . . I believe I'm not the climber I used to be. The last time I tried this I had on an old pair of Dunstan's breeches. It was a lot easier then."

"If you hold on to your sleeping friend there and keep one arm around my neck, I think we can all get down safe enough. Agreed?"

"Agreed," she answered. Her complete trust in the young man showed from behind her round wire frames. She took a step forward, ready to climb lower to meet his outstretched arms. But the branch gave way, and she cried out his name in fear.

Instantly, Taggart grabbed for the closest part of her that came crashing down at him. His viselike grip clamped over her right wrist. He dragged her against his body on the wide, steady branch where he crouched.

A cry of pain escaped her tightly held lips as her wrist felt on the verge of breaking. Still doggedly clinging to Mittens, she tried to halt the tears that stung her eyes when the pain in her thin wrist increased. She made no angry protest because she knew Taggart had done what was necessary. She owed her life to this man. The fall to the hard earth below might have killed her.

How she wished it had taken longer to descend the tree once they were out of danger. Resting her cheek against Taggart's shoulder, clinging to his lean yet strong frame, Millicent felt close to heaven. When he placed her ruined slippers on the green grass below, she felt disappointed at the loss of his arms.

11

"Thank you," she said earnestly. She handed the kitten back to a grateful Edna.

Bowing slightly, the O'Rahilly groom smiled down at the tall English girl. But when he noticed her already discolored wrist he frowned. "Is it hurt ya are?" he asked, forgetting his place and tenderly taking the small wrist in his own large hand. His work-rough fingers had never felt such soft, silky skin.

"I. . . ." Feeling embarrassed, Millicent pulled back her hand. "It's nothing," she said lightly. "Even when I bump into things if I'm not wearing my spectacles, my skin turns all sorts of rainbow colors."

"I'll have to remember how easily ya bruise, *Gealbhan.*"

"You've called me that before," she stated. Did it mean "goddess" or something equally romantic? she wondered hopefully.

"'Tis Gaelic for 'sparrow,'" replied her rescuer.

"Oh." Millicent tried to hide her brief disappointment. She'd hoped for something more earthshaking. Well, she told herself, it wasn't so bad compared to what a few neighboring English children called her, especially Edwin Somerset. And Taggart had said it with affection. Looking up, she gave Taggart an engaging smile. Happier than she'd been in a long time, she blurted, "And I do want you and Edna to come to my party this afternoon."

"Taggart, did ya hear? A party!" Edna cried and jumped up in her excitement.

It was Millicent's first party since her mother died. But why should Taggart look so displeased? she wondered.

Frowning, Taggart turned to his sister. "Shouldn't you be back in the kitchen helping Colleen?" he asked, forcing himself to sound more authoritative than he wanted.

"But . . . the party, surely we can—"

Right now Taggart was more parent than brother. Edna's green eyes narrowed. "Your coat." She handed it over, then turned sullenly and headed for the main house, still clutching her kitten.

Millicent felt her back straighten. Her narrow chin pointed slightly at a haughty angle, a habit which surfaced unconsciously with temper. She felt chagrined at his obvious refusal.

And as much as she tried to deny it, something cut inside to think he wouldn't even come to her birthday party or allow her dearest friend to attend, either. With a toss of her head, she gathered her skirts and proceeded to step around her companion. She'd only gone two steps when Taggart's voice stopped her.

"Lady Millicent," he grated formally, "a moment please." His fingers tightened around the coat he'd tossed over one shoulder. Though his tone was polite, arrogance sparked the "request." When he thought of his sweet little sister's fallen expression, his jaw clenched. This English girl probably meant well, but she was such a child when it came to the way things really were in Ireland. He tried to push down his bitter frustration. Though he and Edna were lucky to have a small thatch-roofed cottage for themselves, most Irish Catholics he knew lived in squalor. They were forbidden to purchase land, teach school, or vote. Not only did they have to pay tithes to the Established Church even though they weren't Anglican, they also had to pay increasing rents to those fat English landlords who sat in their clubs in London living off Irish sweat and toil. His mouth became a grim line when he remembered his father had once been the head groom here. And when the present earl decided to cease being an absentee landlord, one of the first things he'd done was have Taggart's father arrested and hung for treason. True, his father had wanted the English landowners to lower their constantly increasing rents, but his gentle father had never been a rabble-rouser.

Taggart's expression became colder. Who, he wondered, was the Englishman who had informed on his father? Someday, he vowed, he'd find that bastard and pay him back.

When Millicent turned slowly to face the Irishman, she caught her breath. Did he look ready to murder someone? She stepped back a pace, then caught herself. After all, she was the daughter of an earl. How dare he try to frighten her. "Well," she demanded with bravado. "What is it?"

Taggart hadn't missed the uneasiness in her gray eyes. He swallowed his rage, a habit he was becoming very tired of these last two years since her father came here. Did she know how her father treated his servants? How could she think he and his sister would be allowed to sit down for tea and cake with all those snobs?

"Your height makes you appear older," he let slip. "I keep forgettin' what a child ya are. Surely, you must realize your father would never allow two Irish Catholics—a groom and a kitchen maid—attend his English aristocratic daughter's birthday party. Though we're not dirty or ignorant, thanks to Father Michael Collins teaching us to read and write in secret," he went on with sarcasm. "You honestly think 'tis the earl himself will welcome us with open arms this afternoon? Along with all your fancy-dressed English friends?"

So grateful for his rescue and delighting in the warm summer day, until now Millicent hadn't considered anything but her desire to share her happiness with the two people she felt most comfortable with. But now, the truth of Taggart's words slashed her. Gray eyes misted with unshed tears as she realized how hurt and disappointed Edna was going to be and how she'd inadvertently insulted the man before her. "I . . ." Words of apology seemed to fail her.

Without saying another word, Taggart shrugged into his coat and left.

Millicent could only stare after him. It never occurred to her that she could easily have him punished for such insolence. As she walked slowly back toward the large brick mansion, each step gave her more confidence. Rarely did she ask her father for anything, usually more than happy to stay out of his way, but this was an emergency. By heaven, she would have the two O'Rahillys sitting across from her this afternoon.

"Will you join me in a glass of claret?" Geoffrey Fitzroy poured an ample amount of the amber liquid into a crystal goblet.

"Thank you, my lord . . . but I fear it is a little too early in the day for me," John Nolan replied. Nervously, he watched the wide face across from his become redder. Squire Nolan cleared his throat and fidgeted in the brocade-covered wing chair.

Geoffrey shrugged his shoulder and eased his short frame

14

back down on the cushioned mahogany chair. He studied his fashionably dressed guest. "You're a man after my own heart, not just because you've lent me so much money, but despite your unfortunate heritage you have sense enough to rise above it. Years ago you gave up that enemy religion and became Anglican. You act more English than Irish. As a practicing member of the Church of England, you married a wealthy Englishwoman, settled down, became a member of the landed gentry. You've a skilled hand; why, I let you pen all my letters. Never could master a good scroll. These," he added holding up his chubby hands, "are more suited to subtle maneuvers, like hauling the garters off a woman's shanks. Now, I ask, why can't more of your countrymen be like us?"

John Nolan's smile was strained. At thirty, he was a handsome man, with a disciplined body and perceptive hazel eyes. "Well, my lord, you know the Irish can be a bit stubborn at times."

"Harumph." The earl's fingers tightened around the stem of his glass. "Like that bloody O'Rahilly and his two spawn." He adjusted his periwig, which began to slip with his animated gestures. "Ought to handle the lot of them like we did O'Rahilly. And the son's going to be just like him, you mark my words. Why, this very week he had the affront to criticize me. All but called me fat when I went to ride one of my older horses. But I'll beat that insolent manner out of him yet." The man of fifty stabbed the air with his finger, and his jowls moved in agitation. "You have to show these people who is their master. The whole bloody lot of them ought to be drowned in the Irish Sea."

Obviously used to the earl's outbursts, Squire Nolan looked down at the gold buttons on his waistcoat. He brushed a few beads of moisture away from his forehead. His full brown wig was too warm on such a hot day. "Quite right, my lord. Would you like me to have a word with young O'Rahilly about his disrespectful attitude toward you?" the squire offered.

Lost in his thoughts, the earl didn't answer at first. He plunked his glass down on the dark tea table to his right. Then he got out of his chair and walked across the beige-and-black Oriental carpet. His dark coat matched his mood. "Imagine," he demanded from the seated guest behind him. "The chit wanted to ask those two O'Rahillys to the party this afternoon. God's blood!"

"Well," he added, turning back to look at Nolan, clearly dismissing the other man's Irishness. "I put a stop to that in a hurry. It's bad enough I'm forced to live in this godforsaken part of the world. I'll not have the enemy at my table, guzzling my wine, or hurting my delicate ears with their singsong way of speaking. Damn me, if Colleen Mulcahy wasn't such a good cook, I'd toss her out tomorrow with her wastrel husband, that long-winded Fergus. Ask that man the time of day," grumbled the earl, "and it's more than likely he'll go on for an hour about the beauty of the harbor. Man's a blithering idiot."

"I will not ask how your trip to London went."

The earl's shoulders dropped. "God, John, how long will the king punish me? How I miss White's." Geoffrey looked his friend in the eye. "I practically begged him to let me return to London, but he wouldn't hear of it. Said the scandal hadn't died down yet." His watery eyes pleaded with his confidant. "How was I to know the stupid girl was a niece to the King's cousin? Nolan, I swear I wish I'd never set eyes on the minx. I curse the day I met her at that palace ball. And the little slut loved it," he muttered under his breath.

John Nolan sat silently, feeling it was the best approach. The scandal had even reached Ireland. Geoffrey obviously hadn't counted on the girl running to the king when she became pregnant with the earl's bastard. The child had died at birth, but it hadn't erased the damage done to the girl's reputation, or the pain it caused the earl's wife. Shocked at the scandal, Lady Milicent's mother had died giving premature birth to a dead son. London society was closed to him. His landholdings in Ireland were the only concession the king would grant.

"I hate this country," the earl grumbled.

Squire Nolan cleared his throat, clearly attempting to think of something to say. "Two years have gone by swiftly. Why, Lady Millicent is almost a young woman now," he added hopefully.

"Bah, be grateful you don't have children," the earl countered. "That's another thorn in my side." He moved over

16

to his chair and sat down once more. "With a face like the back end of a horse and those damn spectacles she always wears, it will cost me a fortune to marry her off. Who wants a bluestocking for a wife? A plain brown wren, just like her mother. The one saving grace her mother had was lots of money."

"Oh," John protested. "But I've heard such wonderful things about Lady Millicent. Why, the countryfolk admire her. She visits the sick and older people of the village, helps—"

"That's the bloody part about it," complained the earl. "The stubborn chit would rather spend time with those dirty Irish peasants than with her own kind. Says the English children tease her. Well, why wouldn't they? If she'd take more interest in acting like a proper English lady, they wouldn't tease her. I lay that at her mother's door. The fool woman used to do the same nonsense in London, dragging Millicent along with her."

"Mind you," Geoffrey went on, "I'm going to see that she marries young Edwin Somerset in a few more years. And I've told her so. The Somersets are a good English family. Though I've no need of his money now, it won't hurt to have a wealthy son-in-law for my old age."

"Forgive me, my lord, but . . ." John hesitated.

"Well, what is it?"

"I had always imagined the older boy to be your first choice. At twenty-three now, Nigel will be just the right husband in a few years for—" The harsh laughter from his companion slashed his sentence.

"Nigel Somerset? Nolan, you cannot be serious. An Anglican priest for a son-in-law? God's nightshirt, isn't he the imbecile who goes about the ground talking to mushrooms?"

"I believe," the squire remarked with new force, "Nigel catalogues them in a notebook and later makes more detailed sketches."

"Hah!" The earl looked coldly at his friend. "So, the Somersets sent the fool of the family into the clergy. A good place for him. With Millicent for a mother, my future grandson will get nothing in looks. Hang it all, if I do as you suggest and let Nigel hump her, the child will also be without brains."

Geofrey Fitzroy raised his hand, giving the death sentence to John's next words. "No, she marries Edwin. Am I not king in my own house?" the earl demanded.

Unfortunately, at this moment he became a trifle unsteady on his black leather shoes and would have keeled over had not Squire Nolan dashed over to his side in time.

"Thank you, John." The earl puffed as he regained his balance. "We Englishmen have to stick together in this country. Can't have a lot of heathens taking over. We may be outnumbered but we're superior." A loud belch punctuated his sentence.

Chapter 2

Millicent looked down at her piece of cake once more. Though she tried to be the hospitable host, she really wasn't enjoying herself. The two people she wanted were not here.

"So I told Edwin," went on Garnet Somerset to her hostess, "I know Millicent will want to show you Daisy's new foal."

"Yes, of course," Millicent answered softly. She couldn't help admiring Garnet's lovely blue gown. And the Chinese fan on her wrist matched the color of her water-silk gown. Three years older than herself, Garnet had the blond English beauty and blue eyes the boys found irresistible. She turned to her right to study Edwin as he took a pinch of snuff from a small enameled box in his left hand. At fourteen, Garnet's brother was almost too pretty for a boy—with a pouting mouth and long golden lashes. Like the twenty other young guests here, he was dressed in the latest London fashion, eating his fill in the open garden. Millicent tried not to think of it, but she was too aware that many Irish children were starving not far from where they sat stuffing themselves with sweets and punch.

Millicent's father had spared no expense in lavishly decorating the rose garden for her party. She knew it was to show off in front of others rather than any devotion to his daughter which prompted him to have such elaborate food and entertainment, including musicians playing soft music in the background. Her guests's parents were inside being equally entertained and dined by her father. Did he hope these aristocrats would put in a good word for him with the King?

But she had no desire to return to London. There was nothing for her there. And she knew Dunstan felt the same way.

After the musical entertainment, her guests, ranging in age from twelve to sixteen, chatted with each other. Like the other ladies, Millicent was dressed in a sack gown—elbow-length and flounced—with a straw-and-silk slouch hat with wide flopping brim. However, instead of the silks and satins worn by the other girls, Millicent had chosen a more practical, fine, nonlustrous taffeta material for the warm summer day.

The young men dressed in close-fitting coats, brightly colored waistcoats and knee breeches, and black leather pumps with decorative buckles. Some wore wigs; a few opted for their own hair gathered at the back of the neck with a black ribbon.

"Happy birthday." Dunstan Fitzroy bent down and placed a kiss on his sister's cheek. At fifteen he was already six foot, but he was graceful for his height. Unlike his father, he preferred not to wear a wig. His reddish-brown hair was tied neatly behind his neck.

Millicent returned her brother's smile. "Dunstan, have you spoken to Father yet? Surely he won't make you go to London so soon."

Dunstan's smoky eyes became serious. He thrust his hands behind his well-tailored buff coat. "I'm afraid I'll be leaving within the week," he said with finality.

"But you can't," she cried, forgetting their guests for the moment. "You don't want to be a soldier, and we—"

Dunstan took his sister's hand in his. "We have to face it, Millie. We tried. But Father is adamant. All the Fitzroy men do military campaigning." He recognized the signs and put his arm around his sister's shoulders. "Please don't make it harder for me than it is, darling. You must know how much I hate leaving this place."

He glanced about the green, rolling hills, noting again the gray brick and stone of Fitzroy Hall—outside crumbling in parts, yet standing defiantly on the hill overlooking the water. Built more than a hundred years ago, the large house had never been occupied on a permanent basis by a Fitzroy owner until now. It saddened him that his father refused to make any needed repairs on the structure beyond the stables.

"It rains less here than in London," Millicent's older brother mused aloud. "The air is more pleasant. I'll miss our rides, your beating me at chess, and—do you remember the fun you and I used to have playing with the O'Rahillys? God, what Father would have done if he'd ever found out."

Dunstan grinned down at his sister. "It was always more pleasant than playing with the Somersets," he whispered.

The lady gave her brother a wan smile. She was trying not to make it more difficult for him. "You will write me?"

"Of course. And you must tell me all about how my horses are doing."

She would have liked to say more to her brother, but there wasn't time when another guest called for her attention.

"Lady Millicent! I found it!"

The lady looked up to see Nigel Somerset racing toward her and his two siblings.

Oh holiday from Trinity College in Dublin, the gangly Nigel obviously preferred the outdoors to the company of the other adults inside the Hall.

"It's th—the rare sp—spotted one," he cried, holding up the gigantic mushroom for her admiration.

"Really, Nigel," Garnet protested, snapping her older brother across the knuckles with her closed fan. "I'm fair to puking at finding those stinking things all about our house."

"Bless my so—soul, pray do not be so indelicate," Nigel appealed, clearly taken aback by his younger sister's phraseology.

"Oh, give it a rest," Edwin grated. "Lud, look at your silk hose—grass stained, and there is a smudge of dirt on your face. Can't you refrain from grubbing about the ground like some truffle hog?"

Appearing crestfallen at the rebuke from his younger siblings, he turned to look across at Millicent. "Mmm—my lady, do you think the earl would be cross if I took a few home?"

Millicent smiled affectionately at the simple, good-natured young man. "I am positive Father would not mind. Please take

21

how many mushrooms you wish."

Nigel's thin face beamed. "Oh, th—thank you, dear Lady Millicent. I shall collect them straight away." With a gawkish bow, he was off to retrieve his precious samples.

"Stuttering boob," Edwin muttered under his breath. "I'm going over to converse with Percy Bembridge. Shall I put in a good word for you, Sister? Not that the lad isn't already smitten with you."

Appearing not to hear her brother's question before he moved away, Garnet's attention was focused elsewhhwere. "That is John Nolan's driver," she stated.

Millicent followed the direction of Garnet's gaze to see the gray-uniformed driver vault up to the driver's seat of Nolan's closed carriage. He moved the horses closer to the front entrance. The squire's wife came out first, holding a white hand to her forehead. To Millicent, she appeared much paler and drawn than usual. So much so, the woman never acknowledged the two girls as she brushed quickly past them. One of the Fitzroy footmen assisted her up the three tiny steps to the carriage.

"There is John," Garnet whispered breathlessly, her cornflower eyes sparkling. "Is he not the handsomest of men?"

Lady Millicent observed him as he slowly descended the stone steps of Fitzroy Hall. Though tall and muscular, with aristocratic features, no one in her mind could compare with Taggart.

Her gray eyes grew large when she looked back down at Garnet's expression. "But he is already married," slipped out.

"Fiddle-faddle," scoffed the petite beauty. "He only wed that pinch-faced sack of bones for her money. Barren as a board and six years his senior, I can tell he holds no feelings for her."

The younger girl could scarcely believe her ears. "But you already have Percy Bembridge's adoration, and when you see him in his officer's uniform next year, surely—"

"Lud, Percy is just a boy. Besides, he affects that lisp merely because a few silly girls showed how endearing they found it."

Before the taller girl could say another word, Garnet had

stepped directly in John's path.

"Oh dear, my fan," Garnet cried as the blue object seemed to slip from her tiny hands.

Automatically, the gallant gentleman bent down and gracefully retrieved the fan before it landed on the stone entrance at his feet. "Miss Somerset," he greeted, politely returning the wayward accessory to its owner.

"Thank you. Leaving the party so soon, Mr. Nolan?"

Whatever was she about, Millicent thought, shocked by her guest's audacity.

In his neatly tailored brown coat and breeches, with a full-bottomed wig under his three-cornered hat, the squire seemed to take a closer look at the feminine creature in front of him. "Marigold has another of her sick headaches."

"I never get headaches," Garnet pointed out. "I believe it is because I have a healthy bosom."

Hazel eyes darted to the area to which Garnet alluded. He appeared to suck in his breath at the voluptuous sight of the tops of those full, ripe mounds above her tightfitting bodice. "Yes, Miss Somerset, you appear healthy. As well as being a very forward child," he admonished, holding up his right finger in front of her pert nose in the manner of an adult addressing a precocious child.

"I am sixteen, not a child," Garnet defended. However, instead of peering down meekly at the ground as Millicent would have done, she opened her mouth and ran her tongue over her soft, pink lips.

Clearly unprepared for this bolder flirtation, the squire's eyes glinted, showing something Millicent did not understand. He appeared to need a few moments before he could speak. Then his hand raised Garnet's dainty chin, forcing her to meet the penetrating look in his hazel eyes. "Miss Somerset, tell your father he should warm your posterior for your wickedness."

Garnet did not flinch when she replied, "I should much rather you performed that service yourself . . . John."

Millicent felt her face flame with embarrassment, even if Garnet felt no such reticence. She wanted to run, but her slippers seemed rooted to the spot as she stood there not

23

knowing what she should say or do as hostess.

"I've a good mind to—"

"John!" Marigold Nolan demanded, poking her thin face out the carriage window. "I wish to leave *now!*"

To Millicent, leaving was the last thing Squire Nolan desired right now as he studied Garnet, obviously seeing the blond temptress for the first time.

"Coming, my dear," he called over his broad shoulder. Doffing his hat, he bowed from the waist. "Ladies." Then he turned and headed for his carriage.

So aghast by the whole situation, Millicent was almost grateful when Edwin came back over to join them.

"I say, Millicent, I was hoping you'd show me Daisy's new foal now," Edwin Somerset stated. "Dunstan says Charger's new son will win races someday like his father."

Though Millicent looked politely at her guest, she couldn't help noticing Edwin's elaborate costume—fob ribbons, quizzing glass, yards of pristine lace at his immaculate gold silk cuffs. The scent of jasmine was heavy around him. His skin was clear and smooth, almost like a girl's.

"Why, of course," Millicent replied. "But since Star was just born yesterday, I do not think we should all charge in to the stables. If you wish, I'll take you to see him after we dine."

A few hours later some of the other guests had begun a game of croquet on the large lawn. When Garnet bent over to use her wooden mallet, Millicent was shocked to see just how low Garnet's bodice was cut. Did she realize the young men were looking at her . . . her bosom?

When she walked across the lawn near the tallest hedge, from the other side Millicent heard two young men discussing Garnet in low tones. Though she didn't understand what some of the words meant, she was positive it had something to do with Garnet's voluptuous figure. Garnet was beautiful, Millicent had to admit. She looked down at her own flat chest. And it had to be faced, she told herself. She was definitely going to take after her mother's side of the family—glasses, thin and tall—and men would not be smitten with her. "Well, stuff," she muttered aloud. "'Tis not that important," she tried telling herself.

"What did you say?" Edwin asked.

"Ah . . . yes, quite a lovely day. Would you like to see Star now?"

Garnet insisted on coming along with Millicent and Edwin to the stables.

"Phew," Garnet complained, placing a lacy white handkerchief to her nose. "Now I remember why I always insist on having my mount brought to the courtyard at home."

Millicent delighted in the smell of horse and leather. And she knew her father's stables were far cleaner and better equipped than many in England. She hoped Taggart would be in one of the other buildings or getting a horse shod— anywhere but here. After their last meeting, she felt so sorry about the misunderstanding and she still blamed herself.

"Please try not to startle him," Millicent advised.

But both Edwin and his sister seemed to disregard her words.

"So this is the champion Dunstan is so proud of?" roared Edwin. He peered closer into the stall. "He doesn't look very promising at the moment. You don't suppose a mongrel mounted Daisy instead, do you?"

Garnet laughed with her younger brother.

Millicent looked at the wobbly-legged foal with the white patch on his forehead. Daisy stood near her offsrping protectively. Millicent thought they were beautiful, with their reddish brown coloring. "Well," she defended softly, "he was just born yesterday. I dare say I was not a beauty when I was a day old either."

"And you still aren't, my dear," quipped Garnet as her eyes met her grinning brother's face. "Oh," she murmured innocently. "I should not have said that. Pray forgive me," she added, with token sincerity.

Millicent's cheeks grew pink as the barb hit her vulnerable feelings. Her mother's gentle teachings came swiftly to her aid. "Think nothing of it." She even managed a half smile. "You are quite right, Garnet. Unlike you, it appears I am not to be a rose."

"Ah, but a rose is too perfect and cold, with thorns that can

25

tear at a man's heart," said a familiar voice coming out from one of the adjacent stalls. The young Irishman set down the leather harnessing he'd obviously been working on. He took in Millicent's becoming yellow gown and the daisies embroidered on the ribbons of her brimmed hat. For some unexplained reason, all his earlier vexation towards her vanished. He hadn't missed the hurtful things the older girl had said. He'd seen Garnet and her coxcomb brother here before. Where was Dunstan, he wondered, to allow these two jackals to draw his sister's blood this way? Hell, had she been Edna, he'd have—

"'Tis a yellow wildflower a man can feel at peace with and laugh on a clear summer's day." Smiling broadly, Taggart pushed down his sleeves, which had been rolled up while he worked. He came over to stand in front of her.

She was affected at seeing his bare arms, the way the bronzed skin clenched as his muscles worked.

"Happy birthday ta ya, Lady Millicent. 'Tis smooth sailin' I wish for ya always."

"What the devil!" bellowed Edwin. "Who is this Irish lout?"

"Of all the insolence!" echoed Edwin's sister.

Millicent barely composed her features. After all, the Somersets were important to her father. "Edwin and Garnet Somerset, I would like you to meet the gentleman who runs these stables, Mr. Taggart O'Rahilly."

To his credit, Taggart made a formal bow. However, Edwin and Garnet turned their backs on him.

Taggart shook his head and in a mocking tone remarked, "Your friends, my lady, have never learned manners. Of course, I have to remember they weren't raised with all my privileges."

Garnet whirled around first. "You," she directed to the Irishman. "Saddle this horse for me immediately."

Millicent gasped at Garnet's rudeness. Not only was she taking over the Fitzroy stables, but never had she addressed a servant in this fashion. Right now Garnet reminded her of the earl. "Please, Garnet. I should be honored to have you ride any of our horses, but Daisy is not up to being ridden yet. It's too soon."

The blond-haired girl raised her chin to look up at the younger girl. "Having been forced to come to your silly party only because our fathers are friends who conspire to have my poor brother saddled with you for a future wife, I think the least you could do is comply with my request. At our house we would never allow a servant to insult a guest."

"I . . . I am sorry if you feel slighted," said Millicent, feeling at a loss, "but I—"

"Yes," broke in Edwin. He gave the taller man a disdainful look. "We have ways of dealing with this sort at Somerset Hall."

Millicent felt truly afraid for the first time. Would they tell her father on Taggart? "Please, I am sure Taggart meant no—"

"'Tis grateful I am, my lady, but I need no one to apologize for me."

"Yes, quite," Millicent added nervously. "Please. It is my birthday. Let us forget the whole incident. Now, Garnet, you said you wished to ride and I—"

"She said she wished to ride Daisy," pointed out the belligerent Edwin. He brushed an imaginary piece of lint off the round cuff of his silk coat. "You've received your orders, O'Bumpkin, or whatever the devil your name is. Speed it up, man. We haven't got all day." Then he turned back to his hostess. "You are mistress here, are you not, Lady Millicent?"

Millicent swallowed. She was painfully aware that Taggart was watching her reaction. "I . . . yes, I am in charge here," she said with new authority. "And as such, I must refuse your request. Daisy is in no condition to be ridden. My father would not appreciate any injury to his property." She held her back straight, her hands clasped in front of her.

"That's tellin' them, my lady."

Oh, please, Taggart, Millicent begged silently, don't say another word.

As Taggart glanced again at Garnet Somerset, he realized he'd never seen such a gorgeous creature in his life. Yes, she was spoiled, but she was beautiful, with full breasts and a very kissable mouth. His youthful body responded instantly.

Millicent watched Garnet's expression. She knew Garnet was fully aware of the effect she was having on the handsome

Irishman. And for the first time, she felt a real stab of something that both hurt and angered her.

Garnet moved closer to Taggart. Her smile was beguiling. "So, you do not like roses, Mr. O'Rahilly," she cooed, boldly placing her gloved finger on his muscular arm.

Taggart felt sweat break out on his forehead. The arousing scent of roses assailed his nostrils. If he stretched out a hand he could touch her blond curls, run a hand down those ripe breasts. Unconsciously, he reached out to fondle the globes of his desire. Only Garnet scampered away before he could reach her.

She laughed up at him. "You are a bold rascal. Do you really think I'd let your dirty hands touch me, you fool?" Her contemptuous smirk mocked him.

Taggart muttered a Gaelic word.

Millicent assumed he wasn't calling Garnet a rose right now.

"You bastard," raged Edwin. "I can just imagine what you said. How dare you insult my sister!" He made a lunge for the taller man.

"No! Please, stop." Millicent put herself between Taggart and Edwin. Her eyes pleaded with Edwin. "Let us please, dear Edwin, go back to my party."

So obviously angry, Edwin shoved Millicent aside roughly. "Get out of my way."

Taggart reached out instantly to catch her, but he was too late.

Millicent landed hard, bruising her gown-covered knees and the palms of her hands on the rough cobblestones. Not only physical pain rushed upon her but the memory of the way Taggart had looked at Garnet. Tears swam before her eyes.

"*Gealbhan!*" Taggart soothed as he reached her side.

"Unhand the girl," Edwin ordered imperiously. "You are not fit to—"

"Shut yer gob, ya bony little snot, and get out of my way." Without hesitation Taggart gently lifted Millicent in his arms. "You," he directed to Garnet, "make yourself useful and pick up her spectacles."

Such was the tone of his command that the blond-haired girl found herself doing as bidden.

"Thank you, Garnet." Millicent brushed back another tear and accepted her glasses. She felt much better. She was being carried and held in Taggart's arms. It didn't matter where he was taking her; she wanted it to go on and on. Truly, he was her knight in shining armor.

But when Taggart placed her on one of the wooden stools outside, she could barely refrain from protesting after he stood away from her.

The blushing softness of her sweet face captivated him. For a second he lost himself in the depths of her gentle gray eyes. "There now," he finally managed. "Just rest there a minute. None of them can see you from here." He brushed a few strands of hay from the bottom of her gown, then stood up. "I'm sorry darlin', for spoiling your party."

"You didn't spoil it, Taggart. It wasn't your fault. And I am fine," she said, forcing a smile. And to her amazement, Taggart bent down and kissed her on the cheek. It happened so fast, but she felt his warm breath on her face.

When Garnet came out, Taggart glanced back into the stables. His dark eyes narrowed. "You ladies will excuse me for a moment," he said so formally with an added bow that Millicent would have giggled had Garnet not been present.

However, from their position outside the stables both ladies heard the sound of a fist connecting with a cheek. Then there was a loud yelp from Edwin.

Both girls raced back in to the wooden structure.

"Oh, my God," Garnet shrieked. "That savage hit Edwin. You brute," she yelled at the Irishman. "You leave my little brother alone."

Edwin landed a clumsy punch to Taggart's eye. Daisy and her foal merely snorted at the rowdy goings-on.

"Stop this at once!" ordered Millicent in a tone she rarely used. Both men ignored her as they rolled across the floor, oblivious to the dirt and straw.

"Why, that Irishman is going to kill Edwin. I'm getting Papa right now."

Before Millicent could say a word, Garnet was racing for the house. Though she knew Edwin was in no mortal danger, Millicent was not so sure about Taggart. What would her father do to him?

"But, Dunstan, Father will not tell me where Taggart is," Millicent protested. "Edna won't play with me or talk to me. She sits on Colleen's lap and cries. It's been five days and no one seems to know and I am—please," she begged.

Dunstan looked down at his sister. She gave so much away in those gray eyes of hers, he thought. He was sure Taggart had no idea Millie had such a crush on him.

"Dash it, Millie, I thought to spare you. The night of your party—I tried to stop Garnet from charging into the dining room where Father had all his guests, but the girl would not listen to reason," Dunstan went on sadly. "You know, Garnet. She blew everything out of proportion and made such a row that when Mr. Somerset asked, Father readily agreed to turn Taggart over to him for 'discipline,' as old Somerset called it. I got Father to promise to let me go and fetch him back tonight."

"But, Dunstan, what type of discipline is Mr. Somerset talking about?" She felt a sickening fear in the pit of her stomach and knew her brother was keeping something from her. "Why was it necessary for him to go to Somerset Hall?"

"Ask no more, Millie." The strain was evident on Dunstan's face. His troubled gray eyes pleaded with his sister. "Let it be. As it was, Father and the Somersets wanted him held there for two weeks. I had all I could do to get Father to cut the time to five days."

"Do you enjoy being our guest?" Garnet Somerset purred.

Her brother smiled and uncoiled his leather whip once more. "I shall have to make this beating a good one. What do you say to that, Irish scum?"

Taggart knew he couldn't speak even if he'd wanted to. Like other landowners, the Somersets had a prison right in their own home for punishing their wayward Irish servants. This was the first time he'd ever been in such a place, and he vowed it would be his last. Something had happened to him during these five days. It wasn't just the lack of food and slimy water, or that his hands and legs were chained to the wall, or the beatings—he'd had plenty of those from his employer. It was something in his spirit—it raged like a hot iron, tearing at his insides.

"What, no tiresome Irish speech?" Edwin baited. He raised his whip arm and brought it down hard against the Irishman's already tender bare back.

Taggart tasted blood as he bit down hard to keep from crying out. Tears stung his eyes.

Garnet moved closer to the man in chains. "Don't be too hard on him," she advised her brother. "We wouldn't want to hurt any delicate parts of him." Brazenly, she took off a dainty glove and ran her fingers against his arm as she'd done the first time they'd met. "You are a magnificent animal, aren't you?" She touched the top left button of his filthy breeches. She giggled when she looked lower. "I bet you want to touch me, too," she whispered. "Yes, I can see that you do, Irish Stallion. You want me, don't you?" she demanded.

"Yeess," he grated, pulling harder on the chains at his wrists until the broken skin began to bleed once more.

"Good." Garnet made a pretext of lowering the tight bodice of her flowered muslin gown. But she stepped just far enough away so that the man before her could only stare at her. "I think he is ready for you, Brother dear."

Edwin brought his whip down twelve more times, then tossed it to the ground.

Taking this as an obviously prearranged cue, his blond sister made a hasty exit up the long stone stairs. She never looked back.

"Noo!" cried Taggart in his frustration. His loins ached as painfully as his bleeding back. A second time Garnet had teased him, made him lust for her, then left him like this. So lost in his own tormented thoughts, he hadn't remembered Edwin's presence.

"Don't worry," came Edwin's voice next to him. "We need no woman for pleasure."

Oh, God, no! Taggart thought desperately. He tried to move away but Edwin was right after him, his shaking fingers going after the remaining buttons of Taggart's breeches. He felt revolted by Edwin's touch, which now resembled that of a lover.

Clearly misinterpreting the Irishman's reaction, Edwin's voice became softer. "Don't be scared. I've done this dozens of times. I'll be gentle with you. He rubbed his hand across the front of Taggart's breeches. Then he smiled. "My sister was right; you are an Irish stallion."

Edwin stepped back and removed his elaborate purple coat. Then came his canary yellow waistcoat.

Taggart tried to force himself to think of a way out of this new dilemma, but in his weakened condition nothing came. He tugged on the chains once more, feeling frightened and sick at the same time. Edwin was coming at him.

"Edwin!" Garnet Somerset came racing down the stairs. "There is no more time. Dunstan is here. Father says to bring O'Rahilly up immediately."

Taggart made no effort to hide his relief. "It . . . it appears my carriage has arrived earlier than expected," he dared. "Perhaps another time we can settle this between us. When my hands and feet aren't hobbled. Or have you ever had a fair fight?"

Edwin grabbed for his whip once more.

"No!" shouted Garnet. "I told you, Edwin. There isn't time. Bring the Fitzroys' property up at once."

Despite Taggart's protests, Dunstan had his carriage drive right to the small O'Rahilly cottage. Though Dunstan was two inches taller than his companion, Taggart had more muscle. It was not easy getting him into the house. After the Irishman collapsed on the straw mattress at the side of the dirt-floored cottage, Dunstan busied himself with lighting a fire. When he saw the condition of his friend, he was shaken.

"God's blood, old Somerset is ruthless." Dunstan reached into the folds of his coat. "Here, drink this."

Shakily, Taggart accepted the dark bottle of whiskey in his dirty hands. Tilting the bottle back, he took a huge swallow. Then another. "It was the younger two Somersets and not their father I have ta thank for the strips on my back," he said bitterly.

Before Dunstan could comment on this startling news, the wooden door of the small cottage burst open and Millicent rushed in.

"Millie, you should not be here," Dunstan scolded.

Ignoring her brother's words, Millicent quickly tossed off her outer cloak. "I hide food and bandages easier with the cape. I don't suppose you thought to bring anything but whiskey," she quipped, wanting desperately to see Taggart, to make sure that he wasn't dying.

"'Tis the truth your brother speaks, Lady Millicent."

"No one saw me, and Dunstan will be going back to the house, having deposited his servant home. You can play another game of cards with Father. He thinks I am in bed fast asleep," the lady remarked coolly. "Now, please don't argue with me, Brother. I can see to his wounds better, as well you know."

Outmaneuvered, Dunstan had to accept the truth of his sister's words. She was far more practical, for he hadn't thought to bring medicine, bandages, or food.

When they were alone, Millicent took charge of the situation. Angry tears came to her eyes when she saw the deep, bleeding cuts on Taggart's back.

"I stink to high heaven. My lady, you must go," Taggart protested.

"Soap and water will take care of that first. I'll heat it right now. Then we'll get some hot food into you."

Suddenly, Taggart's bloodshot eyes scanned the room. "Where's Edna?"

"Rest easy, my friend. I had her stay with Colleen and Fergus Mulcahy tonight. I knew you would not want Edna to see you this way. When Dunstan told me where you were . . ." She saw how weak and exhausted he was, so she let her words drift off.

She forced herself to concentrate on bathing his back and tending his cuts and bruises. The lady noticed the marks from an earlier beating. Had her father done this? All the time she fought back tears. What had they done to him? How could people be so cruel? What if they learned the truth about her and her mother? Would they do this to her? The thought made her shiver.

After eating the nourishing broth, bread, and cheese—and finishing off Dunstan's whiskey, Taggart stretched out on his stomach. "Ya always surprise me how much older than your years ya act."

Millicent looked about the room. "I'm not the only one," she replied softly. "Your sister keeps this place clean and neat." She refrained from commenting on the sparseness of the room and began cleaning away the dishes and medical items.

The strong whiskey was taking effect. Taggart watched her work as she bent over the hearth. "Has anyone ever told you that you have an adorable bottom?" he slurred.

Shocked, Lady Millicent straightened automatically and almost dropped the clay bowl she'd been wiping out. She whirled about to face him. However, when she saw the silly grin on his face, the English girl realized he was quite foxed and not accountable for his bold speech.

"I . . . I've noticed it before," he blathered on from his position across the room on his bed. "'Tis not flabby like some of the girls' in the village. That day I pulled ya out of the tree, I stole a feel." He smirked like an unrepentant boy in confession. "Yours is a round and firm little rump, a ve—very pleasant handful."

Her face flamed with his blatant admissions. But it was not only Taggart's inebriated state which held down any ranting puffs of "how-dare-you." How could she, for it was so rare when she received any sort of compliment?

Mischief lurked at the corners of her mouth. Did she dare? Hands on her hips, she asked, "And what other attributes of mine have you admired from afar?"

The Irishman watched her, with no attempt to hide the train of his thoughts. "Ya have rich brown hair that glows with a red burnish, graceful hands, and . . ." He could barely keep his eyes open as he tried to focus on the bespectacled girl standing over him. "Best go now, my lady." All humor left his features. "If you're discovered here, there'll be hell to pay."

Millicent had to admit he was correct. "Yes. You must rest. I've told Father you cannot do his bidding until you've recovered your strength."

He chuckled at her words. "Did ya now? That must have been an interestin' sight." Did this gentle-natured English lady have a temper? he wondered in amazement. Was the fire in her hair no lie after all? Then he shook his head. "'Tis a damn shame," he mumbled, his eyes closing once more. "You and Edna had to grow up far too fast. You should be playin' with dolls and pickin' wild flowers, not . . ." A yawn interrupted his meanderings.

"Good night, Taggart," murmured the English girl as she headed for the door. "I . . . I love you," she whispered.

A loud snore echoed across the room.

She gave herself a mental shake. It was obvious he never heard her words.

Chapter 3

"Millie!" The distraught girl sobbed, trying to keep her voice low so Mrs. Halsey wouldn't awaken down the hall. "Oh, please. Dear God, I must see you."

Groggily Millicent came awake. Dressed only in a thin, ruffled nightgown, she went to the door and opened it.

Edna raced into her mistress's rooms. "It's Taggart, my lady. He's talkin' wild. He rode out just now, like the devil himself was after him. Even Father Mike couldn't make him see reason. And 'tis only two weeks since that horrid beating at Somersets. Oh, me lady, please don't let the earl send Taggart back there. I . . . I'm frightened and—"

"He took a horse? Good Lord, if my father finds out—"

"I checked with Fergus. He said your father was still out and would probably come home boozy again. Oh," Edna caught herself. "I'll be beggin' yer pardon."

"Nonsense. It's true." Millicent rushed to the wooden trunk at the foot of her canopied bed. There wasn't a minute to waste.

Taggart had taken Charger, her father's prize horse. To catch up with him, Millicent knew she had to ride this difficult stallion, Hellfire. She held on to the racing animal, praying to God she wouldn't fall off. If only her father hadn't sent Dunstan away to become a "proper soldier." How she needed his help now.

"Taggart!" she cried when the moon came from behind the clouds, and she saw the outline of a rider ahead. "Wait!"

The Irishman recognized her voice instantly and brought Charger up with a lurid curse. He waited for the younger girl to catch up to him. His mouth fell open when he saw how she was dressed. Riding astride, she had on a young boy's coat and breeches, her long hair piled up under a tricorn hat.

"What in blue blazes are you doin'?"

She looked down at her outfit, purposely misreading his question. "They're Dunstan's old clothes. I keep them handy. They are frightfully comfortable."

"You ninnyhammer! You can't come with me."

"Actually, I came here to bring you back."

"Never," he grumbled adamantly. "I'm through with this place. If I reach Cork tonight, I can get a boat for the Colonies."

"But . . . what about Edna?" And me, her heart cried out silently.

"I hate like the devil leavin' her, but she refused to come with me." He ran an anguishesd hand through his thick black hair. "But I'll be back. I swear." He had a score to settle here, and he would never have the means to do it if he stayed. They tore the heart out of a man, these English. He hated them all, he thought savagely.

"My father's death on their hands, and this estate you Fitzroys squat on. It was once my ancestors. It's O'Rahilly land. And it's been ours since the days of Brian Boru." His voice rose with the pain and bitterness he felt. "I tried, God how I tried, but I cannot swallow it any longer. Father Mike and John Nolan, my only real friends here, they tried to help me, but it's too late."

Millicent knew she had to remain calm. She now began to realize Taggart would not be dissuaded. However, she couldn't let him leave like this, with no money or plan of what he would do after he crossed the Atlantic. "Taggart, if you are determined to leave, wait two days. It will be safer then. Father is going up North with some of his cronies to do some hunting. He'll be gone for at least two weeks. That way you'll have a head start. And for heaven's sake, take another horse. I can just see Father hiring one of his lackeys to follow you across the ocean to slit your throat for taking his best racehorse."

At her flippant tone, Taggart couldn't resist a devilish smile. The indentation at his chin seemed more pronounced. "I took the best of the lot. I've always been a good judge of horseflesh."

For some reason the picture of Garnet flashed in her mind. "And besides, I want you to see me in the new gown I've had made for the Somersets' ball tomorrow evening. Just before we leave I'll sneak out to your cottage. I've had a dress made for Edna, too. I . . . I realize she won't be able to attend, but I wanted her to have some new clothes. Please say she can accept them."

He felt his body relax. Some of the rage left him. "For such a slip of a girl, you could charm the fork from Satan himself. With all your smooth words, lass, are you sure you're not Irish?"

Millicent was glad the darkness hid her expression. Unable to join in his teasing, she concentrated on holding Hellfire still. The stallion pawed the earth impatiently.

"You'll break your scrawny neck riding that beast."

Her chin came up at his censuring tone. "I can ride just as good as you, O'Rahilly, as you bloody well know."

He made a clicking sound with his tongue. "Now, is that any way for the daughter of an English earl to be speakin'?"

"Stuff," she countered. But when she heard approaching horses in the distance, all humor left her features. Then the rowdy laughter. With a sickening dread she knew who approached.

"It's my father." She heard Taggart say something in Gaelic.

"You go hide behind that brush, girl. When we've gone, get back to Fitzroy Hall."

"No," Millicent protested. "Let me handle this, O'Rahilly." She surprised herself at how coolly she took charge.

"It's daft you are if ya think I'm lettin' a girl rescue me."

"Oh, be reasonable," Millicent said, almost out of patience. "Do you want him to send you back to the Somersets? God's foot, what use to Edna would you be then? And you'd come back in no condition to survive an Atlantic crossing."

Despite himself, he felt the blood drain from his face. The picture of Edwin Somerset, the putrid smells of their dank cellar assailed him. "But I can't let you—"

"Quiet," ordered his companion. "Say nothing, understand?" She tried to lighten the blow to his pride. "One day you may be in a position to take charge, but tonight it's my turn. Agreed?" she pressed, aware that her father and two of his drinking friends would soon be upon them.

He nodded abruptly.

"Good. Now, dismount. We're switching horses."

This done, Millicent waited until she knew they would be seen. "Father!" she yelled. "Oh, thank God you've come!"

Over the din of laughter and singing, the earl heard his daughter's voice. "What the . . .? Millicent?"

"Over here, Father." She waved in a sweeping motion, giving the impression of eagerness.

Millicent watched as the three riders advanced. Her father's mount was obviously under a great strain from his rider's girth. Calvert Huntington, Duke of Montrose, was as thin as her father was heavy. The spindly legs of the man of sixty-one dangled comically down the sides of his horse. John Nolan was the only one in the group who rode steadily and with any expertise. He could hold his liquor, too, if Millicent was any judge. It would take all her skill to deceive him.

"O'Rahilly! Get down off that horse. At once, I say." Ignoring his daughter, the earl grabbed for his riding crop and dismounted with difficulty. He moved to stand beside Taggart's horse. "This is the last straw, young whelp. Dragging my daughter out here, raping her in some dark ditch, and . . ." He staggered to the right and held on to the horse's bridle to steady himself. He was forced to adjust his powdered wig. "Get down, damn your eyes."

Taggart swung down from his horse. He felt his own temper begin to rise. He wanted to kick the drunken old goat in his fat English arse. Not looking the least bit scared, he stood staring down at the intoxicated man. Even when the overdressed duke and a somber John Nolan came up next to their companion, Taggart refused to give an inch. He was going to die anyway, he mused. He wouldn't go begging for mercy. John Nolan had done a lot for his family already. Taggart knew he couldn't ask the man for another favor.

"Yes," encouraged Millicent. She jumped down from her horse and forced her voice to sound sulky. "This . . . this cur," she said, pointing disdainfully at the Irishman, "had the audacity to come after me when I rode out tonight. 'Tis too late for a lady to be out alone." She mimicked his brogue expertly. "And dressed like a boy says he. The idea," she fumed. "I'll have no potato grubber tell me what to do."

Caught off guard, Taggart looked down quickly at his boots, then back up. To his credit he said nothing.

"Beat him now," Millicent demanded, stamping her oversized boots on the wet grass. "I want to hear him scream."

Saints preserve him, Taggart thought uneasily. This was her great plan to rescue him?

At her words, the earl whirled around and tried to focus his bleary gaze on his wayward daughter. Then he glanced back at his two friends. They appeared embarrassed. He saw the duke's look of censure when he stared at Millicent. John Nolan whispered something to him. The earl saw both men shake their heads and frown. The chit had made a fool of him in front of his friends. He took a closer look at the horse she'd been riding.

"Charger! Be Gad, you took Charger!" bellowed the earl. He appeared close to popping the silver buttons on his blue waistcoat.

Just as she'd expected, her father had little thought for her reputation. The main item that hoisted him over the edge, she knew, was discovering she'd taken his four-legged darling out in the night air. Millicent projected an expression of bored unconcern. "Well," she repeated petulantly, "I want you to spill this churlish Irish hound's grimy innards all over the road."

Calvert put a veined hand to his elaborate neckcloth. "Such language," murmured the shocked old duke.

All right, girl, Taggart thought uneasily. One more grisly request like that and he'd be lucky to escape with all his parts intact. Doing it up a bit brown, wasn't she? The look the duke was giving him right now told Taggart he clearly thought castration was too good for him.

"You," accused the outraged earl. "You . . . you baggage!"

"I don't see what you are becoming so overwrought about, Father. I was bored. I wanted a canter. No one is dead. But I strongly resent this . . . this Irish bog trotter's interference."

Her father seemed to have difficulty getting air. His cheeks puffed out like a bellows at his daughter's insolence. He raised his riding stick high in the air. "You homely little—I'll teach you to . . ."

Taggart was just getting ready to jump to Millicent's aid when Calvert Huntington's thin voice rang out.

"Geoffrey!"

Millicent thought the duke moved rather quickly for a man of his years and supposed frailty. His spindly legs, encased in white hose, brought him over to her father in record time. Expecting a blow, she'd braced her body to take her father's harsh temper. She let out a long sigh of relief.

"You've been in these Irish wilds too long, old friend." The duke took the riding crop out of the earl's meaty fist. "You should be grateful for such a responsible servant. He saved your headstrong daughter and your precious horse."

"You mean you aren't going to beat him?" demanded Millicent, cosying up to her new role as rowdy aggressor.

When Calvert took Geoffrey Fitzroy over to stand near a tree a few feet away, it was John Nolan who continued watching them.

Adjusting his leather gloves and expertly tailored hunter-green coat unhurriedly, the squire came close to Millicent. "Be thankful no one is getting beaten this night, my lady." Then in a lower tone, he spoke to the young man next to her. "And, Taggart, you young hothead, thank God you have such a friend in her ladyship. Rest easy, boy. Both Father Collins and I will keep your secret, but nothing could have saved you tonight from the earl's wrath." He turned admiring eyes on the English girl. "My compliments, Lady Millicent. You have a clever mind."

Millicent smiled gratefully.

"However," Nolan cautioned. "You are not out of the woods yet. Here they come. For God's sake, keep your eyes lowered and your mouths shut."

"Taggart," the earl ordered, "return to your cottage. Leave the horse with me."

Millicent was sorry he would have the four-mile walk back home, but she knew there was nothing she could do about it now. At least he wasn't going to be beaten.

Nodding, though the bile rose in his throat, Taggart handed the reins to the earl. He wanted to ask about Millicent's well-being but he didn't dare.

The earl confronted his daughter. "And as for you, my girl. Be thankful these gentlemen will say nothing of your folly to anyone. Perhaps a day without food tomorrow in your room will give you pause for ever contemplating such outrageous behavior in future. There will be no ball for you tomorrow, and you can bloody well walk back behind our horses. That should cool your desire for clandestine rides in the middle of the night."

Millicent said nothing. Another sigh of relief escaped her lips as she watched Taggart's back disappear in the distance. He was safe. That was all that mattered.

Millicent Fitzroy sat outlining a deep pink rose. Her mother had taught her embroidery, patiently showing her the quiet peace in stitching bright colors on linen.

Other than hunger and the letdown at not attending the ball, the serenity of the day appealed to her. It gave her the opportunity to work out her strategy. She would see Father Collins early in the morning. There was so little time.

When she heard the carriage drive up, she put down the doily she'd been working on and went over to the window. Lanterns lighted each side of the ornate carriage. The footmen were in their best gray uniforms. Her father descended the long stone steps and entered the upholstered carriage.

She'd been looking forward to this night for so long, Millicent had to admit it was very disappointing to be left behind. This would have been her first ball and—she chided herself. It couldn't be helped. No use of looking back. The gnawing at her stomach changed the frame of her thoughts anyway. On her father's orders, Mrs. Halsey had locked her in her room last night. No one had been in to see her. She returned to her sewing.

Then she heard the scraping sound, like a pebble against the heavy glass. There it was again. Curious, she walked to the other side of the room and sat on the window seat. Peering out to the back of the house, she gasped when she saw Taggart O'Rahilly climbing up the elm tree outside her window. He made a motion for her to push up on the window.

She gave a second push upward and the wooden frame moved.

As if this was an ordinary event for him, O'Rahilly jumped gracefully across the tree limb and shimmied himself to the window ledge. Then raising himself on his arms, he hoisted his legs through the open window. "A pleasant night for a climb," he said outrageously.

"You are impossible." But her delight in seeing him overcame her fear for his safety or any thought of propriety.

"Here," he said, offering her something in a checkered napkin. "With the compliments of Colleen. Edna insisted on the pastry."

The delicious aroma of hot lamb pie and cherry tarts assailed Millicent's nostrils. "I am grateful. Thank you." She accepted his proffered gifts. Just as she was about to take a bite from the meat pie, she caught herself. "Have you eaten?"

He was touched by her thoughtfulness. "Yes. And I had three tarts. Go ahead, girl."

Needing no further encouragement, Millicent did justice to the pie and tart in record time.

While she ate, Taggart sat next to her on the window seat, dressed in the familiar gray trousers and frayed shirt, his long legs extended out in front of him. He watched her. She was a strange girl, he thought. "I . . . wanted to thank you for helping me last night. How does one so young have such— You were right about waitin' until your father goes. You risked a lot goin' after me."

She knew it wasn't easy for him to be beholden to anyone English. "You are my . . . my friend, O'Rahilly. The favor was gladly given." She wiped her mouth with a corner of the red-

43

and-white napkin.

He looked down at her plain dark-brown dress. Her hair was hidden beneath a mobcap. The gray eyes looked sad behind her wire frames. He sat up straight as a thought occurred to him. "Your father, he didn't hurt you. I mean, he didn't—"

"No," she answered truthfully. "Other than last night, he is indifferent to my presence." Feeling a little awkward, she blurted, "I meant what I said, Taggart. If you ever have need of a favor, you have only to ask."

"Lady Millicent," he started, then faltered.

"Yes," she encouraged.

"There is a favor I would ask of you. With Dunstan gone . . . you're the only English I dare trust." He stood up nervously.

So serious was his countenance, she came up to stand in front of him. Her heart began to flutter in anticipation.

He took her hand in his. His expression was solemn. Brown eyes captured her gray ones. "There is one I can barely find the strength to leave behind, though leave I must if she and I are goin' ta have any decent future. Will you . . . I mean, will you keep an eye on Edna for me? Colleen and Fergus have already said they'd take her into their home, but Edna is adamant. She insists on stayin' in the O'Rahilly cottage alone. Has some cork-brained notion it's up to her to protect the family's interest here. I can't change her mind."

Millicent tried not to show her regret. What had she expected? Sometimes, she chided herself, she was too romantic for her own good. She forced herself to smile. "Of course I will." Then her expression matched his own. "I swear to look after Edna and protect her as if she were my own sister by blood."

Feeling as if a tremendous weight had been lifted from his shoulders, Taggart's face relaxed. So grateful, he forgot himself and gave her a rib-crushing hug.

Her slippers came off the carpeted floor, and she had to brace her hands on his shoulders to steady herself. As she looked down at his face, taking in the deep depression at his chin, then moving her glance upward, she thought briefly he was going to kiss her. The brown of his eyes took on a warmer hue. But just as quickly he seemed to remember something, and he placed her back down on the blue wool carpet.

He stepped back from her and bowed stiffly. "Thank you, my lady." He touched a hand to his right temple. "And . . . I couldn't remember everything the next morning—the whiskey—I'll be apologizin' if I said somethin' I shouldn't that night in my cottage."

Oh, she thought bitterly, why did he always have to remember that she was an English lady and he was an Irishman? She wasn't the one separating them by class. Why did he? When she saw him brace a leg on the edge of the window, Millicent knew this would be her last time to make certain that Taggart would see the priest.

"Taggart, you will say good-bye to Father Michael Collins before you leave, won't you?"

He looked at her puzzled. "Yes, of course. I'll see him the day after tomorrow. Why do you ask?"

"Well . . . I know what John Nolan told me on the way home. He and the priest have taken a special interest in you. Father Collins would be hurt if you went without saying good-bye."

"Do you know the priest?"

"Not well," she hedged. "But I have run into him on occasion when visiting some tenants." She knew this was dangerous ground, and she wanted no more of his shrewd probing. She changed the subject quickly.

"Please. You will be careful. Try to get a good education. I've read that Virginia is a good port of entry to the Colonies. There is a college there. It is called William and Mary. You have a good mind, O'Rahilly. Do not waste it. Revenge can divert too much of a man's talents."

He shook his head and smiled. "You never cease to amaze me." He chuckled as he eased his body over the window ledge. "You, Lady Millicent, are thirteen goin' on forty," he teased.

She watched him leave. Would he come back? Tears stung her eyes.

"Good-bye, little sparrow." Then he was gone.

Millicent sat at the closed window long after he'd left. Oblivious to the tears on her cheeks, she walked over to her carved dresser. She pulled out a wooden box and took out the key she always kept hidden in a hat box in the back of her wardrobe. Opening the lid, diamonds, rubies, and emeralds flashed before her. It was her dowry from her mother, kept hidden from all but Millicent. She would need those jewels tomorrow. Pray heaven Father Collins would help her prudently.

The lady brushed the tears away from her eyes. It had to be done, and it was the only wealth she had any control over. Even her father did not know of their existence. On her deathbed, her mother had sworn her to secrecy. She must have known just how quickly the earl would go through her money.

Then Millicent pressed a side panel on the wooden box. A drawer opened. In it was Millicent's most prized possession, given to her by her mother. It had belonged to her great-grandmother, handed down secretly to each daughter. No male of the family ever knew of its existence.

In the candlelight Lady Millicent held up the symbol of her mother's legacy gift. The small wooden beads of the rosary moved against each other. "He has to come back," she whispered, for the first time in her life feeling truly alone and frightened.

Chapter 4

"I am not asking you to lie, Father Collins." Millicent placed the box on top of the rough table, unfastened its lid, then returned to the wooden chair. She waited for the priest's reaction.

Father Michael Collins looked younger than his six and twenty years. The black cassock he wore, buttoned from collarbone to waist, contrasted sharply with his short-croped, carrot-red hair. His eyes grew large as he took in the glittering bounty.

"My plan," the lady continued, "calls for your kind assistance as intermediary only. As I have explained, no one else need ever know of this."

The Jesuit ran a hand back to his neck, where the hair just touched his black robe. "But what about Edna?"

The Earl of Holingbrook's daughter glanced down at her green riding jacket. Past the O'Rahilly cottage was the only direct route here. She had not counted on the sharp-eyed Edna to be up this early and outside the cottage playing with her kitten.

From the other side of the table, Millicent finally answered. "Because of Edna's insistence to know where I was going and why, and my dread that her brother would awaken upon hearing his younger sister's shouts, I was compelled to take her with me."

The English girl gave the priest a level glance. "She is waiting outside with my horse. However, I made Edna give me

47

her solemn promise never to reveal the owner of these jewels. Please, Father." Millicent's eyes entreated the man sitting across from her. "There is no one else I dare ask for help. I know this places you in danger. If you do not wish to tell me how to plan to sell these jewels to obtain money for Taggart, I will understand."

The priest's features softened. Slowly, he nodded his agreement. "All right, my lady. Do not worry about the details." He had certain foreign acquaintances from his seminary days abroad who could quickly assist him with discretion. "It will be done as you request."

"Thank you," Millicent replied gratefully. As she rose to leave, for the first time that morning, she felt relaxed. Her smoky eyes sparkled behind her spectacles. "How is Liam coming along with his studies?" she asked, with warm politeness.

When he joined her near the door, Father Michael's face beamed at the mention of his nineteen-year-old brother. "He's head of his class in anatomy this year at the University of Padua."

"How proud you must be. Liam will make a fine doctor."

"It is kind of you to ask about him."

Her reddish-brown eyebrows rose. "But why do you seem so surprised?"

Educated in Flanders, belonging to the Society of Jesus, the young man appeared uncomfortable for a moment. "Forgive me, my lady, but there are few English here who would take any interest in news of a Catholic priest's family."

"Oh, stuff. I am quite interested and pleased to hear of Liam's excellent progress."

His eyes clouded. "But Liam had little choice. Though you are the only Englishwoman I'd dare say this to, in truth, my lady, medicine is the only profession open to a Catholic Irishman here. And if I'm even caught saying Mass, the law here states I will be fined two hundred pounds and tried for high treason." He clearly fought to control his agitation by fingering the black sash that hung from his waist, where his wooden rosary would have rested had this outward Jesuit representation been more acceptable during these difficult times. "My one conciliation is that, like other men in my family's history, Liam really wants to be a physician. And God knows we need him in Ireland."

The lady had to agree. More children and elderly had died of starvation and disease this past winter than the last.

Automatically, Millicent reached out to touch the troubled priest's firm arm. "As you are needed here, too. We must keep praying and doing what we can, Michael. I cannot believe a merciful God, Catholic or Protestant, will abandon us."

So moved by the girl's sincere words, Father Collins found himself squeezing her gloved fingers in a new, closer bond of friendship.

Lady Millicent blushed, then slowly retrieved her hand. She walked back to the table and picked up the patterned cloth, which had served to conceal the wooden box on the ride over here.

When she reached the door once more, Millicent turned back to her companion. The priest was watching her with a bemused expression on his lean face.

"Speed is important," she reminded him.

Taggart O'Rahilly could not believe his good fortune. He'd never seen so much money in his whole life. He brushed back a strand of wavy black hair from his forehead. "I . . . I can hardly take it in."

Father Collins smiled. "But understand this," he cautioned. "The donor made only one stipulation—anonymity. You must promise never to try and find out his identity."

"Sure and shouldn't I be thankin' him, Father?" Taggart looked again at the mountain of coins. "Why 'tis a king's ransom."

His companion chuckled. "Hardly that, lad." He began placing the coins back in the black leather pouch. "But it will more than pay for a good start in the Colonies. Best tie it to your waist to keep it hidden. And on the day you reach the harbor, be sure it's before nightfall."

"But I still feel I ought ta—"

"Your patron is adamant. He wishes no thanks."

Taggart nodded. "I'll do as he asks, then."

After saying good-bye to Father Mike, Taggart started down the dirt path, which headed out of Kinsale. He rode the horse Lady Milicent instructed Fergus to give him. Not as fine as Charger, but the stallion was a strong, even-tempered mount. And he knew the lady had picked the best she could without the horse being missed by her father.

She was a strange girl, the Irishman mused to himself. Practical, yet gentle-natured; intelligent, but ready to share laughter, even at herself. It surprised him to suddenly discover he was going to miss the tall English girl.

Taggart rode along for a few miles. Then it struck him. Why hadn't he realized it before? Of course. His patron had to be the one man who always helped the O'Rahillys. And John Nolan wouldn't want it bandied about that he'd given a lot of money to an Irish groom—especially since Taggart ran away from his employer, the Earl of Holingbrook—who was also Nolan's closest friend.

He slowed his pace, telling himself there was no hurry. For the first time in years, he felt free of burdens and excited about the future. The day was sunny, and the countryside filled his senses with yellow wildflowers, warm, moist grass, and clumps of fragrant pink roses cultivated outside a few Irish cottages. Besides, he now had more than enough money to start a new life in the Colonies. "God bless ya, Squire Nolan," he murmured aloud. He'd never forget John Nolan and his very generous gift.

Taggart arrived at the dock in Cork much later than he'd planned. It took longer to convince the local priest that the horse was actually Taggart's to give away.

As the Irishman walked down the dirty street, he could hear the drunken laughter of both men and women coming from the many pubs along the way. The pungent scent of the harbor pervaded his nostrils. Automatically, his hand went to the inside of his coat to feel the full purse secured to his waist. He quickly rebuttoned the frayed coat. He was hot this way, but it was more dangerous to leave the wool coat open. The sooner he was aboard the *Sarah Anne,* the better.

"Help! Stop, thief!" A man's voice rang out in the distance ahead of him.

Taggart had to squint to get a better view of the scene. Three scruffy boys had just pounced on a shorter, unsuspecting man. Gangs of hooligans were common in these parts. With the English bleeding Ireland dry, it was no wonder men turned to crime. The Irishman tried telling himself it wasn't his fight or his business. Didn't he have more important things to do—like booking passage on the *Sarah Anne?*

However, when the black-haired man saw the flash from an upraised knife, he found himself charging into the foray.

To Taggart's surprise, the frantic victim was putting up a good fight, despite the uneven odds. This well-dressed young man might be a gentleman, Taggart thought, but he sure as hell didn't fight like one. He saw a kick to the groin from a silk-covered knee send a knife to the rotting boards and the first robber howling away in agony.

After pulling the next man away from his prey, Taggart's right fist landed squarely in the second man's belly. It seemed to be enough to give him second thoughts, for the lad took flight along with his compatriot, hurling a loud stream of Gaelic curses behind him.

While the stranger leaned against a wooden beam to catch his breath, Taggart grabbed the third hooligan from behind and whirled him around. He doubled his fist again in preparation for battle.

But for an instant both Taggart and his opponent stopped dead, shocked by recognition. It was Sean Kelly, a boy he'd grown up with in Kinsale.

"Jesus, O'Rahilly, would ya hit one of yer own?" The smaller, freckle-faced lad nodded toward the stranger. "Why, that nob ain't one of us. Sure and ya'd never take his part over me own?"

Taggart unclenched his fist but kept an iron hold on the other Irishman. "Three against one?" he growled. "'Tis not a fair fight comin' up on a man in the dark." So, he thought, this was how Sean Kelly spent those long periods away from his home in Kinsale.

Sean struggled for his freedom with little success. "We didn't even get his purse," he complained. "He won't never miss it." He lowered his squeaky voice. "Me and the lads will split it with ya. Look at the way he's dressed? He ain't even English. Talks like some foreigner. Let go, O'Rahilly."

"You were goin' ta kill him."

"So, what's he ta you?"

"Nothin', but I don't hold with takin' a man's life without cause."

"Like what they done ta your father?" Sean jeered at the bigger man who wouldn't let him escape.

With both hands now, Taggart tightened his grip on his pug-faced adversary. "I'm not lettin' ya kill him," he said with finality. He didn't know why he felt so strong about it now, but his mind was set.

The Kelly boy's eyes sparked hatred. "Then 'tis the worst for you, Taggart O'Rahilly." With a surprising show of strength he wrenched a hand free and grabbed something from the folds of his tattered coat.

It happened so quickly, O'Rahilly had no time to ward off the knife. He felt the sharp point embed in his left shoulder. More angry at his own carelessness than the searing pain, he snarled a Gaelic oath. His doubled fist met the other man's jaw, and the force of the blow sent his opponent reeling backwards. Dazed, the Kelly boy crashed to the hard planks.

Dismissing Sean from his mind, Taggart's face contorted in pain when he pulled the knife from his flesh. He threw the weapon into the murky water. His coat had lessened the depth of the wound, but not by much. And it began to ache like the devil. Hell, he thought, despite the law against Catholics carrying arms, why hadn't he insisted Lady Millicent give him one of her father's pistols? He still had the money under his coat, but at this rate he'd have to sleep with one eye open during the long sea voyage.

"Thank you, suh, for coming to mah aid."

Both men then heard the moans coming from Sean Kelly. Dazed, he put a dirty hand to his bruised jaw.

"Welcome back," Taggart managed to say in a mocking tone.

The Irish ruffian staggered to his feet, eyes raging silent curses. "I've got ya down in me book, O'Rahilly. We Kelly boys have long memories," he spat.

"'Tis quakin' in me boots I am," replied the cocky Irishman. "And there ain't a day when an O'Rahilly can't take on a Kelly. Even with one hand tied behind me back."

But when Taggart watched the Kelly boy limp away, all traces of humor left his dirt-smudged face. Angry at the cut on his shoulder, he'd lost his temper and let his words get the better of him. He knew the clannishness of the Kellys. To them he would now be seen as a traitor against his own. It was a sin far worse than murder in their eyes. And the Kellys lived in Kinsale. "Edna," he whispered as fear crashed over him. What had he done?

So troubled by these thoughts, he'd paid little attention to the stranger.

"I said," repeated the man, "Ah was trying to thank you, sir, for coming to mah assistance." He seemed to let his words sink in a second, then added, "Mah name is Benjamin Abrams."

The taller Irishman blinked, then looked down at the man only a couple of years older than himself. He had light-brown hair and an aristocratic line to his face. His skin gave evidence that he might be more at home with books than outside activities. Torn ruffled lace at throat and cuffs, dark-rose satin waistcoat contrasted with ruined fawn-colored coat and breeches. The ribbon holding back his hair had long since come off. His wavy locks fell about his shoulders in disarray. But where, Taggart wondered, had he learned to handle his fists so expertly?

"No thanks needed," Taggart replied more curtly than intended. Dressed just like the three others who had tried to murder this man, he suddenly felt awkward and ill at ease. This gentleman probably thought he was a vagrant, too, Taggart mused, aware that the other man's piercing blue eyes studied him. "Ya look like ya could of handled it on your own, anyway."

Feeling a little lightheaded from his injury, the Irishman moved unsteadily as he prepared to take his leave.

"Wait, please." The man reached into the pocket of his coat

and took out some coins. "At least let me give—"

Taggart's cool dark eyes narrowed as he looked down at the open palm containing the silver coins. "What I did, I did for me own reasons. Keep yer money, Mr. Abrams."

"I . . ." Clearly embarrassed, the stranger put his money away. "I apologize, suh. It was never my intention to insult you. The mistake was . . . My people do not take kindness from outsiders for granted, for it happens so rarely. Do you understand mah meanin', sir?"

The Irishman had never heard this accent before—the softer "r" sounds, the words drawled gently out from the man's even white teeth. There was no mockery in the face next to him. And whoever this Abrams fellow was, for all his fancy dress and mannered speech, he could fight like an Irish rowdy.

A sharp pain from his shoulder made the taller man wince, and he thrust a hand under his old coat. It came away covered with blood.

"Good God, man, no more talk." Instantly, the stranger put his arm about Taggart's waist. For being three inches shorter, the young man had a lot of strength.

Probably ate better, Taggart thought. To make up lost time, he hadn't stopped to eat since yesterday morning.

"Here, let's get you to my cabin."

"No." Taggart struggled. "I've got ta reach the *Sarah Anne* tonight."

Benjamin smiled at his stubborn companion. "But this is the *Sarah Anne*. I sail in the morning for London, then back to my home in Williamsburg."

Taggart stopped fussing and looked at the good-natured face of the man who still attempted to drag him up the wooden planks. "Williamsburg?" he echoed. "That's where I'm bound. But . . . I have ta speak to the captain about bookin' my pas—" His words slurred as he tried to get a grip on himself. Blood seemed to drain from his face out the gash in his shoulder. He felt chilled despite the warmth of the summer evening. Hell, he thought, gulping air into his lungs, was he going to swoon like a silly maid?

"Don't be such a stubborn ass, O'Rahilly—isn't that what the other man called you?" Taking charge of the younger man,

54

Benjamin practically shoved him up the gangplank. "The first order of business is to see to that wound of yours. Then I'll have mah man arrange your accommodations."

"'Tis the pushiest genteel man I've ever come across," muttered the Irishman as he allowed the new acquaintance to bully him into accepting his help.

Once inside the clean but small cabin, Banjamin would hear of nothing less than tending to Taggart's knife wound himself. He even stood behind the Irishman and assisted him off with his ill-fitting coat and blood-soaked shirt.

"Ah believe you'll carry a scar," Benjamin said, after he had skillfully washed, stitched, then dressed the wound. "Less than an inch lower and it would have pierced your heart. I owe you my life, Irishman."

Taggart touched the cloth dressing at his left shoulder. The man pricked his interest. Polite, yet tough. "Skilled in the art of healin', too," he said aloud. "Is there no end to yer talents, Colonial?"

Abrams clearly took no offense. "My mother taught me a few basic medical skills. Rest does most of the work, along with soap and water. Many of your English physicians, if they can be called that, still bleed and purge their patients to death."

"They ain't *my* English," Taggart corrected.

It was evident to the Virginian that this was a sensitive point. Leaving Taggart propped up on his bed with two down pillows at his back, Benjamin busied himself with replacing the items in a small wooden chest. "I seem," he said from across the room, "to have a knack for getting your hackles up." He tossed off his ruined coat and waistcoat.

There was a knock at the cabin door.

"Enter."

A black-skinned man with tight gray hair came into the room. Dressed in well-cut dark linen coat and breeches, the Negro's reserved expression quickly changed to shock as he took in Mr. Abrams's appearance. "Good Lord, sir, what has—?"

"It's all right, Martin. This gentleman," Ben went on with a nod toward Taggart, "came to my rescue just now when three ruffians attacked me. Taggart O'Rahilly, I should like you to

55

meet mah manservant, Martin."

Martin held himself with proud grace. Bowing formally, he said, "I am pleased to make your acquaintance, Mr. O'Rahilly." The black man's accent added a British clip to his words.

"Same here," Taggart answered.

Stripped to the waist, the Irishman's back rested against the headboard of the comfortable bed. He was well aware of his poor appearance. Uneasily, he watched as Ben spoke softly to his manservant.

A short time later Martin brought food and drink to the cabin and set them on the small mahogany table in the center of the room.

After he'd washed his face and hands in the ceramic basin on the medium-sized dresser, Mr. Abrams retrieved a clean linen shirt from one of the drawers of a carved dresser. Then he put on a brocade robe over his shirt and breeches. "Will you join me in some supper?"

"Mr. Abrams, I—"

"My friends call me Ben. Come. I don't know about you, but I'm starved."

Most of his connections with wealthy gentlemen had never been friendly. In the dark it was different, but here in the candlelight, Taggart was well aware of the shortcomings of his manners and speech. "Thanks, but after I rest here I'll be goin' to find myself a berth below."

"Nonsense. I've taken care of your accommodations. Martin has kindly agreed to share quarters with my cook, and you can have the room next to mine. Though it's smaller than this, it is clean and reasonably comfortable. Our cabins from London to Virginia will be roomier."

"Ya bring yer own cook?" slipped out before he could catch himself.

Ben laughed. "Well, for a quiet fee, His Majesty allows us to have certain privileges. The boats technically belong to England and are manned by Englishmen, but my father does arrange to share the profits, along with having a say in what is shipped."

Then Ben seemed to think of something. He went over to a leather chest at the foot of his bed. "Here, put this on. It should fit you, even if it's a little short in the arms. He tossed the dressing gown to Taggart. At the Irishman's hesitation, he frowned. "If having clothes I've worn close to your skin repels you, suh, I—"

"'Tis not that," Taggart cut in, surprised at the man's sudden defensiveness. "It's just that . . . 'tis too fine a cloth. I haven't washed in a while; I'm afraid I'd soil it."

"Is that all?" demanded his companion. "Put it on and stop being so stiff-rumped, while our food gets cold." The corners of his blue eyes turned up with suppressed laughter.

At first both men ate the warm beef, cheese, and fresh bread in silence. If Ben was shocked by Taggart's table manners or the speed with which he thrashed down the tasty food, he said nothing.

He pushed a plate of carved ham over to Taggart. "I asked Martin to bring this up to you. Of course, I realize this is roughing it, but I hope you will eat your fill."

"God, 'tis a feast." Taggart grabbed two huge slabs of ham, a slice of Cheddar, then wrapped a chunk of bread around them. Between mouthfuls he said, "You call this roughin' it? I haven't seen so much meat in me life, least not at one sittin'."

Something softened in the other man's expression. He looked away for a second and made a pretext at readjusting the hastily tied ribbon that held his light-brown hair away from his face.

Taggart liked the feel of the borrowed robe. He'd never had velvet next to his skin before. "Where's Martin from?" he asked in the way of conversation.

Ben's attention came back to his guest. "Jamaica. My father bought him after he moved his business down from New York."

Taggart stopped eating. "You own slaves?" He spoke so quickly, he was unaware of the censure of his question.

The other man rose from the table; it was evident he fought for control. Ben walked over to the dresser and splashed water on his face once more, then took greater than the time required

57

to towel off his clean-shaven face.

When he returned to the table, Ben's features still held strain.

A few seconds earlier, Taggart thought he was about to feel the other man's fist connect with his Irish snout.

The sound of the chair scraping along the wooden floor was the only noise in the cabin. Ben reached for the decanter and sloshed some red liquid into two cut-crystal goblets. He nudged one over to Taggart.

"I prefer this Madeira from Portugal." Without waiting, he tossed off a long swallow, then set his glass back down on the smooth table.

"Yes," Abrams finally answered, "we do own slaves. But I'll tell you one thing," he bit out, never taking his eyes off Taggart. "We treat our Negroes far better than your protestant landowners treat their tenants—clothes, a bed, care when they're sick, and from the thin look of you, better food I'll warrant than your diet's been. Acquired those stripes on your back enjoying a lusty romp with an Irish lass, did you?" Ben's strong chest moved in and out with his obvious fury.

Taggart had to admire the way Ben stood up for himself. Was he any man's judge, after all? Taggart asked himself. How could he fight the truth of the man's words? And his five guineas a year had barely kept Edna and him fed on a monotonous diet of potatoes and milk.

His companion seemed to accept his silence as acquiescence. Ben shrugged his shoulders and poured more wine into his glass.

"Here, Ben," he said in the way of an apology. "You have ta try this ham. It's wonderful, I'm tellin' ya."

"No . . . thank you, but I'll have another slice of beef."

Suddenly the Irishman laughed, beginning to enjoy himself. "Listen to me, offerin' ya your own grub. Next I'll be wearin' your fancy shirts," he chortled.

"That is not a bad idea, O'Rahilly. I've a coat too long in the sleeves for me. It should just fit you."

Taggart looked embarrassed. "I was only jokin', Ben. I never meant—"

"I know you didn't. Just the same, I insist you take the suit of clothes. It's a small thing. Now," he dismissed, "drink your wine."

When both men finished eating, it was Taggart who rose from the table first.

Sensing his rescuer's exhaustion, Ben opened the door connecting the other cabin. He brought a lighted candle and showed Taggart where to find the things he would need. Before he left, he turned back to the man now sitting comfortably on the edge of his new bed.

"Taggart, before you accept my friendship, there is something . . ." He looked down at the floor. "Something you've a right to know about me."

The Irishman watched Ben turn and pace nervously to the other side of the cabin. Clearly, the man was finding it difficult to confess something.

Facing the wall of the cabin, Ben spoke seriously, with a twinge of bitter resignation. "I will understand if, after you hear me out, you decide to severe our brief acquaintance."

Caught up in the somberness of Ben's countenance, Taggart began to feel ill at ease himself. What had the man done? And for this man Taggart had just made a bitter enemy of an old play chum.

The back facing Taggart became straighter, and pride came through the well-modulated voice. "I am a Jew."

Taggart almost laughed, then cursed, he felt so relieved. "I thought ya were goin' ta tell me you'd killed and ate your parents."

Ben whirled around to face the reclining Irishman. It was obvious he hadn't expected this reaction.

"Ya don't look Jewish, with the gold in yer hair and light eyes. I'm darker than you by a long measure."

"Not all Jews look like Shylock," Ben quipped.

"Who's Mr. Shylock?"

"A character in a play—I'll let you read it sometime." He looked patiently at his new friend. "What I am trying to explain is that we are Sephardic Jews. My ancestors came to New York in the seventeenth century. One of the men in our family later quarreled with his rabbi. That is why my great-grandfather came to Virginia. There are some who still do not accept our right to be there." Then he went on in a lighter tone. "My mother's relatives came from Flanders many years ago. One of my brothers inherited her blond hair; I received her blue eyes."

"I'm a Catholic," Taggart countered. "The men who run this land ain't exactly beggin' me ta stay. Ireland's not my home anymore." Without further explanation, he slowly got off the bed and came over to stand next to Ben. He thrust out a hand. "Here's to a new friendship in America."

Without hesitation, the Virginian accepted the Irishman's hand.

Both men smiled, then they stepped away from each other.

"Think ya could make a gentleman out of me?" Taggart demanded outrageously.

Ben's grin broadened. "When we dock in London, I'll take you to the tailor my father uses on his trips there. Though my side trip here has convinced me Ireland's shipbuilding has been stifled beyond salvage, at least we can go back with a new wardrobe." He headed for the door. "And during the weeks crossing from London to Virginia, we'll have plenty of time to talk about the Colonies. Only . . ." He kept his face devoid of expression.

Here it comes, Taggart thought. The part where he tries to explain why his American family won't want to meet him. "Best say it plain." He tried to keep the disappointment from his voice.

"Mah Lord, I don't know how to tell you this, suh," Ben went on seriously. "But for a beginnin', a gentleman would nevah swear in polite conversation, and absolutely nevah in earshot of one of our Virginian ladies."

"You bastard!" Taggart aimed a fist playfully at Ben. "And here I was getting ready ta . . ."

Ben laughed outright. He heard Taggart say a word under his breath. "What?"

"Sure and does that word sound better in Gaelic, Colonial?"

Lady Millicent Fitzroy sat on the grass, her skirt-covered legs bent as she rested her chin on her knees. She looked out at the sun setting on the calm water. Taggart had only been gone a few days, but already she missed him—the way his dark eyes danced with suppressed laughter, the lilting sound of his voice, his gentle touch as he lifted her down from a tree limb.

A few feet up the embankment, she knew Edna would be preparing for bed soon. Millicent stood up and brushed off the back of her riding jacket. Though she didn't want to, she had to return to Fitzroy Hall.

Edna's high-pitched scream ended her romantic reverie. Then a boy's angry voice shouted something in Gaelic, followed by a feminine cry for help.

Racing to Daisy's saddle, the English girl quickly retrieved the pistol from her leather satchel. Right now she was glad Fergus insisted she always carry it with her when she went out alone these days.

She gathered her heavy skirt in one hand and wasted little time charging up the embankment. However, the grass was slippery and she lunged forward once, barely missing a fall on one of the large jagged rocks.

Frantic and out of breath, Millicent shoved open the door to the O'Rahilly cottage.

Her gray eyes took a second to get accustomed to the dimness inside. "Edna?"

"Here, me lady," came a sob from the back of the room.

A small candle on the oak table flicked shadows across the rough mud walls. The smell of a peat fire and burning mush pervaded the tiny cottage. Millicent took in the scene before her.

The sixteen-year-old held Edna by her long curly hair. He brandished a knife in the other hand.

"Let the girl go," Millicent ordered, raising the flintlock pistol with both hands. "You heard me, Sean Kelly." Those Kelly brothers were a bold lot, she thought. Why had her father insisted on hiring them to take care of his stables? Hadn't she just seen Annie Kelly that very afternoon? Married to Patrick Kelly, the oldest boy, Annie was often on the receiving end of her drunken husband's fist.

"I said," Millicent repeated, "let Edna go." She motioned Sean away from her friend. "Over there."

It was clear Sean hadn't expected this. Nervously, he let go of Edna. "I was only playin' with her. Ain't that right?" he demanded, giving the sobbing ten-year-old a warning look.

Edna massaged her bruised neck, then scraped away at the tears on her face. "Playin', is it now?" she demanded. "Is that what ya call it, Sean Kelly?" She held up the top of her torn shirt with her right hand.

Never letting her gaze slip from the shorter, pug-nosed Sean, Millicent asked, "What did Sean do to you?"

"Nothing, I told ya," the Irish boy added with a belligerent look at Millicent. "Ya can't hold it against a lad for tweakin' a girl's tits before he spills his—"

"Be silent!" the English girl ordered.

"I was fixin' to wash for supper," Edna began. "Imagine me shock when I look up ta see Kelly's weasel face watchin' me through the window. Before I could run for me shawl, the little runt charged into me home and grabbed me, and him reekin' of Fogarty's pub. I cracked me best pot against that wall, missin' his thick skull, more's the pity. Then I screamed and ya come in."

Relieved Sean had gotten no further, Lady Millicent focused her attention back on the now wary lad before her. "The assistant magistrate," she went on in a severe tone, still pointing the long muzzle at him, "is one of my father's good friends. Do you know how Sir Jeremy Cartgrove would handle a troublesome Irishman?"

"Easy now, me lady." Sean raised his hands in supplication. "There ain't no call ta be botherin' his lordship about this. I'll just be goin' back ta the stables, and—"

"You do that. And if you ever attempt to bully Edna O'Rahilly again, you will answer to me."

When they were alone, Millicent lowered the pistol and placed it on the edge of the table.

Edna took the ruined food off the fire, then came back to sit down on a round stool on the other side of the rickety table. "Thank you, my lady, for helpin' me."

In agitation Lady Millicent walked the short length of the cottage, clearly deep in thought.

Edna watched her, immediately reminded of Dunstan and

the way he thrust his hands behind his back when he contempleted a course of action. Finally, she saw the English girl stop pacing.

"Edna, this will not do. I know you wish to stay here, and your gesture is a gallant one. But tonight must have shown you how dangerous it is for you to stay here alone. Can we not come to some agreement on this matter?"

The green-eyed girl looked away. "But I have ta see to the O'Rahilly cottage."

"I want you to come and live in Fitzroy Hall tonight. Wait," Millie added when she saw Edna's mouth open. "Please hear me out. We can bring some items from my rooms over here. I'll even embroider some doilies. We could visit the cottage whenever we wish. This could be our secret retreat," she offered hopefully.

"You . . . you mean like a playhouse?"

"Why . . . yes," she agreed, trying to press her advantage. "You see, you won't lose anything. And I'll have a companion for company. We can fix up a room next to mine."

Edna's dimpled smile faded. "And his lordship? Your father will just love havin' an Irish kitchen maid encamped in the Fitzroy apartments."

Millicent's slender nose moved upward. "Well, I shall handle Father. Companion, kitchen maid—I'll—Maid!" she shouted. "That's it, Edna. You leave Father to me."

As the girls sat across from each other, a question occurred to Edna. "Millie, would you have really shot Sean Kelly just now?"

The taller girl tossed back her reddish-brown head with a saucy laugh. "Hardly. The pistol was not loaded. I've always been skittish around the things. Don't tell Fergus, though. The poor little man would have kittens."

Edna shook her head. "Blessed Mary, you're a game one."

Then both girls burst out laughing.

Chapter 5

March 1749

While Edna O'Rahilly continued with her white-on-white embroidery, Lady Millicent Fitzroy finished the last red rose on a lady's riding jacket. Sitting across from each other in the Englishwoman's sitting room, both young women were similarly dressed—white lawn caps and simple gowns of brown lustring.

Millicent stopped sewing for a few minutes to rest her eyes. She glanced about the once beautiful room. They had her father's gambling debts and high living to thank for their present destitute state. The clock given by Elizabeth Tudor to one of Millicent's ancestors had long disappeared from her mantel; the elaborately carved wooden wardrobe was now replaced by a much plainer but serviceable one. Many nonessential rooms in the large house were closed, with the remaining furniture covered by old sheets. Mrs. Halsey and Benton had been the first to leave when their salaries materialized too slowly to suit them. Only Edna, Fergus and Colleen Mulcahy, along with the Kelly brothers remained.

"Do you have enough light, your ladyship?"

"Quite enough," Millicent replied softly. "And, Edna, I do not wish to yammer on about it, but when we are alone, there really is no need to call me anything but Millie."

Edna returned her friend's smile. Old habits were difficult to break.

"Do you know," the taller girl went on, "it amazes me how much you are able to get for our needlework. Now I am only sorry I did not think of this scheme earlier."

Edna's green eyes focused on her thread. "The English ladies are quite pleased with the crafts. Sure and they're all agog at how fast *I* produce them."

As Millicent continued with her morning session of embroidery, the nineteen-year-old Irish girl couldn't help studying her. Seriously bent over her needlework, Millicent had no idea how little came in from her lovely work. So ready to believe the best in people, her ladyship thought her father's friends were paying extraordinarily high prices for what they assumed was solely an Irish servant's stitchery. But, Edna reminded herself, the Englishwoman was proud. If she realized the truth, Lady Fitzroy would never accept a farthing in charity. In pride, Millie matched Taggart.

"Perhaps we shall receive a letter from Dunstan today," the Englishwoman exclaimed as she tied a knot to the back of a multicolored peacock. She sighed. Dunstan was now fighting the French in India. And it had been ten months since either of them had received a message from the British officer. It was becoming increasingly difficult to hide her deep concern.

The younger woman fidgeted on the worn, overstuffed chair. "Two years without leave seems very unfair ta me," Edna stated with feeling. "Pray Mary, he gets back soon." She crossed herself. "And I vow never ta tease him again about how he looks in his scarlet coat and powdered wig."

When the auburn-haired girl saw Edna brush a tear away from her eyes, she put down her sewing and immediately went over to her friend. Millicent put her arms around the smaller girl, wishing desperately that there was more she could do.

"The waiting is so difficult, I know."

Then Millie's lips turned upward. "But if my perceptions have been correct during Dunstan's last few visits home, scarlet uniform, sash at his waist, and all, not to mention the number of letters which have passed between you," she teased, "I would venture to wager that my brother will ask for your hand when next he returns."

Edna's attempt at courage faltered a little as the words, "if he returns" were left unspoken.

The taller girl rose slowly from her crouched position and headed back to her patched sofa cushion. She tried to clear her thoughts, focusing on something to brighten their spirits.

"I shall burst if you do not tell me of your brother's news from America."

"How did you kn—?"

"Forgive me. I wasn't spying, but when I entered the kitchen this morning, I saw Fergus hand you a parcel. I just assumed it was from Virginia." The eagerness was evident in her tone.

"Blessed Mother, I forgot with me frettin' about the Visc— Dunstan," she amended, clearly liking these times of less formality. She dashed from her chair and moved to the door connecting their rooms. "And to be sure himself even sent ya a gift. I'll be back presently.

A gift from Taggart! Millicent thought with growing excitement. Even if he hadn't written to her personally, she told herself, he obviously must be thinking about her. Not a day passed during these last nine years when she hadn't thought of her Irishman, prayed for him, worried over him, and eagerly awaited any news about him from his sister.

Millicent's gray eyes behind her round frames glowed with anticipation as Edna returned and began reading Taggart's latest long letter. Like many of his others to Edna, the descriptions of his world travels enthralled her. Turkey, Portugal, China—the sights and smells of those exotic places captivated her senses.

"And," Edna continued as she neared the end of the communication, "he says he is well and learning to enjoy the hotter summers in Williamsburg, though his travels keep him away a good part of the year."

"I do hope," Millicent interjected, "his employer treats him well. Your brother is such a loyal servant, not once has he written a complaint at how hard the man works him."

Edna lowered her eyes. Clearly, Millicent had no idea how wealthy Taggart had become. And, of course, thought Edna uneasily, how could she tell this Englishwoman where some of the money for their food and feed for Dunstan's beloved horses came from? Hadn't the lady cared for her all these years, teaching her manners, introducing her to books? And as the earl's fortunes dwindled, so did his days of sobriety. Even Dunstan, away two years now, had no idea how difficult things had become at Fitzroy Hall.

Edna sighed as her deceptions mounted in the barrel. She'd also deceived her own brother by hiding the present living conditions at Fitzroy Hall. She would probably burn in hell, but what else could she do? How could she abandon her proud friend now that things had reversed from years past?

As she came to the last paragraph, Edna tried to keep her expression light. "He ends with some teasing words only an older brother writes his sister." She silently scanned over the section where Taggart brushed off her earlier protests that he was sending her far too much money each month. He then went on to say it was worth even more to have her away from any Fitzroy influences. One thing had not changed, she realized—Taggart still loathed the Earl of Holingbrook. As her brother's education and polish increased, so did the formality of his letters. He finished by writing in a clear, straight hand:

> I understand you think it amiss of me not to write your friend, but I cannot bring myself to initiate correspondence with anyone by the name of Fitzroy. And I must caution you again not to become too attached to that Englishwoman, for you are too trusting. It will, I fear, only lead to your disappointment and hurt later on. Pressed, it is my firm conviction that no Englishwoman would ever take the part of anyone but her own kind.
>
> Pray, dear sister, write no more to me on this matter, for my mind is set upon a course. I will not be dissuaded.
>
> However, your winning ways have persuaded me to enclose a second gift to dispose of as you wish.
>
> As always, your loving brother,
> Taggart

When Edna reopened the leather box that accompanied his letter, she found the two ivory fans wrapped in silk. The first was hand-painted with red flowers and exotic birds—a slip of paper with her name on it was folded across it. The other fan, though of equal workmanship, was a more subdued painting of a tranquil water scene. Obviously, Taggart meant the less pretty one for Millie.

Edna hid the sheet of paper in a pocket of the apron covering her dress. After all, she thought, it was such a small token. She handed the exquisite fan to the English girl.

Unable to contain her pleasure, Millicent rushed over to the window with a cry of delight, clutching the precious gift in her hand. "See how the red and gold catch the light. Oh, Edna, I have never received such a beautiful present!" Tears misted her gray eyes. He did remember her, she shouted inwardly. Pirouetting across the room, she smiled and giggled with uncharacteristic abandon. She posed this way and that, opening and closing the Chinese fan, waving it in front of her as she curtsied low, pretending to accept Taggart's offer for the next minuet.

How had he changed? she wondered. Nine years had added two more inches to her height, accompanied by a rounding of her body. Of course, she knew she'd never have the curves of Garnet Somerset or Edna O'Rahilly, but Millicent was grateful right now for what she did have—Taggart hadn't forgotten her.

From below her ruffled pinner, an unruly black curl tumbled free, and Edna whisked it behind her ear as she watched Lady Fitzroy. Never had she seen her so flushed or animated. It pleased her to see the overworked, lonely English girl this way. Millie always glowed at the mention of Taggart or the delivery of another letter. Though Edna knew it must, at the very least, disappoint her at never receiving a letter from him, not once had the lady made any outward protest.

"Well," Millicent said with a hint of reluctance in her soft voice. "I must get ready for my afternoon rounds." As she reverently wrapped her gift back in the yellow silk, she added, "And, Edna, when next you write, please allow me to add a note of thanks to your brother for his lovely present."

Benjamin Abrams turned the pages of the ship's log. His expression was grave. "As your lawyer, Captain O'Rahilly, it is mah duty to tell you . . ."

Taggart watched his friend from across his desk. "Yes?" he encouraged. Only the corners of his dark eyes gave evidence that he knew his old friend was having sport with him.

Ben grinned at the Irishman. "To tell you that your *Yankee Rose* has just brought back the biggest haul yet from the West Indies and in record time. Congratulations. This even surpasses your last voyage to China."

The sea and dirt from months on the ocean washed from his ruddy skin, Taggart was now dressed fashionably in dark-brown knee breeches, coat, and cream-colored waistcoat over a white ruffled shirt. His thick black hair was tied neatly at the back of his neck. Looking pleased with his lawyer's report, he glanced about his large office. The walls were covered with paintings of ships at sea and there were bookcases filled with seafaring volumes, charts, ships' logs. Three drafting tables with high wooden stools were located at the back of the room, where some of his employees sat drawing his maps and logging in the long lists of goods that he always brought back from his trips.

Up on the hill in the distance, he could hear the sound of workmen pounding boards as they readied his home. Yes, he thought triumphantly, this was what he wanted—Williamsburg Shipping right on the James River with the wharf practically in his backyard. Then up on the hill, in walking distance from his separate office would be the main house, standing proud and tall overlooking the water.

Ben's clear blue eyes sparkled with admiration. "You were born with a head for business, suh."

A sound of deep laughter echoed across the room. The three men working over their high drafting tables looked up and smiled, obviously used to their employer's direct show of emotion.

At twenty-five, Taggart's shoulders had broadened with hard work and Virginia culinary skills. "All right," he added, noting his friend's genuine frown after he turned to the end of the ship's log. "Out with."

"Also as your lawyer and friend, Ah have warned you against intercepting those Spanish galleys. His Majesty will take a dim view if Captain Fernandez complains to the King of Spain."

Thrusting his legs out in front of him, the taller man looked unrepentant. "But there she was, Ben, only a short distance away from us—a fourteen-gun, Spanish sloop. King George won't squawk when he sees the ninety-five casks of sugar, two hundred casks of indigo, and twenty-five bales of cotton I'll be shipping off to London within the week."

"But privateering is not your business, O'Rahilly." Ben lowered his voice so the others in the back of the room would not hear. "You have a respectable shipping business here. You don't need the money, and it's sheer folly to—"

"Don't worry, Ben. Captain Fernandez was so impressed that none of my men robbed his crew of their personal possessions that he treated us all to a feast of roasted ox before we put into port." The dimple at his chin expanded with his impudent grin as he watched the handsome young man pore slowly over the large pages.

Ben's father, Eleazar, was a long-established Williamsburg investor. Both he and his son helped ease Taggart's way into learning the manners of a gentleman. Ben had tutored him for his entrance examinations to William and Mary. Even though Ben was two years ahead of Taggart, he'd helped him through his first difficult year at the university. The razings from some of the other students because of his brogue and awkward manner soon died away when the Irishman learned to use his verbal gifts instead of his fists.

With a quick and eager mind, Taggart had devoured all he could about ships and commerce. John Nolan's generous gift, along with a loan from the Abrams family had started his small business. And how it had grown during the last few years, making it possible to repay both loans quickly.

This last voyage would do it, the black-haired man thought eagerly. Things were ready now.

Ben pulled his nose out from the log. "Will you have dinner with Rachel and me tonight?"

Taggart accepted the well-dressed lawyer's invitation readily. "I would like that. And how is your lovely wife?"

"Marvelous," he answered, then laughed openly. "I am

bursting to tell you. Rachel is . . . that is . . . she just gave me the news this morning—I'm going to be a father."

Instantly, Taggart was on his feet. He came around the carved wooden desk to embrace his friend with open exuberance. "Well, now isn't it grand news." Emotion always caused him to slip back into his brogue. "This is cause for celebrating tonight."

"Yes, and now that Williamsburg Shipping is going so well," Ben kidded, "don't you think it's time you settled down, too? You've got plenty of men to sail the ships for you. Why not stay right here and run the business from your office? Ah know of no other owner with your success in Virginia who still risks his life tearing out all over the globe with his ships."

Taggart didn't take offense. "But I enjoy the sea, and there's a special trip I need to begin planning right away."

Ben blurted, "Edna must have enough money to live like a princess now. She rents a lovely home, has servants, doesn't need to work. You told me yourself she wouldn't leave Kinsale nine years ago. Why not leave well enough alone?" Concern etched across his features as he looked up at Taggart. "Ah remember too well your state that first night we met. There is nothing in Ireland for you; only trouble can come of this."

Taggart's strong jaw clenched. He did not want to quarrel with his friend. They'd had this argument before. Though Edna had never fully agreed to return with him, he was sure she'd come around if he visited her in person. The vision of a little girl with curly black hair and dimples at the corners of her mouth entered his mind. Besides, there were other reasons for going back.

"Have you done as I instructed?" Taggart asked abruptly. "About those notes." His tone was now totally businesslike.

Frowning, Ben went back to his client's large desk and pulled out a stack of papers from a leather satchel. "Ah have gone over all the notes you now hold on the Earl of Holingbrook. The Englishman must be strapped, for his solicitor has become even more careless in his haste to get money for his overextended client. My sources in London tell me many of the servants have left and all but the essential parts of the mansion have been closed off, except for the stables. Apparently the earl

71

refuses to cut back in that department."

"There is a son, Dunstan," Taggart pointed out casually. "Hasn't he done anything to curb his father's ruin?" Sarcasm colored his question.

Ben leafed through some papers. "Let's see, I do recall something . . ."

Despite his attempts to shut her out of his mind, Taggart found himself thinking of Lady Millicent Fitzroy once more. The vision of her riding astride Hellfire in the moonlight, strands of silken auburn hair that broke free from under her tricorn hat and whipped about her delicate face—yes, he often longed to know how she'd fared during these last years. But . . . His body tensed. He'd forced himself to harden his heart. The earl had played a major role in his father's death, as well as illtreating Taggart and his sister when they were under his employ. How could he write the English girl in friendship, while he plotted her father's ruin?

"Oh, yes, here it is." Ben pointed to a scrawled note attached to one of the legal documents. "It appears the young man was an officer in His Majesty's army. Distinguished service in the War of Austrian Succession. He's been home a few times, but for the last year no one has heard from him. He was fighting at Pondichery on the eastern coast of India." Ben stopped reading and glanced up, a look of sympathy on his face. "It appears he died there in a skirmish with the French."

Taggart turned quickly and gazed out the window at the James River for a long time. He had no real quarrel with Dunstan, and this last news saddened him. "May God rest his soul," he murmured softly. Another sin the earl had to answer for. He knew his son had never wanted to be a soldier, damn him. Dunstan's gentle nature had always been better suited to raising the horses he loved. "'Tis a waste. A damn bloody waste."

"Do you wish me to continue? Ah have little information about the earl's daughter, Lady Millicent, isn't she?"

When he turned back to his adviser, Taggart's eyes were hard stones. "No, for I've heard all I can stomach about those Fitzroys this day." He walked about the large office, trying to fight his mounting fury. He saw the three men push their

72

attention down to their work as he scowled past them.

A few minutes went by, then he stalked back to his desk. "I'll depart for London within the week. After I drop off my tobacco and the rest of this trip's cargo, I'm heading back to Kinsale." There was a new, determined set to the smooth line of his jaw. Ben would not put him off this time, he vowed. It was more than time to collect his younger sister . . . and extract payment on the overdue debt Geoffrey Fitzroy owed him.

Chapter 6

After taking leave of Sir Arthur Lyncrost, his affable host, Taggart O'Rahilly headed toward the back of the large reception room. Still holding his glass of claret, he sat down on one of the brocade-covered benches that dotted the periphery of the room.

He usually didn't attend such functions on his trips to London, but it was King George's birthday and private parties like these were taking place all over the city tonight. Besides, he liked his English contact. In his late fifties, Sir Arthur was respected in these aristocratic circles, even though he was a younger son and had to work in trade for a living. Ben Abrams had been correct in advising Taggart to utilize Sir Arthur as mediator for selling his American cargo.

Taggart glanced about the room after taking another sip of wine. From his vantage point he could observe the captivating woman sitting nearby. At least four men paid court to the blond-haired beauty. One, an officer in His Majesty's army, if Taggart had correctly identified the sash, bent over and whispered something in her ear. Looking playfully shocked the petite lady closed her lacy fan and tapped the bold fellow on his scarlet-uniformed sleeve.

"Captain Bembridge," the vision admonished. "You are too bad."

When the young officer stood up, Taggart realized they were about the same height and age, but there the resemblance ended.

74

"Pwease, your grace," Captain Bembridge begged. "Your beauty causes me to loose my sense of propriety. Pway forgive me."

The lady seemed to relent as she looked up at her powdered and painted devotee. Her eyes warmed to the repentant officer, and he sat back down next to her once more. The three other nonmilitary swains appeared to have lost their advantage.

Something stirred in the Irishman's memory as he took in the blond curls becomingly arranged to set off a perfectly oval face, the pink skin, blue eyes, and the low cut of her dark-blue gown which exposed the alluring mounds of her full, ripe breasts. Could it be her? Taggart thought.

Feeling both pulled and repelled, the man from Virginia stood up and headed for the French doors. He stopped a footman carrying another tray of sweetmeats. "The young lady in the blue gown holding court at the center of the room, I believe I've met her before," he whispered, then handed the young boy a gold sovereign. "I feel the perfect fool at forgetting her name. You see," he covered casually, "I've been abroad for a few years."

The thin young man in gray linen coat grinned as he quickly stashed the coin in his pocket. "Why, sir, that's Duchess Garnet Huntington of Montrose."

Garnet Somerset, now Duchess Huntington, dared a glance again at the intriguing stranger. Coolly, she watched him from lowered lashes as he spoke to a servant. He wore dark velvet coat and knee breeches, the latest fashion of a pleated neckband buckled at the back of his neck, pristine ruffles at his wrists, waistcoat in the new shorter length, and silver buckles on his black leather pumps. His blue-black hair tied neatly at the back stood out among the majority who wore elaborate white, pink, and yellow powdered wigs. Handsome face, strong, broad shoulders, tall, and well-formed legs encased in white hose. Unaccustomed to seeing an obvious gentleman with such tanned skin the clear result of outside activities, Garnet's curiosity was piqued. The blue of her eyes became darker as she openly watched him walk out the connecting doors to the outside garden.

Taggart wanted to be alone in the chilly night air. Down the familiar marble steps, he found his way out into the maze of boxwood hedges. The grass-covered earth was hard beneath his shoes, the spring temperature unusually cold, but he'd felt the need to get out of the stuffy room. He breathed the biting air into his lungs. Memories crashed against him—visions of Garnet laughing up at him in the Fitzroy stables, the smell of the damp and dirty cellar at Somerset Hall. However, he could not deny it. Garnet Somerset had become even more beautiful.

Alert, the Irishman suddenly realized he was no longer standing alone. Someone lurked behind the tall, clipped hedge next to him. Without pistol or sword, he hoped this was only an inebriated gentleman relieving himself in the bushes. Cautiously, Taggart inched his way forward, ready to grab the fellow when he came to the place where the hedges veered to the right. His body tensed as he grew ready to defend himself from attack.

"Oh!" squealed a feminine voice. "Sir, you startled me," Garnet admonished. She dropped her fan and swayed, giving full evidence that a faint from shock was imminent.

Just in time Taggart reached out and took the perfumed bundle of silk and lace against his strong chest. He tried to steady her with a gentle touch. "Madam, I am sorry if I frightened you."

His well-meant words seemed to displease her, for instantly she pulled back from his supporting arms.

"Sir, you have made a grave mistake to address me so. I," she pointed out, stiffening her spine even more, despite her tightly laced corset, "am a duchess."

Taggart looked at the ground. "Again . . . your grace," he amended, "I must beg your pardon. I am an American and still learning London ways." With a graceful movement, he retrieved her fan, took out his white pocket handkerchief and wiped the dew from it, then handed the dainty item back to its owner.

After accepting the blue fan in her gloved fingers, Garnet

smiled beguilingly up at the man before her. "A colonial," she cooed. "How exciting. I just knew I had never seen you at one of Arthur's soirees before."

"My relationship with Sir Arthur is also of a business nature. On my trips from Virginia he purchases my cargo." He bowed formally. "My name is—"

"Oh, no," Garnet interrupted. She came closer, allowing her eyes to get a better view of his handsome features. "I . . . I think it would be more exci—prudent if we do not use our own names tonight. Don't you agree?" she demanded with a coquettish smile. "I shall call you . . . my colonial. Yes," she added playfully. "That will suit you. Perhaps . . ." She looked demurely down at the tops of her now damp slippers. "You might tell me more about the place called Virginia later this evening."

Fully aware that a geography lesson was the last thing this petite temptress in front of him wanted, Taggart gave nothing away in his expression. "I shall be most honored to tell you about my homeland. Shall I meet you here in—?" The tinkling sound of her laughter stopped his words.

"Oh, pray forgive me, sir, for I do realize you are a true gentleman. I knew it the instant I saw how fashionably you were dressed, and your articulated speech—Cambridge, is it not?" Not waiting for a reply, Garnet continued. "A woman of my standing can tell good breeding at a glance. However—" A giggle escaped her small mouth as she tapped him on the arm with her fan. "I should not laugh at you so. It is too bad of me, but it is quite clear you are not used to the company of English ladies. We could never meet here," she admonished, a look of mock horror on her pretty face. "Can you ride a horse?"

Taggart cleared his throat rather than let the sarcastic retort escape his compressed lips. He could more than ride her flanks well enough, he thought, if that was what she wished to know. And when she snapped him on the arm once more with her fan, he barely controlled the urge to grab the cursed thing from her pampered hands and break it in two.

However, in an even tone, he replied, "Yes. I can ride, your grace."

"Good. Oh," the duchess whimpered, clutching her glove-

77

covered hands about her arms, where the sleeves of her Paris-styled gown ended just below the elbows. "My delicate skin will be ruined with the cold night air. Now listen carefully." She gave the next instruction like a well-seasoned general. "A few miles from here there is an inn, The Three Cranes. The proprietor's name is Jonathan. When you arrive there at midnight, ask for . . . for Lady Louise's rooms."

Taggart nodded his comprehension.

"Excellent," she purred, slipping back into her childlike voice. "Now, I must go back. Give me ten minutes before you return. You may kiss my hand." Clearly, assuming her companion would be honored by her magnanimity, Garnet thrust her right hand up at him.

The only indication of his reaction was the narrowing about his dark eyes. He took her gloved hand in his. However, instead of placing his lips on the material, he boldly used his other hand to pull down the silk glove so that his warm lips touched the alabaster softness of her skin. He took his time easing the material back over her hand and wrist.

"My . . . you are quite naughty," she admonished half-heartedly. "You will be on time?"

Taggart hadn't missed the eagerness in her sultry voice. "I shall try to be," he replied, "but one never knows what will happen. Your husband might—"

"Oh, do not fret yourself about Calv—my husband, Colonial. He is seventy and only thinks of bed at that hour."

"But, your grace, that is where you shall be also, is it not?" he asked innocently.

This time Garnet replied with a new boldness. "But *we* will not be sleeping." Another quick wrap to his knuckles. Then with a flurry of skirts, she rushed back toward Sir Arthur's mansion.

Taggart watched her expertly maneuver the elaborate maze. Clearly, this was not the first time Edwin Somerset's sister had made her dainty way about Sir Arthur's complicated gardens at night. He saw her stop on the stone stairs to catch her breath. Then in the moonlight, she brushed a hand across the front of her blue gown and composed her features quickly, before walking regally through the French doors.

78

After waiting the ordered time, O'Rahilly felt he'd stayed out here in the cold long enough. However, before he reached the doors leading back into the ballroom, from the shadows a scarlet-covered arm on his coat sleeve halted his advance.

"You are that colonial friend of Sir Arthur's. O'Rahilly, is it not?"

The old O'Rahilly would have answered with his fists. But the new O'Rahilly merely looked down coolly at the long fingers on his arm. "That is correct, sir. I, on the other hand, do not have your insight. Is it now His Majesty's wish that his officers waylay guests at private functions?"

Looking slightly chagrined, the soldier removed his hold on the other man. "I am Captain Percival Bembridge, at your service." He finished with a military bow.

When Taggart would have continued on his way, the officer spoke. "A word of warning, Mr. O'Rahilly. The lady I saw you attempting to take advantage of in the garden just now is inexperienced in the ways of the world. Her sweet nature shelters her from the true ways of men."

The black-haired man heard no lisp now, though Bembridge's voice was rather high-pitched for a man. From the top of Bembridge's powdered white wig, red coat with gleaming gold buttons, to the tips of his shiny black dress pumps, not a minute detail was out of place. With a delicate appearance, this officer looked as if he could never hold his own in a fight. There was a softness in the man's physical form. "Just what the devil are you attempting to tell me, Bembridge?"

Despite his overly powdered face, the officer's features took on color. His voice sounded petulant. "The duchess and I— Damn it, you are an intruder in this matter. I have first claim on the lady's—"

"I should think," Taggart cut off, "those claims would be the sole prerogative of the lady's husband." Before the furious captain could say another word, Taggart deftly reopened one of the glass doors and stepped inside.

Having discreetly borrowed a horse from his host, Taggart finally found the Inn of Three Cranes. When he saw it, he realized why the seclusion of the large brick inn appealed to Garnet. Set far back from the road in a grove of oak trees, the ivy-covered old inn was the perfect place for a clandestine tryst.

He bent his head and entered the dimly lit establishment. Men sat at rough wooden tables puffing at long clay pipes and raising tankards in another round of toasts. A serving girl with a saucy smile came over to him immediately.

Taggart could not help notice that any sudden movement threatened to tumble the young girl's ample breasts out of her loosely laced bodice.

"Can I help ya, gov?"

The corners of his sensuous mouth turned upward at the bold mischief in the girl's brown eyes. "Could you direct me to the owner of this establishment, a Master Jonathan, I believe?"

Clearly admiring the well-dressed man before her, the girl nodded her head backward. "'E be the one standin' in the back with the leather apron around his fat gut."

"Thank you." Taggart made a slight bow, then headed toward the innkeeper. It amused him to feel the girl's eyes on his back.

"Excuse me, sir, but are you Jonathan?"

The rotund man in his late fifties nodded. "That I am, sir. How may I be helpin' ye?"

Taggart leaned closer and said softly, "Lady Louise is expecting me."

The innkeeper grinned, revealing a gaping space where at least three front teeth once called home. "Ah, yes, sir. I understand. Top a the stairs, third door on your left. And not to worry about your 'orse, mate. The girl will see to 'im."

"Ah, why do I always 'ave ta see ta their 'orses," the girl whined behind Taggart. "Why can't the guests see ta their own 'orses. Next ya'll be 'aven me wipe their bums when they use the privy."

"I won't 'ave no coarse talk around my guests. You just watch your speech, miss, or I'll rip your gizzard out and nail it on me wooden sign outside as a reminder that I run a high-class inn."

In answer, his employee clanked the last tankard of ale from her wooden tray down in front of a sodden patron who merely raised his face from his stew plate, smiled at the tavern girl, then plunked his head back down on the rough table.

"Least this time ya managed to miss your food dish, ya donkey dick," the young girl sneered, then looked back at her employer, clearly unafraid of his threats. "Besides, I ain't never seen this one around 'er grace before. 'Es a new one."

The innkeeper wagged a finger at the grumbling girl. "You best be keepin' a civil tongue in your head, my girl. What your betters do is no business of yours. Now see ta the gentleman's 'orse."

The girl's expression brightened immediately when Taggart tossed her a shilling for her trouble.

As Taggart headed for the rickety stairs, the innkeeper called solicitously, "And don't fret yourself, sir. You'll not be disturbed. A pleasant night ta ye."

His tricorn hat and leather gloves under his arm, Taggart knocked softly at the door. Part of him almost wished she wouldn't be here. And when a pretty, dark-haired girl answered the door, he thought Garnet had tricked him. Looking apologetic, he bowed and said, "I am sorry for disturbing you, miss. It appears I have the wrong—"

"Louise" came a familiar voice from within the room. "Answer me, you fool. Is he here yet?"

The large, sad eyes of the young girl watched him. "You are the colonial, monsieur, no?"

"Yes, I am." Taggart liked the soft, charmingly accented French girl's voice. So, this girl was Garnet's maid. How like Garnet to choose the girl's name to cover her own. Clearly, Garnet felt little compunction ruining Louise's reputation by using her name instead of the Duchess of Montrose.

Louise stepped back. "Please come in, monsieur."

Excusing herself after motioning him to sit down, the maid went into another room, obviously to tell her mistress she had a visitor.

Taggart sat on the overstuffed striped chair. Blue, white, and gold predominated the room. The richness of the fabrics and furnishings immediately led him to believe the duchess herself had permanent access to these rooms. He was sure none of the other guests at the inn had such accommodations. A welcoming fire blazed in the marble fireplace across the room. He counted at least three vases filled with white roses. Garnet obviously preferred things French. Gilt-edged carvings on the white-and-gold chest of drawers, the small marble cupid that stood mischievously aiming an arrow at an unsuspecting sleeping kitten, and the paintings on the walls depicted well-endowed ladies in various stages of their toilet. One wood nymph had an uncanny resemblance to Garnet herself.

His observations were cut short when he heard Garnet's angry voice. "I told you never to call me that here, you stupid girl!"

"I am sorry, madam," he heard Louise apologize softly. It was followed by the loud crack of flesh connecting with flesh, and Louise's wounded outcry.

"That will help you remember," growled Garnet.

The maid came dashing out of the room crying. Taggart stood up when he saw the sobbing maid try to move quickly past him. His gaze captured the tear-filled eyes of the younger girl. It was no impatient tap Garnet had given her servant. A dark-red handprint stood out against the delicate white skin of the French girl's cheek. Automatically, he reached out a hand to comfort her, but the girl lowered her head and moved past him to enter a small room. From behind the closed door he could hear her wrenching sobs. Why had he come here? he berated himself.

"I am sorry to have kept you waiting," came Garnet's purring voice behind him. "But I could not rush my bath tonight, for I do so love the scent of roses."

"The maid, she—?"

"Oh, Louise is very bad. So lazy. La, I am worn out with trying to fashion her into a proper lady's maid. But," she added, coming closer to the handsome American, "let us talk of more pleasant things. Would you like a glass of cognac?"

Not waiting for his reply, Garnet led Taggart into the adjoining room. It was a large room for an inn. A fire crackled warmly. Two gold-striped chairs were placed on a blue-and-white Oriental carpet a short distance from the white marble fireplace. The large elaborately carved white-and-gold bed dominated the room. The ethereal fresco painted above the bed caught his brown eyes immediately. Pink-cheek cherubs played musical instruments on fluffy white clouds against an azure blue sky.

It was excellent cognac. Garnet had nothing to drink, and he continued watching her. She was now dressed in another, more revealing gown of blue muslin. It was clear she was not wearing a hooped petticoat or a corset, nor had she sufficiently toweled her body, for the dampness made the soft material cling to every curve of her voluptuous figure. His hand was unsteady as he replaced the glass on the smooth surface of the table on his right.

She looked down at her small hands. "Would you like me to have food brought up to you?" Her blue eyes captured his.

"Thank you, but food is not what I require."

"You forgot to address me as 'your grace,'" she pointed out. Her soft pink lips formed a pretty pout. Then she rose gracefully from her chair. The only sound in the room now was the faint rustle of her thin gown as she floated toward him.

Hands on her hips, she stood in front of him. This stranger from Virginia clearly intrigued her. Darkly handsome, he sat observing her from those cool midnight eyes. The clean spicy smell of his skin combined with the faint scent of leather from his ride here. She knew by the signs that he wanted her, yet it fascinated her to realize he was also fighting to keep in control. This one was obviously not used to being mastered by a woman. Garnet smiled at him provocatively, anticipating a night filled with his adoring attentions.

"For failing to used my proper title, what do you think your punishment should be, Colonial?" With a provocative movement of her shoulders to enhance her companion's view of her breasts, the Englishwoman came to stand right beside his outstretched legs.

Taggart leaned to the right, his lips close to hers as she bent her golden head toward his. "It is for you to say, your grace."

She felt his warm breath on her moist lips, and it vexed her that he did not take the kiss she offered. She tried another tactic. Haughtily brushing her skirts past him, she returned to her chair. "You did promise to tell me about Virginia, did you not? Are there savages? How do they treat their wives?" she rattled off. "Is it true they eat Englishmen?"

He laughed openly. "Where I live I have never heard of the natives indulging in cannibalism, your grace. And . . . I am sure they treat their wives as Englishmen do."

"How disappointing," she sulked. "Then savage women must lead very dull lives."

"Does your husband treat you so badly, then?" He eyed the large diamond necklace at her white throat. One of the shimmering drops nestled lasciviously in the cleft of her breasts, enticing him to take her own fleshy jewels in his hands.

The diamonds at her ears moved when she tossed her blond head in agitation. "I have everything I want but an attentive husband."

His comment held mock sympathy. "How distressing."

Obviously unable to stop herself, Garnet was out of her chair and standing next to her companion once more. "And what do you do in Virginia?" she asked, turning her body in a manner that more than hinted readiness.

Only a moron could fail to read her blatant signal, Taggart mused. Slowly, he eased Garnet onto his lap, well aware that she'd wanted this all evening. "I grow corn and tobacco." Through his velvet breeches, he felt her ample bottom wriggle across the corded muscles of his thighs.

"And that is not the only thing you colonials grow in abundance," she commented as she felt him respond to her close contact. "Oh," she giggled. "That was very wicked of me." Her face came closer to his. "You make me think such naughty things."

The Irishman could no longer resist the soft, moist lips so close to his own. He bent his head and tentatively touched Garnet's pouting mouth. Then, as he felt her heated response when she pressed her breasts closer to his chest, his lips became more demanding. It was Garnet who pulled away first.

"My, you are so forceful." She stopped to fan her flushed cheeks with her tiny hand. Her voice was breathless. "I shall call Louise to undress me."

"That will not be necessary." Skillfully, the Irishman began to unfasten the hooks at the back of her gown.

Garnet did not understand why she was so uncharacteristically docile with this man, but she found herself standing between his strong legs as he undressed her. She had to bite down on her lip to keep from demanding that he remove her gown and lacy chemise with more speed. He left her only in her small-heeled slippers and white stockings.

"Beautiful," he murmured, unable to hide his open appreciation for her full, round charms. It was clear she was proud of her body, for she stood before him, not hiding the gold thatch between her fleshy thighs. She unfastened the diamonds from her throat and ears and placed them casually on the dresser next to the bed. Fully aware that she had his full attention, after removing her dainty shoes and blue-ribboned garters, Garnet bent over and began skimming down each white stocking from her creamy legs. Clearly she wanted him to get the best effect.

Taggart felt the ache between his legs become more intense. This gorgeous English beauty was a mistress of seduction. When he got up from the chair, the movement caused him no slight discomfort. He quickly tossed off his coat, waistcoat, and black leather boots.

He joined her on the bed and pressed her soft body gently into the fluffy mattress. He kissed her eyes, cheeks, then moved his mouth to worship her white neck. Unable to wait any longer, his lips found their heaven as he teased and sucked each hard pink nipple of her beautiful breasts.

"Oh, oh, I may faint," she whispered, tossing her head from side to side.

"No you won't . . . your grace," he added with a devilish chuckle. And to prove his point further, Taggart increased the force of his hot kisses along her receptive flesh. When he felt her body move with the open desire for fulfillment, he pulled back to watch her.

"You are a wicked man," she whimpered. Her azure-blue eyes glazed with arousal. "What are you doing to me?" Boldly, she ran her hand across the front of his trousers. Her smile was wanton. "You will burst those buttons if you keep him so confined. Do not colonial men remove their garments, too?" she asked with intended unworldliness. "What ever could you be hiding in there?"

Taggart rose from the bed and wasted little time returning to his chair by the fire. He took a deep breath and deliberately set about trying to draw out her need as she had done his earlier. He forced himself to slow his actions by taking a long swallow of the amber cognac. Then he stood up. As he walked again toward Garnet, where she sat enticingly on the edge of the white coverlet atop her large bed, Taggart reached behind his neck and unbuckled his white neckband. Never did he take his eyes off her. How long had he waited for this moment? He saw her wet her lips in anticipation. She touched her breast, desire showing clearly on her pretty face.

He gave her an amused look. "Have you no desire to know my identity, your grace?" Right now he was still prepared to tell her who he was and let her choose whether she went the distance with him.

But for the first time she looked cross. She bounded off the bed and stamped one small, bare foot on the carpet covering the wooden floor. "Dolt! What care I whether you be baseborn or nobleman? I burn, fool. Hurry," she ordered, impatient annoyance in her petulant voice. "I will not be kept waiting."

Full ready to give her pleasure, Taggart stopped dead at her arrogant order. He tossed the neckcloth to the carpeted floor. His lips became a firm line. Hands on his hips, he ordered in a dangerously quiet voice, "Come here."

The Duchess of Montrose's blue eyes became large, round circles. It was clear no one had ever spoken to her in this tone. "How dare you address me in—"

"I said, come here!" bellowed the Irishman, his voice now rumbling like the first sound of thunder on an unsuspecting summer day. His index finger pointed to a spot just in front of him.

There was a hint of ice about Garnet's eyes, and her mouth lost some of its childlike pout. She appeared on the precipice of hurling some abusive retort, but then she seemed to catch herself.

Looking down at her bare toes, she confessed, "You . . . you frighten me, sir." There was a sobbing catch to her tiny voice. She sat down on the edge of the bed, giving the impression that she was about to collapse in a swoon once more.

As the sound of Garnet's crying filled the room, Taggart felt the tenseness leave his body. He had no desire to bully any woman, but her remark just now had made him angry. He did find it a trifle amusing at how easily the blond-haired minx could worm her way out of a difficult situation. And it was more than clear they lusted after each other. Sexual frustration had made both their tempers short at the moment.

"There now, your grace, don't cry," he soothed, coming over to the bed. Her right hand was buried under the lacy pillow, while she reclined facedown on the embroidered coverlet. He patted her hip affectionately. "Has no one ever scolded you before?" he couldn't help asking, amazed that such a small thing could crush her. When her cries became louder, he moved even closer, trying to coax her out of her unhappy state.

However, when he reached out a gentle hand to pull her into his arms for comfort, she turned on him, brandishing a jeweled dagger in her hand.

"You insolent whore's son!" she shrieked, her eyes dry, venting blue fire. "No man gives me orders, and you will touch me only when I give you permission." She expertly cut the white material of his ruffled shirt, exposing his left shoulder.

Instantly, she took in the large mark on his bare skin. "So," she added with a triumphant smirk, "you've been pricked by a blade before." Menacingly, she moved the knife lower to hover right above the bulge at the front of his breeches.

Floored by the change in the woman next to him, Taggart answered, "A remembrance from a dock rat, madam. And I've no intention of getting a second one." He lunged at her. With a rough blow to her wrist, Taggart knocked the lethal weapon out of her hand. It landed on the floor a few feet from the bed.

He'd known instinctively from the way she'd held the knife, Garnet was quite capable of using her weapon. "A dainty nosegay to keep under your pillow . . . your grace."

Spitting outrage, Garnet lashed out at him, just missing his eyes with her nails.

Ready for her this time, Taggart grabbed her arms and used his body to pin her beneath him. "My hands aren't chained to a wall this time, Garnet, so be warned."

At this first mention of her name, Garnet's eyes widened in shock. She stopped struggling. "Who—"

"Sure and don't ya know me, Garnet Somerset, or should I be sayin' Duchess of Montrose now that ya bagged old Calvert?" He imitated his former brogue expertly. "And here I'm thinkin' how much I remember yer hospitality when last we met in yer dungeon of a cellar."

Recognition distorted Garnet's pretty face. "You . . . you were that Irish groom at Fitzroy Hall. Terence?"

Still holding her beneath him, he corrected, "Taggart O'Rahilly. How kind of you to remember."

"O'Rahilly!" she echoed, using his name like a curse. "How dare you!" she hissed, looking more incensed. Her struggles increased. "Let me up at once, you filthy Irish bastard. And to think," she raged aloud with disgust, "I let you touch me, even address me."

All humor left O'Rahilly's strong features. Until now he fully intended to let her go. But her scathing words pushed him in another direction. He tightened his hold on her. "You can always cry for Louise," he snarled. "I'm sure she'd love seeing you this way, helpless for once, getting a taste of the rough treatment you so readily dish out to others." He held her down with one strong arm while he quickly tore open the buttons of his breeches. The expression in her blue eyes told him she wasn't even afraid, but her look promised revenge. While he held her wrists easily with his left hand, his long legs kept her still beneath him. He began stroking his hard member with his right hand.

Confusion etched across her features. "I can't open my legs if you're holding me down. Aren't . . . you going to . . ."

He realized full well what she anticipated. Anger as well as lust made him peak in record time. In a deliberate movement, he allowed his manhood to have its explosive release across her full white breasts.

Finished, he wasted little time in rebuttoning his trousers

before he released the furious Garnet. Ignoring her completely, he picked up her knife and headed back to retrieve the rest of his clothes.

"I'll kill you for this!" she yelled as she used the sheet to scrub the sticky liquid off her breasts. A string of lurid curses followed.

"Ah, Garnet," Taggart remarked in his flawless British accent when she was forced to come up for air, "your words remind me of home. One would have to go to the seamiest Cork dock to hear such familiar phrases." He reached into his waistcoat pocket and tossed two guineas on the white side table. "It's less than the girls get downstairs, but I'm sure they usually give a man a warmer departure." With a rakish grin, he placed her deadly knife next to the coins.

As Taggart left her rooms, he heard the loud crash of porcelain hit the back of the door, followed by another stream of oaths and promises for revenge. The sooner he left for Ireland the better, he told himself, not quite regretting his tangle with Garnet Somerset. Revenge did have a certain heady spice of its own.

Despite his desire to see Edna first, Taggart forced himself to stop at John Nolan's estate. He owed so much to this man, he told himself. At the very least, Nolan should receive his hearty thanks before he saw his younger sister.

A few lines at the corners of his eyes, but the years had taken little away from John Nolan's disciplined features. Fresh from riding, John was dressed in a well-tailored coat and breeches, with shiny black boots. Tossing his riding stick and tricorn hat on a nearby table, he rushed over to greet his visitor.

"When my wife told me who was here, I could scarce believe my ears," he greeted warmly. "Look at you!" he demanded, stepping back. "You left a boy and have come back a tall, strapping man." His shrewd eyes took in the expensive cut of his guest's clothes. "And successful to boot."

Taggart moved his eyes from the man's brown wig to the tops of his own leather boots. "I owe most of it to you, Squire.

89

I . . ." Words seemed to fail him, and in his usual direct show of emotion, he went over and gave the man a bearlike hug. "I'll never be able to thank you for giving Father Collins all that money for me."

If John was surprised, Taggart's exuberant embrace gave him time to collect his thoughts.

The younger man stepped back. "If there is anything I can do for you, you must know you've only to ask me. 'Tis more grateful than I can ever say," he added with emotion. "Williamsburg Shipping would never have been started without your assistance. I wanted to thank you sooner but Father Mike said you wanted it kept secret."

"Ah . . . yes, quite. Only too happy to help, my boy." Nolan returned Taggart's smile. "We Irishmen have to stick together and all. But . . ." He hesitated. "I do think it would be better to continue to keep this between ourselves." Nolan rationalized the lie he'd just told, thinking it best to accept Taggart's gratitude now rather than have the young man get in more trouble stirring up things best left in the past. "Relationships between the Irish and their landlords have worsened since you left. Only last week a group of Irish hooligans burned a likeness of the Irish viceroy in effigy. Fools," Nolan scoffed. "And they were hung for their troubles." It was clear his companion took this news to heart. John Nolan shrugged his shoulders. "Forgive me, Taggart. This is your homecoming and should be a joyous time. Join me in a glass of brandy."

Both men were silent for a few moments while they sipped their liquor. Taggart spoke first.

"I meant what I said earlier, John. If there is anything I can do for you— At the very least, I've brought a note drawn on my bank in London for all the coins you gave me nine years ago. And I insist you take the extra as interest." He retrieved a sheet of paper from his inside pocket and handed it over to his host.

John Nolan's eyebrows rose as he read the sum written on the legal document. "I . . . I don't know what to say. You are too generous, my boy. It really is not necessary to repay—"

"We O'Rahillys pay our debts." The black-haired man

grinned at his family's longtime friend. "Besides, not to hurt your feelings, but my shipping business is doing well enough, thank God. You'll be happy to know that amount puts no dent in my profits or straps me in any way. I'm in your debt, Squire. And to be sure I'd not be ungrateful to you. There is more where that came from if you need it." The brogue tinged his voice, for he realized he owed all he had to this man, the man who had given him the only kindness he'd ever received in Ireland.

Trying to regain his composure, Taggart took another swallow of the smooth brandy. Then he placed the glass on the table to his right. "But I must leave you now, for I'm fairly bursting to see Edna. It's a surprise, and she does not know I am here." He looked back at the squire, who now sat staring at him. "The truth is, I don't even have Edna's new address. I suppose it gives her pleasure to have a servant bring my letters to her from Fitzroy Hall, rather like a reminder that she's a wealthy woman now. Kinsale isn't that big of a town, though. I suppose her townhouse is with all the rest of the wealthy toffs," he chuckled. "Are you familiar with Edna's mansion?"

John studied his friend's open expression with amazement. "New home?" he echoed, placing his own glass down. He stood up and joined the younger man.

"Why, yes. I was under the impression . . ." Taggart's words drifted off at the squire's serious countenance.

"To my knowledge a ladies' maid does not earn sufficient wages to rent a home off that road. Forgive me, Taggart, but I think someone has played a joke on you."

"Ladies' maid?" Despite his efforts, his volume increased as his earlier conviviality turned to something else. "Edna is a ladies' maid?" He began feeling uneasy, but he plunged in just the same. He demanded, "Who employs my sister as her servant?"

"Why, Lady Millicent Fitzroy. You did not know?"

A cold fury washed over him, evident only in the lowered pitch of his reply. "No. I did not." He took his leave quickly from the squire.

In spite of feeling tired from his London voyage, the tall

Irishman forced himself to ride to Fitzroy Hall that afternoon. All the while his temper grew hotter. What treachery rooted itself again at Fitzroy Hall? Had the earl stolen his sister's money? He'd heard tales of servants' mail being intercepted by their aristocratic employers. And what in hell was Edna doing as an Englishwoman's maid?

Chapter 7

"Now, please remember, Millie. You must try to be more—"

"Reserved," finished Lady Millicent Fitzroy with a chuckle.

This time Edna did not share her employer's humor. "When Reverend Somerset's wife comes to tea this afternoon, you said she'll be bringing three of her friends from church. Abigail Somerset's maid told me there has been a lot of talk lately about how you treat me. Last week when we were in the milliners you should not have insisted on buying me a new straw hat, too."

Millicent's gray eyes danced with mischief. "Oh, stuff. We both needed a new brimmed hat. Lord knows the old ones are only fit for our garden work."

"And when Sean Kelly stepped in my path and tried to kiss me, you should have allowed me to handle him myself instead of charging to my defense to give him that verbal dressing-down. Millie, you must realize such public displays serve us both poorly. It makes me—my position with the other ladies's maids awkward. Sure and how many titled Englishwomen act as yourself?"

Millicent looked repentant. Edna's speech reversions proved the Irish woman's deep concern. The taller girl pushed her wire frames up farther on her nose and brushed the skirt of her simple muslin gown. It would not be easy to treat Edna in public as she requested. However, practicality forced her to realize Edna was correct. "All right. This afternoon at tea, I shall be just like a few of the English ladies here—a regular

93

tartar toward my maid."

"And do you know what I told Reverend Somerset?" Abigail demanded. "I told him he spends more time with those silly mushrooms than he does with me." Another fit of high-pitched giggles overcame Nigel Somerset's buxom wife. "Mind you, I am quite concerned. Though there are few I'd confide this to," she added in a whisper, "lately when the light hits Nigel's features a certain way, bless my soul, if his face doesn't resemble one of those mushrooms."

After listening politely to her guest, Millicent stole a glance about the room. The three other well-dressed ladies in flowered or striped gowns, powdered and lightly painted faces, sat near the round walnut table, sipping tea and eating small lemon cakes, accompanied by occasional tidbits of gossip and the latest fashion news.

"Susan," ordered the youngest lady in the circle. "Fetch my pills."

Millicent watched the maid haul a large wooden box with leather straps over to her mistress. The young woman with the elaborate wig pawed through the bottles of multicolored pills, before finding the one she desired.

"I have such a delicate constitution," the guest complained. "I never go anywhere without my medicines." But with a surprising show of strength, she barked, "Well, don't just stand there, girl. Take the thing away."

The thin maid lugged the heavy box back to the side of the room and returned to her seat on the wooden bench next to Edna O'Rahilly.

Abigail Somerset watched Edna for a second. "Lady Fitzroy, I've told Lilian," she added, with a nod toward the woman now tossing back a handful of pink pills, "we must set a more English example here in Ireland, regarding the treatment of servants. Don't you agree?" she added pointedly.

The English girl met Mrs. Somerset's question without a flinch. Purposefully, Millicent allowed her expression to take on a haughtier countenance. "I do indeed, ma'am." She thought of how her father might react. "We owe it to our Irish maids to train them properly."

A few moments went by. After Edna nodded, giving the prearranged signal, Millie looked across the room at her and ordered, "Edna, fetch me my fan at once."

"Fetch it yourself, Millicent Fitzroy!" shouted a masculine voice from the hall. "As of today Edna O'Rahilly is no longer your servant."

There were loud gasps of feminine shock as all the ladies present watched the tall, well-dressed gentleman stalk into the Fitzroy sitting room. Instantly, the unannounced intruder seemed to dwarf everything in the large room.

A flustered Colleen Mulcahy waddled behind him. Her usually round, pleasant face was a mask of distress. "'Tis sorry I am, your ladyship. But didn't I try to stop—"

Edna O'Rahilly gave a loud cry of joy and raced toward the stranger. "Oh, Taggart!"

Hardly aware of his words, Millicent had to place her hands on the back of Abigail Somerset's chair to steady herself. How she wanted to race into his arms, too. It had been so long. And now, at last, he was home. Tears misted her eyes as she tried to give Edna and her brother time to greet each other.

Taggart released his tight hold on his younger sister. When he stepped back to look at her more closely, he was struck at how pretty she'd become—rich, curly black hair, and her figure had definitely filled out. He'd come back none too soon, he told himself. At nineteen it was high time a suitable Irish marriage was arranged for her. "Why, Edna, what happened to that chubby-faced urchin?" He shook his head, a touch of sadness in his voice as he realized all the years he'd missed. "You're a woman grown."

Edna laughed openly. Hands on her hips, she looked her brother up and down. "And I could be askin' where's the scrawny, tall drink of water that left here nine years ago?" She reached out to touch his well-muscled shoulder. Mischief sparked her saucy green eyes. "Sure and I'll bet you left many a colonial lass panting after you."

Taggart caught his sister's mood. The corners of his sensuous mouth quirked upward. "I will admit the Virginia ladies are lovely, soft-spoken, well behaved. And not like some of you rowdy Irish girls, with your feisty Gaelic ways."

"What insolence!" Lilian remarked. "The blackguard acts as if this were a tavern. Barging in here unannounced—why, the idea. Susan, my medicine chest. I feel quite faint." Looking scandalized, Lilian readjusted her large periwig. "Is this . . . gentleman a relative, your ladyship? Perhaps you should have your man, Fergus, fetch the magistrate. Sir Jeremy Cartgrove could deal with his sort."

Millicent turned her attention back to the shocked guests. "He is . . . a friend of our family," she replied evenly. "Having been away in the Colonies for the past few years, this is his first trip back home."

"But your maid seems very—"

Lady Fitzroy sighed, realizing she had to tell them more. "He is Taggart O'Rahilly, Edna's older brother."

"The groom? Good Lord, I thought he was killed by those red savages in America?"

After politely excusing herself from the chattering women, Millicent took the first tentative steps toward Taggart and his sister. He must have been in a hurry to get here, she mused, for he wore no hat or gloves. Her heart fluttered in anticipation. Had he missed her so much, too? She smiled and brushed a tear of happiness away from her cheek, making no attempt to hide the welcoming expression on the fine-boned features of her face.

No longer the thin, scruffy boy, Taggart had grown taller since he'd left Kinsale. Millicent caught her breath as she observed him. His shoulders had broadened, his face was strong and tanned. He was even more handsome than before, dressed in the latest London fashion. In speech and manner right now she realized he'd fit easily into the most prestigious English club.

When Taggart saw Lady Millicent Fitzroy, his first reaction was to take her in his arms for the warmest of greetings. But then something happened to him. The vision of Garnet with her French maid flashed across his mind, and he remembered Lady Fitzroy's order just now to his sister. How many times, he wondered, had Millicent struck Edna?

Her smile and salutations were abruptly cut off as she looked up and read his expression. Why was he looking at her with such cold contempt?

Completely ignoring the English girl, Taggart looked down at Edna. "Get your things. We're leaving this house at once. You are no longer at the beck and call of another of these spoiled English bitches."

"Taggart!" Edna admonished, knowing full well Millie had heard his scathing words. Of course, he might be a little upset to realize his sister had misled him, but just because she was Millie's maid was no reason to be so—cruel.

"Edna," he said in warning, for the first time addressing his sister in an uncompromising tone. "Please do as I say, for I am in no mood to mince words, especially standing in this place. I've a carriage waiting outside to take us to an inn. We need to talk."

Millicent found her voice first, realizing the strong, angry Irishman looked quite ready to bodily haul his reluctant sister out of the house in a second. Surely, there would be time to speak with him later and straighten out any misunderstanding. "It is all right, Edna," she forced herself to say. "Come, I will help you pack."

"Is his lordship about this morning?" O'Rahilly asked his old friend.

Fergus Mulcahy shook his gray head. "No, the Earl of Fitzroy came home dru—he's a little under the weather this mornin', still in bed." The short, older man grinned. When he saw Taggart dismount the fine black stallion, Fergus piped up, "Well now, lad, then it must be her ladyship you'd be wantin' ta see. And I don't mind tellin' ya me and Colleen think it's about time ya paid Lady Millicent a call." Fergus sauntered over and took the horse's reins. "I'll see ta your mount."

The taller man frowned. "You don't have to wait on me, Fergus." He made a motion to take back the reins, but the little man raised a protesting hand.

"Not a t'all, me boy. You just go back around the house. Her ladyship could use cheering up. And I'll see yere not disturbed," he tossed at Taggart's back.

Not disturbed? What the devil did Fergus think he'd come for? Taggart thought. During the last few days, Edna had said little about the Fitzroys, but she made it clear she had stayed on as Millicent's maid by choice. And she'd vehemently pointed out that Lady Fitzroy had always been kind to her. However, the Irishman knew Edna was keeping something from him, but the stubborn girl would not say more. And when the unexpected invitation to Calvert Huntington's birthday celebration had arrived this morning, Edna had wrangled a promise out of him to ask Millicent to attend with him. He suspected John Nolan had thoughtfully gotten the duke to invite him, using the guise as colonial shipping owner. It was doubtful any English aristocrats would recognize a former Irish groom, or ever admit the fact at a polite soiree. And how would Calvert's wife, the Duchess of Montrose, greet him? The thought of Garnet's expression when he showed up with his proper invitation intrigued him.

A good thing he had money, Taggart thought cynically as he walked toward the back of the mansion. It would cost a great deal to get this place in shape. He glanced about the unkempt grounds. The earl had certainly let the place go to seed.

Good Lord, Taggart mused as he continued slowly across the lawn, past a grove of overgrown shrubs. He stopped abruptly at the scene before him. Was Lady Fitzroy getting as eccentric as Nigel Somerset and his mushrooms?

Oblivious to everything but her work, Millicent knelt on the hard ground, dressed in an old serviceable gown and apron. The cloth gloves she wore had long since seen better days, but they served to protect her hands.

After using her small spade, the English girl retrieved another potato from the dark soil. Taking little interest in such matters, the earl had no idea his daughter had converted a hidden patch of the once lovely rose garden into a more practical use. What wasn't used in the house, Millie gave to the needy tenants on the estate. Thank God, the potatoes were better than last year. But now that Edna was gone, there was even more work to do.

*   *   *

The grass and moist earth muffled his approach. What could he say to her? Sighing, Taggart wondered if Millicent would scoff at him when he asked her to the ball. He cleared his throat.

Still on her knees, Millicent expected to see Fergus. She turned and was surprised to observe a pair of shiny black boots. She looked up and found burgundy knee breeches, then higher to take in a rose waistcoat and matching burgundy coat with expensive buttons.

Removing his gold-braided tricorn hat, Taggart nodded a tentative greeting. Then the dimple at his chin deepened with his suppressed laughter when he noticed the dark smudge of dirt that ran from her slender nose to her right cheek.

Transfixed, at first Millicent could only stare up at him. For nine years she had dreamed of this day, the day her O'Rahilly would come back to her. She would be dressed in a red silk gown, there would be flowers entwined in her long hair; perhaps the straight hair would even manage a curl or two for the occasion, and she would be carrying a huge bouquet of yellow flowers.

The English girl blinked, then stood up awkwardly, for the contents of her large apron weighed her down. The features of her delicate face took on a pinkish hue as the actual picture she presented washed over her. It wasn't flowers she carried right now. Hastily she shoved the muck-covered potato in the front pocket of her canvas apron.

Taggart couldn't explain why he felt tongue-tied as he watched her. It irritated him. He noticed the gray eyes behind her glasses looked hopeful, yet a little apprehensive. Her figure, though not as voluptuous as Edna's, had definitely rounded during the last few years. Her breasts strained against the tight material of the obviously outgrown dress she wore. Even smudged with dirt, her skin was smooth and becomingly pink as she blushed. The old straw hat she wore against the sun was frayed on one side. Yes, he had to admit it—he'd missed her, though he'd tried to fight softer emotions toward anyone named Fitzroy. "I . . . it is good to see you, Lady Millicent."

Her mouth quirked upward. "I . . . how kind of you to call." Then emotion made her forget her formal manners. "I . . . oh,

Taggart I can't tell you how happy I am you're back." She took in his appearance. "Virginia certainly agrees with you" popped out before she could catch herself.

What was it about this Englishwoman that always attracted him? He studied her face. "I came here this morning," he began more coolly than intended. "That is, will you accompany me tomorrow to the Duke of Montrose's residence? A formal ball is being given to celebrate his seventieth birthday."

Unable to hide her delight, she looked up into his dark-brown eyes. "Yes, Taggart. I will be happy to attend the ball with you."

Refusing the temptation to tease her about her English eccentricities in this sort of garden work, Taggart decided it was better to leave. "I will call for you at seven. Is that suitable for you?"

Why were they so formal with each other? Was he shy at seeing her again, too? she wondered. Millicent's gray eyes became softer. "Seven will be most agreeable."

"And what in blazes am I to tell Edwin?" The Earl of Holingbrook's bloodshot eyes bulged even wider as he glared up at his daughter. "God's blood, you've lost your senses. Knew it would happen with all that reading you do. An uncluttered mind, that's what gives a man peace. Look at me," he demanded with obvious pride. "I spend my time in other, more rewarding pursuits. John Nolan takes care of my correspondence, and I've a solicitor to read things for me, though the cheeky fellow had the nerve to ask about his salary." Clearly aware he was digressing from the matter at hand, the earl stopped speaking and gave his only daughter another malevolent stare.

As was usual in front of her father, Lady Millicent was successful in hiding her emotions. "Father, I have already accepted another invitation to the Duke of Montrose's party."

The earl shook his meaty fist. "Haven't I got enough to fret about, this place mortgaged to the hilt, not knowing where my next bottle of claret is coming from, and now this. And I

100

assume this colonial has no money, or does the fool think you've got some?"

She didn't want to have a scene with her father, not tonight, the happiest night of her life. Better to let her father see Taggart on the dance floor at the duke's Irish residence. The earl could not make a row in front of the other English guests. "He is not wealthy, Father, but I suspect he earns a decent living as a ship's captain for a wealthy American." Her father's belligerent features caused a pleading catch to her voice. "Please, Father, this will be my first ball. Couldn't I . . . well, would it be so bad if I went with someone whom I chose . . . just this once?"

"Harumph." Geoffrey looked down at his attire. "Had to wear this bloody dark silk for the second time. Binds in the crotch. Well," he finished, scowling again at Millicent. "You can have your man of mystery this one night, as long as you say you'll dance with Edwin most of the evening. But mind you, Edwin Somerset's family won't take damaged goods, my girl. See that you keep those long legs of yours together. Your maidenhead must be intact for young Somerset. His father and I plan to post the bans for your wedding shortly. And there'll be no long engagement, not after all the time you've made me wait for this day."

Aware that she was lucky to get this brief concession to attend the ball with the escort of her choice, the English girl stifled her true feelings about this constant scheme to get her married to Edwin. Edwin had seemed as little interested in the match as she. However, both parents were adamant, and it appeared inevitable that they would, indeed, marry in the late spring. Best not to think about that now.

"Thank you, Father." She tried to remember this rotund, overindulged man before her was her father, and she did owe him a certain civility. But it galled her that he worried more about his own attire than his son, and they hadn't heard from Dunstan in so very long.

The loud knock at the door cut into her worried thoughts about her older brother.

"Hang it," the earl grumbled, "don't expect me to greet the savage. Probably has feathers in his hair, like some aborigine

101

and knows nothing about the proper way to tie a cravat. And don't let the clod pate piss on the carpet; the blasted thing is frayed to strings now. Uncivilized country," the earl went on, venting his spleen. "Can't see why anyone would ever want to leave England. If I had the chance I'd be out of Kinsale this very day," he muttered. Another knock sounded, this time louder than before. "God's death, will the fellow run the brass lion through the door?"

Silently praying her father would leave first, Lady Millicent stood rooted to the spot without speaking.

"Well," he demanded, glaring back at his daughter. "Expect me to shuffle about as butler, too? Fergus is getting the Kelly boys to bring my carriage around. And do not think for a moment I shall offer you and that iron-handed sailor a ride." Clearly, her serious mien unnerved him. He turned and headed for his library. "A pox on you and and the Colonies," he tossed over his shoulder.

An audible sigh of relief escaped Millicent's soft lips before she straightened the skirt of her brocade gown. She congratulated herself on her needlework in embroidering colorful butterflies on the strip of white velvet at her throat. Quickly, she opened the large wooden door.

Unable to hide her happiness, yet feeling a little shy at their first outing together, the young woman could only stare appreciatively for a moment. A warm smile played at the corners of her pink mouth. The Earl of Holingbrook could not have been more mistaken about her colonial's appearance.

Tall and handsome, Taggart was dressed in a cream-colored coat and breeches. At the throat of his pristine neckcloth was a diamond stickpin that had to be worth a small fortune. And she knew the elaborately embroidered waistcoat was the latest fashion in London this season, according to Abigail Somerset. When he signaled his increasing agitation by unconsciously tapping the gold-tipped walking stick on the marble step, she apologized for her tardiness and bid him come in.

Taggart's strained smile faded when he looked closer at Lady Millicent's attire. Retrimmed lace of a poor quality, plain and unadorned. Though he had to admit the colorful ribbon at her slender throat was quite enchanting, he was versed enough in a wealthy lady's proper attire for this sort of occasion to realize jewelry would have been more appropriate. The gown she wore had definitely seen other seasons. And he was well aware the old reprobate, her father, still dressed to the nines, indulging himself at every turn. No, there was money to be had, he told himself, with growing irritation.

Why was Taggart scowling at her? Though pale pink was not her favorite color, this gown was the only one left without patches that still fit. "Taggart," she said tentatively. "Is there something amiss?"

His lips thinned as the truth hit him. "Amiss, Lady Fitzroy? Though I should have been prepared for this insult." Anger sparked from his cold, dark eyes.

"Insult?" Millicent could not hide her dismay. "What ever could be the matter?"

The words rushed menacingly from his tightly held features. "That I had once been in your employ, I am not ashamed. I worked harder for you cursed Fitzroys than any dumb beast on this estate. But, my lady." He made the last words sound like swearing. "To dress in your shabbiest apparel just to humiliate me in front of your English friends, because I'd once been your lowly groom—not one whit of jewelry to properly adorn—"

"Jewelry?" she tossed back at him. The word seemed to burn her tongue.

"Yes." The low timbre of his voice rose an octave. "Not to mention your deliberately wearing that poor excuse for a gown when I know full well you've probably got a wardrobe upstairs stuffed with Paris frocks. It is the most despicable act I can imagine." The picture of Garnet flashed before him. His hand tightened around the mahogany cane. He pushed air into his lungs, determined not to lose control.

"All right, madam." Taggart's voice had almost returned to normal. "You've had your little folly. Now, I shall give you fifteen minutes to change into something more suitable." He removed his tricorn hat, and placed it under his arm. The cane, however, still remained in his right hand. When she didn't move, he looked across at her. "My patience is not without limit, my lady. I'm not one of your milksop neighbors, with their perfumed manners. My sister's kind heart makes her

103

blind to your ways, Millicent. But you're a Fitzroy, all right, and I am not so easily duped."

For the first time Millicent realized there were other changes, not just physical, in the man before her. The last nine years had brought a ruthless, hard streak to him.

"I believe I can find my way," he remarked, brushing past her. "Shall I wait for you in the drawing room?" Anticipating her compliance, O'Rahilly's tone was quite civil now.

Her initial embarrassment was replaced by something more heated. Millicent made a fist with her right hand rather than give in to her uncharacteristic urge to grab the nearest object in the starkly furnished hall and hurl it at the imperious form behind her.

"Well," the Irishman demanded. "I am waiting."

Pride came to her rescue, and she held her body straighter before she moved closer to him. "Mr. O'Rahilly, you can wait until spring turns to summer, but this is the gown I choose to wear for this evening's party."

His lips became a grim line. Though difficult, the taller Irishman managed to get a firmer grip on his temper. "Then you choose not to attend the ball with me. And having participated in so many during the last nine years, a pity this one will be such a trifling loss to you." Without another word, he turned his back on Millicent and headed out without even taking his leave of her. The heavy door rattled on its unsteady hinges when he slammed it loudly behind him.

Lady Millicent Fitzroy stood staring at the closed door. She hadn't missed his Gaelic curse. Little did the Irishman realize her work with the Irish tenants had increased her understanding of his native language. He'd called her a "spoiled English bitch"—for the second time.

Impatiently, Millicent swiped at the tears on her cheeks. Never, she vowed, would she ever tell him the truth—about her gown or her jewels. She clutched the pink marble banister as she proceeded slowly up the stairs toward her room. There would be no first formal ball for her tonight. She felt cold when she remembered the way he'd looked at her. It would be hard to forget his look of betrayal, then hatred.

*   *   *

Taggart was not prepared for Calvert Huntington's reaction.

"So, you've done well for yourself, young O'Rahilly. Delighted," he added without guile. A raspy chuckle followed. "Do some of these complacent fops good to get shaken up a bit. In my day young men didn't spend all their time preening themselves and learning the latest dance steps. These young bucks are becoming too soft. What?" the Duke of Montrose demanded, his blue eyes twinkling. "You look surprised, my boy."

Despite his efforts to appear contrary, Taggart was bored with most of these English aristocrats and their pro-Crown Irishmen, like John Nolan. Calvert Huntington's moderate leanings were a refreshing change. "I . . . the truth is, your grace, I never thought to hear such words from you."

"You forget." The seventy-year-old man raised a thin but firm hand. "Unlike many around you here, I live in Ireland as much as I can out of choice. I love this country, Taggart. When John Nolan asked me about inviting you, I was pleased to do so. I'll wager you didn't know in my younger days I was known as quite a radical in the House of Lords. Tried to plead more leniency toward you Irish, but they wouldn't hear of it." He eyed his companion shrewdly. "I was about your age when my father forced me to give up my seat, under the guise of ill health. Wealth's hard to forsake, O'Rahilly. Offered a choice between what you believe in and the abrupt halt to your standard of living—well, I guess you wouldn't listen, anyway. Can't say I ever did."

Taggart was surprised to find he was beginning to like the Duke of Montrose. There was more depth to the man than he'd ever expected.

The shorter man took a generous pinch of snuff, then sneezed into his lacy handkerchief, before stuffing it back in the wide cuff of his silk coat. "However, I'm looking forward to Geoffrey's expression when he sees you." He looked up, recognized someone, and motioned the person over. "Here is a new friend of mine that I should like you to meet, my dear."

Dressed in a gown of shimmering silk which matched her eyes, Garnet, Duchess of Montrose, held out a small gloved hand automatically to Calvert's companion. "Any friend of my husband's . . ." When the gentleman turned to face her,

Garnet's beguiling smile became a trifle more set. ". . . is welcome at our party," the duke's young wife managed as her husband handled the formal introductions.

"Your grace." Taggart bowed formally, only the glittering coals of his eyes gave evidence of the amusement he felt at the situation. The scent of white roses assailed him, and he couldn't help notice the more than generous view he received of the tops of her breasts—the gown was just a tad away from being scandalous for such an occasion. Calvert, he mused, was certainly a tolerant husband. "You are very lucky, your grace."

"How gallant of you," Garnet purred, lapping up the compliment.

The Irishman's mouth quirked upward. "I was speaking about his lordship," he corrected. "Surely a kind, even-tempered husband is something any woman would cherish."

Garnet looked taken aback. "Why . . . yes, of course." She fluttered her open fan and smiled, then slipped a dainty hand into the crook of Calvert's thin arm.

The look the old duke gave his wife showed clearly he worshiped her.

Playfully, the duchess tapped her husband's forearm. "Would you be a dear and fetch me a glass of ratafia?" She fanned herself, the slight puffs of air gently moving her blond curls closer along the smooth skin of her oval face. "It is so crowded in here I may swoon." Her pink mouth pouted.

The duke appeared enraptured. "Wait until my hundred-year birthday party, my pet. I suspect the Prince of Wales will attend that one."

Taggart knew the prospect of her husband lasting that long, even in jest, did not sit well with Garnet, for she frowned, then caught herself. "And what age then shall I be, sir?" she teased.

"Ever young, my angel." Then her husband was off on his errand.

"Old fart."

Taggart alone overheard the lady's muttered words as she watched her thin husband walk slowly over to the elaborate tables of cold beef, salmon, and cream pastries. The Irishman became aware that Garnet was observing his own expensive attire. She wet her lips, and the blue of her eyes sparkled even more radiantly. To those around them, it appeared they were making polite conversation.

"You did not finish your wine," she pointed out, as Taggart placed his glass on the silver tray when a footman passed.

"You sound perturbed," he replied in a pleasant tone.

She looked at him, then smiled. "I do not like things unfinished. They keep me awake evenings."

He read the clear meaning of her words. And in truth, his healthy body was still affected by her beautiful presence. "I am sorry I disturb you, your grace. Perhaps your husband can assuage your tormented spirits."

The blue eyes narrowed at his sarcastic barb, before the duchess hissed, "You may be dressed for the part, O'Rahilly, but you'll always stink of the stables." Her expression mocked him. "I should give up any pretext at being a gentleman if I were you. It might fool some of your naive colonials, but after I explain to a few of my friends just exactly where you came from, I doubt we'll be seeing much of you or your sister in London or Kinsale."

The taller Irishman stood staring down at her calmly. "I like your husband. A pity if I'm forced to tell him about his wife's—what shall we call them, Garnet? Or does he know about your little rooms at The Three Cranes."

"He'd never believe you." But her face lost some of its smugness.

"Then you have nothing to fear."

"You son of a—"

"An Irishman," he finished smoothly. "We O'Rahilly men pride ourselves on not taking any sh—any impertinence from anyone. And that includes a street rowdy, or an English duchess of rather dubious virtue. Your servant, madam." he bowed gracefully, and turned his back on a furious Garnet.

However, as the Irishman walked to the edge of the candlelit room, his smile faded when he spotted Geoffrey Fitzroy talking with Edwin Somerset. The years had not been kind to the Earl of Holingbrook. Though dressed fashionably in black silk, his jowls sagged on his meaty face. There was an unhealthy grayish tinge to his flaccid skin. He hadn't remembered the rotund man in the powdered bagwig being so short.

When Taggart saw Calvert walk over to the two gentlemen, he fought the urge to leave. Was Ben right when he warned his friend against this venture? As the Irishman observed the twenty-three-year-old Edwin giggle with his friends—in powdered wig, black patch on his cheek, dressed like many of the other dandies here—Taggart suddenly felt Garnet might have been right. Would he and Edna ever fit in here? And did he really want this life for his sister and himself?

He admitted it now, after his anger had toned down. Millicent's joke at his expense tonight had cut him. Of all the English he'd ever met, she was the one he thought would never make fun of him. His lips compressed as he stared across at the approaching earl and his two friends. Yes, she was a Fitzroy all right. You couldn't change blood. "Damn both their eyes," he cursed under his breath.

Chapter 8

"Oh, Millie's got some sort of headache," the earl explained to the Duke of Montrose and Edwin Somerset as the duke led them over to be introduced to the unusual guest from America. Even this short walk made the overweight Englishman puff. "Damn me, this gout is worse tonight. I need a brandy. Millicent doesn't know what pain is. A tiny headache and she can't come," he grumbled. However, Geoffrey did manage a slap on the back for the young man next to him.

"Of course, you'll soon learn about all those female complaints," he added raucously to Edwin.

Dressed in a pale-lavender waistcoat and breeches, the hint of rouge on his fashionably powdered cheeks, Edwin merely smiled politely at the earl. "I dare say Lady Millicent and I will have ample opportunity to attend other social functions together."

This seemed to please his lordship, for his wide face split into a grin.

"Do I detect an announcement in the air?" The Duke of Montrose teased his longtime friend.

"Yes," Geoffrey replied with obvious relish. "Edwin's father and I, with Edwin's encouragement, of course, had a long talk this very afternoon. We have reached an understanding."

"And the lady in question, your dear daughter?" The duke's expression softened. "How does Lady Millicent feel about this splendid news?" he added in a cordial manner.

All affability departed from Geoffrey's features. "My daughter will do as she's told. And mark you, Edwin, Millie will soon come to heel if you handle her right. Her mother was the same way when first we wed. Stubborn lot, the females of that family. But I soon brought her around to my way of thinking." He elbowed his future son-in-law in the ribs. With a lecherous wink, he continued. "And such sport heats the blood. You probably can't wait to mount her, right, lad?"

Appearing embarrassed at how the earl spoke about his absent daughter, Calvert cleared his throat and interrupted. "I'd like you both to see an old . . . acquaintance of yours," he said, looking at his two companions. Then he explained Taggart's business.

Geoffrey squinted. "But I don't know any colonial shipping owner," he mused.

"You knew me as your groom," Taggart added in an even tone.

"Groom?" Edwin echoed. His mouth lost much of its pleasantness as he recognized his former adversary. "Is this a joke?"

Taggart felt the old resentments begin to boil his blood as he studied his former enemies. They both looked at him as if he were something unpleasant they'd found caked to the soles of their boots.

"God's teeth, Calvert, what in blue blazes can you be thinking of to let this—"

"Geoffrey, calm yourself," admonished the older duke. "Taggart is no longer an Irish groom. According to John Nolan, he is now a successful American businessman."

"But it is hardly proper to have . . . his sort . . . mixing in with polite society," Edwin added, looking up disdainfully at the man he'd once whipped in the dark cellar of Somerset hall nine years ago. "I can't think what the King would say."

As the duke straightened his narrow shoulders, again Taggart was reminded of the inner conviction and strength of the man of supposed frailty. "Though it is not my habit to divulge the contents of conversations between polite gentlemen, John Nolan tells me that Mr. O'Rahilly has been received at Court. The Prince of Wales was especially taken with our

110

colonial guest and his seafaring ventures. And as Taggart O'Rahilly is a guest in my home, gentleman, I trust you both," he said, eyeing the earl and the heavily perfumed Edwin, "will treat him accordingly."

The tense moment went on as Taggart used all his self-discipline to remain calm, despite the remembered injustices and cruelty that suddenly came crashing at him, things he thought were long buried with the years. Yes, he told himself, he had to stay calm. His revenge was too close at hand to jeopardize with a brief spark of temper. By the middle of the week, the Earl of Holingbrook would know he was ruined. He smiled to himself. Yes, he'd waited this long. Two more days would not matter. "You will excuse me, gentlemen." He nodded politely at Calvert. "The air has become too close for me in here. So used to my home's more pleasant aroma in Virginia, I feel I must take my leave from your party this evening." He looked across the room. "Ah, I see John Nolan and his wife. I must pay my respects." With a formal bow, he left a smiling duke and his scowling companions.

Taggart departed without looking back. The next party, the Irishman vowed, would be in his new home here in Kinsale—the former Fitzroy Hall.

The following Tuesday, Geoffrey Fitzroy, the ninth Earl of Holingbrook, sat scowling down at the large legal document on his study desk. It couldn't be true, but there it was. He'd had no idea the size of his debt was that much. The figure made him feel sick. It was all that stupid solicitor's fault, he told himself. Just because he hadn't been paid for over a year, he'd grown lax and not watched out for his financial affairs. "God, what am I going to do?" He put his head in his hands. Then he poured himself a huge brandy and gulped it down in one, uninterrupted swallow.

Dressed only in his nightshirt, a brocade dressing gown, and matching round cap on his bald head, Geoffrey Fitzroy knew things were desperate. Unless the huge amount owned to the undersigned was paid within the week, all the contents of Fitzroy Hall, its properties and environs would be lost. His

111

horses, too, would be taken over by the exclusive owner of all the earl's outstanding notes. In bold scrawling handwriting, the future owner's name glared at him like the muzzle of cannon:

Taggart O'Rahilly, owner of Williamsburg Shipping.

The earl could not believe how easily he'd been tricked. His fist slammed down on the carved wooden desk. "Damn his Irish spleen," he cried aloud. Grabbing the most available item—a Chinese vase—he pulled back his wide arm and sent it crashing against the marble fireplace. Colorful pieces of porcelain went flying about the room. Ignoring the havoc he'd created, the earl stood up and began pacing slowly back and forth on the frayed Oriental carpet. Damned if he'd let that . . . colonial upstart have Fitzroy Hall.

"Bloody gout," he swore, an excuse to vent his fury on something more concrete. His doctor was an idiot, telling him to reduce his drinking. Brandy was sustenance, any fool knew that. He hobbled back to his leather wing chair on the other side of the room and tenderly raised his slippered foot to rest atop the pillow-covered footstool in front of him. What could he do? he asked himself. He'd borrowed already from every friend he knew. In truth, some of them had become former friends as the time lapsed, and he couldn't find the money to pay them back. Only John Nolan still called here, and Geoffrey knew even Nolan couldn't give him any more now—he'd read the signs a week ago when he'd handed over the sack of gold coins. No, he couldn't tap that source anymore.

"Father?"

Bleary-eyed, the earl squinted in the dim light of the fire.

Holding a candle in her slender hand, Millicent stood in the doorway. A ruffled cap held her long auburn hair away from her face. Out of bright light she wasn't quite so homely, the earl mused. And she'd filled out a little in the last couple of years. He removed his round cap and scratched his head as a plan for his salvation began to materialize. "Come in, my dear," he said in a totally uncharacteristic attempt at sweetness. "I should like to talk to you."

Cautiously, Lady Millicent came into the room. Her slippered feet hardly made a sound. She placed her candle on a side table, then, clutching her heavy wool shawl about the gray flannel nightdress, she came to stand before her father.

"Bring the chair closer to the fire."

His daughter obeyed but sat watching her father with a wary air. She saw the strewn remnants of one of the last expensive vases in the house, but she said nothing. Hands folded in her lap, she waited for him to yell at her for not telling her father that Taggart had been the ship's captain she'd intended to be her escort at the party this evening.

One thing the earl felt was in his favor, Millie hadn't attended the ball with that Irishman. Headache? Merely an excuse, for he knew his daughter probably had the constitution of an ox. He eyed her more shrewdly. The red puffiness about the eyes told him she'd been crying, something he'd never actually seen. And no one else, least of all Edwin, had any notion Millie had even considered going to the party with O'Rahilly. Yes, he mused, feeling happier, Millie might just be malleable now. A woman spurned and all. O'Rahilly probably never had any intention of taking her. Had to admire the man's deviousness.

"Are you cold, child? Would you like a little brandy?"

"No. Thank you," she added, once over her surprise. An eagerness to please from her father was rare. Her instincts told her the man across from her wanted something. Millicent stared at the glass-paneled French doors, which led to the terrace and darkened garden outside. She turned her head and gazed at the fire once more. Without her glasses, the flames softened this room, causing it to take on a welcoming atmosphere. "It is better to say it plain, Father. You know the social amenities have not existed between us for some time." Her gray eyes were serious.

"Quite. Though your future husband may not discover your straightforwardness as a compliment to your sex, I do find it to my liking tonight. Well, then, Millie, here it is. My fool of a solicitor has just presented me with a document that will stand up in any court of law. You know I have been having . . . ah, certain financial difficulties." As if he'd expected some sympathetic mew, the earl paused.

She was a cool one, he thought with a twinge of irritation.

113

Just sitting there staring at him from those grave eyes of hers. He shrugged. Nothing to do but press on.

"Well, the long and short of it is that one man now holds all my outstanding notes—it's a huge sum, Millicent, and there is no way I can raise even a quarter of that amount. And if the heartless fellow doesn't get his money by next week, we will lose everything—house, land, livestock."

Silence.

"God's nightshirt, girl, do you understand what I'm saying? Everything will be lost!"

"Would you have me play at being surprised, Father? For years I have watched you squander the Fitzroy legacy, including Mother's wealth. It is only an enigma that it has taken this long."

"Don't get pert with me, miss." His voice reverted to the usual menace. "I've often thought a taste of the whip would improve your disposition."

Knowing her father was quite capable of carrying out his threat, Lady Millicent tried to subdue her speech.

"And with Dunstan gone," the man across from her went on, "well, who knows when he'll be back from India. Might as well be the moon for all the help he's given me these last two years."

Millie bit down on her lower lip rather than remind her father it was his insistence that made Dunstan take that cursed commission in the Army in the first place. "Colonel Shelby wrote me that he is investigating the matter. I should hear something in a month or so."

"Bah, that will be too late. I—we need funds now. And only you can get it for us."

So that was it. "Am I to plead your case to this Englishman for you, beg him to spare us from Newgate?" she asked, her spirit returning. "If you give me his name, I shall—"

"It's of no concern who this man is," he cut in briskly. "And I'd kill you myself if you went and begged anything from him. Man has no principles at all. He isn't a gentleman, that's all you need to know." Geoffrey took a deep breath, clearly attempting to recapture the sweetness in his voice once more. "Daughter, I know we haven't always dealt well with each other. Perhaps it's because you've always been so much like your mother. You know, my dear, a man likes a woman he can laugh with and have a good time. You're far too quiet; you read too much." He eyed the high neck of her gray flannel nightwear. "Damn me, a man would need a horse rake to get you out of that thing you're trussed up in. And you should learn to dress better, show a little more of yourself off. A man enjoys stealing a look at a woman's secret charms."

The lady dug her nails into the palm of her right hand rather than divulge her thoughts. The man squatting on his comfortable chair had no idea how very much she liked lovely things. So little did he know her, he thought she wore these shabby old garments by choice, not economic necessity.

Misinterpreting his daughter's silence, Geoffrey smiled indulgently. "There now. Of course you're embarrassed at how you dress. But I have a friend in town, a lovely lady who can help you choose a suitable trousseau."

One of his trollops, no doubt, but Millicent only said, "A trousseau suggests a wedding, Father." Something lurched in the pit of her stomach. She'd thought to put this off, but now it appeared there was no way out this time. "Edwin?"

"Yes, my clever girl. He and his father have agreed to the terms. They will get Fitzroy Hall and our lands. And we will receive—"

"The Somerset money," she finished. Though Edwin was not demonstrative in his affections, nor had he even spoken of love or kissed her, Lady Millicent had always known what was expected of her. "And," she pressed, "Edwin has agreed, Father? No one coerced him. It is important to me. I must know the truth, for I am well aware of . . . of my shortcomings," she added, brushing back a strand of straight auburn hair.

Her father knew she wouldn't be duped in this area. "Well, we both know you're no beauty." He tried to find a safe harbor. "But Edwin said your sensible nature is exactly what he desires in a wife."

Millie closed her eyes, understanding full well what the words meant. In other words, she would not interfere in Edwin's life or his pursuits. Did he have a mistress? Probably, she told herself. With his blond handsomeness and expensive dress, if a little too foppish for her taste, he was a "catch" according to many of the ladies in Kinsale and London.

The earl read his daughter's initial reluctance, and therefore, he pressed, "Will you allow a stranger to take over this land? And he's got no charitable qualities, girl. Probably would sell Dunstan's horses, drive off the tenants. He won't live here I'll warrant. Probably bleed the place dry."

The tenants? Millie thought, suddenly afraid. Though poorly fed now, they would die if they lost their right to work Fitzroy land. And they depended on her for the food she could spare and the little help she could offer. How could she abandon them?

The earl added, "And I don't have to tell you there are no other husband prospects for you. It's this or spinsterhood. Even John Nolan says this is the only salvation for us."

The twenty-two-year-old woman had to agree. Her eyes misted at the thought of Taggart. It had all been a child's fantasy. For years she'd deceived herself with her romantic dreams of a future with the darkly handsome Irishman. But she was no longer a child, and she forced herself to face the truth: Taggart O'Rahilly felt nothing for her. He'd only come to Kinsale for his sister, Edna.

Damn it, the Earl of Holingbrook thought, she couldn't falter now. He had to get Millicent tied to Edwin. He knew the Somersets would be more than ready to fork over the money he needed—old Somerset had desired the Fitzroy lands for years. "Time is running out, miss. I need your answer this night."

Millicent blinked and stood up quietly. "Then you shall have your answer, Father." Successfully, she hid her true feelings behind the mask of gravity. Her voice was soft yet firm. "You can post the bans in the morning. I . . . I agree to the terms." She turned to leave, while her eyes were still dry.

"Fine, my dear." The earl was in his element. "That's it, you run along to bed. Leave everything to your papa. We'll have the wedding in two weeks time. I shall speak to the Reverend Somerset."

The girl stopped near the door. She turned to face her father. And Nigel Somerset was to perform the ceremony—it

116

was to be Anglican, she had no doubt. The way all the plans fell into place, it seemed she was the last person to hear the news of her impending wedding. How could she have expected more? she admonished herself. "But so soon, Father? Surely, that will not be seemly. Your friends might . . . well assume I'm—" Her father's harsh laugh cut off her embarrassed words of protest.

"That Edwin's got a brat in you? Well, that wouldn't hurt at all. Old Somerset's whispered to me that he's a trifle worried about the boy's abil— Here now, those are not proper thoughts for an earl's daughter." He turned to waddle back toward his desk. "You concerned about gossip? Hah!" Geoffrey added with exasperation. "Had you been sensitive to what people thought of you, you'd have spent more time with your betters, instead of gallivanting about Kinsale wiping snot from the noses of those filthy Irish—" The loud sound of his study door closing caused the earl to look up. Well, he'd let her go this time. He reached for his decanter of brandy. It was time to celebrate. He'd gotten everything he wanted.

As he toasted himself with another huge tumbler of the amber liquid, he murmured pleasantly, "Here's to O'Rahilly and all those stupid Irishmen in Kinsale, may they end in Hades. God save the King and White's until I return." This would do it, he told himself with glee. With the Somerset money now behind him, he'd buy his way back to Court. He glanced about the room. And this estate in Kinsale and all the Irish on it could rot for all he cared. Thinking about how O'Rahilly was going to be livid when he learned the earl had turned the tables on him, Geoffrey began laughing out loud. His generous swallow of brandy careened the wrong way, however, and he began to cough and curse in unison.

"Taggart, why don't you say something?" In exasperation, Edna grabbed the newspaper out of her brother's hands. Her green eyes flashed as she tossed it to the carpeted floor.

Her brother scowled as he looked up from his position on the brocade-covered settee. Edna stood with her hands on either side of her waist. The black ringlets of her recently coifed hair bounced up and down. She was dressed in the latest fashion, a becoming yellow-and-white striped gown, but when she spoke again, her brogue was as thick as a London fog. He'd never seen her so angry.

"What would you have me say?" he demanded at a lull in her tirade. He got up from the couch. His own irritation rose as he thought once again how the earl had outmaneuvered him. According to the cursory note from the earl's solicitor, the money was to be paid to him in a week's time. And what did Millicent think of him, now that she realized his manner of revenge against her father? Did she hate him? he wondered as he looked out one of the windows of their expensive suite of rooms. It was more than likely, he mused, especially visualizing the picture her father probably painted of him. Though he didn't know why, the thought bothered him.

Clearly at the end of her patience, the nineteen-year-old girl stamped her foot. "Since the bans were posted a week ago, you've not said a word about it."

At the mention of Millicent's wedding, Taggart whirled about to confront the pretty girl. "What would you have me say or do, Sister? The matter is out of my hands." The earl had taken away his weapon for revenge. He'd never considered a father could so easily sell his daughter to save his own neck. God, how he'd underestimated the earl's penchant to be such a bounder. And to Edwin? The Irishman gave a bitter laugh. Edwin would be about as useful a husband as a gelded sheep. "The Fitzroys can go to the devil for all I care. Edwin and Lady Fitzroy deserve each other."

Hardly believing her ears, Edna was at him like an angry bulldog. "Oh, that my own brother, after all her ladyship's done for ya, you'd abandon her to a life— Dolt!" she shouted. "Millie sold her dowry for you. I know you didn't mean to harm her, but do ya think 'tis you alone has all the pride?" The words having escaped, instantly Edna clamped a hand over her mouth as the realization of what she'd just done hit her. She'd broken her promise to Millie never to reveal the truth. However, when the short, raven-haired beauty would have backed away, her brother's strong hands at her shoulders held her still.

118

"Dowry?" he demanded. "What are you talking about?"

"Nothin'. I was just—"

"Edna," his tone was firm. "I want the truth."

She met her brother's gaze head on. "Yes. It's time you knew." It was actually a relief to have it out. Then she told her brother about how Millicent had sold her jewels so he could get a start in America. Deciding it was best not to tell him what she had done with the money he'd sent her, she ended with a comment on how worried she and Millie were about Dunstan, whom they had not heard from in so long. And she made a point of telling him how hard Millie had worked to help the tenants as best she could.

So floored by this new information, Taggart missed the look of deep emotion in his sister's eyes when she spoke of Millie's absent brother. Right now, he decided not to tell either girl that Dunstan was dead. After all, he'd received the report from Ben Abrams who warned him the French sources could not always be trusted. Best to wait until he could investigate the matter further. His head was still reeling from this unbelievable news that Lady Fitzroy had been his . . . patroness.

The tall Irishman slumped into a nearby chair. He knew his sister did not lie this time. "Good God," he mumbled aloud. "Millicent." The picture of her on Charger as she switched horses to save him years ago, the gentle way she'd tended to him that horrible night he'd come back from the Somersets—a long sigh escaped his lips when he remembered the way he'd treated the lady upon his return. Shame filled him. Yet, he shouted to himself, what the devil was he going to do now? Then another question occurred to him. Why had John Nolan allowed him to believe he'd been the one to give him the money nine years ago? And Nolan had accepted the returned wealth that was rightly Lady Fitzroy's. Though the money meant little to Taggart, he promised himself to ask the squire about this later.

He vaulted from the chair in mounting agitation. "This is madness."

Instantly, Edna's face became softer. She reached out a small hand and touched her brother's arm with affection. "Sure and don't I know we'll think of something. Why not go talk to Father Mike on the matter? He often helped you see the right of things before."

Nodding, ready to grasp any thread of help, Taggart headed for the door of their rented accommodations. "The ride will clear my buzzing head, if nothing else."

"Millie will never speak to me again."

Taggart came back to put an arm around his younger sister's shoulders. "Why, you know as well as I do the lady must have a kind heart. I was a blind fool not to recognize it." It bothered him to see his sister so upset. "Now wasn't it yourself who told me not to worry a second ago." His voice was teasing as he coaxed, "Sure and I'll straighten it out with her ladyship." He hid his own uneasiness about this startling turn of events. Forcing himself to smile, Taggart handed his sister his cambric pocket handkerchief. "There now, you don't want to ruin those pretty green eyes. What would these Irish bucks say when they start coming to ask me for your hand? And didn't Kevin O'Hara ask about you this very morning?"

Though Mr. O'Hara was a handsome young man and congenial, Edna was uneasy at the way her brother kept hinting in this direction. No, she decided this wasn't the time to tell him she and Dunstan had an understanding. Best get her friend, Millie, out of trouble first. She smiled shyly up at her brother. "The Somersets aren't fit for Millie. You . . . you won't let her marry Edwin, will you?"

Taggart winced, wondering what the devil she expected him to do about it. Yes, he'd pay her back every penny of her dowry, but he wouldn't stop the marriage. "You haven't considered her ladyship might be marrying Edwin because she chooses to."

Edna's small nose wrinkled in disgust. "But he is so fastidious. And he doesn't seem to like children."

A good thing, Taggart thought with sarcasm, for Edwin would hardly father any. He was quite sure neither his sister nor Lady Fitzroy knew the truth of Edwin's preferred inclinations. And from what he could discern the other evening at the duke's party, Edwin's taste still had not changed. And a few discreet inquiries with the right coin had confirmed his suspicions.

"You will see Father Collins, then?"

Taggart shrugged. "I hardly think—" He caught the hopeful pleading in Edna's green eyes. "Oh, all right."

"You look like you could use something stronger than tea." Father Michael Collins went over to a high cupboard and grabbed two cups, along with a half-empty bottle of whiskey. Nine years had not changed the tall, robust priest very much. Only the muted touches near his temples hinted that time went on, even for Kinsale's parish priest. However, when Taggart studied him closely, he saw the deeper lines near his eyes. "Edna told me about the bad harvest. Will you tell me more? I've seen few happy faces since my ship docked here. The people look even more worn and ill-clothed than I remember on the estate. Part of that Fitzroy bastard and his pampered daut—"

The Jesuit plunked his half-filled whiskey glass down on the rough wooden table. "Do not speak of her ladyship in that manner. Irish friend or not, Taggart O'Rahilly, you'd best watch your tongue concerning Lady Millicent, especially around the townfolk here. I know a few Kinsale men who'd give you more than the warning I'm offering you. Not a week goes by that she doesn't visit the sick and old, giving what comfort she can. And working that land—why, she does the chores of at least two men, and—"

"But . . ." Taggart let his words drift off, for there was little he could deny now. So, his sister had not exaggerated. Things began moving in place at such a rapid speed, O'Rahilly felt as though his horse had kicked him in the stomach. The garden work that morning was not an eccentricity as he'd blindly assumed. And the dress. He felt color suffuse his face, experiencing more shame at this moment than at any other time in his twenty-five years. Never in the years he'd known the lady had she brought him down because of his poor attire or the work he did. Now he realized it had been the best gown she had, and he'd—God, what had he done?

"Well," the priest added, setting the worn cup back on the table. "I knew the truth would come out some time, though I was certain her ladyship wouldn't be the one to tell you. A strange, gentle—"

"Thoroughly exasperating woman," Taggart completed with feeling. Why hadn't Edna or Millicent told him how bad things had become at Fitzroy Hall? But his logical mind sorted the answer quickly. It was clear Edna and Millicent felt sisterly affection for each other. And pride was strong in the Englishwoman. Would he have done less, or begged for help? But he wasn't so sure he'd have ever been so generous to anyone English. "To sell her whole dowry," he said aloud. A hand went unconsciously to his temple, almost as if he still couldn't take it all in. "My God, Geoffrey Fitzroy would kill her if he ever found out."

"And that's the truth of it," the red-haired priest remarked. "And I can think of a few of his friends who would applaud the act. The lass has courage."

The thirty-five-year-old priest grinned at his companion before he continued. "Yes, I'd have to say that, though she appears sedate and always ladylike, there's the touch of something . . ."

"Touch of the Irish hellion in her," Taggart added with the first shout of laughter since he'd learned the truth of her secretive actions from nine years ago. Then he looked bemused as warmer thoughts of Lady Millicent Fitzroy washed over him. Her long silky auburn hair, the gentleness of her hands when they touched him the night she'd risked more than her reputation to come to nurse him, the laughter in her gray eyes and soft voice when he'd teased her about— How could he let her marry Edwin Somerset? The man wasn't capable of being any real husband to her. At best he'd never touch her, but he did have a sadistic streak. What if he harmed her? "No, she can't marry Edwin!" Taggart rose so abruptly that the wooden chair almost toppled to the rough planks at his feet.

He looked embarrassed at the way he'd confided so much of his feelings to his former confessor.

The black-robed priest sat watching the younger man calmly. "You know, she and I have talked a lot while you've been away. Oh," he hastened, "never about you directly. But about life, and what she believed in. She's an intelligent woman. You already know how kind she is," he added, clearly wishing to push this home once more. A few silent moments passed. The priest had the barest smile when he saw the tall Irishman come back and sit down at the table. "You know, we were so busy catching up on all the news of Kinsale I never asked you, have you married?" The question was nonchalant, given as he raised his earthenware cup to take another sip of the strong liquor.

"No, I have not married, Father."

"Really? Why, at twenty-five, do you mean to say no Virginia lady has snapped you up?"

Well aware at what the priest was getting at, O'Rahilly was not sure he wished to head along with him. True, he'd always liked Millicent, and he did not wish to see her tied to that . . . foppish Edwin. Hell, would Edwin and his young Italian boy all live at Fitzroy Hall with her? He might have known the earl wouldn't give tuppence for his daughter's feelings. But she was a Fitzroy, daughter of the man who'd sent his father to the gallows. Lady Fitzroy's life was none of his business.

"I will not ask Lady Fitzroy to marry me," he blurted.

The older priest's expression mirrored shock. "Why, I never said you should. Besides," he added, straightening the black sash at his waist, "it's too late. The bans have been posted. The . . . ah, Anglican wedding is only a week away." His tone was casual as he added, "And I doubt she'd have you anyway. Hardly suitable for an English lady and all that. Mind you, I think you're the salt of the earth," the priest added outrageously, while maintaining his serious countenance. "But she is an English aristocrat, you realize. Probably have you tossed out on your as—fine London breeches before you had your booted foot in the door."

The chair scraped the wooden boards once more as Taggart bounded to his feet. "Oh, you think so, do you?" His strong jaw tightened. "I'm no man's judge and I have my faults, but I'm bloody well as good as any of those toffy-nosed English boobs around here. And any wife I choose will be well provided for—both materially and in the bedding department," he said, before grabbing his tricorn hat off the table. "If you will excuse me, Father Collins. I have a call to pay at Fitzroy Hall."

devilish grin on Father Michael's boyish face as he bade his long-time friend godspeed. Then the priest pulled out his rosary, bent on saying some serious ones for the difficult cause that lay ahead for both the Irishman and his English lady.

"She says she don't want ta see ya. And I can't blame her," Colleen Mulcahy added, holding her wool shawl closer about her heavy shoulders. The bed cap, tied under her chin, was askew, giving full evidence she'd been wakened out of a sound sleep. "And if Fergus hadn't been so devout at Fogarty's Pub tonight, he'd be shooing you away with the end of his boot. I heard her up there cryin' her eyes out behind those locked doors. All for the likes of you. You think I don't know how you went prancin' about the Duchess of Huntington at the duke's party. And wasn't me lady's future bridegroom over the next mornin' just grinnin' ta tell her all the sordid details."

The news caused him no joy. Just what had Edwin said about him? But did it matter at this point?

Taggart forced himself to modulate his voice. "Colleen, you must know I'd never harm her ladyship. I merely wish to talk with her. Now, will you kindly let me in. It's cold standing out here in the night air."

The older woman's face seemed to relent a trifle when she noticed Taggart wore no hat or gloves once more. "Well, you can come in and warm yourself in the library by the fire for a moment. His lordship is upstairs in his room, so be quiet."

Taggart did as bidden. Though he wanted to race here after seeing Father Collins, he'd forced himself to stop at his rented rooms first. Bathed and dressed purposely in a more subdued attire—dark-brown coat and breeches—he wanted his clothes to match his speech tonight, simple and direct. Besides, he preferred this unadorned attire. However, instead of heading for the room to his right, he darted silently for the stairs, trying to ignore the portraits of Fitzroy ancestors that adorned the stairway wall on his left.

"Taggart!" the horrified Colleen hissed. In a frenzy she waddled after him as fast as she could. "Saints preserve us, you'll have us all brought before the magistrate."

Hearing the fear in the kindly old woman's voice, he stopped just short of the first step. "Don't worry, Mrs. Mulcahy. I protect my own." He smiled, looking like the mischievous lad of years ago. Then he bent down and gave her a quick kiss on her wrinkled cheek.

Despite herself, she smiled and touched the spot where the handsome man had kissed her. Colleen shook her head as she watched him walk silently up the marble staircase. "'Tis the devil, ya are, Taggart O'Rahilly, and no good will come from this night's work," she whispered to herself. Shrugging her shoulders, she turned and walked slowly back to the warm comfort of her bed.

"Is that you, Colleen?" Millicent went automatically to the door and opened it. "I told you before, I don't want any food, thank you." Dressed for bed in a thin muslin nightgown and soft ecru slippers, Lady Fitzroy could only stand mutely for a second. "You!" she accused. So shocked by his new boldness, words failed her for a moment.

Taking advantage of her astonishment, Taggart entered her room and shut the door behind him. He couldn't help noticing the starkness of the room compared to years ago. But he quickly came to the point. "I wish to talk with you, and since you have refused to see me, this seems my only method—"

"I have nothing further to say to you," she snapped. It was impossible to ignore the way something inside her automatically responded to his presence. His height and strength seemed to dwarf her room. How easy it would be to tell him how happy she was to see him. But anger at their last meeting replaced some of her elation. "You will leave this room at once," she stated, in a tone used only on rare occasions. Without her glasses, she knew he could easily read the unyielding steel in her icy glare.

Undaunted, he folded his hands across his chest and enjoyed the enchanting picture she presented. How could she be so unaware how lovely he found her right now? The light from the bedside candle gave him a provocative outline of her long legs covered only by the floor-length nightwear. Ruffles and bows at her throat, long auburn hair, straight but silky as it flowed riotously about her shoulders, color in her cheeks as she showed clearly what she thought of his audacity. Something stirred inside of him. *"Gealbhan,"* he whispered aloud. His hands reached gently out for her, only to have her step back.

The way he was looking at her made her suddenly aware of her lack of clothing. Hastily, she grabbed for her heavier wrapper at the foot of the bed. Her fingers shook as she tried to fasten the row of cloth-covered buttons. Millicent heard his Gaelic name for her. But to call her "sparrow" now only caused her pain. It reminded her of a time long past and dreams that had no basis in reality.

She attempted to keep her voice cool. "Will you kindly leave here at once." His expression of patient amusement incensed her. "Or must I toss you out of here bodily?"

"You and what other four men?" Lord, he thought, as he read the jutting angle of her slender chin. She meant it. Unrestrained laughter overcame him.

In an instant, she was standing right before him. "Will you be quiet," she ordered, trying to give him a rough shove, then became more vexed when she couldn't budge him. "My father is just down the hall. Do you want to get yourself killed?"

His laughter stopped, and before she could get away he captured her shoulders. "Then you do care what happens to me, my lady?"

Trapped, she looked away. "I . . ." Then she met his gaze. "My father would not spare me, either." She began struggling to be free. Though he wasn't hurting her, she did not like the weakness in her knees that he was making her feel. "And a woman engaged to wed in one week does not entertain strange men in her boudoir at night. Now, let me go," she commanded.

Fully intending to release her, Taggart now felt irritated as he watched that haughty way she held her head. Not only did he continue to hold her shoulders, he slipped his left arm about her waist and hauled her closer to his body.

She began struggling in earnest now, pushing and straining

against his soft velvet coat. Always considering herself a strong woman, it amazed her how firmly muscled he'd become. She might have been trying to push on the elm tree outside her bedroom window for all the effect she was having. "All right," she warned. "This is your last chance. Do you give up, sir?"

Taggart's black eyebrow rose, then his mouth quirked upward, but this time he stifled his laughter. He had her pinned to him, and she dared ask him to yield? "Sometimes," he whispered, "I don't know whether I want to kiss you or spank you, Lady Millicent Fitzroy." When he saw the blush creep up her slender neck to her delicate face, he knew quite certainly he wanted to kiss her. He smelled the enchanting scent of her lavender soap, felt the warmth of her slender body. But then he glanced down at the pleading in her gray eyes. No, he told himself with regret, this was not the time or place for him to seduce her. He released her reluctantly.

Stepping back, he tried to regain some composure. "I did not come here to engage in fisticuffs."

"Well, you should have because it is the only reaction you'll get from me this night."

He was surprised at her angry retort. "So, the sparrow has a temper." The realization did not displease him, though at the moment he couldn't say why. Looking amused at her show of bravado, he stood his ground.

His humor did nothing to assuage her emotions. With a toss of her head she turned her back on him. "Please do not slam my window on your way out. I trust you can still climb down trees. I will refrain from telling my future husband of your ungentlemanly actions if you leave by that window at once."

"Now is that any way for the daughter of an earl to be actin'," he teased. "And here I'd come to ask you a very important question."

She whirled about to face him as he mimicked his former Irish speech. "No doubt another invitation to a party you've no intention of escorting me to."

Though he knew she'd tried to hide it, Taggart had not missed the pain behind the words. He came back to stand close to her, taking care to keep his booted feet away from her bare toes. His brown eyes softened. "Have you ever attended a formal party?" He saw something change in her expressive face.

"I . . ." She looked defensive. "Of course I—"

"No hedging, no 'I dare say.' The truth, sparrow," he added in a gentler tone.

Gray eyes met warm dark coals. "No." Her smile was rueful. "It appears circumstances always conspired to keep me away. But in the scheme of life, I've come to realize it is not that important." She thought for a moment, looking perplexed. "Is that the question you came charging into my boudoir to ask at this unholy hour?"

"No, Lady Millicent Fitzroy." All traces of humor left his handsome face. "I have come tonight to ask you to marry me."

Chapter 9

After Millicent regained some of her composure, she realized the Irishman was quite serious. The dark eyes studying her so intently were warm and gentle, like her O'Rahilly of years ago. The arm enfolding her shoulders gave comfort and strength. He was talking quietly to her. However, she could barely discern the words, for joy radiated through her body, touching and gliding across her heart like the welcome rays of a forgotten sun. *He loves me,* her mind shouted.

Taggart reached for her fingers. "You have the loveliest hands, my sparrow." His lips touched the smooth skin of her hand, then turned it over to place an intimate caress on her palm. "We will deal well with each other, Millie."

Her voice was breathless. "But you have always been able to read too much of my thoughts, dear Irishman." She saw affection in his eyes, yet there was also the evident sign of triumph. Millicent sighed, wondering if she would ever understand this complicated man. "I know if Mrs. Halsey were still here, she would chide me to be standoffish, to demand the courting, and put you through all those unsure agonies men usually go through. Yet . . ." Her gray eyes met his. "You should be warned that the English here have often found me unconventional. In truth, my father despairs of me, for I am too direct, he says. But I . . . I do wish to marry you, Taggart. I cannot play games with you."

He couldn't help but smile at her disclosure. "It is not a fault in my eyes, *Gealbhan,* for I, too, prefer the direct approach."

Now even more secure in her feelings, she let him see the love shining from her eyes.

Unable to resist, he pulled her closer, liking the feel of her tall, firm body. Again, without fully comprehending why, Taggart found himself drawn to this woman. She gave so much away in her expressive face. The scent of lavender from her soft skin assailed his welcoming nostrils. He reached across the short distance and took her chin gently in his fingers. "Will you have me bend a knee and ask for your hand? For truly, my lady, I am prepared to do this honorably, if at least unusually."

Her smile began at the corners of her mouth as her heart overflowed with happiness. She had always loved him, and now her feelings were returned. Truly, he did want her to marry him. "I would never ask you to grovel at my feet, Taggart, for it is a husband you would be, never a servant."

Her words pleased him. Tentatively, he leaned his body forward. His eyes studied her sweet face, taking in her slender nose, smooth forehead, and well-formed cheekbones. With a combination of shyness and affection, he felt her hand on his recently shaved cheek, then she ran the satin tips of her fingers along his angular jaw, lingering in the cleft at the center of his chin. When her fingers touched his lips, he found he could not stay so passive and reached out to press the slender fingers to his mouth.

She inhaled deeply, not only to steady her tumultuous emotions but also to take in the welcome fragrance of the man before her. There was none of the heavy odor of jasmine as Edwin was so overly fond of wearing. Her Irishman carried the scents of soap and leather, combined with the night aroma from riding fast and hard through a dense forest. Would he kiss her? Her bare toes rested right in front of his black boots. "Is it not customary to shake hands during these negotiations, sir?" the lady asked, impishness showing on her face.

He marveled that she obviously had no idea of the seductive picture she presented and how difficult it was for him to show restraint.

"Well," Millicent continued, when he did not answer either verbally or physically, "I shall just get parchment and quill."

She made a motion to turn away. However, a muffled cry of surprise escaped her lips when she felt him haul her back easily against his hard body. This time his embrace was more forceful.

"English hellion," he growled, only half in jest. His warm breath fanned her parted lips. "We Irish seal our bargains with more directness than stuffy English fops." Without another word he pressed his lips to hers—firm, yet gentle at first, for he sought to learn her ways, determined not to frighten her. But it surprised and delighted him when he felt her own fiery response as she opened to him. Warm and soft, her mouth was both shy and a trifle awkward as she returned his embrace. Perhaps, he mused, marrying Lady Millicent would not be such a sacrifice after all, for this first kiss between them did, indeed, hold many possibilities.

The young Englishwoman felt the room spin as his smoldering kiss consumed her. Yet, something inside wanted her to burn, for the first time to feel the touch and desire of the man she had loved for so long.

At six foot, Taggart liked the way Millicent was only three inches shorter. It pleased him to reach across to hold her. In the past there had been a lot of stooping and bending over to kiss petite young women.

His large hand caressed her long silky hair, as it tumbled about her shoulders in enchanting disarray. He could feel the firm mounds of her thinly covered nipples as she unconsciously pressed herself deeper into the folds of his open coat and linen waistcoat. If he didn't stop soon, his mind warned—

Reluctantly, he pulled away first. Never had he experienced such passionate giving from a woman's kiss. He forced air into his lungs, trying frantically to master the desire to take more from the woman before him, who clearly had no idea the havoc she was creating within him. It had been weeks since he'd had a woman—the London encounter with Garnet had left him far from satisfied. Hell, he wasn't made of granite. "I must go," he managed, his voice ragged.

She looked flustered. Had she displeased him? "Yes . . . of course." She stepped back, remembering. "I would never forgive myself if Father took his whip to you again." Silently, she admonished herself for forgetting about his safety.

"Oh, sparrow," he said, shaking his head. "I must leave because I find you far too tempting," he admitted in a husky whisper. But he was touched by her concern for his safety. Until now he hadn't realized how his hatred for her father had obsessed him. Sadly, he wished he had written her during those years, for he suddenly wanted to know her better, yet there wasn't time. There was no help for it now, but it was a tempestuous way to begin a marriage.

She blushed at his bold speech, then couldn't help smiling. "My lady, you do not appear too repentant for causing me such anguish," he scolded in a playful tone.

"Truly, I am sorry, sir, but it is just that . . ." Her gray eyes sparkled. "No man has ever said those words to me before."

Open, without guile. God, he groaned inside. She needed protection. "And that is precisely why I must speak to your father," he confessed aloud.

All humor left her face as more practical considerations forced their way into her romantic thoughts. And what of Edwin?

She began tugging at the taller man's sleeve. "You must leave at once. I shall try to slip away and meet you at your rented rooms tomorrow night. We can make our plans then." Millicent knew she was talking rapidly. Fear for his safety always did this to her. "I will need at least a day to pack and write Edwin and Father a letter of explanation. We can go to your home in Virginia within the week," she added, as her old habit of taking charge with him took over. She smiled to ease him past her words. "I shall enjoy being a sea captain's wife, with a small cottage, and—"

"I will not skulk about with the earl," O'Rahilly countered. Irritation at her suggested plan showed on his face, and he decided not to correct her inaccurate assumptions about his finances. The earl might have duped him out of any revenge, but the Irishman certainly wasn't going to play the coward in wedding his daughter. "I'll marry you openly, for there is nothing either of us has to hide. Do you imagine I'd allow you to steal away in the middle of the night, leaving Edwin Somerset to be the victimized man of honor? Your reputation

132

would be in shreds." His dark eyes narrowed as old insecurities came up to jeer at him. "Or are you ashamed of becoming my wife openly, with honor in a church wedding and our friends about us?"

"Of course not," she countered, unable to hide the edge in her voice, for she wondered how he could think her so shallow. However, she tried to remain calm, reminding herself they needed time to become reacquainted. "But it seems more logical to show a little prudence in this matter. I'll have no blood spilled, yours or my fathers, to become your wife." She held up a hand in supplication. "Please, dearest, swallow that Irish pride of yours and think of the end result. We will be married and safely away from here."

He looked disgruntled. "Yes, as I've had to swallow all I've felt when dealing with you English. By God, madam, this time it will be on my terms. I shall call on your father in the morning and ask him for your hand. This will be done properly."

After reading his unyielding stance, the lady decided it would be better to move her future husband away from this topic for the moment. Perhaps she might use other ways to dissuade him. She almost giggled, just beginning to understand what other powers might be hers. Hadn't she observed on a few occasions how Edna coyly moved Dunstan to her way of thinking? Deliberately, Millicent lowered her gaze in an attempt at meekness. "As you say, my love."

She saw his body relax, so she continued speaking. "It still amazes me that you . . . when you first returned to Kinsale you seemed so distant. What caused this change in your feeling for me?" Yes, it was true, she wanted to hear the three words. "Please tell me," she encouraged. "It is important to me." She would cherish this moment always, she told herself, and the words would come back to warm her romantic heart in the years ahead.

Having dreaded this direct question, Taggart searched his mind to find some way to avoid hurting her.

She felt his withdrawal, despite his attempt to conceal it. His wary expression was not what she'd anticipated. "Please, Taggart," she pressed, moving a little away from the arms that now reached out to embrace her once more. "I wish to know the truth."

What is wrong? she shouted at herself. No, it wasn't shyness holding him back. "You do love me?" escaped her lips.

His eyes met hers. "We seem comfortable with each other."

"That is not what I asked."

"Let it be, Millie." The strain of the last few days was taking its toll on him.

"Answer me."

When he saw her chin come up at that familiar angle, he blurted, "No, I do not love you. Must you always hurl yourself at things head-on?" he demanded, yet unable to wait for her answer. "Damn it, Millie, you might at least be a trifle grateful that I'm willing to save you from the demented Edwin or a life of martyred poverty with that lecherous father of yours." The harsh words out, he lifted his hand automatically to pull them back, but he knew it was too late. He cursed himself for thrusting the truth at her with the callousness of his lost temper.

It was difficult to hold her head erect, but Lady Fitzroy managed it. His words cut deeper than any blade. Physical pain buffeted her slender body, but she clenched her hands at her sides, vowing to die on the spot rather than let Taggart see how deeply his words affected her. "If marrying me appears such a loathsome task, sir, why did you ask me to be your wife?"

Her eyes right now reminded him of two gray stones as she confronted him with that cool English reserve. Damnation, he cursed, angry at her for making him feel like such a loathsome cur for his outburst. Let her have the whole of it, then. He told her what Edna had confessed.

The scant fire had gone out by now, and Millicent shivered. Without saying another word, she turned away from him.

The Irishman watched as she walked slowly over to the fireplace. She faltered, but when he made a motion to come to her aid, Millicent raised a hand, waving him back. Understanding her pride, he stayed where he was but kept his brown eyes on her. He breathed easier when he saw that she appeared to steady herself by reaching for the cold marble ledge. Even in the candlelight he observed that the hands now gripping the rose-colored stone were shaking and drained of color.

"Edna is very upset that you will never forgive her," he tried, wanting to hear her voice, to know she was all right. For all her height and supposed strength, right now he thought she looked small and fragile, like a reed swaying in a storm at sea. Part of him wanted to go over, take her in his arms, and let the devil take both their pride. However, he knew at the moment she would probably scorn any offers of direct comfort. While remaining where he stood, he tried words once more. "Edna only had your best interest—"

"I understand friendship, Taggart." Millicent cut him off from her position across the room, yet she could not look at him. "Tell Edna not to fret herself. I know she was only thinking of my welfare." God, Millicent pleaded, please don't let me cry in front of him. I couldn't bear his pity on top of everything else. Fool, she scoffed at herself. This would surely cure her tendency toward romantic illusions. Of course, he did not love her. Nor could he be blamed for trying to do his duty. Duty— The word choked her. She raised a cold hand to her aching temple.

After a few silent moments, Millicent turned to look at him. How she loved him, but the thought only taunted her now. Unbidden, the picture of Garnet fluttered across her tortured mind, along with Edwin's gleeful tale of how his sister had captured the Irishman's fancy the night of Calvert's party. "I never wanted you to know where that money came from."

He looked perplexed. "But why ever not?"

Sadness tinged her reply. "Because of the way you are looking at me now. What I gave, I gave freely, O'Rahilly. You owe me nothing."

"The hell I don't. If you think I'd take—" He stopped, reminding himself this was not the way to handle the proud woman before him. "Damnation," he growled under his breath. He'd bungled the whole thing when he'd lost his temper.

At once the truth rushed over her. If she married Taggart, even without meaning to, he would break her heart. And wouldn't he take mistresses as her father had done, ignore her, bring her nothing but pain the rest of her life? She'd look at him every day, loving him, only to realize he felt nothing for

135

her. No love, but a squaring of accounts. That was all she meant to him, and in the end, he would hate her. No, she shouted inwardly, she could never be passive in this area, like her mother.

Having made her decision, Millicent felt calmer, though it took all her self-control not to give in to the tears that threatened. No, she would not bind him to her out of duty. None of the women of her family had been able to marry for love. Why, she demanded bitterly, had she considered herself different? Clasping her hands in front of her, she straightened her back and walked over to the man who stood watching her warily from across the room.

"Thank you for your offer of marriage, Mr. O'Rahilly. However, I must decline the honor."

His own body tensed at her words. Not only her refusal but her formal manner vexed him. "I suppose you'd rather I lied, waxed lyrical, and spouted my undying devotion."

"Don't be ridiculous," she snapped at his sarcasm. "I value the truth as much as you, O'Rahilly. However, I will not marry you, thank you just the same."

"And that's all?" He tried to control his mounting irritation. "For all your talk of a preference for directness, is it pretty speeches you'd be wantin' then?"

She hadn't missed the emotional return of his brogue. "No," she answered. "My mind is made up. I will marry Edwin Somerset as planned on Saturday."

"The devil you say." He reached out and grasped her shoulders, this time roughly. "Look me in the eye and tell me you love Somerset."

Unflinching, even though she knew there would be bruises on her arms, she said calmly, "I have told Edwin I do not love him. We understand each other. Edwin and I accept the duties expected of us."

Hardly believing his ears, Taggart almost shoved her away from him. "'Tis the typical English marriage," he said derisively.

"And is it the typical Irish marriage you are offering me? Without love they are both the same."

"At least you would be marrying a man, not some English

136

fop." Then he eyed her warily. "Perhaps," he grated, "Mr. Somerset's wealth holds more allure for you than I'd suspected."

"Oh, that you could think—you Irish hooligan!" she shouted. Her right hand came up, but his reflexes were quicker. She bit her lip rather than cry out as his fingers encircled her wrist and applied a measure of pressure.

"No, my lady, you shall not. No Fitzroy will ever hurt me or mine again." He released her, then stalked to the door. "Go to Edwin Somerset, then. A bank note in the amount to the penny will be deposited in your name within the week." He flung open her bedroom door. "Then the debt is paid between us. We owe each other nothing," he finished coldly.

"'Ere, what's this?" came a woman's voice from the hallway.

Taggart looked down at the scantily clad woman of about thirty-five. He noticed she eyed him up and down, obviously appreciating what she saw. Who the devil was she?

"Where are you, my dove?" Dressed only in his nightshirt and embroidered cap covering his bald head, the Earl of Holingbrook sauntered out from his bedroom down the hall.

The overblown woman's charms spilled freely out from her dirty nightgown. "We was out of wine and I 'eard voices. Didn't think her 'ighness entertained gentlemen friends in 'er bedroom. Not the hoity-toity miss." A coarse laugh followed. "Seems your daughter's had us all fooled, and what will young Somerset say? Poor Edwin."

Despite his gouty foot, the earl increased his pace down the uncarpeted hallway. "O'Rahilly!" he shouted, then charged after the man. "Devil's spawn!"

At the commotion, Millicent came outside her door immediately. "Father, this is not what it appears." She clutched a thick bed quilt around her shoulders.

"In a pig's eyes," the earl's companion spat. "And you, always lookin' so saintly, the perfect lady. Hope he paid ya enough, dearie." She cackled at Millicent's look of outrage. Her smile was lopsided due to some missing teeth. She eyed Taggart again. "Or maybe the wench 'ad ta pay his honor for 'is service, 'e bein' the better lookin' of the two."

137

"I hardly think my father's latest whore should toss aspersions on my character," Lady Fitzroy tossed back at the shorter woman. "There have been many before you, and I dare say by next week your place will be usurped. Of course, Mrs. Mulcahy will have to delouse the place first. Father," she directed, "can't you at least find one not terrified of soap and water?"

"Why, you ugly little—" The woman's filthy hands thrust upward for Millicent's throat.

Millicent took this opportunity to toss her coverlet over the woman's head, then gave her a calculated shove.

She fell backward into Geoffrey Fitzroy, who let out a loud curse as his bare feet went out from under him. The earl and his paramour fell in a tangle of scantily covered bodies and expansive coverlet.

"Taggart, get out of here," the English girl hissed under her breath. "They will not stay this way long."

"Will you stop rescuing me," Taggart shouted.

"Then cease acting like an Irish ass and leave here at once." She gave him a forceful shove, ignoring the why of her actions. Despite everything, his safety still mattered to her.

It was no playful push she's given him. Well, damn it, he thought, let her solve the whole bloody mess. "All right," he bellowed, at the end of his patience. "Marry Edwin." He headed for the staircase, now in a rush to be gone from this cursed madhouse. The earl and his bedmate were shouting at each other, reminding Taggart of two buffoonish actors from a Covent Garden play he'd seen recently in London. A stream of curses could be heard throughout the house. The earl shoved the bedcovers away from his face, while he leaned on the marble banister in a feeble attempt to stand up. "I'll cut your balls off for this, O'Rahilly!"

"Oh, Father," Millicent's tired voice interceded. "He did not have his way with me."

At the foot of the stairs, Taggart looked up, seething with a cold fury. His eyes held Millicent's. "Go to Edwin Somerset. And the lot of you can go to the devil for all I care!"

But when the Irishman reached the darkness outside, his shoulders slumped against the cold bricks at the exterior of the

Hall. For all his fury, he was well aware Millie had impetuously saved him once more. But she would never consent to wed him now. And he could not explain the disappointment and sorrow that engulfed him.

"Oh, sparrow," he whispered aloud in despair.

Millicent shivered against the unusually cold morning air. April it might be, but Kinsale felt like a London day in the heart of winter. The sun peaking out between the heavy clouds seemed to mock her dark mood. How long before she would be allowed to enter the church?

Her father and Edwin stood next to each other. Like most of the other men here, Edwin was dressed in his finest coat and breeches, a dress sword at his side. The ladies were kaleidoscopes of bright colors, plumes, and jeweled wigs. The scent of heavy perfume permeated the crowd. But it was obvious many had been drinking heavily, even for such an early hour. And Millicent did not know many of the guests here, including her future husband's supporter.

"This . . . is the first wedding I've attended," lisped Edwin's best man, "where the groom was prettier than the bride."

Laughter filled her ears as Edwin and her father joined in the rowdy goings-on. Edwin looked as if he might not be able to walk up the aisle on his own power. Garnet had been chosen as her matron of honor, and it was transparent to Millicent she was making the most of her opportunity. Dressed in a gorgeous gown of bright yellow satin, ribbons in her curly blond hair, the Duchess of Montrose appeared the picture of radiance as her husband and many of the young bucks here paid homage to her with their eyes. Yet, Millicent saw that Garnet's attention was focused on the handsome Irishman, John Nolan.

Only Abigail Somerset, the vicar's wife, seemed to pay the future bride any mind. Millicent was at least grateful for her assistance in helping her dress this morning. With corset and hoops under her mother's wedding dress, Millicent knew poor Mrs. Mulcahy would not have been able to act as ladies maid. And despite her frivolous ways, Abigail seemed truly to want to help. Nervously, Millicent touched the simple flowered circlet she wore over her brushed but straight auburn hair. Instead of wig or other adornments, she'd chosen to wear her hair about her shoulders in this manner. And both her father and future groom were far too tipsy to notice or protest her choice.

Abigail readjusted the short train at the back of Millicent's ecru-colored gown. "Do not worry, my dear," she tried to soothe the girl before her. "I shall speak to the vicar to herd these men inside. Disgraceful," she added, taking another baneful glance at the inebriated wedding party.

Millicent could only watch as Abigail hustled over to Nigel, who stood awkwardly in his black robes, the white squares of cloth at his throat flapping in the gusty breeze.

One of Edwin's friends slapped him on the back saying boisterously, "I'll be happy to lend you a ladder, old boy, for she's a tall fortress to breech." The other young men joined in their friends' rowdy laughter. Even some of the well-dressed ladies tittered behind their lacy fans. Of course, Edwin and her father were too foxed to take any offense. Only Reverend Nigel Somerset and his wife looked displeased at the lack of decorum among the guests.

Lady Millicent shut her eyes, praying to God this dreadful day would soon be over.

"Well," huffed Abigail Somerset, her ample bosom rising in outrage. "A fine state of affairs, I must say. Mr. Somerset," she hissed, with a frantic motion at her worried-looking husband.

"Bless my s-soul, I fear this is getting out of hand." Nigel nervously fingered his prayer book. "What ever sh-shall we do? We must get everyone inside."

"Nigel, stay calm or you will start that awful stuttering again." Abigail sniffed. "His lordship certainly knows some odd people. With the exception of the Nolans, the Duke of Montrose, and lovely Garnet, I must say not all of these people are known to me."

"I believe many have come from London, my dear," the vicar explained. "And Edwin has some of his old chums down from Oxford."

"I have never seen such carrying on before the ceremony, at such a sacred occasion. And this poor creature cannot stand out here in this cold morning air."

Pity was something Millicent could not abide, especially the way she felt today. Never would she see the man she loved again. Hope was lost to her. If she steeled her heart to face the truth, she could weather this, she told herself. "Perhaps," the bride offered, "if the three of us walk in now, the others will follow. Come, let us—"

The sound of horses' hooves cut off her words. Millicent's eyes grew large behind her spectacles when she recognized who led the five young men into the open churchyard of St. Multose.

"Good morning," Taggart O'Rahilly shouted down to the throng in a hearty greeting.

The earl's bloodshot eyes focused on the man sitting astride the black stallion. O'Rahilly and his companions were dressed properly enough. Probably at the expense of the Irishman, thought the earl, for he knew none of these Irishmen had that much money. "Well, a father can be a little magnanimous on his daughter's wedding day. You are welcome to stay, sirs." These Irishmen were outnumbered by Englishmen who carried swords. The earl told himself he had nothing to fear. Do them good to see how their betters married in style. None of that popery here.

Unable to move or speak, Millicent could only stare while Taggart and his friends dismounted, tied their horses' reins to nearby trees. Appearing quite elegant, they walked over to her. She could not help but notice that Taggart, unlike his companions, wore a heavy gray cape over his attire. Quickly, she forced herself to look at his companions.

She recognized the young men with Taggart. Hadn't she visited their families often enough? They looked happy. She was touched by the efforts and expense they'd obviously gone to be with her today. "I . . . I do thank you for your good wishes this morning, gentlemen." Though she dared not look Taggart directly in the eye for fear he'd read her true feelings, the Englishwoman tried to be gracious, for he clearly was here to show his support of her decision.

The earl held up a pudgy hand. "But be warned, Colonial; you and your friends will be expected to act like true Englishmen here today."

"Now, if we do that, your lordship," Taggart drawled, mocking his former brogue as he looked pointedly at some of the young bucks about Edwin, "sure and we'd be so far in our cups we wouldn't be able ta stand."

"Your insolence will not be tolerated here, Mr. O'Rahilly." Nigel Somerset looked severe. "If for no other reason, her ladyship," he went on, looking with sympathy at the young woman, "deserves our courtesy."

"Quite so, Vicar." Taggart nodded as he accepted the rebuke with uncharacteristic meekness. After removing his right leather glove, he doffed his tricorn hat and bowed deeply to Lady Fitzroy. "Your pardon, gracious lady." His manner was as neat and correct as the most polished English aristocrat.

Nigel regained much of his composure. "Then we will proceed," he said in a louder tone, sweeping his hand toward the stone stairs of the large church. Many of the guests began to head into the building.

The earl came to stand next to his daughter. "Well, be Gad, then let us proceed." He offered her his arm.

"Yes," Garnet complained. "I am freezing in this light gown. Let us have done with this farce."

The taller English girl placed a gloved hand on her father's arm. There was no turning back now. Because it was appropriate that all the guests be settled in the church first, she and her father stood waiting for Taggart and his friends to enter. She felt the muscles of her father's arm tighten, signaling his growing impatience.

"Sirs, if you will please enter the . . ." The Anglican priest appeared irritated. "Mr. O'Rahilly, you are dressed for a wedding, are you not? Now will you kindly . . ."

Taggart grinned like a man sure of himself. "Yes," he said in his clear baritone. "I am dressed for a wedding—my own."

Chapter 10

Many of the guests, some halfway through the large wooden doors of the church, stopped immediately, ignoring the jostled press of elaborately dressed bodies. There was a resurgence of guests pushing their way back out the huge doors as it became suddenly clear more interesting events were about to take place outside. Ladies gasped in shock at the Irishman's audacious words; only Calvert Huntington looked amused as he reached for his wife's arm.

"Calvert, what are you doing?" The duke's wife clearly thought her husband had taken leave of his senses. "I must precede the bride."

"My dear wife, are you so certain there is to be a wedding today?"

"Oh, there will be a wedding," Taggart interjected with a mocking smile in Geoffrey Fitzroy's direction. "But with a few slight alterations in the proceedings." He walked leisurely over to Millicent and her father. "Such as a change in groom and place for the wedding ceremony."

"Taggart," Millicent protested, feeling this folly had gone on long enough. "This is no time for one of your jests." His behavior was making civility difficult for her. "Will you kindly leave with your friends now." She was aware all eyes were on them. "Is there no end to your desire to humiliate me?" she demanded under her breath.

His dark brows rose. "Humiliate you?" he echoed in a louder tone. "Why, I intend to marry you."

143

Someone must have raced down the aisle to fetch Edwin, for the former intended, now appearing quite sober, came charging down the stone stairs. "By God, O'Rahilly you go too far." He began drawing out his sword from its ornate scabbard as he walked. Men and women moved out of his way. "You may be an American now, but you'll always be that same Irish scum." He glanced at Millicent. "My dear, you will excuse me for a few moments while I rid the earth of one more Irish bastard. Then, dear Brother," he directed to Nigel, "you shall marry us as planned."

"Now, Edwin!" Millicent shouted, frantic that things were getting so out of hand. She recognized the cruel twist of Edwin's smooth lips. "These men are unarmed." She nodded in Taggart's direction, aware Edwin knew it was against the law for any Catholic to carry a sword. "And I will have no blood spilled on my wed—"

The words died in her throat when she spotted Taggart tossing off his outer gray cloak. He handed it to one of the Irishmen next to him. She took in his cream-colored silk coat and breeches, white waistcoat with gold embroidery, white hose, and gold buckles on his black leather shoes. But it was the sword against his left hip that caught her complete attention.

"I'm an American now, not an Irishman," O'Rahilly stated firmly. "I've worn this sword in the presence of King George, and I will wear it now as my right." Without another word, he shrugged out of the well-tailored coat. His hand clasped the handle of the sword as he slowly pulled it out of its sheath.

Millicent thought she must be losing her mind. Was she the only one intent on stopping this madness? "Taggart," she entreated, reaching out to touch his free left hand. "Leave now while you and your friends have the chance. Edwin is an expert swordsman." At his unmoving stance, she lost some of her composure. "Do you think Edwin will let your five companions go free when you are dead?" Frantically, she glanced about the sea of faces, begging for someone's aid in stopping this duel. Garnet looked smug, confident her brother could easily fell O'Rahilly. The others backed away, anticipation of an already decided victory for Edwin marked clearly on most faces. Millicent watched as a few of the older men hustled their

144

reluctant wives back into the church, then proceeded to return to the church's courtyard. Her eyes fixed on John Nolan. Standing next to his thin wife, John's expression was serious and intent. He'd helped them before. Silently she begged God for his intercession. A glimmer of hope flickered inside her when she saw Nolan bend down and whisper something to Marigold. Then he made his way to Millicent through the crowd.

"Oh, John," Millicent pleaded when the handsome man reached her side. "Can you help me stop this insanity?"

He shrugged. "My lady, I believe it is now in God's hands. Look at them," he directed, one large hand gesturing toward the two men approaching each other. "They're both bent upon a course, a course charted years ago, and the devil himself would not be able to stop them."

The truth of the Irishman's words wrenched at her. John Nolan could not help her. She was alone.

"This has gone far enough." Nigel Somerset came to stand near the earl and the two adversaries.

"Stay out of this, Vicar." Geoffrey Fitzroy grabbed Nigel's billowing black sleeve. "This is a day I've been waiting for, and neither you nor my stubborn daughter will cheat me out of it. Thought you could ruin me, did you, devil's spawn?" he taunted. "A titled English lady is not for the likes of you, O'Rahilly."

Edwin began flexing his sword arm, after handing his satin coat to his supporter. "Sorry, old boy," he jeered at the somber-looking Taggart, "Lady Fitzroy is mine. You'll have to content your bed with that Irish hedge drab, your sister."

Millicent gasped at Edwin's vile insult. Only the straightening of Taggart's shoulders and the grim set to his mouth told her how incensed he was at that remark. Having done none of Edwin's elaborate postures in preparation to cross swords, the Irishman, she was convinced, knew nothing about handling the weapon. After all, O'Rahilly had gone from groom to ship's captain. What opportunity could there have been to master this type of fencing?

She raced over to Edwin. "Please, dear Edwin, do not do this. He is rash and foolish," she pleaded, grasping at anything to save Taggart's life, for she read the expression on Edwin's face. He meant to kill the Irishman. There would be no call of "satisfaction received" with the first bloodletting. "I will keep my pledge," she assured the blond-haired man before her. "We will marry today."

"Of course we will, my dear," Edwin remarked in an unpleasant manner. "But it will be after this Irish cur is dead."

Tears pricked her eyes at Edwin's remark. So lost, Millicent wasn't aware that Taggart had stalked over to them. "Please, dear Edwin, I beg—" She gave an outcry of surprise when the Irishman's strong arm clamped about her waist. Her embroidered slippers were hoisted off the ground as he carried her effortlessly against his hip. It all happened so fast, there was no time to struggle or protest.

Away from the others, Taggart placed her back down on the dew-covered grass. He still brandished the sword in his left hand as he glowered down at her.

On the offensive she blurted, "I told you last week I would not marry you. Nothing, least of all this, will cause me to consent to be your wife." Despair for his safety gave way to anger.

His smoldering eyes burned her. "I asked you properly once, and I'm damned if I'll make that mistake again of *asking* you. Your consent, my lady, is of little consequence here." The muscle along his lean jaw tensed as he bit out, "And if you dare go racing over to beg for me one more time to that . . . popinjay, I swear by Saint Patrick I'll turn you across my knee right here in front of the vicar, your father's guests, and God Almighty!"

Lady Millicent Fitzroy could not hold back the shocked gasp or rush of blood to her face at his insolent manner. However, something held her back from the temptation to race right over to Edwin just to spite the swaggering man before her. After attempting to save his life, this was his gratitude, she fumed, only thankful no one else had heard his words. The Englishwoman stepped back, not sure right now what she felt or wanted to do.

"Nolan," Taggart called over his shoulder. "Will you see that Lady Fitzroy stays back?" John Nolan was the only guest here he could trust right now, and he wanted no accidents if Millie took it into her head to "save" him once more. He tried to rid himself of the rage he'd just felt when he saw her race over to beg Edwin for him. He would need a cool head during the next few minutes. Watching Edwin's confidence made him feel better. Powdered and painted, a black triangular patch on his right cheek, Edwin seemed not the least interested in how Lady Fitzroy was faring. After John led Millicent away toward the crowd, the black-haired man quickly went over to Edwin. He waited patiently while the Englishman completed his fancy warm-up. To Taggart, he seemed to be posturing for the crowd. Patience, he reminded himself.

Both men circled each other. Edwin's expression was that of a boy anticipating a treat. Taggart, on the other hand, gave nothing away. His dark eyes never left Edwin.

"On guard," Edwin said as he took the proper position with practiced ease. "If you need any assistance untangling your feet from your sword, you will let me know, O'Bumpkin."

Taggart held the gleaming foil in his right hand and raised his left, knees bent, as Ben Abrams had taught him during their countless fencing lessons in the open fields behind the College of William and Mary. "I shall keep that in mind, old boy."

Surprised, Edwin didn't seem to lose any of his good humor. "Well, at least you won't look too ridiculous when I kill you. Appearance is everything, you know."

"Is that why you keep your Italian lover, Prince Ronaldo, hidden away in the country?"

Taggart's barb appeared to meet its mark, and Edwin gave an angry growl, lunged at the taller man, coming too close for a direct riposte.

O'Rahilly quickly countered and thrust.

Edwin looked astonished, then angry to discover his opponent was skilled in swordsmanship.

Millicent's face was contorted in anguish. If it hadn't been for John Nolan's strong hands restraining her, she would have wrenched free to stop this dangerous business. The gleam and loud clash of steel against steel tormented her with sickening dread. She would take no joy in having either man hurt this day. "Please, John." She struggled without success. "Please

147

let me go."

"No, my lady. I cannot let you be injured, too." His hazel eyes held a gleam of something Millicent could not describe. He watched the swordplay with an intensity that reminded her of a cat watching two birds fight to the death. Which man was he hoping would win?

Advance, recovery, lunge, attack. The sky grew darker as the two men went at each other relentlessly. Taggart dodged Edwin's fifth attack, but not before he'd delivered a grazing cut along Edwin's lacy sleeve. It was only a superficial wound, but the tear to his immaculate shirt, now stained with drops of blood, seemed to incense the blond-haired man. Somerset charged after him, the niceties forgotten as he began to tire.

Both men sweated from their exertions. Strands of Taggart's coal-black hair escaped from the taffeta ribbon at the nape of his neck. Green stripes from the wet grass stained his white hose. But Taggart's countenance was mocking when he realized Edwin fared no better. Spatterings of mud were visible on the Englishman's satin breeches.

No longer smiling, Edwin fought to regain his breath. "Are you man or bull?" he whined, clearly angered by his opponent's stamina. Aware his friends looked at him, Edwin glanced down to see his sword arm shake from fatigue.

Taggart lowered his sword, for Edwin appeared ready to fall at his feet. He almost pitied the Englishman now; he looked totally defeated. "Let's call an end, Somerset, for—"

Edwin lunged hard, ramming his sword for the kill.

Berating himself for letting his guard down, the taller man just managed to escape Somerset's blade aimed for his heart. It wasn't a pretty move on his part, but it saved his life. Taggart's dark eyes narrowed as he took the offensive. Strong and swift, without mercy he pushed Edwin to the very limits of his endurance.

Edwin was almost sobbing with exhaustion. And when his stop thrusts got sloppier, he backed farther away from his opponent. His black patents slipped on the wet grass, hurling him down to the ground. The Englishman could only watch as his sword landed a few feet away. The low rumble of distant thunder seemed to make him shake with fear. He closed his eyes, obviously waiting for Taggart to finish him.

A triumphant O'Rahilly stood over Edwin Somerset, the point of his blade at Edwin's throat. When he glanced lower, he saw the wet stain soaking the front of Edwin's breeches. Weak kidneys under duress, he mused. This was the man who had chained him to the Somersets' filthy cellar and whipped him without mercy. And now, he thought, Edwin was helpless at his feet. A little pressure and the twisted man beneath him would be dead.

But . . . Something held the Irishman back. Why couldn't he kill him? The reason stole softly into his consciousness as he watched the terrified man on the ground. There was a small part of him that did not want to kill the quivering Edwin now. An inner voice warned it would be a hallow victory.

"Taggart!" Millicent cried, tearing herself free when John Nolan's fingers slackened at the outcome. She raced ahead to the middle of the circle, her angry eyes focused on Taggart. "If you kill this man, I will hate you until the day I die. And I am a Fitzroy," she stated proudly, not an ounce of pleading in her voice now. "You know how treacherous we can be. And this has all been for naught, for I would never marry a murderer."

Though he was already determined not to slay Edwin, Taggart did not remove his sword from the man's throat. Her words pricked something in him. His smile was menacing. "No doubt your next threat will be about killing yourself to save your honor."

The lady did not flinch. "On the contrary, it might be you who would feel a dagger in your ribs . . . or elsewhere," she added, with a meaningful look at the area between his long legs.

It took effort not to let the bark of laughter escape his lips. She was a firebrand, with her flashing gray eyes behind those studious glasses and auburn hair that billowed about her shoulders when a gust of cold wind tousled her. At his reaction, he saw her face suffuse with color before she lowered her eyes. By God, she was a scrapper, for all her usually outward demure. Their eyes locked. He forced an expression of ruthlessness on his features, before he reached out his free hand to force her chin up. He wanted to see her eyes clearly, those serious, gray jewels of fiery reproach that gave her whole soul away. "Well, my lady, then it is up to you." He glanced down at Edwin. "Agree to marry me or I send this Englishman to Hades." He applied a hint of pressure, just nicking Edwin's throat enough to ooze a thread of blood. "Your answer, Lady Fitzroy," he bit out in a savage tone.

Millicent's stomach lurched when she saw the thin line of blood run down Edwin's neck to splatter his lacy shirt. It was impossible to miss Edwin's unsuccessful efforts to hide his fear. Never expecting this turn of events, she frantically sought a way out. At first she could not believe there was no other logical solution.

"I am not a patient man," growled her adversary, cruelly pushing her to the limit, for he saw his only chance. Silently, he prayed she would take the rope he was tossing her. He had no wish to kill the pathetic Edwin now, and this would give her a way to save her pride in front of all her fellow Englishmen. He chanced a contemptuous glance at them. There they stood, waiting like spectators at a cockfight, not caring about the fate of the participants, their only interest to be entertained. Didn't Millie realize none of these people, save perhaps Nolan and Calvert Huntington, were her friends? He took an impatient breath, vowing that one way or the other it would soon be over. Enough of this verbal parrying.

With a nod of his dark head Taggart signaled his Irish friends. As he'd instructed earlier, they headed slowly back toward their waiting horses.

For God's sake, take the rope, O'Rahilly shouted to her with his smoldering brown eyes. It was hard to maintain his unfeeling stance when he saw a tear escape from behind her spectacles. "Then it is to be Somerset's death," he snapped, giving her no quarter. "Let it be as you wish," he growled, pulling back his foil in both hands, in a gesture designed to prove he was prepared to sever Edwin's neck.

"Stop!" she screamed. "Please." Then Lady Fitzroy nodded her acceptance of the bargain. Though her voice was weaker, she knew all present heard her say, "I will marry you, O'Rahilly."

Thank God, he thought, breathing a sigh of relief. But he knew there was little time to waste. This stunned herd of sheep

150

would soon loose their lethargy. With an ancient Gaelic war cry, as a symbol of victory he plunged his sword deep into the ground, directly opposite Edwin's head. All this seemed too much for the Englishman, for his upper body lifted up, only to fall back down on the damp earth as he fainted.

A hundred emotions hit Millicent at the same time. She knew he was still acting out of duty, not love. How could she marry him on these terms? His methods angered and appalled her, showing her a side to his character she had never witnessed before. The gentle, friendly boy of her youth was now ruthless and dangerous. But she had given her word in front of all these witnesses, and she suspected this was Taggart's intention. She tried to strangle the hidden part inside still drawn to him. It taunted her with images and dreams from the past. But the actions of this day left no place for romantic reverie, she told herself.

In a quick motion, Taggart pulled his sword from the moist earth, wiped it on the unconscious Edwin's sleeve, then clamped a firm hand about Millicent's silk-and-lace-covered arm.

Her father, John Nolan, and the Reverend Somerset reached them first. Garnet and Calvert went over to minister to the groggy Edwin. The Duchess of Montrose, noted Millicent, looked furious at the outcome of events.

"Whoreson!" bellowed Geoffrey Fitzroy. "Give me your sword, John." He would have taken it, but Nolan managed to hold back his shorter friend by gripping him by the shoulders.

Lady Fitzroy did not appreciate being dragged behind Taggart like a recalcitrant child. "Unhand me," Millicent ordered. "I have given my word, and though I should like nothing better, I shall not try to escape. Perhaps you would feel more secure to have me in chains." She held herself regally despite the fearful pounding of her heart. "There is no need to truss me up like a prize you've bagged from a morning hunt."

Taggart released her. It was time to tell the earl about his plans. "For your . . . acquiescence," he added, looking straight at the puffing Earl of Holingbrook, "I will pay all your debts. You may continue living at the Hall. And since you are my future bride's father, I will provide a reasonable allowance for you for the rest of your life. But everything you possess, including your daughter, now belongs to me."

The earl shook off John's restraining arm. "As if I'd take anything from the likes of—"

"Or I can legally toss you out on your fat arse without a farthing," Taggart thundered.

The earl rubbed a hand across his flaccid chin. Hadn't his fool lawyer warned him of Taggart's popularity with King George? His Majesty was so delighted with the booty from intercepted Spanish and French ships that he was only too happy to add his stamp of approval to a loyal subject from the Colonies. Borrowed to the hilt and out of favor at court, the earl came to the bitter realization that he had no recourse. And in truth, this colonial's generosity was far more than he'd ever expected.

At his former employer's expression of angry defeat, Taggart felt a twinge of satisfaction. Not a bad day's work to vanquish two old enemies at once. Completely dismissing everyone but Millicent from his mind, he turned to her.

However, when Taggart saw the paleness of her cheek, the way she bit her lower lip, clearly in an effort to steady her emotions, something inside made him want to reach out and take her in his arms, to assure her that he would have a care for her, that he would answer for her future. He reached out a hand to her, but Reverend Somerset's voice stopped him.

"Wait!" cried the vicar. "Bless my soul, we cannot allow . . ." Nigel looked even more frustrated as he darted his eyes back and forth from Nolan to the earl, clearly expecting either one to protest. "I will not ma-marry you," he said with surprising finality.

Taggart laughed aloud. "I do not remember asking you." Without another word he went over to retrieve his coat. He shrugged back into it, straightened his stock clip, took his time putting on his leather gloves and tricorn hat, then headed back to Millicent. "Come," he directed, holding out his hand to the woman standing in front of him.

Lady Fitzroy stared down at the masculine hand that invited her to concede. There was more than politeness in Taggart's gesture, and she knew her response was important. If she placed her slender fingers in his hand, he and everyone here would see the action as compliance. Yet, she would keep her promise, she knew. Thunder rumbled louder in the distance. Hers was not to be the streaming sun and blue of an early spring wedding day—the sky was now black and foreboding. The wind cuffed her face, but with a defiance for the elements and the man standing in front of her, she tossed her head and swept her voluminous skirts to the side of him, just as a lady might circumvent a pile of refuse on a cobbled street. From a few feet away, she stopped and turned to look behind her. She could not hide her satisfaction when she saw him color slightly at her deliberate affront. Let him learn she was no whey-faced girl with water in her veins.

But just as quickly, she saw his dark eyes narrow, and his expression took on the characteristics of the threatening weather.

However, she stood her ground, especially in light of his new humiliation of her. Taggart seemed unconcerned that Nigel would not perform the ceremony. Yet, he'd proclaimed to all present he intended to marry her. Was it now his plan to forgo any legal ceremony? "Which horse am I to ride?" she asked, forcing a normalcy in her voice which belied her emotions.

Taggart made himself remember she probably spoke from apprehension and fatigue. She had no way of knowing he'd been planning this for a week. "Here, Daniel." He tossed his sword and scabbard up to the young Irishman closest to him. Then with little ceremony, he ended the distance between them and scooped Millicent up into his arms.

Not wishing to be the brunt of more jokes, Lady Fitzroy compressed her lips rather than give way to the struggles and angry retorts tempting her.

"Taggart," Nolan called, his sympathetic gaze on the woman looking so grave in O'Rahilly's arms. "Even if the rumors are true and you have the King's favor, surely when word reaches his ears that you have dishonored the earl's daughter—"

"There's no disgrace in what I'm doing, John." Though Taggart's arms tightened about his feminine bundle, he kept his voice to a whisper, but his manner lacked some of his usual warmth with his family's long-time friend. There were unanswered questions between them. "I know it was Millie's money that paid for my start in America." He saw the blood wash Nolan's face, then a look of guilt crossed his strong features.

"Taggart . . . I know I should not have accepted that note from you, but I—the earl owed me money that I'm now sure he would never have been able to pay back, and I've made some rather poor investments of late." He bowed his head. "I was too ashamed to ask you for the money, but you can have it ba—"

"Keep it," he cut off curtly. It wasn't the amount and he knew the O'Rahillys owed Nolan more than they could repay in coin. However, it was Nolan's underhanded manner that severed something in the way he felt for the man in front of him. "You can return the favor by being my best man." Since Ben Abrams wasn't here, John would be his second choice.

Millicent thought John hesitated, then he seemed to catch himself. His smile looked strained.

"Yes, of course, my boy. My lord," Nolan directed to the rotund man who hovered near Edwin, Garnet, and her husband. "Will you say nothing on your daughter's behalf?" The wind became gustier, and John was forced to clamp a hand to the hat over his long brown wig.

Millicent saw the anger in John Nolan's expression. Until now, she hadn't realized her welfare meant so much to him. Had that been the reason for his look before accepting the offer of Taggart's supporter at their wedding? Of all the people here, John Nolan remained the only one left with the courage to stand up for her. It touched her deeply, and she reached out a hand to him. "Dear John, I—"

"Lord Holingbrook," John shouted forcibly, clearly aware he'd just cut off the lady's show of gratitude. "This young woman is still your daughter."

Geoffrey looked unconcerned. "O'Rahilly," he yelled back. "You thought to gain your revenge through taking Millicent, didn't you?" Not waiting for an answer, the earl went on. "Then the laugh is on you, for she comes to you penniless, and I don't give a hang what you do with her."

Of all that had occurred today, Millicent thought she had steeled herself to accept embarrassments from her father. But this final blow in front of all these people made her turn her face into Taggart's coat. She wanted to be away from here, to hide from everyone.

Taggart felt some of his earlier irritation with the young woman in his arms vanish. For John and the lady he carried close to his chest, he whispered, "Lady Millicent will come to no harm, Nolan. I swear." Then he turned and headed for his horse, placed Millicent gently on the black stallion's saddle, and swung up behind her.

To Millicent, he seemed quite at ease arranging her skirts and petticoats across his saddle, but she did not like this close proximity, so she grabbed the pummel of his saddle and tried inching herself away from his legs.

"Oh no," he whispered with a chuckle against her ear. With ease, his ruffle-covered wrist came around and moved her back to where she'd been before. "You will break that lovely back if you hold yourself so straight, haughty sparrow," he teased. "Then you might miss where you're headed."

Her hair fluffed across her face in the wind as she turned around to glare at him. "I would as soon ride to hell with the devil."

Taggart's mocking laughter filled her ears as she snapped about to look straight ahead. His lips came close to her ear once more. "Why, Lady Millicent, I thought you realized that he rides behind you now."

She confronted him again. "Yes, he does, and why has he gone to such lengths merely to repay a debt?"

"This involved less paperwork than having my solicitor come up with hidden ways to return the money to you. Besides, who better to run Fitzroy Hall? You come from sturdy English stock and already know where the wine cellar is located. I can hardly run two households from my home in Virginia." Taggart became more serious. "Though I'll probably never love any woman, it is time I married, for I want a home with children."

Millicent was not satisfied with his answer, but before she could press him further, she saw that his attention was focused on the crowd of unfriendly faces.

"You are all invited to our proper wedding about an hour's ride from here—at the Catholic chapel nearby," O'Rahilly said. "You all know of it, though you pretend not to. And there will be feasting, wine and music at Fitzroy Hall this night. All are welcome." Then he pressed his knees to the horse's flanks, and he and his five companions, along with the stolen bride, were off in a flurry of shouts and threats from the Englishman, with returned Irish male laughter.

Never, Millicent vowed, would she forgive the O'Rahilly for this day's work.

Chapter 11

And one hour later Millicent Fitzroy's vow was even stronger. When she saw all the Irish guests dressed for a wedding filing into the thatch-roofed Catholic chapel—Edna O'Rahilly in apparel resembling a maid of honor, Father Michael Collins in his best vestments—she knew a rage so powerful it almost chocked the breath from her. The look she gave Taggart when he lifted her down from his horse would have quelled any ordinary mortal.

However, her future husband merely grinned before commenting pleasantly, "You'll have to excuse the feast after we take our vows. My servants from the *Yankee Rose* and the townfolk here had little time to get everything over to the Hall while you and your father were absent today. We only had a week to prepare, you understand."

Spots of color stained her cheeks. "You . . . you son of a . . . a . . . !"

"An Irishman," Taggart interjected, with a hearty chuckle at her uncharacteristic but interrupted display of spirited language. There was fire in this proud Englishwoman, he mused as he glanced at her long shiny hair. However, his expression became more serious when he saw the disdain in her gray eyes. "I know this is not easy for you to accept, sparrow, but you gave me little choice. No Anglican vicar would marry us, you must know. Nor will they probably recognize the legality of our marriage. But a Catholic ceremony before witnesses is all I can offer you." At her continued tight-lipped silence, he grew more uneasy. "I am not ashamed of being a Catholic, Millicent."

She appeared surprised at his words. "It is not your religion, sir, but your methods in acquiring a wife that have vexed me so."

Taggart accepted her rebuke, but it did not make things easier right now. "I . . . I just assumed you'd want Edna to be your maid of honor. If this is unacceptable, please choose whom you wish, and I'll have Daniel fetch the lass. Of course, only if she is willing," he added, raising his hands in defense at her quelling expression.

The condemning words for his underhanded behavior died in her throat when Edna came over to them. Dressed in a lovely pink gown, the black curls brushed back from her pretty face, Edna was a picture of dainty loveliness.

"Oh, Millie," she cried, giving her friend a warm hug. "I've been so worried. That brother of mine wouldn't hear of me going with him and his friends this morning. I wanted to be there so you wouldn't be afraid. Are you all right? Do you still hate me for tellin' Taggart about your dowry? Would you want some wine?" she babbled in a nervous rush. "Oh, Taggart," she admonished, "for shame. Look how ready to swoon she appears? Have you been bullyin' poor Millie? Sure and I'll take a shillelagh to that thick skull of yours if you've frightened her."

"Poor Millie" could not hold back a wan smile at the way Edna ranted at her older brother, reminding her of a snapping terrier confronting a huge black wolf. "I have missed you, dear Edna," she said truthfully. And though she would never admit it to Taggart, with no one seriously injured, suddenly a bit of humor at the whole situation hit her. Quite plain, her father despairing she would ever wed, for a brief time this morning Millicent had two intended husbands. And Edwin, Garnet, and her father had planned to have a small, subdued gathering at Somerset Hall after the ceremony. It had been a gesture of beneficence on Edwin's part, for he knew her father had not the means to pay for an elaborate celebration at his own estate. Would any of the English guests actually come to Fitzroy Hall this evening? Then a troubling thought echoed within her.

Taggart was almost a stranger to her now. Tonight, would he demand his husbandly rights?

Concerned that the English girl did indeed appear lost and forlorn as Edna had pointed out, the Irishman reached for her cold hand and tucked it in the crook of his arm.

As she allowed him to lead her to the rustic structure to take their vows, Millicent searched the small group of familiar faces. It delighted her to see the priest's brother heading her way. Automatically, she freed her fingers from Taggart's arm and reached out to greet the man who had come to mean so much to her during these last few years. "Dear Liam," she cried, emotion making her voice shake.

Surprised, Taggart watched as the handsome, red-haired Dr. Collins bent his head to place a kiss on Millicent's soft cheek. Though Liam was only three years older and a couple of inches taller than Taggart, the black-haired man realized he lacked some of Liam's subtle gentility. For a reason he did not understand, Taggart did not like the way Liam was looking at his intended at this moment.

Fully prepared to ease Millicent over the awkwardness of an unfamiliar Catholic service, Mr. O'Rahilly was taken aback when his bride answered automatically and correctly in Latin. His questioning look at Father Collins merely caused the priest to smile. How, Taggart wondered, had an Anglican aristocrat learned so much about Catholicism?

When the formal ceremony was finished, Taggart turned to his bride and offered her his left arm.

Millicent saw the warmth in his expression. There was no arrogance in him now. Shyly, she placed her right hand on his outstretched arm. "Thank you," she said softly, then began walking with him back down the bare earth floor of the small chapel. Mrs. Mulcahy was sniffing into a handkerchief, while Fergus winked at the newlyweds.

"I am proud of you today," he whispered to his new bride. Their eyes met. "You are lovely, Mrs. O'Rahilly."

For the first time that morning, Lady Millicent felt a warm glow hover inside her. Despite the circumstances that led her here and the many unanswered questions between them, she could not hide her pleasure at his words of praise.

Millicent could not believe the change in the great hall. The large room was decorated with flowers and colorful banners. Long tables were filled with platters of roasted mutton, pork, and freshly caught salmon. The scents of recently baked puddings and bread permeated the hall. Candles lighted the banquet room brighter than she had seen in years. Though the room was rather bare, she was relieved to see that Taggart's workers had stowed away some of the more threadbare pieces. Of course, there wasn't time to clean and tidy any of the other rooms, but at least this one sparkled like the old days. Footmen dressed in gray velvet, with white gloves, offered wine to both the Irish and English guests.

Millicent could not hold back a grin. Probably the promise of free food and drink had induced many of her father's friends to come to the reception. Or was it mere curiosity or a hope that there would be another scene like this morning to give more fuel to the gossips? No matter, as Taggart had said, all were welcome. Elaborately dressed Englishmen and their wives sat across from the more simply groomed and boisterously jovial Irishman and their ladies. White-wigged musicians sat along one side of the huge room playing one of Mr. Handel's latest compositions. They would probably, Millicent thought with delight, be playing some lively Gaelic jigs and reels by evening's end. She had not missed the fiddle and round Irish drum with brush that two Irish tenants carried in with them.

Aware of her duties, Millicent greeted each guest with polite warmth. However, after a few hours she began to feel the strain of the day's surprising events. Excusing herself, she quietly slipped out into the corridor for a few moments of solitude.

"Well," said a familiar voice. "You have certainly surprised us all."

Millicent saw Garnet Huntington coming out from one of the small anterooms under the stairs. "It has astounded me also, your grace."

Garnet adjusted her elbow-length white gloves. "That is

160

better. In truth I should not drink so much wine. It makes me wet a stream. Oh," she squeaked, placing a small hand to her perfect lips. "I should not use such words in your presence. I must recall how sheltered your life has been until today."

Millicent's eyebrows rose. Sewing until her eyes ached, virtually running her father's huge estate alone, sheltered indeed! "Your grace, I should hardly call the last few years sheltered," she countered, her gray eyes sparking behind the wire frames.

"Yes, of course. But, it is too bad," the shorter girl mewed in sympathy. "I am merely concerned for your happiness, my dear. And, of course, my poor brother is crushed." She reached under her gown for one of the small bags tied about her waist, pulling out an embroidered pocket handkerchief. "Father and I had to restrain him from doing himself harm, he was so distraught."

Though she knew this was hardly likely, Millicent's features softened. "Garnet, please convey to Edwin I never meant to cause him injury or embarrassment. And if it is any consolation, relay I have not gone unscathed in this matter."

"Oh, I will tell him." The handkerchief was hastily put away. "You may depend upon it."

Millicent felt uneasy at the way Garnet now studied her.

"For who more than I knows the trials of the marriage bed. Now, pray do not let me fluster you, my dear. It is just . . . well, you are quite thin . . . down there, I mean." Her cornflower-blue eyes lowered. "And men are such beasts." Her voice became a whisper as she moved closer. "It is only my protective feelings for you which prompts such a disclosure, but after all, you were to be my dear sister-in-law, were you not?"

The taller woman's expression became more wary. "Garnet, I should not like to be the cause of your divulging another's secret. It is quite—"

"Oh, but I must make that sacrifice. Besides, the private matter is mine to bestow." The duchess looked about her, clearly to be sure they were alone. "In London I swear that Irishman almost rent me in two with his huge . . . weapon. Were I not already married to dear Calvert, upon my honor, my maiden's blood would have been everywhere. Indeed, he has earned his name of 'Irish Stallion' very well."

Millicent could not hide her shock. It couldn't be true. "You do not mean to say you actually . . . ?"

The teary look entered the blue eyes once more. "Would that it were not. However, Calvert wasn't feeling well that evening but insisted I attend the party given by Sir Arthur Lyncrost, an old friend of his family's. Imagine my horror when I saw that upstart there, dressed in the latest English fashion, talking with all our friends as if he had a right to be there, or even on the face of the earth for that matter. When he forced his attentions on me, threatening to tell such vile lies to my poor husband if I did not submit, well, I . . ." Further declaration appeared too much for the petite woman, for she burst into tears.

Moved by such suffering, automatically Millicent reached out to comfort the smaller woman. Had Taggart become that cruel, so bent on revenge for his treatment by Garnet's father in their cellar years ago? "Rest assured, Garnet, I shall let none of this information pass beyond these walls."

"And my torment goes on," wailed the duchess. At Millicent's puzzled look, Garnet's lovely brow furrowed. "You stupid twit! I mean—" Catching herself, she coughed, then buried her face in her small hands once more.

"Garnet," Lady Millicent soothed, "you must stop or you will make yourself ill. Is . . . is there nothing I can do for you? Shall I have a footman fetch the duke?"

Almost instantly these words seemed to affect the distraught woman, for when she turned her beautiful face up toward the English girl, all traces of sobbing had vanished. "You're so kind, however, you need not take Calvert away from the festivities. I know how dearly he loves cavorting with those Irish rustics. But . . . you can pray for my deliverance from your husband, for he continues to debase me as his mistress. Oh," she added in a rush, "and you must never tell him you know of this for he threatened to tell those filthy lies to Calvert if any should find out that on my . . . my various travels to visit relatives I am forced to meet that . . . that loathsome Irishman in secret. Promise me," she added, taking Millicent's

162

hands in desperation. "Promise me, you will not tell anyone my shame."

"But surely, the duke would believe you over such monstrous lies."

"How trusting you are," Garnet sniffled. "You know little about men similar to Mr. O'Rahilly. My dear, do you not realize the stories cruel people make up about an older man with a young wife? Why, even your own father, it is said, goes—"

"Yes, I dare say," Millicent broke off, realizing the point the other woman was about to make. She clasped her hands in front of her after Garnet released them. Too overwrought to eat this day, it was not only lack of food that caused her stomach to lurch. Her body felt drained of warmth as strong emotions buffeted against her. Was Taggart just like her father where women were concerned? "Be assured, your grace, I shall tell no one of this." Millicent realized years ago Garnet was pampered and frivolous, but why would any woman lie about so intimate a matter? Surely, if Millicent were in Garnet's shoes, she would be devastated by such an encounter.

Silently, Millicent fought her own private battle. She remembered only hours ago Taggart stood next to her and appeared kind and gentle. Yet, hadn't she seen how ruthless he could be? His methods in forcing her to marry him—the boy of nine years ago was now a man, with a man's desires and determination.

"I knew you would understand." Garnet seemed to regain much of her composure. "Now, it is time we joined your guests."

Clearly, the duchess appeared to read the uncertainty on Millicent's features. Just before they entered the ballroom, Garnet turned to her companion and said sweetly, "Taggart does get angry if you mention the scar on his left shoulder. Just a caution, my dear."

"I . . . I shall bear it in mind." The only sound Millicent heard was the pelting rain against the heavy window glass. The lightning and subsequent clap of thunder made her shiver. Just what sort of man had she married? The young man of sixteen who had cared about his little sister, defended Millicent at her party—was there nothing left of that gentle Irishman?

The lady rejoined her guests, hardly aware that Duchess Huntington had left her side. So many questions plagued her, but she forced herself to make conversation with the vicar and her father, then Edna and her friends. However, when she happened to look up half an hour later, Lady Millicent saw the handsome bridegroom talking with the Duchess of Montrose. She could not hear what they were saying, and Taggart's back was to her. However, the charming smile and occasional laughter from Garnet told the taller English girl the duchess was certainly enjoying the Irishman's company. Hardly the reaction, Millicent mused, of a woman who was forced to submit to the Irish Stallion, as she'd named him. Had Garnet lied to her?

"My lady?"

Millicent blinked, then stammered an apology as she looked up to see the face of Dr. Liam Collins. They were alone now, for the other guests had wandered over to the buffet and liquor tables once more. She forced a smile. "The last to greet me, but the most welcome." She held out her hand.

Liam's gray eyes warmed her. He bent his auburn head and kissed her slender hand, holding it longer than necessary. "Don't worry," he whispered for her ears alone. "The Garnets of this world have only fleeting moments."

"I . . . I had not meant to give so much away," she confessed to her long-time friend.

"Ah, it is time to lead the first dance."

Clearly, the young doctor was trying to put her at ease. However, his pleasant words had the opposite effect. Anxiously, Millicent became aware of the other couples watching her as they waited for the time when the bride and groom would lead the first minuet. Would Taggart add to her humiliation by dancing with Garnet first? Surely, he would not—a quick glance in his direction confirmed her worst fears, for Garnet had closed her fan and was looking up at him with what appeared to be inviting anticipation.

Her gray eyes searched the crowd and saw Calvert Huntington enjoying some congeniality with her father and Reverend Somerset. The duke looked quite prepared to talk

164

for hours.

"Just once I wish I had Garnet's ability to deal so well with men," she whispered aloud, then blushed at her unrestrained admission.

"No, you don't," the young doctor challenged as he watched the eyes behind her spectacles mist with tears she fought to control. "I should hate to see such a lovely lady change." Obviously aware of her distress, despite her efforts to appear detached, the doctor exclaimed, "Would you do me the honor of dancing with me? It appears the lad I used to play with as a boy has become a bit of an ass in his maturity."

A giggle of rich amusement escaped Millicent's lips. "Dear Liam, promise me you will not change either," she said. "I do not think I could have survived the last few years without you or Edna." Let Taggart dally after Garnet's skirts if he wished. When she saw Garnet move closer to Taggart and run her closed fan along his arm, Lady Fitzroy's chin lifted. "I shall be delighted to dance with you," she told the handsome doctor.

Taggart was scarcely paying attention to Garnet's chatter. His dark gaze flickered across the room to find his wife and former childhood playmate. It was not necessary for Liam to hold his wife's hand so long, he told himself. And he'd have sworn there was a reproachful challenge in the doctor's expression just now. He felt relieved when he finally caught Calvert Huntington's attention, and the older man joined them to request the first dance with his own wife. Taggart was well aware Garnet wanted him to ask her to dance. The conniving little minx was still up to her usual mischief; he hadn't missed the brief spark of open lust in her blue eyes. And irritating as it was, he still felt a physical response whenever he was near her. Of course, he could never trust Garnet, especially after how he had humiliated her. The vision of her brandishing a stiletto near his private parts was even now sufficient to make him break out in a cold sweat. Dangerous but oh so tempting, he mused, as he watched the duchess saunter away on the arm of her devoted husband. Her earlier exuberance looked a trifle subdued, Taggart surmised in amusement. It must be hard work for her to act the dutiful wife. Poor Calvert, he thought with sympathy. The duke had no idea his charming wife was such a treacherous little slut.

Well, it was time to collect his bride for the first minuet. Taggart's features softened when he thought of Millicent. How sweet she looked saying her vows this morning. Once over the surprise of today's events, he was sure she would accept the situation with her usual gentle practicality. And this was for her own good. He owed her the protection of his name and the material comforts he could provide. He might not love her, but he would treat her far better than her life would be if she stayed either under her lecherous father's control or that twisted Edwin's influence. And as her father said, she had always been a malleable creature. Quiet. He turned around to head across the room to collect her for their dance.

However, all congeniality departed from Taggart's face when he discovered the Englishwoman was not waiting for him as he expected. His dark brows rose in astonishment to find his "malleable" bride dancing the first minuet with that . . . doctor. The Irishman's lean jaw tightened as he fought down his irritation. He saw her smile—no, it was a smirk as she danced past him near the back of the room. How dare she insult him this way! At the very least she should have saved the first dance on her wedding day for her husband. All here knew the custom.

"They make a handsome couple, don't they?" Geoffrey Fitzroy jeered at his new son-in-law, before taking another gulp of the free-flowing wine. It was followed by a swig from the tankard of ale he held in his other chubby fist. "Well, you may be Irish, but you certainly know how to throw a party, hey, Nolan?"

John Nolan did not join in the earl's levity. He stood watching O'Rahilly's expression. "I am sure there is nothing improper between her ladyship and the young doctor," he said pleasantly to his host.

"Who says there is?" Taggart snapped far too quickly.

"Why, no one, my boy. I merely desired to set your mind at ease."

With a crystal goblet in one hand and the silver tankard in

166

the other, the earl's attention clearly veered to the conversation between his old friend and the bridegroom. "Harumph. Why not tell him the truth, Nolan."

Taggart's expression became cautious. "What truth?" he demanded.

"Nothing." Nolan gave the earl an admonishing stare. "His lordship is . . . fatigued after the long day's events. That is all."

"Fatigued? God's teeth, I'm drunk," growled the earl. "And bloody glad of it, too. Why the devil should I be up-upset?" Then he focused his bleary eyes on the tall Irishman. "My debts are paid, I get a sizable allowance from my generous son-in-law, who has relieved me of my homely daughter. Damn me, a good day's work." He took another gulp of ale. "And . . . what does O'Rahilly get out of all this? Do you know, Nolan?"

Appearing ill at ease, John looked down at the tops of his leather pumps. He touched one side of his full-bottomed brown wig. "I am sure I do not know, my lord."

Grinning broadly, Geoffrey Fitzroy confronted his former groom. "Tell you what he don't get, Nolan. He doesn't get any revenge. Thought I cared a hang about this pile of rubble I live in or that bride of yours? The joke's on you, Irishman, as I told you at St. Multose. For you can take them both and go hang for all I care. Of course," the earl continued in a casual tone, "her ladyship does go out often. Though she doesn't think I know, my spies tell me things. Seems Sean Kelly, one of my grooms, has seen her often in the company of the good doctor. If the stories are true, you might get something after all out of your wedding night—a good dose of the clap." Then the earl's raucous laughter echoed throughout the whole room.

Aware both English and Irish attention focused in their direction, it took all of Taggart's self-mastery to keep from choking the earl with his bare hands. He saw John Nolan's look of sympathy, then tried to remember the earl was drunk and probably wouldn't remember what he'd said. But was it true? forced its way into his consciousness. He towered over the earl. "If you dare repeat the vile things you have hinted to anyone, I swear I'll kill you," he growled. "And I know many ways to kill a man slowly, with excruciating pain, something a ship's captain easily learns at the exotic ports he frequents."

His words seemed to sober the earl a bit, for his fleshy jowls drained of color.

Taggart took further advantage of having his new father-in-law's complete, if fearful, attention. "And from now on you will meet your doxies outside my home. There will be no string of whores prancing through the upstairs apartments in various stages of debauchery. And you will treat my wife with the respect she deserves. Willingly or not you'll learn I protect my own. Though you may lack affection for your daughter, sir, by God, you'll not abuse her again either by your actions or your revolting speech."

Without another word, Taggart turned his back on the rotund Englishman and stalked across the room to reclaim his wife from Dr. Liam Collins.

Lady Millicent eyed her plate of uneaten food. Despite her irritation with Taggart's methods in wedding her and his clear preference for the Duke of Montrose's wife, Millicent had forced herself to appear polite during the rest of the celebration. She admonished herself for not being able to hide her obvious pleasure in dancing with her new husband. It had felt so right to be with him, even if his request to dance had been a trifle curt and his greeting to Liam civil but restrained. Though the Irishman was attentive to her the rest of the evening, Millicent was aware something troubled him. Gone was his earlier open amusement and the gentle teasing. The coolness in his voice when he'd leaned over just now to inform her it was time for her to retire to their bedroom caused the brief rays of hope to die within her. The hint of command in his tone was not lost on her. However, there was really no way out of it now.

She rose gracefully from her place beside him at the long table. But then a disturbing thought occurred to her. Where did he intend for her to sleep? Her own room had a bed in it for a single maid, not a married woman. The thought of the master bedroom caused an inward shudder. Her father's rooms were dark and depressing, the green colors and heavy draperies never having been to her liking.

When he read the distress and confusion on his wife's face,

Taggart lost some of his earlier irritation. He reproved himself for letting her father goad him. "Caleb," he called over his shoulder.

Millicent watched as a young black man appeared. Dressed as the other footmen, this man wore no wig over his black short-cropped hair. And there was an air of dignified authority for one of about thirty. He leaned down as Taggart spoke to him. Then he nodded and stepped away from his employer.

"Caleb will direct you to our quarters." Then he added in a gentler tone, "I hope it is acceptable to you, but I have chosen what Colleen said would have been your mother's suite of rooms had she lived. They get the morning sun, and I thought the cheerfulness of the rooms would appeal to you. There was only time to bring up the new bed and highboy," he said, almost in the way of an apology. "But later, if you wish, you can choose new furnishings and colors for the rooms."

She smiled her gratitude at his thoughtfulness. "Dunstan will be pleased, for he so regretted that Father let the Hall go without attention. Thank you . . . very much," she added, moved by what she assumed was Taggart's wedding gift to her. Without waiting for his reply, she turned and followed Taggart's manservant out of the hall. Clearly devoted to her mistress, Colleen Mulcahy trailed behind them.

God, Taggart lamented at the mention of the viscount. He looked down the table to see Edna rising to follow Abigail Somerset to the bride's rooms. He could not find the courage to tell her the truth, not today. They had no idea Dunstan Fitzroy was dead.

Some of the guests still remained downstairs when Taggart left the hall. Just before she left, the voluptuous Garnet finally maneuvered a dance with him. She whispered to him that he'd never be happy with what she called his "plain English wife." And Liam wasted little time telling him he "was a lucky man to have her ladyship for a wife." His thoughts were a mass of confused emotion. Knowing it was time for him to join his bride upstairs, he suddenly felt apprehensive. Yes, he'd had women before but this was Lady Millicent. Until now, he'd thought of her as the lady of the manor—at first gentle, yet beyond the reach of an Irish groom, later as the supposedly selfish daughter of the man he despised, the man responsible for his father's death. And his sense of duty had caused him to force her to marry him when she refused verbal persuasion. He knew she was still upset with his methods. But how would she receive him tonight? He had no wish to be cruel, but he did not believe he loved her, if he was even capable of loving any woman. Millie, he knew, was not a woman who tolerated empty words or insincere flattery. He winced when the next question jeered up at him. And was his bride's heart and body already given to Dr. Liam Collins?

Taggart had all he could do to keep some of the rowdier Irishmen from following him into the bridal bower. He realized, well meant as they were, some of these abundantly aled men might embarrass his new English bride. There would be many a sore head in the morning if he was any judge of the wine, whiskey, and ale that had careened down both English and Irish throats this night.

If only he could make amends tonight, bury the past and start a new life. He knocked softly on the carved wooden door of their room and walked in slowly.

Chapter 12

When he entered the candlelit bedroom, the Irishman found his bride sitting up in bed. Her auburn hair was about her shoulders. It pleased him that she wore the nightgown he'd had Caleb bring from the *Yankee Rose*. When he'd seen the yellow flowers on the gossamer cloth, he'd thought of Millicent. Edna was correct when she told him straight out Millie would need even a new bed gown, not to mention a whole new wardrobe. It had shocked him this morning when he helped move the bed in here. He'd glanced into his bride's old room, amazed at how meager her wardrobe and belongings were. There was hardly a gown unpatched.

As Taggart watched his sister adjust Millicent's long auburn hair against the fluffy white pillows, his full attention came back to his bride. Brushed and with a reddish hue, the straight shiny hair made him want to suddenly run his fingers through every inch of it. Abigail Somerset fussed with the lavender-scented coverlet. Only Colleen Mulcahy looked displeased. When another clap of thunder fairly shook the room, he saw Colleen cross herself.

"'Tis a fearful thing, ya do, lad," she told the tall Irishman.

The old woman's words made Millicent's spine tingle. Had Colleen felt this dread, too? Despite the fire blazing at the side of the room, she shivered.

"You've forced the girl ta wed ya," Mrs. Mulcahy went on in warning. "She was never meant for the likes of you, O'Rahilly. The marriage is cursed from the start."

171

When Millie saw Edna cross herself, too, she clutched the heavy coverlet close to her chin. Both Irishwomen were suddenly acting as though this were a funeral, not a wedding night. Even Abigail Somerset, who was a staunch Anglican, appeared ready to bolt from the room. Though she knew it wasn't possible, suddenly the bride wished she were far away from here, someplace where it was safe, not here in a wedding bed with a groom who did not love her—a man who probably wished she were Garnet, another man's wife.

"Now, Colleen, we'll have none of your superstitions this night," he rebuked, both amused and irked that she was frightening the two young women this way. But when the raging storm outside increased in ferocity, he felt the hairs on the back of his neck bristle. Then he saw Millicent pale after Colleen whispered something into her ear. With brisk politeness, Taggart hustled the three women out of the room.

When he looked back at his new bride, his thoughts turned to more pleasant things. How silly he was to let the earl goad him with lies and the old Irishwoman make him uneasy with her superstitious nonsense. As he'd directed, he saw Caleb had placed the cognac and two glasses on the table next to the bed. He was determined to cause Millicent as little pain as possible. He walked closer into the room.

Though Millicent thought him the handsomest of men in his well-tailored clothes, she was so confused and apprehensive, there was little room for admiring Taggart's attributes.

Sensing her shyness, Taggart slowly removed his outer coat only. He went over to the side of the bed and began pouring the cognac in two crystal glasses.

"I know this has not been an easy day for you," he began again. "Let us hope," he added, "this night will be a smoother passage."

She felt heat suffuse her face at the double meaning of his words. As a result of the wedding ceremony before witnesses, she was now his, and he could do whatever he wished with her. Submit, that was her lot, and the word taunted her. Something wrenched within her as he leaned over to hand her the goblet.

172

She smelled the heavy, sweet scent of white roses—Garnet's perfume clung to the upper part of his clothes. Her hands shook when she accepted the amber liquid.

False courage, she said inwardly, then took a large swallow. However, her body made her instantly aware it was not used to strong liquor. Her eyes watered and she began to cough as it careened a fiery path down her throat. Having eaten little all day, the strong liquor seemed to settle in her stomach with an echoing splash. Quickly she replaced her glass next to his on the silver tray of the bedstand. When she looked up, Taggart's amused features were quite evident. How could one keep one's dignity in such a situation? she lamented. Especially after what would surely follow? Her bridegroom seemed to dwarf the large room. No, he did not appear to be a man who would accept a marriage of convenience.

This last thought and Garnet's warning about his . . . his size, sent rivulets of terror through her veins. Desperately, she searched her mind for a way out.

"Like many things in life, cognac is better appreciated when taken slowly," he advised, the low timbre of his voice now gentler. His wife looked so adorably flustered right now, he had all he could do to restrain from his urge to take her in his arms and kiss her sweet face, run his hand along that slender neck, to nestle in those small, yet well-formed breasts. For all her height and earlier unruffled poise, right now, sitting there in this huge bed, she looked so fragile and young. Never had he felt so protective of another. But he knew he couldn't help causing her pain this night no matter how gentle he'd try to be, and the thought saddened him. Feeling nervous himself, he wasn't paying complete attention as he started to replace the delicate cut-glass stopper of the decanter. It teetered on the silver tray and to steady the bottle, he let the top escape his fingers. It crashed downward, the small chips scattering about the floor.

At that instant, a strong gust from the violent storm outside forced the double doors open that led to a small balcony overlooking the gardens. Millicent automatically got out of bed to shut the French doors.

"Have a care of the glass." Taggart was on his hands and knees gingerly picking up the few pieces of shattered glass that had landed away from the frayed carpet near the bed.

Rain pelted her as she had to use all her strength to close and this time latch the glass doors. The old draperies cut at her like thick weeds on the rocky shore a few miles below the hill. When she felt strong arms encircle her waist and extract her from the tangled, wet curtains, automatically she tried to move back, but his warm hands on her arms foiled any escape.

"Easy, sparrow, I'm merely trying to untangle your wings," he teased against the back of her head. "It would never do to have you catch a chill on our wedding night. Come, I'll show you a delightful way to ward off the stormy night." But when he turned her about to face him, Taggart was startled to see the horror in her gray eyes. There was more than a bride's timidity in her look just now. Trying to be patient, Taggart let her go back under the covers alone. It was then that he reluctantly decided to sleep on the sofa at the other side of the spacious room. He should have known a lady of Millicent Fitzroy's demeanor would need more time, time for them to become reacquainted first. Despite what her coarse father hinted, right now, looking at her, he was certain she was untouched by any other man. God, he thought with self-deprecating humor, how his men would laugh if they could see him tonight. Never one to talk of his feminine conquests, he still knew some of his workers and a few of the women themselves, if the truth were told, took delight in embellishing his encounters.

However, tonight it was difficult to see any humor in this situation. Millie was watching him across the room, reminding him of a rabbit ready to bolt at the first hint of danger. Of course, he told himself, she was no tavern wench to be rolled quickly in the hay. But, damn it, he'd never intended to be anything other than gentle with her. What the devil did she think he was, an uncivilized barbarian? Sighing heavily, he bent down to be sure he'd gotten all the broken glass. The last thing he wanted was for either of them to cut their bare feet in the morning.

Satisfied, he stood up. His smile was self-mocking as he

174

attempted to put her more at ease. "It seems my occasional awkwardness has not changed. More at home with large ships and horses, it appears dainty crystal is not safe around me."

Though her look was strained, Millicent tried to match his tenor. "With so few pieces left, please try to be more careful around my father's meager treasures, or we'll all soon be drinking out of tin cups."

He frowned, misreading her tone as one censuring a clumsy servant.

Millicent put his expression down to nerves from the trying day. Despite their usual ease in conversing when they'd been adolescents, right now they were like polite strangers.

"Irish lout that I am, my lady," he remarked in a clipped manner, "I shall endeavor to be more careful in future."

At the cold sarcasm in his tone, her chin came up slightly. "Please see that you do. The furnishings are old in this house, and many of my father's possessions are fragile."

"They are no longer your father's possessions," he pointed out with inner relish. How could she look so surprised? he wondered. Surely that old reprobate had wasted little time whining to her of how badly he'd been treated by his former groom. What game was this Englishwoman playing with him?

Her gray eyes narrowed. "What do you mean? Though my father had to sell most of his possessions to raise money, there are a few items left to him, thank God."

Two strides and he was back to bed. He grabbed her silk-covered shoulders, forcing her to look up at him. Then he told her about Williamsburg Shipping and how he'd paid off all her father's debts and was now the rightful owner of Fitzroy Hall.

Astonishment etched across the delicate bones of her face. She could only watch him now, with no attempt to struggle away from the arms that bit into her narrow shoulders. And all this time she'd assumed Taggart was a mere ship's captain, when in fact he was the wealthy owner of his own company. And he was the man who held all her father's debts. Did that mean she was part of the revenge, too?

"Everything," he growled, capturing her gray eyes with

175

smoldering intensity, "in this room of mine *is mine*, and that includes the Earl of Holingbrook's daughter."

Almost instantly, Taggart regretted his hasty words. At the look of horror on her pale face, he freed her arms and placed the glass of cognac back in her trembling hands. After only a few seconds, he was relieved to see the color return to her soft cheeks. "Take another sip, there's a good girl."

But Lady Millicent could not hear his words. A possession, that is what he called her. Outrage replaced her shock, and with a jerking snap of her wrist, she thrust the entire contents of her glass up at the man hovering over her.

O'Rahilly bolted away from the bed as if scalded. Most of the generous contents missed his face and splashed across the white ruffles of his lawn shirt.

Suddenly appalled at her own lack of control, Millicent could only watch as the amber rivulets made wet spirals down to the top of his cream-colored breeches. One stride from his long legs brought him back to the edge of their bed. She cringed when she saw the barely controlled fury in his dark eyes. His right hand clenched and unclenched as if he were fighting some demon that tempted a more physical response to her blatant insult.

Something seemed to hold him back, but he growled a few Gaelic words too rapidly for her to translate. She didn't protest when he took the empty glass from her fingers. He set it down hard on the gleaming tray next to the bed. Then he went over to retrieve a cambric handkerchief from the inside of his silk coat.

In the candlelight Millicent again saw the grass stains on his once pristine hose. They reminded her of the duel he'd fought only hours before. Was she mad to do such a thing? Usually the mistress of her emotions from years of necessity around her father and running the estate, these multifaceted unleashed feelings unnerved her. At this moment, she realized it was her former groom who was showing more restraint.

He came to a decision quickly. "It is time we straightened out a few matters of conduct between us, wife." Taggart tossed the cognac-stained handkerchief on the chair where his coat had been placed. He removed his now-rumpled neckcloth, then hastily unbuttoned his shirt. In his anger, he realized he needed to set the tone of their marriage right now or forever he would continue to be her former groom, a servant in her eyes. He'd never been cruel to a woman or child in his life, but by God, he vowed, he'd not be this Englishwoman's doormat.

When Millicent raised her gray eyes to apologize, the words died on her lips. The raging storm outside was nothing to her sudden reaction when she saw the pink scar on the left side of Taggart's chest, where the wisps of coarse black hair had not grown back. The Duchess of Montrose had accurately described it. The implication of that scar taunted her. There was only one way Garnet could have seen it. She had not lied—Garnet was Taggart's mistress.

Millicent ran a hand across her throbbing temple. She shivered, feeling sick and hurt with despair. Until now there had always been a faint spark of hope left over from nine years ago, a hope that one day Taggart would love her. But he had made it perfectly clear his honor was more important than love.

A bitter smile crossed her soft lips. Fool, she raged at herself when the real vision of her marriage rose up to mock her. She was a built-in mistress who could run his home for him. Her life would be just the same as all the Fitzroy women. Unconsciously, Millicent's hands became fists as she remembered how her mother had suffered in silence while Geoffrey Fitzroy made little effort to hide his infidelities.

The English girl felt the bed move when Taggart sat down next to her. He was naked except for his breeches. The ribbon at the back of his neck had been removed, and his thick black hair just touched his shoulders. What had Colleen whispered in her ear before being hustled out of the room tonight? She glanced at her husband's handsome face, concentrating on his chin. Oh, yes, Colleen had given her one of those ancient Irish proverbs: "A dimple in the chin, a devil within." How apt, Millicent thought bitterly.

Taggart studied her but with little success this time. Deliberately, he thought, she was building that wall of cool reserve between them again. He reached out to brush a strand of auburn hair away from her face. His motions were more deliberate now. When she flinched away from him, he took her chin in his fingers.

Forced to look up at him, Millicent tried to still her pounding heart. She saw the cleft in his chin narrow with the clenching of his lean jaw when she'd tried to pull away. His eyes were almost black in the candlelight, which combined with the crackling fireplace to send ghostly shadows along the worn silk-covered walls. She tried to keep her voice steady when she remarked, "Since this is your room, sir, I concede it to you. I . . . I should like to sleep in my old room. Please," she added.

"Impossible. Edna has taken your old room, since you will no longer need it. A wife's place is in her husband's bed." Still holding her chin, with his free hand he began tracing a silky pattern along the alabaster softness of her cheek. Then he ran his fingers along her neck, fluttering away the soft folds of her sheer nightgown.

She had such expressive eyes, he thought, looking up at her. High cheekbones, smooth skin with just a hint of a pinkish hue, a soft mouth—he leaned closer, delighting in the smell of the lavender soap that clung to her warm body. *"Gealbhan,"* he whispered before capturing her lips.

Millicent felt his arms go around her, and despite her resolve, her body and heart began to betray her. When she made an initial attempt to pull away, his strong hand had firmly but gently brought her back to where he clearly wanted her— just beneath him in the center of the large bed.

"Oh, sparrow, I want—" His words were lost as he captured her moist lips once more in another searing kiss.

Through the soft material of her nightdress she felt her nipples grow taut and hard as they made contact with the coarse hairs on his chest. When he took one of her firm small breasts in his hand, she had to bite down on her lower lip to keep the primitive moan of sensuous pleasure from escaping her lips.

Taggart had not expected either of them to react with such ferocity to this kiss. He was breathing hard when he allowed her to finally pull away, but he could not hide the smile that tugged at the corners of his mouth, for it surprised and delighted him that she should respond to him this way. "Why, you've rounded out quite pleasantly," he blurted. "Sure and I'll wager your adorable bottom is still as—" He stopped, realizing his desire for her had unguarded his Irish tongue once more. An English lady would never appreciate such blatant language. You lout, he yelled at himself. He apologized immediately.

Unable to keep the crimson stain from suffusing her face, Millicent looked away, never quite hearing his words. For she was only painfully aware that she had just responded quite wantonly to her husband—the man who did not love her, the man whose mistress was downstairs at this moment. No, she shouted to herself, she was not like her mother. She could not turn her head away meekly while Taggart and Garnet engaged in an affair. No, she would not allow him to make love to her this night or any other night while he made love to other women. Wife or not, she belonged to herself first, and her mind could outwit this cunning Irish wolf.

Unconsciously her chin came up, but she forced her body to relax. She even managed to smile, while reaching for the top button of his breeches. "Two days is such a long time between—well," she mimicked Garnet's little-girl voice expertly. "And what do we have here?" God, she thought, if Taggart didn't fall for this humbug, what would she do next?

At first he was too keyed up with arousal as her slender fingers worked at his breeches. But through the maze of his pleasurable physical response, her first sentence hit him. Two days since . . . ? Abruptly, he pulled back from her eager fingers.

"Oh, now don't be shy, Taggart dear." Her large eyes became a mask of playfulness. "I shall be gentle with you." Her gaze traveled lower to the receding bulge between his legs. "You're a bit smaller than—oh, well, no matter. It's how you use the garden tool that makes the cabbages bloom, as they say."

His brows moved up toward his hairline. Could this be the shy sparrow saying such bawdy things? And though he'd be

179

first to admit he wasn't every woman's ideal, until now he'd received few complaints in that department.

Picking up steam, his companion congratulated herself at not having lost her ability to talk her way out of a delicate situation. She reached out to entwine her arms about her husband's neck. "And pray do not fret about your face, Taggart. With my glasses off I can scarcely make you out." Deliberately, she lowered her voice to a whisper. "I can pretend you're . . . him." Still clinging like a barnacle, she looked down at the floor to hide the stab of inner pain as she realized he would probably have closed his eyes with her, dreaming of Garnet.

All amorous feelings, along with his physical ability to perform them even if he'd wanted to, departed in a rush. Taking his wife's arms from about his neck, Taggart hoisted her out of the bed, none too gently, and stood her in front of him. "What did you say?" He felt as though a horse had kicked him in the stomach. Had her father been correct?

"Taggart," she admonished, giving him a pout as they stood toe to toe with each other. "You'll bruise my tender skin."

"I'll do more than bruise it if you don't tell me what you were hinting at just now."

"Well," she drew out, keeping her voice calm with effort, for he did look dangerous at the moment. "You would find out soon enough, I dare say." She shrugged, trying to think what a woman of the world would spout. "I am not a virgin. But, then," she added, holding his shocked gaze with her own level stare, "neither are you."

His hands fell limply to his sides. Was this his innocent sparrow? He couldn't explain it but his first reaction was sadness. But then he happened to glance at the two glasses on the night table. God, how Millicent must have barely choked to restrain her jeering laughter. He'd been such a gullible fool, concerned that he'd hurt her, awkward as a green lad as he tried to ease her way into accepting him as a husband. He ran an anguished hand through his black hair as the first sparks of fury and injured pride started to fire in him, and he let them grow unleashed. It was better than feeling those soft emotions that had first hurt him at her taunting words. He glanced back at his "bride." She looked damn smug, he thought.

And why not? he raged. She'd just rescued her father and made Mr. O'Rahilly the laughingstock of Kinsale.

Gone was the gentleman when he hauled her next to him. "His name," he demanded, a tight-lipped scowl on his face.

Her act departed with speed, for she now realized it may have gone too far. "Please." Tears pricked her eyes at the excruciating pain in her arms.

Moving to hold her about the waist, the Irishman's right hand came about her slender throat. "I will have his name, my lady," he spat. "Though English whore would seem a more apt form of address."

But there was no name to tell, raged in her fevered brain. When he increased the pressure of his fingers, she knew death was imminent. Never would she give an innocent man's name to save herself. But what would the English do to Taggart if he murdered her? "I cannot tell you," she choked. "Even if you do kill me."

The ringing in his ears seemed to stop, for he heard her words and suddenly became aware of what he was about to do. She wasn't fighting him but lay limply in his arms. Her angry struggles would have pushed him over the edge, but he knew her docility right now hurled him away from the dangerous precipice his fury had led him. As if her flesh burned his fingers, he let her go, watching with torment and anger as she slumped down at his feet. "The debt is paid today, madam—your jewels nine years ago for my protection and wealth as my wife today."

Rubbing her bruised throat, she could only stare up at him. "I never asked you to marry me. The jewels had no conditions. I tried to tell you that the night you asked me to marry you."

"Yes, I was more the Irish fool for attempting to help you. My biggest mistake was forgetting you're a Fitzroy, my English wife. Be assured I shall not make that mistake again." Without another word, he snatched up his hastily strewn clothes, tucked them under his arm, and quickly left their suite of rooms.

Unable to hold back her tears any longer, Millicent, still on the floor, buried her face in her hands. Yes, Taggart would not make love to her tonight, nor any other night. He was probably going to Garnet Huntington at this very moment.

What had she done? "Nooo. Taggart," she cried softly. "Oh, Taggart."

But the only response came from the logs crackling in the fireplace.

Chapter 13

Taggart O'Rahilly felt more at ease here in the servants' hall. "To the new owner," he toasted, holding up the dented pewter mug toward himself. There was a sardonic pull to his sensuous lips, before he tossed back another swallow of the strong whiskey.

The two other people in the room clearly saw something amiss with their new employer. Colleen whispered something to her husband. Fergus nodded, his look of disapproval matching hers.

The old man cleared his throat before addressing Taggart. "Most of the guests rushed out a here, shortly after . . . after ya went upstairs. Fear of the storm gettin' worse, I suppose. There's only about six of them earl's drinkin' friends left— England's noblest gentry snorin' their boozy heads off," he added with a chuckle. "Not wantin' ta disturb ya, we thought it be all right ta drape 'um over some of the sofas and chairs in the hall and the earl's—I mean, your study," he corrected.

"Quite right," Taggart said, his voice dripping with sarcasm. He downed another gulp of the dark liquor. "I shouldn't want my father-in-law's friends to say O'Rahilly was inhopit— inhos—shit."

"It took them two giant blackamoors to get his lordship up ta his room," the little man volunteered. "They related?"

"They're brothers," Taggart answered. "Samuel, the younger one runs my stables. And Caleb—he's my valet."

"Valet, is it now?" Fergus' amused glance met his wife's. "I

183

could never see how a grown man needed another man just ta hand him his drawers."

"You don't know what you are speaking about," the younger man cut off, the strain of the day depleting his patience. A scowl distorted his handsome features. "They are the ways of a gentleman."

"Gentleman, is it?" Colleen's question was scathing. "It don't seem the courtly thing to do ta leave a young bride alone on her weddin' night."

"Shh."

"Don't you be shushin' me, Fergus Mulcahy." Then Colleen eyed her employer once more. "Down here in the servants' hall long after midnight—polishin' off that huge tumbler of whiskey like it was tea on Sunday—'tisn't right. The poor lamb upstairs and himself abandonin' her, shovin' his head in a bottle."

Fergus looked flustered. "Remember your place, woman."

"Oh, well, then. Since me husband has seen fit ta remind me of me place, I'll be asking, Is there anything I can get your honor—like a bucket ta puke in?"

"Colleen." Fergus rolled his eyes heavenward.

Taggart's expression showed clearly his distaste for "your honor." "I won't stand on ceremony with you two," he snapped. "You know you can call me by my name."

"As well we might." With an impatient hand, Colleen swiped at a strand of gray hair that had dared come out from her mobcap. "And wasn't it meself that tended to your cuts and black eyes from all them fights ya got into. I never seen such a lad ready to use his fists." From her position against the stone wall, she eyed the young man sitting alone a few feet away on the long bench before the fire. "I told ya the marriage was cursed, lad. Her ladyship is not for the likes 'a you." When no response from the Irishman in question was forthcoming, she ventured, "Tossed ya out, did she? Well, 'tis no more than ya deserve after kidnappin' her the way ya did, and in front of all them snicherin' English with their superior airs. Good for Lady Fitzroy!"

At Colleen's triumphant outcry, Taggart's fingers tightened around the handle of his tankard. He set it down with a loud thud against the worn oak table. Her words, combined with others this night, made the blood pound before his brown eyes. "Though she keeps her title in England's eyes, my wife's name in Virginia will be Mrs. O'Rahilly. And, Fergus, you would be wise to tell your outspoken wife to mind her own business."

Fergus shrugged his shoulders. "Might as well tell the River Bandon ta stop runnin'." He gave Taggart a sympathetic smile. "You must know you've always been her favorite, lad. But Colleen's also come to care for her ladyship these last few years. You've been away a long time, and ya ain't got a notion how hard 'tis been for the lass—ya can't treat her ladyship like . . . well, like—"

"Like an Irish wife," Taggart bit out. "I'm supposed to grovel at her feet, thank her for consenting to marry such a low sea slug, is that it?" His strong emotions combined with the whiskey and made his brogue noticeable. "Please pardon me shadow, your ladyship," he mimicked, bowing so low he almost whacked his forehead on the edge of the rough table. "Well," he added, coming to his full height, "she's the wife of O'Rahilly now." And by God, he vowed to himself, she'd know it before the night was over. Millicent had fooled them all with her soft speech and gentle manners. Did Fergus and Colleen know their "lamb" had taken a lover? But who was he? And had he gotten into her room the same way he'd climbed in years ago?

Taggart wanted to demand more information from these two old retainers about his wife's prior escapades, but pride stifled his questions. What did it matter? He knew the truth already. And it had come from his wife's own lips. She was as treacherous as Garnet Huntington, with a bedchamber that had probably seen more traffic than a dockside alehouse.

When both servants came over to stand near him, Taggart saw the worried expressions on their faces. "Not to fret. I am quite capable of making it upstairs on my own." He was miles from being drunk. The large whiskey had just swept his mind of some confusing decisions, he told himself.

Colleen snorted. " 'Tis me lamb I'm worried about. You're in no condition ta—"

He shook off their restraining arms easily. "Your English lamb is safe, Colleen, for I'd as soon bed a viper." He walked back over to the hearth and slumped down once more on the old wooden bench. However, this time, he didn't reach for the pewter mug. He just brooded into the dying embers, his shoulders bent.

A few minutes later when he glanced back over his shoulder, the Irishman saw that Fergus had placed his bony arm around his wife's ample waist. Colleen rested her head against her husband's shoulder. He saw Fergus kiss her lined cheek, then whisper something in her ear.

Taggart watched as the older woman smiled, then stood up with her husband. Fergus patted Colleen's wide buttocks across her homespun gown, then he tucked her hand under his arm and began leading her out toward their small room beyond the spacious pantry.

When he heard Colleen giggle, Taggart looked away. Obviously in love after so many years, they still found pleasure in each other. He could not understand why but he felt something ache inside. Their marriage seemed to mock his, for he envied the ease with which the Mulcahys talked and laughed, their understanding of each other so acute, words were not always needed. On the other hand, he felt the way things stood between him and Millie, they would never know such contentment. It was now clear she despised him. He put his head in his hands, despairing that his well-meaning plans to save her from marriage to Edwin had gone so awry.

The image of his wife's expression when he'd demanded to know her lover's name came back to taunt him. Yes, the defiance in her eyes had won out over her fear. That vision of her stayed with him, until finally he came to a decision.

Taggart stood up slowly, then went over to a small table on the side of the room and poured cold water from a pitcher into the chipped basin. After splashing his face, he grabbed a clean linen towel next to the basin and wiped his stubble-covered skin. His eyes focused on the narrow back stairs that led to the bedroom on the floor above.

Dozing fitfully, Lady Millicent came fully awake at the sound of someone trying to gain entry to her locked door. The fire was low, the room dark. She doubted it could be Taggart—his contemptuous declarations before he left hours earlier assured her that her ploy to escape sleeping with him had worked—perhaps too well, for she was now convinced he hated her.

When the sound at her door occurred again, she sat up. Could it be one of her father's drunken friends from the wedding feast below? She remembered a time a few months back when one had stumbled into her room, looking for a place to relieve himself. Since then, she'd taken to locking her door at night.

Without hesitation, she reached down to open the bottom drawer of her nightstand. The brass handle of the pistol was cold against her warm skin. Better to be cautious. No telling what one of these inebriated reprobates might try. Bribing a servant to force the lock wouldn't surprise her. The young women raised the pistol with both hands.

For a moment Taggart only stared stupidly at the unyielding door. But when the truth hit him, all his earlier resolves to have a serious talk with his bride vanished. Lady Millicent had dared lock her door against him! By hell, this was the last insult in a whole day of humiliations—her first dance with Liam, her father's jeering, her glib manner when she informed him she had lovers—said as calmly as "pass the scones," and now locking him out of their bedroom on their wedding night—treating him like some baseborn servant, not fit to clean her boots. He grabbed the brass knob and gave one massive push with his left shoulder.

The old hinges gave way far easier than he'd expected, and O'Rahilly went catapulting into her room, giving the full appearance of a sotted rummy being pitched from Fogarty's pub. Dignity was not to be his as the force of his entry caused him to lose his balance; he went sprawling on the blue carpet in front of the bed.

There had been little noise since the weak door made no more racket than if it had been opened quickly, and her worn carpet muffled the sound of his descent to the floor.

Tentatively, Millicent inched her way on her knees down the long expanse of the new bed. Without her glasses, but still holding the pistol Fergus had insisted she carry years ago, the lady peeked over the edge of the carved wooden frame. When she saw the outline of a man struggling like an upended turtle on the floor, she forced herself to stay calm. If she couldn't handle this alone, she would give a loud cry for help as a final resort. But the last thing she wanted was to have it known her husband chose to sleep elsewhere on their wedding night. The increased comments about her lack of beauty would no doubt be mortifying. There had been enough indignities this day to last a lifetime.

Squinting, Millicent could tell this was not one of her father's older friends. This was a big brute of a fellow.

"You have made a mistake, sir," she forced with cool reserve. "This is not the privy. Kindly leave my rooms at once." With satisfaction, she saw the stranger get up slowly. However, when he made no motion to depart, she pointed the flintlock pistol at him. "If you do not withdraw this instant, I shall be forced to shoot you."

Chagrined at his own less than masterful entrance, Taggart was outraged that this slip of a girl would point a pistol at him. Unbidden, the picture of Garnet and her knife entered his mind. So much for properly raised English ladies, he thought. Hell, they were about as helpless as two gunnery sergeants. Was Millicent just like Garnet? But this arrogant snip was his bride, no less.

Taggart walked over and shut the door. He shoved a patched, overstuffed chair in front of it, for he was going to make damn sure no one came in on them tonight without warning. Any former lover would have to look elsewhere for comfort from now on. This particular charity of his wife's was now at an end. His movements were determined and self-assured as he came back to stand next to the bed. "I've no intention of making you a widow—at least until I've sampled your wares, the ones it seems everyone in Kinsale has tasted. Now, put that damn pistol away," he ordered.

"Taggart?" Relief swept through her, and she barely paid

attention to what he was saying. She placed the unloaded weapon back in its hiding place. "Oh, Taggart, I'm glad you came back." Now she would have the chance to apologize and explain—"We do need to talk, and I—"

"There's been too many words between us already," he cut off, a new menacing tone to his low voice. Without another word, he began undressing hurriedly in the darkened room. Naked, he came over and sat next to Millicent on the edge of the bed.

"It appears we've come this far before, wife." He reached out and slipped his hand down the front of her nightgown. The soft material moved easily away in his powerful hands.

Her nose wrinkled at the smell of strong liquor. This was not the Taggart she had come to love. This man was a stranger. Silently, she berated herself for her hasty tongue. Whatever had possessed her to goad him with taunts of other lovers? When she tried to inch away, his strong arms brought her back. Bending her over his left arm, he forced her to look at him.

"No more words tonight." He cupped her breast in his hands, bent his head, and took one of the small pink peaks between his lips. Despite his resolve to stay unmoved and not let anything inside him be touched by her, Taggart found he was affected by Millicent's body. The sent of lavender clung to her clean skin. Her breasts were small, each barely the size of an orange, but they were firm, one for each hand. He cupped the globes, discovering he enjoyed the feel of her skin against his mouth.

Millicent could not suppress the moan that escaped her tightly held lips when she felt his light kisses along the smooth line of her jaw, then he moved lower to the slender column of her throat, before concentrating on her breast once more. She could not stop herself from reaching out a hand to run along the back of his neck, feeling his long black hair as it ruffled about his shoulders. Shyly, she placed her other hand on his chest. "Taggart." She said his name softly, like a caress. This was what she had dreamed about, wanted for so long. When she felt his hand on her thighs she gasped at the blatant

189

pleasure he was giving her.

Taggart was astonished at her giving response. It was nothing like the English lady of ice he'd come to expect. And her actions right now were passionate, if a little awkward. It was perplexing. She touched him like an inexperienced maid, yet her pleasure at his preliminary actions was quite evident.

Wanting to blot out the tormenting questions and emotions that plagued him, Taggart increased the pressure on her shoulders and raised her upper body closer to his. In the dim light of the flickering candle next to the bed, he studied her lips for a second. Had this saucy mouth that had laughed with him long ago now betrayed him, lied to him? He clamped his lips on hers; he didn't want to think right now. He wanted only to feel her body under his, warm and soft.

The forcefulness of his kiss took Millicent's breath away. Once she tried to pull back, a little frightened of her own response to such a blatant kiss, but she discovered she wasn't to be allowed to end the embrace. Her face suffused with color when she felt his hand caress the round planes of her bottom as he firmly pressed her lower body into his pelvis, making her well aware of his aroused state. However, the beginning fears of Garnet's warning suddenly quelled much of her heated response.

After experiencing her initial passion to his embrace, Taggart slackened his hold on her arms. When she pulled away from him, he was surprised to see the change on her face. But it couldn't be fear, he told himself. What game was she playing with him now?

For a few silent moments he watched her, like a fox waiting for his dinner to tire so he could pounce. She moved back against the headboard in a clear attempt to put as much distance between them as possible. His initial confusion was replaced by annoyance. "I'm getting bloody tired of your play-acting, my lady." He bit the last two words out like a curse. "You change from hot to cold with the practiced ease of an actress slipping into a costume."

"I . . ." She wanted to confess her apprehensions to him, to ask for his patience, but the unyielding look in his midnight

190

eyes told her he would not believe her this time. What was she going to do? Frantically she tried to think, but nothing came.

Tension knotted her stomach. "Noo," she whimpered, then bounded off the bed in a desperate race for the door.

"By God, that tears it." With lighting speed, Taggart reached her. He grabbed for her but only caught wisps of nightdress. In the downward motion to catch her, he rent the gossamer in two, but it effectively stopped her retreat.

They were both breathing hard when their eyes collided. At first Millicent could only look down in horror to see her apparel cascade about her slim ankles in a flowery pool of ruined material. Then her shock turned to something else, and in an instant her right hand shot back in an arch.

The sound of flesh hitting flesh reverberated in the room. Taggart's head snapped back with the unexpected force of her blow.

Unconsciously Millicent's chin lifted. "I am sure there are women who would find your barbaric tactics to their liking," she spat, thinking of Garnet Huntington. "But I am not one of them." It took all her determination to hide the alarm she felt as she saw the red imprint of her fingers along the bronze skin of his cheek. But she told herself, he deserved it. Faith, she wasn't a riverside doxy to be stripped like a piece of fruit.

Astonishment, pain, then rage etched across his handsome features. Lady Millicent had not administered any ladylike tap. She was just three inches shorter than himself and she possessed a strength he hadn't realized until now. But any musings about the discovery of the young woman's temper were shoved aside by his own strong emotions.

"English virago," he snarled, then scooped her up forcefully in his arms before she could utter one word of protest. He strode to the bed and dumped her in the center across the downy coverlet.

The wind was knocked out of her but before Millicent could catch an even breath, Taggart's hard body landed on top of her.

"Don't ever raise a hand to me again, hellion." His expression was menacing. "That's right, push against me all you want. It will make you realize all the sooner exactly what

191

your position is in this house. Hate and despise me if you wish, but tonight you're mine." Without preliminaries, wanting to hurt her as much as he felt betrayed and angered by her disdain, the Irishman forced his knee between her legs. "Look at me," he commanded.

The tone of his voice made her open her eyes. She shuddered at the unleashed fury she saw contorting his features.

"You may refuse to give me your lover's name. But from this night on you'll share your bed with no one but me. It's been made quite clear how unworthy I am," he grated as he held her down with his hips, his hands tangling in her straight auburn hair, "but by God I am your husband, not your Irish servant. You are my wife; you belong to no man but me." Then he thrust angrily into the soft folds of her pink flesh.

Despite her resolve, Millicent could not hold back the excruciating cry of pain that wrenched from deep within her.

He hadn't even entered her fully, yet Taggart felt her firm impediment to his manhood, "What in blazes . . . ?" He pulled back automatically, all earlier anger dissipating at his wife's outcry, like the sound of a trapped animal in pain. Shock, then remorse buffeted him. He'd had women who pretended to be virgins when in fact they were not, but this was the first time he'd ever begun to make love to a women who affected the guise of a seasoned campaigner when in truth she was untouched. *"Gealbhan"* came out as both a soothing balm and a scold. Despite her attempts to fight him, he took her into his arms.

"No," he said gently, "you'll not be running away this time, so you might as well save your strength. You can always shoot my head off in the morning." He continued cradling her quivering body in his arms.

From the comfort of his embrace, Millicent found herself clinging to him as sobs wracked her slender body. It was more reaction from the difficult day, combined with her fear of lovemaking, "She was right," she blubbered into his chest. "You might have killed me with that . . . that thing."

"What's this?" He stifled a laugh when he saw the wariness on her red, tear-stained face. His wife was quite serious. Then

— FREE —

B O O K   C E R T I F I C A T E

ZEBRA HOME SUBSCRIPTION SERVICE, INC.

YES! Please start my subscription to Zebra Historical Romances and send me my free Zebra Novel along with my first month's Romances. I understand that I may preview these four new Zebra Historical Romances Free for 10 days. If I'm not satisfied with them I may return the four books within 10 days and owe nothing. Otherwise I will pay just $3.50 each; a total of $14.00 (a $15.80 value—I save $1.80). Then each month I will receive the 4 newest titles as soon as they come off the press for the same 10 day Free preview and low price. I may return any shipment and I may cancel this arrangement at any time. There is no minimum number of books to buy and there are no shipping, handling or postage charges. Regardless of what I do, the FREE book is mine to keep.

Name _____

(Please Print)

Address _____ Apt. # _____

City _____ State _____ Zip _____

Telephone ( ) _____

Signature _____

(if under 18, parent or guardian must sign)

Terms and offer subject to change without notice.

12-88

his eyes narrowed as he realized someone had needlessly frightened her. Without a mother, and he'd seen to Edna being out of her company, it was beginning to be clear Lady Millicent hadn't learned about the act of love between a man and woman. "I appreciate your compliment on my . . . my abilities," he teased, "but I'm hardly the disfigured giant you seem to think."

She pulled back from him and looked up into his amused face. "Irish Stallion" came to mind. However, she had promised Garnet not to give her away. If Garnet truly was his mistress against her will, Millicent would have to find more proof herself. Right now her husband did not look so formidable. She took in his cleft chin, then moved her attention higher to read the gentleness in his eyes that she had thought never to see again.

He took her chin in his hand. "I'm so sorry I hurt you just now, sparrow. But why in heaven's name did you lie to me? Was the thought of sharing my bed so loathsome to you?"

He said the words so earnestly, Millicent felt suddenly ashamed at her earlier deception. "Oh, no, I've always lo—" She caught the word in time, reminding herself that such an admission would only make things worse, for her husband did not love her. Part of the truth would suffice so she said, "I was angry at your methods in getting me to marry you." She inched away from his hand but was surprised to feel only comfort when he shook his head and gently pulled her back to the circle of his arms once more.

"Here, you're cold. Get under the covers and we can talk." He brushed back a few strands of her long hair, then kissed her temple as he settled both of them under the mound of blankets and fluffy coverlet. "And my Irish temper didn't help matters. My motive was to save you from marrying Edwin, and it angered me when you refused to accept my offer to protect you as your husband. I know." He raised his hand as he read the rebellion in her gray eyes. "You did not want a husband out of duty." His smile was rueful, "I was honest with you about my feelings," he sidestepped, not wishing to cause her pain again. "Even though I did deceive you as to my ownership of

Williamsburg Shipping."

The English girl's body relaxed as she rested her back against his chest. Automatically, she reached out and touched his left cheek with her fingers. "I am sorry I slapped you. As a rule I'm considered softspoken and gentle-natured. Everybody says so," she added with uncomplicated honesty. She welcomed the rumbling laughter from the man holding her. "However, on those rare occasions I am ruffled, I have a tendency to become a trifle arrogant. Father Collins says it may stem from my feeling inadequate in certain areas," she chatted on. "But that was the first time I've ever struck anyone."

"You needn't sound so pleased about it," he chuckled. "You've a right, my dear, that would be the envy of every successful pugilist in London." His mouth hovered near her ear. He ran his tongue along the fleshy part of her lobe. "But I'd advise you not to make a habit of that maneuver. 'Ruffled' would be too mild a word to what I'd do to you if you clout me again," he warned, only half in jest.

The lady in his arms shivered, not from his words but the sensuous feel of his teeth as he nipped the soft flesh at her ear. "Taggart," she began shyly, "can we . . . start again?"

He sighed, misreading her question. "Yes, if you wish, my dear. Though a marriage in name only does not sit well, I will not force you to—"

"Oh, no," she interrupted. Her whole body turned with the true force of her feelings and she blurted, "It would break my heart to live that way. I want to be a true wife to you, and I want you to teach all the ways of pleasuring you." Aghast at her boldness, she felt the heat in her cheeks. She was practically throwing herself at this man, when he did not love her.

"Why do you look away?" He saw the tears in her eyes. "Darling, don't cry."

She looked up at him. "But I know how you feel. You would rather be in bed right now with your mistress, not me. I know your heart, O'Rahilly."

"Mistress?" He shook his head in disbelief. "I've not lived a monk's life, but I don't have any mistress. Don't be so daft." When she didn't pull away, he took this as a positive sign of her trust.

Could she believe him? She looked at his face, seeing no guile or evasiveness. Was Garnet lying?

"But the scar?"

"I'll tell you another time how I let my guard down, not tonight."

"But how did Gar—?"

"Not tonight."

Her desire for the man she had always loved pushed Millicent's doubts to a more hidden place in her mind. She rested her face against his cheek, then shyly moved away after a few silent, contented minutes.

He looked down at her features, frowning when he saw the pink marks where his face had scraped her alabaster skin. "God, I need to shave or I'll tear your sweet face to ribbons, my dear."

The old insecurities popped up. "You don't need to make an excuse if you'd rather not—" Her words were cut off when he gave her a little shake.

"Now, we'll have none of that talk." What the devil had they done to her these last nine years? he thought in exasperation. It was becoming clear to him she was vulnerable in this one area. True, she might not be a beauty in the classic sense, but damn it, he had always found something about her that intrigued him. "Sometimes, my lady, you can be a very perplexing woman." Without waiting for her reply, he got out of bed, stoked up the fire, and went over to the large wardrobe. He pulled out two of his dressing gowns.

Taggart walked back to the bed. "Please move on to your knees."

Millicent knelt on the bed while her husband bundled her into the soft folds of the dark-blue robe. The thick velvet felt comforting as it enveloped her bare skin, and she smiled her gratitude.

"That should keep you warm while I shave and wash. Then he added, giving her a pointed leer, "If you agree, I intend to make love to my new bride until dawn."

"I dare say, one can hope," she said with a saucy grin.

"English brat," he teased, glad for her returned humor. He realized he liked her this way.

"Bog trotter," she countered at his back. I love you, she thought, feeling warm and protected for the first time in many years. Would it be enough, even though she knew he did not love her?

Chapter 14

Millicent glanced at the blazing fire her considerate husband had remade for them. She burrowed deeper into the covers, unable to hide her enjoyment as she watched Taggart shave. The occasional smiles he sent her way added to her warm feelings. "You are a very handsome man, husband."

He was surprised to feel himself color at her open admiration. He bent over the porcelain basin and splashed the remaining soap from his face. "After your exaggerated claims on my prowess, you may be disappointed with the size of my—" He stopped teasing when he looked up to see her reflection in the mirror—the fear was back in her gray eyes.

Dressed only in his light brocade robe, he put down the linen towel and walked back to her.

"Sparrow, will you trust me? You did once when I pulled you out of a tree." He sat on the edge of the bed and took her hand in his. "I swear to cause you as little pain as possible this first time. And if you want to stop, you've only to say so." Silently, he prayed for the self-control to allow her to set the pace in their first encounter together.

Millicent met his gaze. "I . . . I want to trust you." This time the room was lighted, and she did not pull her fingers away. She breathed in the pleasing scent of his spicy soap. With the blue-black stubble removed, the strong planes of his face showed clearly. His skin gave evidence that he'd spent time outside, both in the sunshine of Virginia and on the sea-tossed deck of one his ships. Her eyes traveled to the area just below his collarbone, where his robe had opened to reveal the wisps of dark hair. "I will try to trust you," she whispered.

"Then that is a start." He watched her in silence for a moment. "You've the most expressive gray eyes I have ever seen, *Gealbhan*." He never took his own dark eyes from hers as his right hand went automatically to her long hair. "And I told you long ago how I've been attracted to the fire in your hair, your graceful hands, and—well, I will get to that adorable part later, for there is no hurry, sweet sparrow." He stroked the auburn tresses with his hand.

Lady Millicent took in all his compliments, like a parched flower in the desert receiving the unaccustomed but most welcomed drops of rain. She could not hide the smile that lighted her whole face. "I fear it will never be curly as the style dictates."

"You have always been special, above the others," he said truthfully. His hands dropped away from her hair and he reached for her slender hand, then brought it to his lips. He kissed the smooth skin below her wrist, then turned it over to bestow an intimate kiss along the palm.

His gentle yet deliberate touch sent shivers of delight down Millicent's spine. And when he cupped her chin in his hand once more, she knew she wanted the kiss he was about to give her. His lips were warm and coaxing as they sought to learn her secrets. The touch of them on her receptive mouth started a turmoil in her blood. He was holding her so close now that she could feel the hard-muscled strength of him through his robe. When he began kissing her eyes, her cheeks, down to that pulse beating rapidly at her throat, Millicent thought she was going to swoon from the strong emotions he caused her to experience. The large room seemed to spin as Taggart shut everything out for her except his arousing presence.

Passionately he kissed her again, but this time his mouth opened on hers, and it surprised and delighted him to feel her small tongue meet his. He heard her whisper when he pulled away, but he needed a moment to steady his own raging emotions. Never had he expected to feel such a strong desire for this woman. But he had to go slowly, he told himself. Breathing hard, he now realized it was going to be difficult, for he was beginning to know her—she had a fire within her that until now he'd never dreamed existed. He felt her ardent response and was unable to resist taking her into his arms once more. He removed the sash that held his velvet robe about her body. In the candlelight and blaze from the fireplace, he let his eyes roam leisurely over her naked form, delighting in the firm, small breasts, the slim waist, and those lovely long legs. Her smooth skin had a faint pinkish hue to it. He looked lower, taking in the reddish-brown triangle between her legs. When her hand went there to hide it from his gaze, he looked back up to her face. And this time he was able to read the uncertainty in her eyes.

Millicent found she could not meet her husband's eyes. Would he find her not to his liking? Old perceptions were hard to break.

"Sparrow." Taggart brought his face close to hers. "Don't use the mirrors of the past to see your reflection." He kissed her lips with genuine affection. "Look at me," he commanded.

She opened her eyes, trying to hide her apprehension. "I'm not a coward, Taggart. I can take the . . . physical pain. It's just that . . ."

"I think I'm beginning to understand. But you must learn to use my eyes as your mirror, sparrow. What a ninnyhammer you are," he said, but his tone was gentle. "Did you expect me to go charging out of here for sanctuary in some friary or turn to stone upon looking at your naked form?" His appreciative gaze traveled the length of her once more. "Faith, my dear, what I see pleases me. Pleases me very much."

At the sincerity in his voice, Millicent lost some of her timidity. Surely, he wasn't making sport of her? Or was he merely being kind? "Please know that I do not wish you to say words you don't mean. You have my promise to be your wife, a true wife," she amended, "and you have no need to use overblown flattery to get me to your bed."

He sighed, realizing it was going to be a difficult task to undue the past. "My words were plain and honest," he defended. But when he moved away he brought her body up with his. As if she weighed little, he swung her up and round to sit across his outstretched legs.

Had he misinterpreted her words as a rebuke? But explanations did not come easily, especially the way her senses were reeling from the feel of her soft curves across the sinewy coils of his strong thighs.

Her robe was open, giving him a marvelous view of her whole body. "We both have much to learn about each other, Millie, and I'm not just talking about what takes place in our bed. I now realize I should have written you during those nine years as I'd been tempted to do. I should have found another way to keep you from marrying Edwin."

The words made Millicent cringe inside. Did he regret marrying her after all? But she hadn't forced him, and—no, she told herself, it was best not to think of that now. But she did agree with him on one thing. They should have had a courtship. It wasn't just her romantic side that craved this, it was the practical realization that they hadn't had the time to get to know each other as adults.

What was she thinking now, he wondered, for she looked so serious. "But you must learn to accept my compliments."

"Only if they are—"

"Yes, I promise they will be genuinely meant, for I know you are an intelligent women and will not be fobbed off with empty speeches. All right?"

She smiled. "Yes, and as long as you meant those earlier words, would you mind writing them down with your signature? A woman of my . . . position does not often receive such truthful praise," she added, deviltry lurking at the corners of her mouth. "It will be something for me to keep in my dotage."

He couldn't help hugging her as he laughed at her audacious suggestion. It pleased him to discover they both enjoyed his touching her. "What a handful I have for a wife," he added, at ease with her impudence. "Hellion," he teased, then kissed her slender nose. Close to her lips, he savored the feel and scent of her satiny skin. "A delightful handful," he breathed, before bending her upper body back against his arms. This time his kiss was more demanding, with a new fierceness.

She welcomed his kiss, meeting his growing passion with a spark of desire that threatened to consume her. Yet, she knew right now she didn't want to flee the fire. Her hand splayed across the coarse dark hair of his chest. "Oh, Taggart, it feels so right to be here in your arms. I so wish to please you."

Moved by her open feelings, he prayed silently he would never hurt her, either physically or inside that delicate heart, which right now seemed far more fragile than her firm little body. She was so vulnerable. His sister was right. Millie was not like the other English he'd known. As his hands became bolder, he was aware of her heated reaction, but then when he placed his fingers between her legs, he felt the tenseness return to her body, despite her obvious efforts to hide it from him. Damn, he cursed. At this moment he'd have gladly chocked the person who had terrified his sweet bride with obviously gory tales about a wedding night. It was a cruel joke, just the sort of thing her father would delight in, the old reprobate. And beginning to know this proud Englishwoman, he knew she'd never ask him to stop, for she'd given her word to be his true wife. He had to make her relax. But how?

She was starting to trust him now; he could read that in her gray eyes. But the old fears still lingered there, even though she was trying to prove otherwise. It reminded him of a skittish colt he'd once tended to as groom here. The analogy suddenly made him think of something. Could it work?

"You won't need this," he said slipping her out of his oversized robe. "You're far too tense; lie on your stomach." His displeasure at this thoughtless prank to his bride made the words come out more abrupt than he wished.

Despite her efforts, her eyes grew large at what she interpreted to be an order. Was the time upon her so soon? All she had ever seen were the livestock mate. "You . . . wish to do it like the horses?" came out in a timorous squeak.

"By Saint Patrick, madam, do you think I intend to skewer you on a spit?" This evening of alternate arousal and holding back was taking its toll on him, both physically and emotionally. "Sure and those large doe eyes would try the patience of a eunuch. The position you refer to can be most pleasurable on occasion, but do you think me such a boorish lout to make it your first journey? There have been many women in the past who have delighted in the instrument

201

between my legs," he bit out. "No doubt you'll be happy to hear none of them are deceased."

He hadn't meant to blurt out—and he was slipping back into the brogue again—would he ever learn to control his unguarded tongue? But hell, she wasn't the only one who felt tense right now. Yet, he tried to remind himself, a lady like his wife would not see the humor of his exasperated statement. He sighed heavily when he saw her do as commanded, giving herself up to him like a sacrificial lamb. By God, he promised himself, if he ever had daughters he'd make bloody sure they didn't grow up with this terror of the marriage bed.

He pushed a long breath of air into his lungs. "Well, first off, we're going to relax those tense muscles of yours." He felt the bed sag with his weight as he knelt beside her reclining form. He kept his robe on, deciding to take this slowly. He began kneading the coiled knots along her shoulders. His fingers moved intently down her back, while he tried to soothe her with his voice. "Yes, that's right, sparrow. Let your body follow where it wants to go."

Millicent felt the tingling sensation across the surface of her skin. Down the full length of her legs, even the arches of her feet were attentively cherished. "Ohh, that feels marvelous," she purred. "No wonder the horses love you."

"Brat," he teased, happy that she was feeling at ease enough to laugh with him. He moved his palms down to the fullness of her hips.

With maddening accuracy, he seemed to know just when to increase the pressure of his fingers. Millicent felt her blood fire as his touch became more intimate. Her toes curled deeper into the mattress, and she failed to stifle the low moan that rose from deep within her throat. When he turned her over, she felt a growing heat between her legs. Something was pulling inside of her down there, and it caused her pleasure, yet it made her ache for something more.

His erotic massage progressed with a feathery softness from her forehead to her toes. When he started kissing all the areas his hands fondled, she felt the flames mount in the center of her body. "Oh, Taggart, you must stop. I cannot take any more of this."

202

"Yes you can, *Gealbhan.*" His voice was low, like the sensuous timbre of an oboe. Running his tongue across her flat stomach, his hand stroked the sensitive area between her thighs. However, this time he felt her moisture on his fingers. He teased the soft brown curls, rubbing the upper part of his palm in a coaxing motion across her sweet mound. He smiled when she unconsciously lifted her hips up to meet his hand.

Millicent was feeling dizzy with arousal. Her body throbbed with desire for his touch. A few times in the beginning she tried to escape his skillful fingers because she was embarrassed by the wanton things his touch was making her think about, but he allowed no quarter, keeping her right near him as he continued his gentle conquest.

The Irishman's own body responded to her immediately, and he knew he had to change his strategy or he'd lose control. He forced himself to think of the ship's log entries from his last voyage. Anything to keep from taking her the way his body was demanding right now. Sweat broke out on the top of his upper lip, and he moved his attention back up to her breasts. Taking one firm globe in his right hand, he ran his thumb lightly over the dusky-pink nipple. "Your breasts just fit my hand." He bent his head and took the turgid peak between his lips.

When she felt him suck and gently pull the nub of her breast, Millicent was unable to hold back the primitive, low moan which came from the back of her throat. Her mind, her very soul cried out for release. "Please, Taggart," she begged, not knowing what she wanted, only aware that she needed something more right now.

Reading the extent of her arousal, O'Rahilly moved lower to position his head between her parted thighs.

A trifle shocked at this unfamiliar attention, Millicent automatically wriggled her bottom away from him. "Oh, no, you mustn't. Surely, it is not proper."

His smile was patient as he stayed right where he was. "Yes, it is quite proper, lovely sparrow. Why not come back to me, or must I just stay here, alone at the lower half of our bed all night?"

A giggle escaped her lips at his forlorn expression. "Colleen was right," she teased. "You are a devil, Taggart O'Rahilly."

Yet, she found herself moving down to him.

"At times," he agreed, not taking offense. His warm hands caressed her legs and hips. "Now, let's see where was I? Oh, yes," he added, deliberately slowing his actions to draw out her pleasure. His lips found the treasure he sought. "Ummm, you taste delicious," he said, his voice a husky whisper. "You do please me, wife. Never forget that." Provokingly gentle, he kissed her most intimate part.

"Oh, Taggart, I—it feels so wonderful! Please . . . I can't wait." Her words came out in small gasps as the small nubbin between her thighs throbbed and heated from his skillful lips. His hands held her hips while he continued this delightful torment.

The sound of her passion-filled voice seemed to spur him on, and he increased the force and speed of his mouth on her sensitive skin.

She felt her pelvis convulse as wave after wave of electrifying pleasure pulsed throughout her body, and it took moments for her to return to earth. "Oh, my, that was—I never knew anything could feel so beautiful."

He could not hold back a chuckle of delight at her open pleasure. He'd never known such passion in a woman, let alone a virgin. Had she any idea how endearing he found her? Her arms reached out to him, and he knew he was lost to her. Impatiently, he tossed his own robe on the floor.

In an instant he had her in his embrace. Taggart's lips claimed hers in a long, heated kiss. His hands seemed everywhere, moving down the length of her soft body.

It aroused Millicent even more to smell the faint scent of her own body on his mouth. She pressed closer to him. The strong muscles of his chest made her nipples harden as he moved his body across hers. With a new boldness, her hands pressed along his back. She buried her face in his neck when she felt his throbbing maleness press into the fleshiest part of her legs.

"Darling *Gealbhan*," he murmured between hot kisses along her face. "My sweet, dearest sparrow. Sure and you've blazed the fiercest fire within me." He fought his own body's need once more and focused on increasing her desire so thoroughly that even if she tried, she wouldn't be able to forget the pleasure when she thought of this night. Never, he vowed, was she going to be afraid of him again.

Wanting her husband right now was almost painful in its intensity. "It's all right. I . . . I mean you may proceed now."

The corners of his mouth turned upward at her words. Even in the heat of arousal, her proper English ways influenced her way of asking for what she desired. But he would not press the point. Later, he could teach her new words to use. But there was something endearing about her ways right now. He felt her wriggle impatiently beneath him, and he could not hide his look of male triumph. But he couldn't resist prolonging the moment, so he resumed kissing her, stroking her moist, throbbing skin, while he murmured endearments in Gaelic. And when she reached out to guide him down to her, he pulled back, still wanting to be sure she was ready for their ultimate fulfillment.

"Stop," she cried out in frustration. "Why are you punishing me so, making me want you then . . . ?"

He'd wanted both of them to be positive all her fears were dispelled, leaving only her desire for him, but immediately he was sorry for having pushed her so far. How fragile she looked, he mused, tenderly brushing back a damp stand of auburn hair from her forehead. She appeared so flushed and desirable, he suddenly felt he'd be hard pressed to deny her anything. And the truth was, his own body felt ready to explode in vehement protest for his enforced restraint.

Taggart claimed her mouth with a sweet fierceness. Millicent experienced his unspoken promise that her waiting was at an end. He entered her pink flesh, but when he felt her maidenhead once more he forced himself to remain still, trying to allow his bride to set the pace.

"No," she protested, mistaken about his reason for not pressing further. "Please, I want this. I want you." She blushed at her own boldness, yet she could not refrain from begging, "Please, Taggart. Love me."

He moved again within her, his hands on either side of her head as he used his arms to keep from crushing her with his weight. "Sweeet sparrow," he rasped. "I doubt I could leave you now even if Tara's kings ordered it." He kissed her lips as he quickly thrust past her maidenhead. Then he stopped, hoping with all his heart her pain would soon recede. He felt moisture in his own eyes. "Darling, it will never hurt after this time," he said for both their sakes.

Something was happening within her. The pain had only been slight, nothing like Garnet had caused her to dread. On the contrary, as she felt him grow inside her, she found the return of earlier pleasurable sensations, including the mounting tension she'd felt when he had kissed her there. She moved against him tentatively, trying to encourage him to begin the thrusting of his hips once more. "Oh, yes," she breathed against his face when she felt him respond to her unspoken plea. She moved with him, matching each stroke with an urgent need of her own. "Taggart. Oh, Taggart," she whispered near the brink of her second release.

"Let go of yourself, darling," he coaxed, realizing he wanted to watch her take her pleasure first. "I'll catch you."

Crying out his name again, Millicent's body convulsed as the consuming pleasure coursed through her veins. It only added to her excitement when she felt Taggart increase the pace and strength of his thrusts as he followed her over the edge.

They were both breathing hard, their bodies damp from their pleasurable exertion.

Taggart came down next to her, still cradling her body protectively in his arms. It only gave him joy to realize he was responsible for her now. With infinite tenderness, he studied her face. She looked lovelier than he'd ever seen her.

"I never knew it could be so wonderful. The only regret I have," she added with an impish twinkle in her eyes, "is having waited so long to discover it. Father almost despaired of my ever marrying."

"I'm glad you are my wife." He placed a soft kiss on her cheek, surprising himself that he did feel this way. Even if he didn't love the woman in his arms, he knew he did care for her. Perhaps he would never love any woman, but Millicent pleased him. It was a good beginning.

They fell asleep quickly in each other's arms.

*   *   *

Taggart came awake first. He studied his bride's face in the faint light of dawn. When her long lashes fluttered and she looked up at him, he murmured, "Yes, I am glad you're O'Rahilly's wife." His kiss was sweet and welcoming.

She stretched, then snuggled closer in his arms, allowing him to pull the scattered covers up over them. "You're just saying that to be polite," she teased, her new trust giving more confidence to be herself. "Does this mean I'll have to wrestle the snake of Ireland again?"

"You little devil," he countered, giving her a playful nudge. "Where did you ever hear that naughty joke?" He was only half jesting, astounded that the proper Lady Fitzroy should know this ribald Gaelic story. It was a funny one but highly improper for a lady's ears and an English lady at that.

She chuckled outright. "My contact with the tenants allows me certain accessibilities. I overhear Fergus and Mr. Fogarty talking. They have no idea just how much Gaelic I understand."

He gave her a mock look of displeasure. "What a termagant my wife is turning out to be. Why, you are not a little mouse at all," he went on, laughter in his voice. "Sure and I'd think you were an Irish elf with all your mischievous ways."

This time she didn't join in his amusement. Her serious gray eyes captured his. "Well, the truth is, O'Rahilly, I am part Irish."

"What?" He laughed. But then he realized his wife was not joking.

She moved away from the protection of his arms as she tried to explain. "It happened during the time William of Orange sent my great-grandfather to Ireland. He was a widower in his fifties, a rough soldier with an eye for one of Queen Mary's ladies-in-waiting, a poor but gently bred girl of seventeen. The girl, however, did not reciprocate the older soldier's amorous attentions. But with an earldom for past military services, the king also gave him choice of bride. My great-grandmother's pleas to her father, the king and the earl himself fell on deaf ears. And when the earl was sent to put down the rebellion in Ireland, he took his reluctant young bride with him," Millicent's voice lowered. "It was in the spring when the earl had a recurring bout with gout. His own doctor hadn't arrived from London. However, the increasing pain made him order one of the local Irish physicians to attend him." Millicent wondered if she was doing the right thing, but Taggart had the right to know the truth now that he was her husband.

"Go on," Taggart encouraged, and he put his arm about her shoulders.

"My mother told me they hadn't meant for it to happen, and it didn't occur right away. But the Irish doctor was summoned more often as his treatment helped the earl. In his twenties, the Irishman was immediatley attracted to the sad, gentle Englishwoman. The Irishman found excuses to check in periodically. Once when the earl was away visiting his troops before the battle of the Boyne, my great-grandmother summoned the doctor secretly. So starved for affection, she was also instantly attracted to the kind Irishman, who was so different from her cruel husband. When the earl was killed at the battle of the Boyne, the English court mourned the general's passing, and his widow was ordered back to London where the King and Queen could protect her. When my great-grandmother found she was to bear the Irishman's child, she was frantic yet overjoyed. She knew the doctor would insist on marrying her, but if the truth were known during those troubled times her Irish lover, along with herself and unborn child might have been killed. After all, her dead husband had been a valued general, a close friend of King William and victorious against the crown's enemies, while she had betrayed them all, in their eyes, by taking an Irish lover, and a Catholic at that. There was no money of her own here in Ireland to raise the child properly alone; her own family would have disowned her if the scandal came out. Reluctantly, she went back to England. It was her plan to go quietly away, perhaps to France. However, the king insisted she would be better off under their care at court. When the King and Queen assumed the child was the earl's, my great-grandmother remained silent. The girl was born a few months later, and she secretly raised her to be Catholic. None of the women in my family returned to Ireland until I came here. However," Millicent went on, eyeing her husband with a level stare, "Father Michael baptized me years ago at my request. No male ever knew of this secret—only the women of our family, and my mother swore me to secrecy. She said I could do more good, have more influence to help the Irish if we kept this hidden."

"Then you are Irish?"

She nodded. "Yes, not only is there Irish blood in my veins but I have freely chosen to be a Catholic as well, though I must practice my religion in secret."

Astonishment etched across Taggart's features. "Do you know what Irish family your great-grandmother was a descendant of ?"

"No," Millicent interupted, never meeting the look in his eyes. "It happened so long ago, and I suppose Great-grandmother was afraid the English would harm the Irishman and his kinsmen if anyone ever learned his name."

Taggart sat silently taking in this amazing news. A part of his bride was Irish and that pleased him, but these times were just as dangerous and if the English found out—her father would probably murder her on the spot, incensed that her mother and she had deceived him. All knew of his contempt for Ireland and Irish Catholics.

The lady's husband took her hands in his, concern on his face. "Promise me you will not tell anyone else about this, Millie. Not even my ties with the King could save you from those English nobility if word got out of your ancestry. The Fitzroys in London are just as mean-spirited as your father."

"Of course. I am aware of the danger, Taggart. My mother and her mother lived with this for years, I dare say I can."

"Don't be flippant," he admonished. "It is a serious matter. I know these Englishmen here in Kinsale, and I learned their reactions to the Irish Catholic daily when I lived here. They'd not take kindly that an English aristocrat, one of their circle had—well, in their eyes and most of the Irish here you'd be seen as having made of fool of them, and one thing the stuffy English conscience cannot abide is being made to look ridiculous to the world." When he saw her lose some of her reserve, he knew he succeeded in making sure she would tell no one else this secret. The thought of what might happen to her if the English got a hold of this information frightened him more

209

than anything he'd ever experienced.

His features softened at her expression. "Well, then that is settled. Now, go back to sleep." Without waiting for her compliance, his arm about her waist brought her naked body down to his. Her back was to him, and shortly he felt her breathing deepen as she fell back to sleep. However, it was a long time before he followed. He wasn't sure if it was concern for her safety with this change of events or the close contact of her soft skin next to his that kept him awake until morning.

Chapter 15

Taggart observed his sleeping wife. She looked so sweet and vulnerable, he was tempted to hold her in his arms once more. However, he knew where that would lead, and he suspected she might be a bit uncomfortable so soon after her first time. There would be other mornings to awaken her slowly with his loveplay.

He couldn't help smiling when he recalled her passionate reaction the night before. What a complex women Millicent O'Rahilly was turning out to be.

He left their warm bed reluctantly, reminding himself he had much to attend to as the new owner of this estate.

After a hearty breakfast, followed by instructions to his valet and Colleen Mulcahy, Taggart went over to the stables.

The last thing he'd expected was to hear the usually quiet Samuel arguing.

"As if me and me brother would take orders from the likes a you."

Taggart recognized Sean Kelly's voice. When he heard the sound of a fist slamming into flesh, he quickened his long-legged stride.

"What the devil is going on here?" the new owner of Fitzroy Hall demanded. Dressed in brown breeches, coat, and riding boots, he scowled as he took in his young groom's bloody face. Samuel was attempting to rise from the hard stable floor.

When the Irishman saw Sean's older brother Patrick come from behind the wooden beam, he knew why Samuel had been bested. Fergus had told him about this arrangement of the earl's only this morning. Well, he hadn't planned to start his first day confronting old adversaries, but it couldn't be helped.

"I am waiting," Taggart pressed. He was relieved to see Samuel make it to his feet. "Up to your old tricks, I see." He eyed the belligerent faces of Sean and Patrick Kelly. "Samuel, can you make it to the house? Colleen will tend to your injuries. When you feel up to it I'd like to hear your side of this."

"Ain't no need to hear that heathen's words. He hasn't got a story," Patrick interjected.

"I don't need to wait, sir." His face contorting in pain, Samuel put a hand to his ribs. "The older one held me while the runt beat me. It seems they resented my interference. I found these two taking a whip to that old horse over there." He pointed to the chestnut stallion to his right.

"That horse is a lazy bag of bones. He's bitten my hand before." Sean's pugface appeared triumphant. "But he won't never do it again, I'll be thinkin'. Her ladyship's too soft on Star."

So this old horse was Star, the colt he'd delivered years ago. By the looks of him, Star had been on the receiving end of this cruelty before. Taggart knew Samuel ran his Virginia stables without abusing his property. These Kelly brothers had a surprise coming if they thought O'Rahilly would allow this brutality to continue. He sniffed in disgust. And if his olfactory senses were accurate, the place could use a damn good cleaning.

The taller man's brown eyes were cold when he turned back to the smirking pair. "Pack your things right now and come to *my* study for your wages. I want you both off my property by noon today."

Mouths open, the brothers gawked at each other. Patrick spoke first. "O'Rahilly, ya can't fire us, his lordship—"

"Has no further say in the matter," Taggart cut in. "I own Fitzroy Hall, with all its land and livestock, in addition to paying the wages of the hired help." Dismissing the Kelly

212

brothers from his attention, he turned back to give a hand to the injured black man.

"Samuel, I'll supply you with the names of some locals you can pick to help you run things while we're here. If you find one who stands out, we'll put him in charge before we leave for home."

"Ya haven't heard the last of this," Patrick Kelly shouted at Taggart's back. He swiped the air with his fist.

"Devil's spawn," his brother added, before he spat on the muddy ground. "You'll pay, O'Rahilly," he muttered under his breath.

Ignoring the retreating pair, Taggart concentrated on helping Samuel walk toward the manor house.

"But, sir," Samuel protested. "Shouldn't we notify the authorities. I do not like the likes of those two. That sort will make trouble, I'm sure."

His employer continued to support him as they walked. He grinned at his twenty-year-old servant. "They're just full of hot air, similar to a lot of us Irish."

Millicent came awake slowly. The storm had abated during the night, and the sun streamed through the French doors. She felt a brief disappointment to find herself alone but remembered Taggart probably was being considerate to allow her more sleep and a little privacy.

Thoughts of last evening assailed her, and she couldn't help smiling and blushing when she recalled Taggart's expert lovemaking. However, when she moved, certain parts of her did feel a bit stiff and tender this morning.

"Come in," Lady Millicent responded to the light tap on her door. She pulled the covers up to her chin.

Edna O'Rahilly sailed into the room carrying a tray of steaming chocolate and buttered toast. Dressed in a rose, watered-silk gown, she was the picture of spring radiance, with dainty pink ribbons holding her thick, curly black hair away from her face. Her smile showed the deep dimples at the corners of her mouth. "Good morning. I thought you might like some breakfast. Taggart said I was not to disturb you until you rang." She made a face and giggled, before setting the tray on the night table. "I didn't have the heart to tell him you never would dream of having poor Colleen tackle these stairs with all the other work she has to do. As if you or I ever rang for a servant in our lives. But Taggart has just hired thirty servants to work at the Hall. It will be like the old days, with footmen, parlor maids, help in the stables, laundry, and kitchen." She became more serious. "But he did ask me to remind you to engage your own maid soon. I've already got mine, one of the Kelly girls. You know the Kelly women are nothing like the father and their uncle Sean. She has a sister, if you're interested. They say she is very good, with an eye for gowns and hair arrangement. The poor thing is hardly suited to working in the fields. That's her father's doing. He's a cruel man, that Patrick Kelly. When I think of how he treats his poor wife, I—well, let's talk of more pleasant things."

Millicent couldn't help chuckling as Edna rattled on in her usual method of skipping rapidly from one topic to the next. "Yes . . . ah . . . I dare say." She felt her face flame, wondering where the velvet robe had gone. Never had she slept without garments, and it was a bit disconcerting in the light of day to be so unattired. She was relieved when Edna went automatically over to the chair and retrieved Taggart's light brocade dressing gown. However, she barely stifled a gasp when she spied her torn nightdress on the floor near the bed. Whatever would Edna think if she saw it?

Without comment Edna bent down gracefully and picked up the gown, folded it, and placed it on the chair. "How are you this morning?" she asked.

Despite her cheerfulness, Millicent saw the concern in Edna's green eyes. The Englishwoman's expression was reassuring when she answered truthfully, "I am well . . . and happy, dear Sister."

True to Edna, the shorter Irish girl bounded on the bed next to her friend in a flash. "Oh, that's grand. I'm so pleased you and my brother have worked things out."

Millicent could only laugh and manage a quick hug for her rambunctious friend. "I can truly call you sister now."

"I've missed you, Millie. It's good to be back at Fitzroy Hall.

Though my brother feels differently, I've always liked this house, the land, and Dunstan's beautiful horses. Taggart may never understand that I have no desire to leave. And I'd never be happy just languishin' on a settee stuffing chocolate truffles into my mouth; it goes against my upbringing," she added, only half in fun. Edna moved back to look at her friend. "Forgive me for bringing it up now, but have you heard any news about Dunstan?"

A little ashamed that her happiness with Taggart caused her to forget about her brother this morning, Millicent sadly shook her head. "Nothing yet. But I am sure we shall hear from Colonel Shelby soon. He wrote last month he had arranged to have an emissary sent to India specifically to find Viscount Fitzroy."

Edna tried to smile. "Would you like me to have them come in now?"

"Good Lord, who?"

"Before Taggart rode out to inspect the estate this morning, he left word that Caleb was to have the brass tub brought up here." When the taller girl said nothing, Edna spoke again. "My brother thought you might wish to soak in a warm bath after . . . I mean—"

Despite her efforts, color suffused Millicent's face. She could not comment right away. After putting on Taggart's robe, she busied herself with replacing her spectacles. It was very thoughtful of him, but his perceptiveness was a little unsettling. It made her realize just how familiar he was with a woman's body and its functions. "Yes," she said, trying to sound less embarrassed, even though Edna seemed perfectly at ease with such things. "Please tell Caleb the tub and water can be brought in now."

Just before Edna left, she asked, "Did your brother say when he would return?"

"No," the raven-haired girl answered. "But I suppose it will take most of the day to cover the estate. Oh," she added, her hand on the brass knob, "he did say he wondered if you would arrange to have your father's overseer bring him the account books to go over."

Overseer? Millicent almost burst out laughing. Obviously

Taggart had no idea who had been running this estate practically single-handed these last few years. "I shall see to it." she answered, knowing full well Edna realized the truth.

After Edna left, all humor left Millicent's features. Well, if her bridegroom was going to put in a day's work, so would she. Without hesitation, she swung her legs over the side of the bed. She looked down at the meager breakfast. Ham, potatoes, and eggs would suit her better. Had Taggart given this order to Colleen? So, he thought her the fragile Englishwoman, did he? Well, she'd have a bath, dress, and go down to the kitchen to eat her usual hearty breakfast, then it would be time to do her rounds.

"Mrs. O'Rahilly . . . I mean, my lady," Samuel amended awkwardly. "I'm sure the master will be worried." He looked up at the Englishwoman who smiled down from her sidesaddle across the chestnut filly. "And I'd be happy to have one of his men accompany you in the carriage." He eyed the sacks of foodstuffs hanging down either side of the leather saddle. "Assistance might also be required in carrying those parcels," he added in his soft-spoken, Jamaican accent.

After getting over the shock of poor Samuel's bruised face, she was certainly not sorry to hear Taggart had fired the Kelly brothers. "Thank you, Samuel, but I shall do splendidly on my own." She tried to reassure the concerned young black man. "Not to worry, for I've been doing this for years." Without another word she pressed her knees into Buttercup's flanks and they were off in a flurry.

The wedding feast had provided a higher quality of food than usual. After visting the last tenant and giving the grateful woman with a brood of children what food she could carry away from the Hall's kitchen, Lady Millicent headed back down the dirt road where her horse was tethered. Even for April, it was cold, and she hugged the worn red cloak close to her. It didn't quite reach her ankles anymore. She must ask Taggart if she could purchase a new one.

The thought brought warm images of her husband. It was pleasant to be called Mrs. O'Rahilly this morning. Lost in thought, Millicent didn't notice Annie Kelly's condition until she was upon her. Clearly not wishing to be seen, the small woman brought her shawl up over her head. Three young ones pulled at her tattered skirt, while the babe on her arm emitted sickly whimpers.

"Annie?" Millicent saw the women limp. While only two and thirty, Annie Kelly looked like a woman twice her age. A long black pipe protruded from the edge of her cracked lips. Her skin had a gray pallor, the listless eyes stared straight ahead. That she came to a stop was the only indication she'd heard Millicent call her name.

As the Englishwoman took in the discolored, puffy bruises on the frail woman's features, something began to boil inside her. She made herself take it all in—the arm not holding the baby looked broken. The woman breathed with a wheezing sound, as if the movement of her rib cage caused pain. "God's blood," Millicent swore. "Damn that Patrick Kelly."

Forcing down her rage until she could air it effectively, the taller women led Anne Kelly and her children back to their cottage. Then she sent the oldest boy on her horse for Dr. Liam Collins, with instructions to bring him back immediately. She made him take the coins in her purse to also fetch meat for a broth.

In record time the boy returned with the doctor.

"Liam, I do appreciate you coming," Millicent greeted. She told him what she managed to pry out of Mrs. Kelly. "And I thought the jostling on my horse would make it worse." The fine-boned features of her face softened when she looked up at him and read the surprise in his eyes.

"Only married yesterday—I hardly expected to see you here today." But then he seemed to catch himself from making any further intimate comments, for he turned and wasted little time in tending to Mrs. Kelly's injuries.

As was her custom when she was able, Millicent assisted the doctor. Occasionally she glanced across to watch him as he worked. Liam Collins was indeed Kinsale's most eligible Irish bachelor. Unlike his older brother, Father Mich el, Liam's features were more aristocratic—with a darker burnish to the fire in his hair, well-formed, angular face, broad shoulders and trim waist. With wit and graceful charm, many an Irish girl, even some English ladies, had barely controlled their sighs when he passed them in town.

If Liam noticed the unusual anger that sparked from behind her glasses, especially when she found out Annie was pregnant with her twelfth child, the tall Irishman made no comment.

Without squeamishness, Lady Millicent followed the doctor's instructions with the same practical efficiency she carried out her daily life at Fitzroy Hall.

"There," Dr. Collins said, after he'd set Mrs. Kelly's arm and taken a few stitches to close the wound in her right hip. "I'll be by in the morning to check on you." After he washed his hands in a basin Millicent provided, he rolled down his sleeves and reached for his dark-gray coat.

For the first time, Annie looked ready to burst into tears. "Oh, no. Best not, Doctor, for me husband might see ya, and he'd make such a fearful row. Beggin' yer pardon, but he don't believe in doctors."

Liam sighed, clearly used to the way of Patrick Kelly. "As you will, then." He held up a hand in warning. "But keep off that leg for a day or two, else you'll open the wound again."

"But me work, the children, and—"

Millicent spoke up. "Edna and I will take turns helping out here for the next few days. Lord knows you've assisted us many a time with taking in our washing."

"Oh, but your ladyship. 'Tis not fittin' for ya ta—and you just married and all—"

"Stuff. Not another word, now." Millicent studied the toes of her serviceable riding boots. Deliberately, she kept her voice casual. "Annie, could your oldest boy watch the others for about an hour? I have one more call to make, then I'll return."

Annie nodded, her bruised face showing more animation. "And Kathy, me second oldest, can watch the children at night. Why, that'll be grand. I'll be thinkin' I'm a regular duchess, bein' waited on and all." She even managed a half smile. "There is one thing . . . ."

"Yes?" the other woman encouraged.

"Bridget, me oldest girl. She's out workin' in the fields again. 'Tis fearful hard work, me lady, and the sixteen-year-old ain't as strong as the others. Edna took Caren, and the girls have always been close. Miss Edna, she said I was ta ask if ya wouldn't mind takin' Bridget, if you needed a maid. Oh, she's a good girl, your ladyship," Annie went on in a rush. "She can fix hair, and she knows how to stitch, and she's clean. Father Mike got a few of the English ladies ta lend him some of them fancy sketch books from London. Why, ya should have seen Bridget studyin' 'em, and she can copy the gowns and styles just like a London seamstress. And—"

"I'm convinced," Millicent interjected with a laugh. "Please tell her to come to the Hall when you can spare her." She'd seen Bridget here before and had liked the girl. And Annie was right; Bridget had been ill many times with chest colds for the last two winters. That grueling outside labor would kill the girl if she kept it up. And it seemed Taggart wanted her to have a maid.

Outside, Liam turned his head to watch the woman walking beside him. When he adjusted the leather satchel containing his medical supplies over the front of his saddle, he assisted Lady Millicent in mounting her horse. "You would not care to tell me where you are headed, my lady?"

She adjusted her skirt to accommodate the sidesaddle. "I would not."

Dr. Collins looked up at the Englishwoman. "For a woman of only two and twenty, you have a seasoned English dowager's ability to put a man swiftly in his place."

"I dare say," she replied, with a saucy smile. "I learned at a young age to look after myself. But I thank you, Liam, for your interest. Rest easy, for I know what I am about. Besides," she added, lowering her gaze. "What could a mere woman do? The Kelly brothers hardly did a tolerable job running our stables, and many a time I've noticed one or the other is nowhere to be found. Patrick Kelly is probably with your brother at his prayers right now."

"Prayers, is it?" The doctor clearly bristled with disgust. "More than likely Fogarty's Pub."

Sitting gracefully atop her horse, the Earl of Holingbrook's daughter appeared pleased. "Thank you, Liam. With so many taverns in Kinsale, it would have taken most of the day to find him."

"You tricked me!" Liam Collins shouted, clearly more angry at himself for being duped so easily. He glowered up at the bespectacled Englishwoman. "Lady Millicent, Taggart O'Rahilly had better have all his wits about him, for you'll soon be managing his life before the poor sod realizes it."

"I shall do my best." She giggled openly with self-satisfaction.

"But," the doctor added with affectionate exasperation, "sure and he'll be liking it, too, I imagine."

"I dare say," she replied, with mischief in her smile. "And a good day to you, Dr. Collins." Without another word, she turned Buttercup around and started toward the town at record speed.

"But my lady. Wait. Come back here—at once I say!" Liam Collins' clear voice rang out down the mud covered road. "Damn fool woman!"

An old farmer passing by minutes later sidestepped the angry young man who stood in the center of the road shaking his fist and yelling at no one in particular.

"A bit early for the bottle, young Collins," the old man admonished as he walked past the Irish doctor.

"Damn it," Liam roared. "I have not been drinking." He stormed back to his own horse. "But you've given me one bloody good idea." He grasped his horse's reins and swung up. "Hang it," he muttered again. He had Mrs. Hogan's baby to deliver. He couldn't go after her, and stop her. "Oh blast it."

Her cloak still around her, Lady Millicent entered Fogarty's Pub quietly. The late-afternoon sun streamed through the only window. She looked up at the ceiling. Like many a thatched cottage, this place probably leaked when there was a good rain. The air was heavy with stale pipe smoke and spilled ale. But the rumbling sound of male voices stopped abruptly when they spotted the figure of a women—a sacrilege in this male sanctuary.

She pushed back the hood of her faded red cloak. Keeping her eyes straight ahead, the Englishwoman walked directly over to the wooden bar.

"I am here to speak with Patrick Kelly," she stated in her no-nonsense tone.

Fogarty, the round man in his sixties who owned the bar, looked horrified. "God in heaven, me lady, ya shouldn't be here. Where's that husband of yours ta allow ya ta—"

"My husband is inspecting the estate this morning." She paused as she tried not to lose her nerve. "Circumstances, Mr. Fogarty, have left me little alternative." She glanced about the sea of unfriendly male faces. "As soon as I speak to Mr. Kelly, I assure you I will depart without fisticuffs."

"Well" came a gruff voice behind her. "And what might ya be wantin'? Come to beg me and Sean ta come back?"

She turned quickly, chin pointed up. "It is not your work or Sean's at Fitzroy Hall that I am here about."

"Hah. As well I know, for me and Sean kept his lordship happy with his horses." The huge man smirked, puffed out his wide chest and looked at his companions. "And the earl himself so glad ta hire us, after his former groom run off and all, without even so much as a 'kiss-me-arse.'" Ignoring Millicent completely, the burly Irishman addressed his friends, who now crowded about him. "Sure and didn't I tell me own brother, Sean, me boy, ya can't never trust them O'Rahillys. Just see how long the new owner lasts. The earl will have that O'Rahilly out of the mansion quick enough."

Despite her attempts at self-mastery, anger made the delicate feature of her face turn pink. But refusing to give an inch, she craned her neck to meet the Irishman's mocking features. "I have spoken to you about this before with little success. Today I have come here to order you to cease beating your wife. Annie is not able to stand up for herself. Without parents or brothers, she is alone in Kinsale. This abominable treatment must cease immediately."

Millicent glanced around the room once more. "And I wager I am not the only one well aware of your bullying ways toward your wife. However, today was the worst, especially since she carries your next child in her belly. Why . . . a dog's a

221

better mate."

The broad face of the man in his late thirties turned scarlet. He raised a meaty fist and slammed it full force upon the edge of the wooden bar. Pieces from the curved front molding shattered to the floor. "Nobody tells Pat Kelly what ta do," he bellowed," least of all a scrawny, pasty-faced English spinster, who only got married because the O'Rahilly lusted after Fitzroy Manor."

Prepared, Millicent reached into the folds of her wool cloak.

When the others saw the pistol, many began backing away. Only Mr. Kelly stood still, a belligerent scowl on his face. But there was a hint of unease in his puffy eyes.

She cleared her throat, ready to speak in a manner the man before her would understand. "If you ever lay an angry hand on Annie Kelly again, I swear I'll blow your Irish cock off." She aimed the pistol at the threatened area.

An audible expression of male shock reverberated about the room, clearly not only as result of this English lady's actions but also her uncharacteristic, coarse language.

"You'll not get away with this." Kelly took one pace back, unable to hide the sweat that popped out on his brow. "I'll have—"

"I am the Earl of Holingbrook's daughter," she countered, forced arrogance emanating from the steel of her eyes. "You could do nothing, Irishman, as well you know."

The truth of her words clearly hit Kelly harder than any blow to his midsection. But a new emotion entered his eyes. "Devil's bitch," he swore.

Aware that she was close to winning, Millicent pressed further. "I'll have your oath, Kelly. Though you've little scruples, I know a sacred oath upon your mother's name in front of all these witnesses will bind you. Swear that you will never beat your wife again."

His lips clamped shut, and Patrick Kelly folded his brawny arms across his chest. Strands of close-cropped hair stood out on one side.

"A pity," Millicent replied. "However, I think Annie will be better off as a widow." With both hands, she began to squeeze back on the flintlock of the pistol.

"Jesus, she's gonna do it!" cried one of the men as he ducked behind the bar.

As the seconds went by, the odor of unwashed bodies and fear permeated the small tavern.

"All right, damn your eyes, I swear," shouted Kelly. "And may ya burn in hell, ya she cat."

Instantly, the lady lowered the heavy pistol. Without hesitation, she slipped it back into the folds of her cloak. "Thank you," she added, all mannerisms of the polite, well-bred lady in place. The tension had affected her also, and she brushed aside a strand of her straight auburn hair that had come away from the upsweep at the back of her head.

The barkeeper mopped his brow with a gray rag. "Best be careful puttin' that weapon away, me lady. A cloak's no place for a loaded pistol."

Lady Millicent rearranged her frames to a more comfortable position across the bridge of her slender nose. It was her turn to look cocky. "Since it contains no ball or powder, sir, I scarcely see the danger."

"What?" roared Patrick Kelly. "Ya mean ta tell me ya never—the cursed thing wasn't even—?"

"She's got ya there," shouted the older man who now came out from his crouched position behind the bar. "And there was Kelly himself," the man guffawed, "standin' up, ready to piss his britches off."

Boisterous laughter shook the oaken walls of the old pub.

"And ya gotta keep yer word, Kelly," another chuckled, "for we all heard ya take the oath." More laughter. "And," added a third scruffy young man, "wouldn't we be comin' after ya if ya break it."

Patrick Kelly's eyes glowered with hatred, for it was clear what this Englishwoman had done to him in front of his mates.

Millicent did not share in their laughter, especially when she read the promise of revenge in her adversary's cold blue eyes.

"No woman makes a fool of Patrick Kelly," he said under his breath, before storming out, slamming the door behind him.

"Please," the auburn-haired woman shouted, holding up her hands to the other men at the bar. "Be silent, please." It took a few moments for the din to settle down.

223

"Most of you know me," she began in a softer tone. "I have a favor to ask you today."

She lowered her hands to her sides. "I have come to regard Kinsale as my home. But the favor I ask is this: Please, for Mrs. Kelly's sake, do not tease Patrick about today's events. No," she added, waving away their protests, "I know a little about your ways. I'll leave, and tomorrow the story will be about the town that Kelly was bested by a woman. Please," she entreated again, "it will only go worse for Annie. You are plain-speaking men, I know, but none of you has ever beaten your women, not this way." Her control slipped as tears misted her gray eyes. "If my actions resulted in your joking about today, can't you see a whiskey-soaked Kelly taking his anger out on his wife?"

"The lass speaks the truth," old Fogarty interjected, wiping his hands on his leather apron.

"Yes," added another from the side of the bar. "I've known Kelly all me life, and 'tis a fearful temper he has."

After a few moments, the little man who owned the bar acted as spokesman. "We agree to be silent, my lady." Fogarty's expression dared any of his patrons to disagree. "And if any of ya ever wants a drink in this pub again, he'd best agree, or I'll be havin' Father Collins read his name on Sunday next."

Suddenly the wooden door of the tavern crashed open.

Frantically, Dr. Collins scanned the room. "Good God, have you killed her?" he cried. Then he groaned with obvious relief when he spotted the tall Englishwoman standing unharmed in the center of the dimly lighted room. In such a hurry to get here, he hadn't even put on his tricorn hat or coat. He looked uncharacteristically disheveled with his neckcloth askew. "Come, Lady Millicent," he said on a ragged breath. "I shall take you home now."

Liam noticed the looks of admiration on the faces of the men who now cleared the path for the young woman.

"We agree, my lady," Liam heard the men murmur as she moved past them.

"Thank you. Indeed, I am grateful, gentlemen." Millicent's affectionate smile came easily as she left with the Irish doctor.

Chapter 16

"You mean to tell me she went out alone, without so much as a groom?" Even a Virginia lady, Taggart mused, would never go out riding such a long distance without a maid at the least.

Edna did not look upset. "But Millie always goes out on Sunday afternoons like this."

Taggart was beginning to see just how unconventional his wife and sister's lives had become these last few years. "But isn't she usually back by dusk?"

Edna's green eyes showed wariness. "Well, it's only a couple of hours later than usual. But I'm sure there's an excellent reason. She plays with the Kelly children and talks to old Mrs. O'Hara, and—"

"Kelly?" Taggart cut off, not liking the sound of this. And he'd just fired both brothers this morning.

"Why, yes."

Without another word, Taggart rushed to his stables, intent on saddling his horse to make a hasty ride to town.

And the hour it took him at breakneck speed from Fitzroy Hall did nothing to allay his fears. He was shaken by the recurring vision of his bride lying facedown in some peat-strewn bog with her slender throat cut from each delicate little ear. There wasn't time to analyze why he felt this strongly about his wife's safety. He only knew he had to reach Kinsale before nightfall.

*   *   *

As they walked toward their horses, Liam shook his head at the woman beside him. "My lady, please be more careful in future. The Kelly brothers have long memories."

Heady with success, Millicent smiled at her friend. The dimming sunlight could not hide Liam's handsome features. She took in his white neckband and gray waistcoat. "I considered my strategy before acting, Liam. And you have to admit it went well." The lady was reassured when she heard her companion chuckle. She touched his arm briefly in a reassuring gesture, then said, "Now, please put your coat on. Kinsale cannot afford to have its ablest doctor come down with the ague."

After Dr. Collins did as she suggested, he reached out to assist the Englishwoman with her horse.

"But I was relieved when you showed up," she confessed, holding on to his shoulders as he settled her on Buttercup's back. "Thank you for coming to my rescue."

Clearly, he wasn't aware that his hands still lingered on her slender waist as he looked up at her. His voice was gentle when he added, "I've always found it easy to care what happens to you, my lady."

From a few feet away, O'Rahilly sat atop his black stallion, Laidir. His initial inclination was to bound off his horse, race over to his unharmed wife, and smother her with warm kisses. However, his brown eyes narrowed when he took a closer look at the picture before him. The good doctor had lifted Taggart's wife with a practiced ease that proved he'd done this service before. Damn it, he fumed, there was no need for Liam to keep his hands on his wife—she was already on the blasted filly and needed no support. His fingers tightened on the leather reins in his hands as he attempted to suppress his vexation. He'd been out of his mind with worry for her safety and—of course, he was pleased to be her first lover. But just what other services had this Irish doctor performed for his wife?

"Oh, Taggart," Lady Millicent greeted with warm surprise when she glanced up to spot him a few feet away. She felt Liam's hands move from her waist. "Edna told me you would not be back until late. How nice of you to join me."

"So it would seem." The words snapped out of his tightly compressed lips before he could bridle them.

Millicent looked puzzled, for she could not understand why her husband should look so cross. Had someone blabbed already? "Now, Taggart, you must know I should never make it a practice to frequent Fogarty's, but this was a necessity."

Her husband blinked as his strong emotions careened up a steep curve in another direction. "Am I to understand, madam, you spent the afternoon in a pub?" He saw the doctor's shoulders shake, which did little to ease his attempt at a practiced English reserve.

Oh, bother, she hadn't meant to tell him, especially since he obviously hadn't known about the matter. But then what had made him so cross? Oh, of course. The answer hit her when she saw the frothy sweat on the black stallion he rode. Her husband was a ship's captain, used to a rolling deck beneath his long legs. And he'd been all day on a horse. She gave her husband a sympathetic look. "It was of no consequence, and I have seen to the matter," she dismissed, with a graceful sweep of her gloved hand.

From atop Buttercup, O'Rahilly's wife looked down at the doctor. "I am confident Liam would not mind taking a look at you, and I'm sure he has something that could relieve your discomfort," she added, trying to assist her proud husband over the delicacy of his condition. Sensitive practicality seemed called for here, she mused, congratulating herself on being able to deal so successfully with her new husband.

"What the devil are you babbling about?" Taggart looked clearly at the end of his patience.

His wife began to feel a trifle miffed by his tone. After all, she was only trying to spare him any embarrassment. It hardly seemed logical to suffer when a remedy was available. She suddenly wondered if the years of Virginia polish had gone so deep that he'd never admit to needing assistance. "I thought Dr. Collins could give you some salve."

"Salve?" her husband echoed, looking across at her as if she'd taken leave of her senses. "What in bloody hell would I be wantin' with salve?"

Oh, this was quite intolerable, she thought in exasperation. "To relieve your difficulty," she tossed back. "It occurred to me that you may not be used to so many hours' riding, and . . ."

His dark brows rose with comprehension, but it did nothing to improve his mood. "My lands in Virginia are three times the size of this estate," he grated. "I am quite accustomed to the feel of a horse beneath me. What I am not used to is having my wife traipsing about Ireland alone doing her philanthropic work at Fogarty's Pub."

Millicent read the amusement in Liam's eyes when he looked up at them with the eager anticipation of one enjoying an evening at a London opera. Her chin lifted. "My day was busy, also. Since you saw fit to work today, I thought it best to carry on my usual activities. You needn't sound so testy."

"Testy, is it?" Much of Taggart's cultivated speech hurtled to the brogue side. "If I'm testy 'tis more than likely because I returned home to find my bride missing."

"Stuff," Millicent countered in a disdainful voice. "I wasn't missing. You make it sound as if I were a crate of limes misplaced from one of your ships."

"*Dailtín!*"

It did not sit well being called "brat" in front of the Irish doctor, and the Englishwoman's chin moved higher. Unfortunately, the position caused her to lose sight of her husband's quick actions. With an outcry of surprise and indignation, she felt herself being hauled unceremoniously off her horse.

Taggart didn't give his wife a chance to move from his grasp after he placed her scoffed riding boots on the dirt road.

"Sir, your gratitude is beyond measure," she hissed. "And after I'd only sought to relieve your discomfort."

"The discomfort I feel," he countered, giving his wife a shake that made her frames rattle on her nose, "would be relieved by finding my bride at home in my bed where she belongs."

Her husband's blatant words caused Millicent's face to take on a reddish hue. And she felt his loud baritone voice must surely have carried throughout Kinsale. Sensitive to his touch, she knew Taggart had lifted her off her horse as if he had every right to the action, as if she was his . . . his property. The thought made her squirm to be free of his grasp.

"Steady, Taggart." Liam came around to stand next to Millicent, all traces of laughter having vanished from his angular face. "The only transgression her ladyship may have done is perhaps been a little rash in defending those less able."

"I require no outside assistance from you, sir, in handling my wife." His clipped speech was back in place, and his tone was scathing as he looked at the man he'd once played with as a boy.

After his curt dismissal of the doctor, the black-haired man glared down at his wife. "Just what were you doing at Fogarty's?"

"Tossing back a few pints and learning a few tavern hymns for the choir," she snapped. His rudeness to dear Liam still irritated her. "And you'll be happy to learn I've hired a maid."

"Old Fogarty himself, no doubt." The fight in those gray eyes behind her glasses suddenly touched something deep in his memory, and he loosened his hold on her. How, he wondered, had he ever thought this girl was meek and shy? She appeared ready to lift her fists in a boxing stance to go another round. It had to be her Irish blood, he mused but grinned despite himself.

Liam looked pleased with Taggart's reaction. "Well, it looks as if my services won't be needed after all. So, it's good night to Mr. and Mrs. O'Rahilly," he finished, before he mounted his horse. "Why don't you finish this argument at home where it's more confortable?" His laughter could be heard for a long time after he rode away.

They took their time riding back to Fitzroy Hall. To Taggart, his wife seemed strangely quiet and subdued. He put this down to fatigue, and therefore he made no effort at conversation. Explanations would keep until morning. He was confused by his own feelings—he'd never met anyone who could instigate such volatile feelings in him and with such rapid changes.

* * *

229

Taggart certainly had a myriad of moods, his wife mused as she pulled up the embroidered sheet and coverlet. Millicent heard the muffled sounds of her husband and Caleb, his valet, in the next room. It was obvious he followed her lead in taking a bath before retiring. The sloshing water and his voice rang out as he sang a few snippets of an Irish melody. He seemed frightfully pleased about something. Well, she concluded, it was best to be grateful he was no longer miffed at her, thus saving her any need to explain her day's actions.

Glancing about the room, she took note of the added new wardrobes, the lovely upholstered furniture that had arrived while she was out today. When she'd peeked in her sitting room opposite their larger bedroom, she couldn't hide her pleasure at seeing the new smaller bed, writing desk, and settee. And the predominant color was yellow, Millicent's favorite. It was wonderful to see the renovations begin on Fitzroy Hall. And despite her father's obvious dislike of her husband, at least the earl was keeping more to himself these days. Of course, she thought, it was unlike Geoffrey Fitzroy to be so passive. Was he plotting trouble for his new son-in-law? She made a mental promise to speak to him in the morning to see how he was faring under these sweeping changes.

Lady Millicent got out of bed and put a lacy dressing gown about her mauve-colored nightdress. She had found her wardrobe filled with new clothes when she'd returned tonight. Taggart was very nonchalant when she tried to thank him for his generosity. It seemed to embarrass him, so she reasoned he didn't like a lot of fuss.

It was now clear Taggart took longer at his bath than she did. Therefore, she decided to go down to the library for a book. Before she could reach the library door downstairs, her new maid, Bridget, rushed over.

The shorter girl was too thin for her sixteen years, but she was pretty. With brown hair and blue eyes, she looked like Annie must have appeared in the bloom of her youth, thought Millicent.

"Oh, your ladyship, I was wonderin' if I should disturb ya." Bridget held out a folded sheet. "Me and the other servants were having our supper and a gentleman came ta the back door. All dressed in black, he was and wouldn't come in. He asked fer me. Imagine me?" Bridget's light blue eyes rose in fright. "I wouldn't a gone, but he said it concerned your ladyship. His voice was gravelly, like he had a scarf across his mouth. He handed me this and told me ta give it ta no one but her ladyship."

Millicent smiled and took the note. It was probably a thank you from one of the tenants or an anonymous request on behalf of a too-proud friend. "Thank you, Bridget."

"I didn't read it, my lady."

"I know you didn't," Millicent sought to reassure the worried girl.

She scanned the brief note. Why . . . it appeared to be Dunstan's writing:

> Dearest Sister, if you wish to see your brother alive, come to the house just off the Teran Road outside of Kinsale at one this morning. A Franciscan nun, Sister Alice, will assist you when you arrive. Ask her to take you to Captain Bembridge, whom you met once through your persistent and most cherished endeavors to rescue me. We owe the Captain my life. Tell no one and come alone or I'm a dead man. I will explain all when we meet tonight, dear Millie. Dunstan Fitzroy, April 20, 1749.

The scrawl gave evidence he'd had to write it hastily. Her eyes misted. Dunstan had come home at last. But why the secrecy? Her brother must be in danger, else he would never ask her to do this. And was he gravely ill? She studied the small map he'd enclosed, showing her directions to the unfamiliar place. Even at a fast clip, it would probably take her over two hours to get there. Color drained from her face when she looked down at her maid. "And the stranger who gave you this would not give you his name?"

"No, my lady. Is it bad news? Did I do wrong in givin' it to you?"

Millicent forced a calmness she didn't feel into her reply.

"No, Bridget, you did exactly what I would have wanted."
Instantly, she started to work on the difficult plan to leave the house in secret. "Bridget, there is one favor I need from you."

"Anything," the girl replied, affection for her mistress showing clearly in her young face. "Why, after all you've done for me and my family, why I'd die fer ya."

Millicent smiled at her maid's loyalty. "That will not be necessary, but please tell no one about this message you have delivered to me."

"I will do as you say, my lady."

There wasn't a moment to lose. Therefore, Millicent dismissed her maid, telling her she would not need her any more tonight. "And I've told Colleen you are to have free run of the larder whenever you wish."

"I'll weigh another stone if Colleen doesn't stop trying to fatten me up with her excellent cooking." The maid returned her ladyship's smile, then curtsied before going back to the servant's hall.

After reaching the top of the stairs, Millicent said a silent prayer when she spotted Caleb. Casually, she called his name.

The black man looked clearly ill at ease. He focused his gaze over the top of her head.

Instantly, Millicent remembered that she was dressed only in her nightdress, slippers, and robe. Even though everything was covered, she realized Taggart's proper Jamaican valet probably thought it scandalous for the lady of the manor to be dashing about the house so attired. "Ah, I . . . you have been with my husband for a number of years, have you not?"

"Yes, my lady, five years."

Why did this man make her feel like an awkward schoolgirl? "It occurred to me that it might assist me in keeping my husband's schedule smoother if you could enlighten me about . . ." Get on with it, she prodded herself. "How long does my husband usually take with his bath and such?"

Caleb's features relaxed. He seemed clearly pleased that the new mistress was trying to help his employer. "He usually takes at least an hour. Once he told me he enjoyed a good soak because as a boy there was only cold water hastily fetched in a

232

wooden—" The black man seemed to catch himself. "I beg your pardon, my lady, I meant no criticism. Mr. O'Rahilly had confided he worked for your father, and—"

"I do understand. Thank you, Caleb." She quickly returned to her bedroom. Thank heavens Edna had retired for the night. She dashed to her adjoining sitting room and shut the door. So, Taggart would be occupied for at least another half hour. When she saw her old wooden trunk had been moved down to their suite of rooms, she almost shouted for joy. Now, if she hadn't lost her ability to climb trees all would be well. Of course, she hated not leaving any message, but there was no choice. Her brother's note was clear—secrecy was imperative for his safety. Explanations simply had to wait until morning.

A few hours later, Lady Millicent was nearing the road indicated on the map. Dressed in Dunstan's old breeches and coat, with her auburn hair pinned up under the felt tricorn hat, she knew her countenance resembled a reedy lad. There was no moon tonight, and while it assisted in her escape, it had made her ride here more scary. Having never ventured this far from Kinsale, she was unfamiliar with the terrain. Once when the road was more twisted and rocky, she'd almost fallen off Buttercup. It made her wish for an instant she'd asked Taggart to come, too. But just as quickly she chided herself. How could she risk her brother's life by telling anyone? Was Dunstan wounded or on some secret mission for the King?

She sighed when she spotted the candlelight from the large structure ahead. This four-story brick building was more a mansion, not a small family home as she expected here in the woods. Now, if only Captain Bembridge would be waiting for her. Obviously, there was a party here this evening, for she saw the line of carriages in the long drive.

After a few anxious moments, Millicent decided to slip around the back gate. With nothing about the house except dense forest, no wonder she'd never heard of this place before.

After tying Buttercup to the low-hanging branch of a nearby tree, Millicent walked up the cobblestone path to the rear entrance.

A burly servant answered her knock. Dressed elegantly in

black velvet and white gloves, his face looked the opposite of gentility. " 'Ere," he said in perfect Cockney, "I told you boys to stop pesterin' us. The ladies don't cotton to a beardless lad without coin."

What ever was this man talking about? "Excuse me, sir," she tried, lowering her voice with a cough. Realizing her English accent might give her away, she added an Irish lilt to her speech. "No need ta disturb the family's party. Sure and I was told ta ask fer Sister Alice so she could take me ta Captain Bembridge."

The name seemed to strike a chord, for the giant opened the door wider and grinned. "Well, why didn't ya say so?" He eyed her up and down. "You must be a new one. Most of the captain's guests usually come to the front door. 'Es busy upstairs, but the good sister will know what ta do with ya." Then the Englishman laughed heartily, as if he enjoyed some private joke.

Millicent had no choice but to follow the servant down a long corridor. She heard male and female laughter coming from various rooms along the way. There were certainly a lot of rooms. Why, even Fitzroy Hall didn't have all these separate entry doors.

"Sister Alice," the man called. "It's arrived."

Millicent could not hide her surprise as she took in the beautifully dressed woman. "Sister Alice?" she squeaked. This was no gray-robed nun.

"Yes," the bejeweled woman replied. Taking charge with a pleasant smile, she directed, "Follow me. Captain Bembridge will visit you shortly."

Left alone, Millicent sat on the wing chair "Sister Alice" had abruptly indicated before she left. Glad for the chance to rest, the Englishwoman leaned closer to the fire to warm her shivering body. Everyone had a right to their own decor, but she decided this elegance was a little too overstated for her taste. Red drapes, upholstery, along with a red-and-gold rug was just a little overdone. Stretching her legs out in front of her, she hoped the captain would not keep her waiting much longer.

Concern for Dunstan made her more impatient as the minutes ticked by. She got up and walked back over to the door, deciding it was time to find the captain on her own.

Millicent tried the brass knob, but with a start, she suddenly realized it was locked.

Chapter 17

After vigorously scrubbing his body with a large beige sponge, Taggart slowly got out of the oval brass tub. When he put on his velvet dressing gown, he was instantly aware of Millicent's faint lavender scent, which still clung to the material from when she'd had it about her. He smiled as he inhaled her fragrance. Strange, he thought, mocking his own feelings as he vigorously toweled his shoulder-length hair. He'd promised himself to have a firm talk with her tonight, including a command that she take her maid or Edna with her when she went out from now on.

Yet, here he was musing about her pleasant charms instead of scolding her. But, he admitted, it was a good sign when she agreed to allow him to pay one of the sturdy lasses in the village to help Anne Kelly, instead of going herself, but why were Millie and Edna so secretive about everything?

All during his bath Millie had played about his thoughts. The expression on her face when she smiled, the searing, moist feel of her body when he'd made love to her throughout the night, and the impudent challenge in her smokey eyes when she refused to be cowed by his temper—never had he expected to be drawn to her this way. His thoughts of her right now were anything but complacent. It did please him that part of her was Irish, but he quickly realized her lineage made little difference in the way he was beginning to feel about her. He did desire her; the tightening in his body right now pressed that message home to him. And this time, there would be no pain for her, just pleasure for both of them. He pictured her waiting apprehensively for him. Poor sparrow. Perhaps her demure attitude on their ride home meant she was afraid of his retribution for her outburst in front of Dr. Collins. Taggart's features softened. How sweet and vulnerable she could be. Her dealings with her father and Edwin Somerset must have made her wary of men. And, he reminded himself, she did need time to get to know him, then she'd be reassured. He would take her in his arms and allay her fears, and then make sweet love to her. His pace quickened near the door to their bedroom.

"*Gealbhan?*" he called softly as he opened the door to their large bedroom.

However, when he saw their massive empty bed, then walked into her adjoining sitting room, he began to feel the hint of unease.

And after he searched the length of the upstairs, Taggart realized he was going to have the humiliating task of asking his servants, for the second time in one day, just where the devil his wife was.

Aroused from sleep, both his sister and his groggy-eyed house servants adamantly denied his accusation that they were keeping something from him concerning his wife's whereabouts. Still dressed only in his hastily tied robe, Taggart saw Bridget, his wife's new maid, quake as she kept her eyes lowered. He wasn't a bully, he told himself, and he didn't want to frighten children. He tried to modulate his tone. "All I wish to know is if her ladyship may have mentioned some urgent appointment." The blankness of their expressions unsettled him. "God's teeth, I know she couldn't possibly be curing hams or putting up jellies at this ungodly hour. Now, has my wife been acting peculiar lately?" As if the brat didn't usually act different from most females he'd known, he shot back at himself.

Colleen Mulcahy adjusted the nightcap tied under her chin, then gave her employer an open look of censure. "My lamb is a proper lady, and if she did leave the house, 'tis me own opinion she was forced to it. The girl was awfully quiet tonight when I served your supper in the dining room. 'Tisn't like her not ta talk to me and Fergus." There was a compressed set to the old woman's lined lips. "Sack me if you've a mind, but I'll say me piece. Did ya thrash the wee lamb then, ya lumberin' brute?"

The man towering over Mrs. Mulcahy appealed heavenward for patience but it wasn't forthcoming. "I've never beaten a woman or child in my life," he answered, his voice rising an octave. "And that includes yer wee lamb, who on our wedding night, I might add, cuffed my jaw so hard my teeth rattled." Hands on his hips, he walked up the line of standing servants as they stood condemning their employer with their morose faces. It was more than clear to O'Rahilly they blamed him for Lady Millicent's odd behavior of late. "You'd think I was an ogre because I used . . . unusual methods in showing Lady Millicent it would be in her best interest to marry me," he directed to no one in particular.

His impish sister looked ready to burst into peals of laughter. "Oh, Taggart, of course, we all know you are not a beast. And Caleb was just snuffing the candles, so he would have heard someone leaving by the front door. I'm sure Millie is about the house, perhaps in the wine cellar . . . reading. Why, she'd have to be a bird to leave without going throught the door."

Her playful teasing had the opposite effect on her brother. He was thinking about his name for her, and it trigged a vision from the past. The window. She'd probably climbed down that blasted elm tree.

Still in his bare feet, his chest hairs glistening with moisture from the recent bath, Taggart O'Rahilly let loose a string of Gaelic words he hadn't used in years. Ignoring the gaping mouths and looks of astonishment at such coarse language, he stormed back up the stairs, clattering the door on its hinges with the force he slammed it.

Colleen Mulcahy turned to her husband. "Well, she's done it this time." All present heard the thumping about upstairs as their master hastily dressed.

In riding breeches and unbuttoned linen shirt, Taggart bounded out of the room to shout down over the marble banister. "Caleb, have your brother saddle the fastest horse in the stables. Laidir isn't up to another ride tonight." Then he popped back into the bedroom to finish dressing.

All the while he thought of a slew of things he was going to do when he got his hands on Millicent. Was this her way of getting even with him for yelling at her in front of Liam Collins? And with everyone in bed, the little minx had slipped out the window. But where would she go? he demanded, stomping on his black riding boots. Half in irritation, partly from fear, he grabbed his leather satchel and stuffed some bandages, ointment, and a flask of brandy into it, then slung it over his shoulder.

When he heard the sound of someone walking past the door, the tall Irishman raced to it, silently hoping it was his wife who had come back after a brief pout in the cellar or an attic room.

"You needn't glower at me, O'Rahilly, just because I came up the back stairs. I haven't brought a woman with me." The Earl of Holingbrook staggered to the right. "I've been out with a few friends." He tried to straighten his coat in an obvious attempt to appear more sober.

"Have you just come from Kinsale?" Taggart couldn't hide the anxiety from his voice.

The earl nodded, with a silly grin. "And a pleasant time I had with a lovely young thing; she had breasts the size of ripe melons."

"Did you see Millicent on your return?" Taggart moved closer to the earl.

Geoffrey seemed to enjoy the implication of his son-in-law's question. "Heard about her little encounter at Fogarty's. Fool girl should know secrets can't be kept by an Irishman in his cups. Kelly was more than happy to spill his guts to me and Nolan. But I told him you were the master now." The earl's sarcasm matched his gesture when he swept Taggart a courtly bow. The effect was lost when he just missed tottering over after he lost his footing.

Taggart's arms steadied the rotund man, but he was in no mood to tolerate the earl's usual baiting. "Where is my wife?" he demanded.

"So, she left you again, did she?" Clearly, the earl enjoyed this tidbit so much he failed to pay attention to the cold look in his son-in-law's dark eyes. "Seems you're having a spot of trouble keeping your bride satisfied. Have you thought about hiring help? I'm sure the good doctor would gladly offer his stud services. Irishmen are usually short of funds, don't you know."

With a low growl, Taggart had his hands about the earl's flabby throat. "If you value your next breath, you'd better tell me where she is." His voice became more menacing when he added, "God knows I've reason enough to kill you after what you did to my father."

"Taggart!" Edna raced up the stairs. She pulled at her brother's hands, begging him to let the earl go.

From far away, Taggart heard his young sister's pleading. Contempt in his obsidian eyes, he pulled his hands away.

Less belligerent than before, the earl rubbed his bruised throat. "Well, what the devil are you all gawking at?" he damanded of the servants who stood below stairs. "Damn me, haven't the lot of you anything better to do than stare at your betters? All this silliness over Millicent."

Not waiting for an answer, the earl turned back to his son-in-law. "I didn't see the chit. God's nightshirt, how should I know where she is? Why not ask Dr. Collins where your wife is?"

"No." Edna placed herself in front of the earl when she read her brother's intent. "Can't you see he's just goading you? He doesn't know where Millie is, either. Oh, Taggart," she added, fear in her green eyes, "what if Millie is in trouble or hurt somewhere?"

His sister's concern mirrored his own, though he tried not to face it. It was easier to blame his wife for her defiance rather than think about the uncomfortable alternative. God, he thought, for the second time she'd done this to him; she would kill him with these fears for her safety. He ran an anguished hand through his disheveled black hair as he watched the earl make an unsteady retreat to his rooms at the end of the hall.

As he led his sister back downstairs, Taggart forced himself to appear more calm. With an apology for acting like a lunatic in waking them out of a sound sleep, he then advised his sister and his servants to go back to bed. Covering his own fears, he told them his wife had probably ridden to one of her Irish tenants after their lover's quarrel this afternoon. "And you know newlyweds always have certain adjustments to make with each other," he added as they left the room. Then he headed toward the study.

The fire still blazed in the marble fireplace. He tossed the leather pouch on a nearby chair before going to stand in front of the double doors on the left side of the room. The signs of spring were hidden by the night and his worried state. He placed his aching forehead against one of the cold glass panes. Did she hate him so much that she preferred the danger of riding on these roads alone at night rather than share his bed? Was she afraid to face him after their argument? But her response last night and later when they'd talked—how could he have been mistaken about her? These thoughts saddened him, causing him again to question the wisdom of having forced her to marry. Would it ruin both their lives?

Lost in his troubled thoughts, Taggart was ill-prepared when the glass shattered above his head. In a reflex action he ducked to the floor, thinking someone had fired a shot through the glass doors. And, he thought with disgust, here he was without sword or pistol, presenting a perfect target in the well-lit room.

In only seconds, Caleb was at his side, assisting him to rise. "Master O'Rahilly, sir, are you all right?"

Taggart felt the left side of his forehead, where the missile had grazed him. There wasn't any blood, but the lump forming hurt like hell when he touched it. "Nothing broken. A good thing it hit my head or there might have been serious damage," he quipped.

The Irishman shook his head and got to his feet, then rushed back to the glass doors. He flung them open and felt the cool air strike his face. The sound of hoofbeats in the distance made him realize the nocturnal visitor would be long gone before he could catch him. He looked about the floor, then spotted the stone under a tea table. There was a mud-stained note tied to it. The unfamiliar flourishes resembled a woman's hand:

An unwilling wife pays her husband back in kind. If you seek your English bride, ask Captain Bembridge at Mistress Alice's.

241

It was unsigned. He placed the paper closer to his nostrils and inhaled. There was a faint scent, perhaps from the garden. He couldn't place it, but . . .

"Sir?" Caleb questioned. "You look ready to drop. Perhaps I should send for a doctor.

"No," Taggart said, the word coming out in a rasp. "Have you asked Samuel to ready that horse for me?"

"Yes, sir, but won't you want some of us to go with you?"

The thought of witnesses sickened him, "Certainly not." His refusal was adamant, without the usual politeness he used with his servant. "I will be ready in a few seconds. You may go, Caleb."

"Yes, sir," Caleb answered with more reserve. "Shall I have one of the men nail some canvas over the opening in the door, until we can have it repaired in the morning?"

"Yes, of course," his employer answered absently.

Alone, Taggart walked slowly back to the fireplace. The earl's study suddenly mocked his presence, reminding him he was an intruder, a usurper in this English domain of Ireland. He put the note in the flames, wishing he could blot out the words and their implication as easily as the parchment scorched to ashes. Why was he always such a gullible fool where Millicent was concerned? But whatever began to hurt inside, he suddenly buried with brutal force, replacing it with the new reaction he felt for his wife's actions this night.

Quickly he rose from the leather wing chair. Was she hoping to humiliate him in front of English and Irish alike? Was her need for revenge so limitless? His earlier anger returned to give him the impetus for action. By God, he'd bring her back, dragging her by that auburn hair of hers if necessary. There was more of the Earl of Holingbrook in her after all. Well, an Irish groom would teach an Englishwoman to be a proper lady. Willing or not, she'd soon learn what it meant to be his wife.

Taggart bounded to the stables without a word of explanation to anyone.

No wife of his would spend the second night of her marriage at Mistress Alice's. It might be the most opulent place in Ireland, with clientele boasting the cream of His Majesty's

242

officers, but it was still a bordello and no place for O'Rahilly's wife.

When Taggart saw all the carriages and horses outside Mistress Alice's, he realized this was going to be harder than he'd anticipated. The place was swarming with redcoats. A colonial, and an Irishman to boot, wasn't going to be able to sashay in, collect his recalcitrant wife, and leave. He spotted Buttercup tied to a nearby tree. His lips formed a grim line. All during the hard ride here he'd secretly hoped she wouldn't be here, that it was only a mean-spirited joke she'd played on him after writing the note herself, and he'd find her back home asleep in her sitting room. But the truth was forced upon him. "Damnation," he muttered under his breath. Had the reckless hoyden merely come to such a place out of pique, without any thought to the danger?

Aware that he'd need a cool head to untangle them from this quagmire, O'Rahilly stalked cautiously through the tall shrubbery as his mind formed a plan. Bending down, he rubbed some dirt into his immaculate shirt, breeches, and coat, loosened his hair from the ribbon at the nape of his neck, and tossed off his tricorn hat, before grabbing the leather satchel across his saddle. Next, he strode purposely to the front door, praying to all the saints he could pull this off. Then, by God, he'd wring that English brat's scrawny neck.

It was Mistress Alice herself who answered the door. Taggart was suddenly relieved he only knew this place by reputation, not practice, for it gave him the anonymity he required.

He made a formal military bow and emulated the proper British tone expertly. "Your pardon, ma'am, but I have urgent dispatches for Captain Bembridge."

The woman in her forties was still handsome, with honey-blond hair and merry violet eyes. "But, sir, where is your uniform? How do I know you are not a French spy?" she teased but gave no appearance of alarm. She smoothed an imaginary wrinkle from the skirt of her gold silk gown. Her eyes moved along his physique. Then something else seemed to occur to

243

her, for she frowned. "You're not one of those Irish fanatics, are you? Just last week one of them almost shot Colonel Shel—" She caught herself, clearly not wishing to divulge one of her patron's identity. "Well, no harm was done and the officers shot the fool Irishman. He's buried in my rose garden," she added with undisguised glee.

"No, madam, I am not a fanatic. But with these Irish rebels about and highwaymen on the byways, my superiors felt it wiser for their courier to carry such important papers under the guise of a nonmilitary person. I've ridden hard from Cork."

All contrite, she mewed, "Poor man. Do come in. You must forgive me for being so cautious," Mistress Alice continued, "but these outbreaks of Irish rebellion cause me to pine for my old house in London. But we must go where our duty lies," she added, before taking his arm. "You will find the captain upstairs, last door on the right. Oh, and I would advise you to knock first. The girl with him is shy."

With a swish of her silk skirts Mistress Alice went past him, her well-endowed form making contact with the front of his body. He was prepared when she turned her head coquettishly to wink at him. His answering smile of appreciation seemed to reassure her.

However, when she was out of sight, he wasted little time in heading up the carved wooden staircase. The few sconces in the corridors, he knew, were deliberate and not from any lack of funds. Few English officers wanted their identities bandied about, especially if word filtered back to their wives. He knocked softly, then once more when there wasn't a response. Something knotted in his guts. Would his wife be in there?

Taggart heard a woman giggle. Then a man's high-pitched voice called out, "Dash it, this room is occupied. Please go away."

The Irishman cleared his throat. "I'm sorry, sir, but I have urgent dispatches from—" Hell, he thought, who the devil can they be from? "From Colonel Shelby," he added, tossing out the only English colonel he'd once met at Sir Arthur's home.

"Oh, confound it. All right, just a second."

Taggart felt his breathing return to normal when he realized Shelby had been a lucky guess. When the door opened, he moved swiftly into the room and closed it.

"Well, what is it? You!" Bembridge accused when he clearly recognized not a fellow officer but the colonial, that irritating gnat for Garnet's affection from the London party only months ago. But any call for help was silenced when his intruder shoved him against the wall.

"All right, Bembridge, where is my wife?"

"I don't know what you're talking about," the English officer squeaked.

"The Earl of Holingbrook's daughter, Lady Millicent," snarled the intruder.

The captain's playmate cried out in Gaelic.

He couldn't deny being relieved she wasn't Millicent. Taggart reassured the young girl automatically in their native tongue, and she looked down at the wooden floor. Color washed over her face when she discovered the stranger was also Irish. Well, Taggart thought, he wasn't here to lecture an Irish girl on the morals of abetting the enemy for profit. A pretty Irish lass could make more money here than digging the roots as a farmer's wife. He returned his attention to Bembridge by tightening his hold on his neck, only to realize the overpowdered, painted officer was telling the truth. The stark fear in his eyes could not be faked.

A knock at the door and Mistress Alice's voice startled the Irishman into a desperate move. He saw the frightened captain open his mouth to cry out, but Taggart cut him off with a right cross to the Englishman's jaw. Bembridge hit his head on the thick edge of a wooden chair on his descent to the floor.

The captain's feminine companion screamed alarm, but Taggart's warning look silenced any further hysterics.

"Captain," Mistress Alice called from the other side of the door. "Is something amiss? are you all right, Lisette?"

"Answer her," Taggart commanded in a whisper.

The young girl gulped, then did as told. "Yes, ma'am. I am unharmed."

"Yes, quite," Taggart added, mimicking the captain's speech expertly. He looked down to the man at his feet. "Sink me, I tripped over the cursed chamber pot." The female laughter on the other side of the door told him his mimicry had not aroused her suspicions.

"Your little surprise is getting impatient downstairs. Milo tells me she is making a rowdy fuss in the anteroom. Your men have already paid me for arranging this birthday gift for you, but do you wish us to send her away? My other guests are asking questions about the noise she is creating."

He crouched down quickly and was relieved to feel a steady pulse at the officer's throat. But he'd be out for hours. Now what? He looked down again at the man, whose height matched his own. Of course, Bembridge had blond hair and was pouchier about his soft middle, but a bit of padding might pull off the deception. He eyed the wooden box on the nearby table. Such a fop, it was true what he'd heard in London. The captain went everywhere with his powder, cosmetic box, and patches. "No, please don't send my gift away," he answered in Bembridge's high-pitched voice. "I shall be downstairs presently to collect it."

When he heard Mistress Alice's footsteps as she went back down the hall, Taggart tossed off his coat. "Here," he directed to the wide-eyed girl who now had a thin wrapper about her nakedness. "Help me get his clothes off, then we'll hide him under the covers."

After he was dressed in Captain Bembridge's uniform, Taggart stared down at the make-up kit with undisguised revulsion. But there was no help for it now, he told himself. He cursed his rashness in giving the captain a facer to silence him. With a groan, he sat down at the mirrored dressing table and reached for the wooden blockhead to take off the neatly powdered white wig. As he adjusted his own hair under the wig with the rolled curls on each side, black satin bow in back, he spoke to the Irish girl. "We both know you're not French and Lisette isn't your real name. The truth I need is whether you've bedded the captain before?" There was no accusation in the question, but he saw the girl look guiltily down at her bare feet. She nodded.

"I've reason to believe someone I care about is being held here, most likely against her will. Now, you can help me if you tell me some of the captain's mannerisms and the way he puts this abominable muck on his face. Please. I won't be able to pull this off without your assistance. I've only met the fop once. Will you help me, a fellow countryman?"

The girl's features softened, and she smiled, exposing the gap in front where two teeth were missing, not an uncommon sight for a poor girl in these parts. 'Sure and I'll be glad ta help ya, for you've a kind face. Besides, the gold piece ya give me will pay for . . . for me assistance," she added, with an impudent grin.

More than half an hour later, Mistress Alice saw the captain saunter down the shadowy stairs. "Well, I am glad you finally came out. Pray forgive me Captain, but I have never known any man take so long at his toilet, save you. Only your generosity refrains me from giving you a stern lecture on punctuality." She raised a finger to him playfully. "But where is your courier?" she asked with a squinted look behind him.

"Gad, madam, I couldn't pry the rutting whelp from Lisette." Looking bored, Taggart reached into one of the pockets of his scarlet coat and gave the proprietress a handful of coins. "That should more than pay for the girl's extra duties."

The woman took the coins with a satisfied smile. "As always, Captain, you are generous."

"It's part of my nature, madam, along with taking the time necessary for proper grooming. Sink me," Taggart mimicked the captain's manner, "quality takes time, don't you know?" He eyed the woman up and down, using the quizzing glass attached to an elaborate gold fob on his military waistcoat. "But I should feel positively naked without face and hair adorned according to fashion. I may not be in London, m'dear, but that is no excuse to let myself go to seed."

The dimly lighted room showed little chance for any escape except through the way Lady Millicent had come in. And the locked wooden door wasn't going to give way. Her shoulder ached from the hard shove she'd tried a moment earlier. "Look here," she shouted for the fifth time, "open this door. Immediately, I say!"

"Quiet. 'E'll be down in a minute to take care of you." Then there was boisterous laughter.

Millicent compressed her lips when she recognized the voice

of the man she had heard called "Milo." "My brother is an officer, and I'll have him clap you in irons," she countered, even though the rising din probably made it impossible for anyone to hear her. "He'll have your guts for garters," she hoisted for good measure.

On the other side of the door she suddenly heard approaching sounds of more rollicking males. Probably boozy in the bargain, she fumed. With only the small amount of light coming from the dying fire, she felt her way farther into the room, intent on finding something to use as a weapon. God, it was like being back in her old room at Fitzroy Hall, with her father's drunken guests stumbling their way into her bedroom. A pity, she thought, in her rush to get here, she'd forgotten to take her unloaded pistol.

Then her hand clamped about a heavy brass candlestick. She raced back to the front of the room and hid herself beside the closed door.

Taggart hadn't expected the six other men to accompany him after Alice had gleefully handed him the key to this room. In various stages of undress, the officers were drinking and spouting lurid jokes as they ushered him to collect his birthday present.

"It cost us a lot to find a lass willing to hide her charms in boy's clothes for your special treatment," said a lieutenant, before he tilted back a wine bottle and took another swallow. "Alice said none of her ladies were willing to do it. Had to give this girl's father the price of a good hunting dog, but the greedy old fellow wasn't hard to convince. We know you have a penchant for Irish girls, and we made sure this one was clean."

Taggart felt someone clap him heartily on the back. "Well, lads, I think I can handle things from here," he said, in an attempt to get them to leave. But it was now clear these rowdy sots wanted to stay and watch the show. There was no choice now but to proceed in this charade. After turning the brass key in the lock, he stepped into the room. The entourage followed.

It was dark and his eyes took a second to get accustomed to the unfamiliar surroundings. The Irishman couldn't call her name, for he was supposed to be Captain Bembridge. God, he thought, had she discovered the truth of this place and killed herself rather than face dishonor? His frantic musings were cut short when he felt a body hurl itself at him. Just in time, he grabbed a pair of upraised hands and applied enough pressure to cause his attacker to drop the weapon. The heavy object thudded to the floor.

This little struggle seemed to delight the other men. "Best be careful, Bembridge, these Irish girls can be dangerous." The man who spoke went over and retrieved the candlestick, before making his way to the fireplace. He lighted the candle from the drying embers and brought it over to the man struggling to defend himself from his feisty birthday present.

"The old buzzard didn't say anything about her wearing spectacles. Well," one of the younger lieutenants went on, "you can always take them off if they bother you, sir."

In her fear and anger, Millicent had forgotten to imitate an Irish brogue. Her clear English voice rang out when she shouted at her assailant, "Unhand me, sir. You have clearly made a grave error." She followed her command with a rousing kick to her captor's shins.

Still in control of his role, if nothing else, Taggart stifled what he wanted to yell and tightened his hold on his spitfire of a wife. "Now, now," he admonished in Bembridge's insipid tone, "Pwease don't be frightened, m'dear. Captain Bembridge will take care of you, there's a good girl." He grunted when a bony elbow crashed his ribs but forced himself to smile at his rapt companions. "Everything's splendid here, gents. I mustn't keep you from your own pleasures, delightful chaps, and thank you so much for the gift. It's better than a tea cozy."

Bawdy guffaws rattled the small room. But Lady Millicent saw little cause for amusement. The added candlelight afforded her a slightly clearer view of her captor. Never, she thought, had she seen such a pompous, overdressed, rouged creature. "Gift?" she almost screeched. "How dare you! I am no man's plaything—least of all to a sissy-faced boob like yourself. What did you do, fairly drown yourself in violet water?" she scoffed, hoping this new tactic would end his obvious intentions. However, when the clownish fop didn't release her, Lady

Millicent resorted to her earlier physical defenses.

"Begging your pardon, sir," interjected a rotund soldier in his fifties, "don't you think she might be a little too much for your . . . delicate nature?"

More masculine laughter.

"Nonsense. I enjoy viragoes." But another low grunt escaped O'Rahilly's heavily rouged lips when he felt her land a fist to his midriff. "She does that very well, doesn't she?" he asked, the air of empty-headed joviality coming with more effort this time. Out of the corner of his eye he saw the Englishwoman raise her right fist once more.

Ready this time, Taggart bent down and easily hoisted the outraged woman across his left shoulder. Clasping her booted legs to his side with his left arm, he used the other to press her upper body down across his body.

The wind was knocked out of her with the force which she landed across the officer's scarlet military coat. Painted milksop he might appear, she fumed, but his upper body was as hard-muscled as any laborer on her estate. She tried twisting and lifting her body upward but found she couldn't move, let alone get a deep breath of air. For a captain in His Majesty's forces, this officer had the manners of a Bow Street bully. When her tricorn hat flew off, her upended position caused the pins to follow suit. The straight auburn hair fell across her face, shutting out even the view of the floor. "Captain Bembridge," she whimpered, "I cannot breathe." Instantly, she was grateful to feel him slacken his hold on her. However, the blackguard still kept her in this humiliating position.

"But, sir," commented the young officer with the candle as he came closer to his superior. "I'm familiar with the Irish manner of speech. This girl doesn't sound Irish. I think she's—"

"Just imitating her betters," Taggart cut off. "There now," he simpered to the girl hanging facedown across his back. "We'll have none of your antics. Besides, I like the way you Irish girls speak—so lilting, so sweet. Damn it, if you clout me just one more time, I'll—" He caught his slip and pretended to clear his throat, then smiled with strained affability at his comrades while he retightened his grip on the bundle of fire in

250

his arms. "Thanks ever so much, lads. Don't let me keep you from your own pleasures upstairs," he tried again.

All but the candle-holding officer seemed ready to leave. Taggart then realized the young man's eyes were riveted on his wife's upended derriere. Dunstan's old coat had flapped up her back, exposing her encased lower charms to all present.

"Cor, what a nice tail she's got. I can see why you like these young girls in their tight breeches." The officer reached out a hand, clearly intent on touching the artwork he admired.

Taggart moved back a pace out of the other man's reach, trying hard not to show his outrage.

Twisting her upper body, Millicent could never remember feeling so indignant in her life. "You call yourselves officers? Why, you're nothing but a herd of randy mules, not fit to wear the King's uniforms."

The Irishman groaned inwardly when he saw the faces of the men turn ugly at this "Irish" girl's dressing down. They came right back to join their companion in the center of the room.

The large-bellied soldier muttered, "Here now, Bembridge, I think you're going to need our help taming this one. And I like an Irish lass with a wide seat. Gives a man something to hold on to during the ride. And this one looks like she bucks."

Quickly, Taggart thought of what Lisette had told him, but he winced when he realized his proud wife would never forgive him for what he was about to do. But, he mused, she had only herself to blame.

O'Rahilly ran his right hand slowly across his wife's firm buttocks, first one round cheek then the other, then across her hips, outlining every curve and separation with unhurried ease. "Well, sink me, the little baggage is my present. Don't you think I should have her first?" In correct anticipation, he increased his hold on Millicent, even though he doubted she was now able to breathe properly both from rage and the strength of his arm. But he could take no chances.

Unhurriedly, the Irishman fondled and stroked his wife's firm, round backside once more. When he glanced back at the men, he breathed a sigh of relief. The audience appeared more than satisfied with the show. Their intent on violence had changed to a glassy-eyed stare of arousal. "Well, it's way past time for my evening pwayers. Beddie bye for us," he told his birthday present. "And you men, I know, will want to see the ladies upstairs."

Other pressing things clearly on their minds, the six grinning officers left quickly.

When they were alone, Taggart leaned down and none too gently deposited his wife's booted feet on the carpeted floor. "For such a gentle creature, Millie, you've the strength of two scrapping Irishmen."

Millicent blinked, initially unable to take in that the man scowling down at her was her husband. She could not find her voice until he'd locked the door and lighted two more candles.

"Taggart?" She gaped at his appearance. More unfamiliar than the British officer's gold braid and red uniform was the flower-shaped black patches on his cheek and indentation at his chin, the white powder on face and wig, along with a nauseating stench of violets that clung to his skin and uniform. But when she saw the furious expression in his dark eyes and heard his low voice once more, she knew the man was indeed her husband.

But her relief was too overpowering to be cowed by his anger. "Oh, Taggart," she cried, rushing to him, "I'm so glad you came to rescue me. How did you know where to find me?"

His arms rose automatically to embrace her, but something triggered his memory and he stepped back. "We will discuss this later. Right now we've got to get out of here." He turned his back on her coldly and proceeded to the window, opening it quickly. "I'll go first, then catch you. This should be less of a climb than your escape out that blasted tree at Fitzroy Hall. Perhaps you'll set a new trend and we can do away with the front door," he growled in derision. "Come along. Be quick about it."

Reading the state of his emotions, Millicent nodded and silently did as commanded.

However, when they neared their horses, she stopped, a look of horror marring her features. "Oh, Taggart, we have to go back. Dunstan is in there." She made a darting motion to turn around, but two bands of steel halted her instantly.

"No. You're even more a fool if you think I'll allow you to

enter that place ever again."

Her struggles became more frantic. "But my brother is in there. The note said—"

"Then it was a lie, you little idiot."

"No, it was Dunstan's handwriting. Let me go."

"It was a clear forgery, that's all." Out of patience with her, he snarled, "Damn it, your brother is dead!"

Chapter 18

Never had Taggart meant to tell his wife this way. Something replaced his earlier feelings when he saw the haunted look in her large gray eyes. "My lawyer, Ben Abrams, has the letter from India. I'm sorry," he added, reaching out to hold her.

But Millicent moved away from him. The truth pushed aside all the hope she'd clung to these last few months. Tears swam before her eyes when she thought of her tall, gentle brother. And dear Edna. This would be a mortal blow for her.

"How long have you known?" she demanded when she could speak.

"Months."

"Why did you wait so long to tell me?"

He shook his head sadly. "Things have been so unsettled between us. The time never seemed right, and I thought to spare you as long as I could. Come, I'll take you home."

After he went over to help her mount Buttercup, he said nothing when she stepped away from his bent knee and cupped hands. He watched her jump up on her horse unassisted. That straight profile. Yes, he mused, her English upbringing again—to bear all without emotion. A pity she hadn't remembered it earlier when she'd pummeled him with her fists.

"But I have the letter from Dunstan right here," she pressed again, reaching into the folds of her brother's old gray coat. She handed it down to Taggart.

He moved back, trying to capture light from one of the black iron lanterns which lighted the cobblestone driveway to the house in the distance. It was definitely not the same hand on his note. "As I said, a clever forgery."

"But that . . . that Mistress Alice. Upon my honor, she is no gray-robed nun, or it is certainly an order I've never encountered."

"Because in coarser circles, my innocent wife, nunnery is another name for a brothel. I'm sure the fellow and his accomplice worked together. I was sent a warning that my chaste little bride was cuckolding me at this . . . establishment."

"Oh, that is monstrous! I would never do such a thing."

"When my temper cooled, I realized you would not. Honor goes deep in you, my lady," he added with more gentleness.

The Enlishwoman lowered her gaze. Then it was becoming clear someone wished them harm. But why? "It . . . it was quick-witted of you to think of imitating Captain Bembridge. How did you convince him to agree to your deception.?" When she saw her husband's arched eyebrow as he smirked at her, she realized he must have used a more physical argument. "Oh, I see."

"Yes, hellion, you do see. Now, we're going home."

"But I still don't comprehend why this happened," she stubbornly went on. "I cannot inherit Fitzroy Hall, and Dunstan was my father's only male heir. Besides, the Fitzroys don't own the estate now. Why would anyone play such a cruel joke on us?"

"I don't know, but perhaps from now on," her husband advised as he mounted his own horse, "if either of us receives any future messages we'd better tell the other. First a pub, then a brothel." He moved his horse close to hers. "I can only wonder, madam, where next you'll fly off to without using the brains God gave you."

In answer, Lady Millicent tossed back her tousled auburn mane, but there were tears in her eyes. "I dare say, another wife would have suited you better." Then she led Buttercup back in the direction of Fitzroy Hall.

Despite her attempts, Taggart knew his wife was grief-stricken about her brother's death. He was tempted to force

255

her to accept the comfort he wanted to give her instead of hiding her feelings behind that stubborn English reserve.

The urge became even stronger when he watched ahead to see her rein in her horse to give money to an older farmer who was dragging his reluctant daughter up toward the house they'd just left. His wife thanked both parties but told them the girl's services would not be required. By their looks, Taggart knew the coins Millie gave them more than compensated for any inconvenience. His lips quirked upward at the dressing down she gave the father for even considering the sale of his daughter "for such indecent purposes."

But after they were alone once more, just as Taggart was about to end the physical distance between them, he stopped when she turned about. That look separated them far more than paces in a road. Sadly, he knew she would accept nothing from him. He let her proceed, staying just far enough behind to keep a close watch on her safety. But he'd never forget the strain in her smokey eyes as she clearly fought so hard to keep the tears at bay. He tightened his hands on the leather reins. Why wouldn't she let him help her?

As he rode his horse through the still night, the Irishman couldn't hold back a heavy sigh. They were both too exhausted to talk tonight. He'd give her the time and privacy she obviously desired to work out her grief. But later, he promised himself, he had to set down some rules for this headstrong wife. He wasn't a snob, but by hell, he couldn't allow her to go traipsing about Ireland at all hours of the night alone. And damnation, what was she doing in Fogarty's Pub, anyway? What would she be like in Willamsburg? he wondered. Probably gallivant up and down the banks of the James River and badger the Royal Governor to instigate reforms for poor orphans.

"But she has been cloistered in her room for two days." Taggart looked across the table at his wife. "She won't come down to meals, and I heard her crying again last night when I passed her door. Dunstan was your brother and my friend, but why is she so completely devastated by this news?"

256

"Edna is young, but it will take her time to get over this shock." Millicent pushed her chicken in cream sauce to the side of her plate. In truth she had little appetite, but she felt Taggart's behavior the last few days warranted her support. He never mentioned the other evening after she explained why she was in the pub, nor had he protested when she left each night to sleep in her adjoining sitting room. He seemed to understand her need to be alone. But a small part of her began to wonder if he was actually relieved to have his bed to himself.

Behind her wire frames, she watched her husband. He held the crystal stem gracefully in his fingers, while he studied the dark-red liquid, his thoughts obviously on something else. He was dressed in dark-blue coat and breeches. The white of his ruffled shirt and lighter waistcoat accentuated his tanned skin. Unconsciously she bent closer to the table, enjoying the opportunity to study his handsome form unobserved. She breathed in the faint scent of the spicy cologne he wore.

The Englishwoman glanced down at her new frock. As yet her husband had not commented on her choice to wear one of the lovely gowns he'd given her, but she had seen the appreciation in his eyes when he held her chair tonight. And dear Bridget had done magical things with pinning up her hair. The girl was a treasure, Millicent decided.

She now realized Edna had never told her brother about her feelings for Dunstan. Well, she would honor Edna's wishes. There was no point mentioning it now that Dunstan was dead.

"What did you say?" Taggart saw his wife's anguished face and thought she was about to speak, but then his voice seemed to cause her to suppress something.

He looked closer. The emerald-green gown complemented her coloring, he thought. Perhaps he might ease her thoughts to something more pleasant. "You should dress in these vibrant colors, not those pale shades in fashion for the ton's Englishwomen of London. Their ways do not show you to the best advantage."

"But I happen to be one of those Englishwomen."

He hadn't meant to make her defensive. "You're not like them at all. Edna was right in that."

The servants weren't about so she decided now was the best

time to make something clear. She set the silver fork down across her china plate. "You had better know this, Taggart. I am proud of my heritage—both English and Irish, and I offer no apology to anyone for it." The wooden legs of her brocade-covered chair scraped against the wooden floor when she pushed herself from the table.

"Oh, no, Millie, you're not running away this time." Scowling, Taggart bounded after her. "It's more than time you learned you can't just toss your shells at me, then retreat in a cloud of haughty English ice."

Millicent increased her pace to avoid her husband's outstretched arm.

However, she had just placed her green satin slippers on the first stair leading to the next floor, when she and Taggart heard the commotion in the hallway.

Fergus was shouting and Colleen shrieked in Gaelic, while Caleb tried to restore some order.

Instantly, Millicent and her husband raced for the front entrance hallway.

Shocked, the auburn-haired woman stopped a few feet away from the man standing near the door. Dressed in white wig, scarlet uniform, carrying a curved wooden cane, stood her brother. She mouthed his name but no words came out. She clutched her hands in front of her for support.

As if any further movement on her part might send the unbelievable vision away, Millicent felt rooted to the spot. "Dunstan? Oh, is it really you?"

"Yes, Millie." Despite the haggard appearance of his thin face, he smiled. "What? No hug from my favorite sister?"

Tears swam before her gray eyes as she raced to hug him before another moment slipped away.

Colleen wiped her eyes on her apron. "Blessed Mary, the young master is home." She smiled and leaned against Fergus' supporting arm.

Astonishment crossed Taggart's rawboned features when he realized Dunstan was alive. Then he had the taller man by the shoulders as emotion gripped him also at seeing his longtime friend alive after so many years. "We thought you—my reports from India said you'd perished at the siege of Pondichery."

"And so I nearly did. The monsoon forced Colonel Shelby to call a retreat. Unconscious from a ghastly blow on the head, with a festering ball in my leg, I was left for dead in all that mayhem. If one of the natives hadn't experienced a twinge of remorse when he saw I was alive after he tried to rob me, I might never have seen Kinsale again. Later, when I wasn't delirious with fever, I learned my rescuer's name was Kumar, and he'd hidden me in his village so the French soldiers wouldn't find me. Even stained my face with musk. Came awake dressed in rags with a cloth wrapped about my head like some exotic turban. You wouldn't have known me, Millie."

Taggart knew Dunstan's joviality came with difficulty. And when he felt the taller Englishman lean against him, he wasted little time clamping a firm arm under his arm for support.

Millicent took his lead and supported her brother on the other side.

"I had to come home," Dunstan tried to explain. "Gave my doctor the slip, but the voyage from London tired me more than I thought."

"Words will wait," O'Rahilly cut him off. He continued leading the ill man toward the stairs. "I'll have Samuel send for Dr. Collins. Mrs. Mulcahy," he called over his shoulder, "can you please get the viscount's room ready?"

"Oh, that I can, sir," she answered. And Fergus followed his wife's bustling form up the stairs, while Taggart and his wife moved slower to allow Dunstan the time he clearly required.

Millicent called down to Caleb. "Please bring my brother's portmanteau and . . . walking stick."

There was a sardonic twist to Dunstan's lips. "Might as well call it the cane it is, for I believe it will be an extension of my right leg from now on."

Millicent bit her lower lip. "Well, we'll face that later. Right now I want you to go to bed. I'll bring some food up to you presently." A look from her husband made her stop to give her brother a chance to catch his labored breath a second time.

Her smile was nervous. "Oh, and I think you should know

259

I'm married now—to Taggart," she added, waiting for her brother's astonished reaction.

However, Dunstan's gray eyes crinkled at the corners. "Finally," he stated with a chuckle. "Edna and I always knew you were meant for each other." He turned to his right to grin at Taggart. "What made you discover at last that you were in love with my sweet sister?" Delight at the news showed on his drawn, pallid features.

Millicent looked down to study the embroidered red rose on her slippers. How could she inform Dunstan her husband did not love her? Or the method of their marriage? Good Lord, how could she tell her protective older brother that?

She was saved from this task when the door of Edna's room opened.

Millicent did not miss the way Dunstan's eyes sparked when he saw Edna O'Rahilly.

Shrugging off the arms that assisted him, he limped over to the shorter girl.

Dressed in a ruffled nightgown and wapper, she looked even more petite. And Edna's eyes were puffy and red from days of sobbing.

Disbelief washed over the Irishwoman's face. "Tag'— Taggart said you were dead, " she whispered. She gripped the large brass doorknob as if to steady herself.

"There were times when I thought I'd never see the sweet dimples in your face again." The tears in Edna's eyes matched his own. "My doctors thought I'd never survive the trip back from India," he mused, a tortured look in his gray eyes. Instantly, he had his arms around the smaller girl. He nestled his nose in her black curls. "Oh darling, don't you know I'd even come back from hell to have you?"

Millicent smiled through her own tears as she watched the lovers kiss. But when she happened to glance at Taggart, all joy left her delicate face. It was clear he'd never expected his sister to feel anything but friendship for Dunstan.

The black-haired man frowned, then stated curtly, "Edna, the viscount must be tired. We should all take our leave so he can rest." Without waiting for anyone to comment, he turned and headed back below stairs, leaving Dunstan in the care of the women.

An uneasy feeling began forming in the pit of Millicent's abdomen as she watched her husband descend the staircase.

"Well, Dunstan, these last few days have done wonders for you." John Nolan looked sideways at Edna O'Rahilly. "And from what I hear the man has you to thank, eh, my dear?"

Edna blushed and smiled at the handsome older man. She noticed that Marigold, Nolan's wife, the earl, and Millicent were also looking happy. Only Taggart frowned and looked away at the squire's comment. "You are kind, sir, but I believe Viscount Fitzroy has his stable of horses to thank also. Spending the afternoon helping Samuel," she teased, "has put the color back into his face. Sure and I think he'll make a fine groom someday."

Though she was convinced Edna had said these playful words with the best intention, Lady Millicent saw her brother wince at the words. Was he remembering that he was no longer the heir to Fitzroy Hall? The title of earl would someday be his, but that was all.

Dressed in a new suit of brown clothes, Dunstan cleared his throat, then smiled at the woman he obviously adored. "The lady has performed a miracle, John. Though I shall always walk with this blasted thing," he added, looking down at the straight mahogany cane with the carved gold handle. But he appeared resigned to this part of his future. "However, I do have many things to be thankful for."

Marigold Nolan's pale face appeared strained as the silence in the dining room lengthened. "I believe Mrs. Mulcahy has outdone herself tonight, though I cannot bring myself to spend so freely on culinary items. One meal and it is gone. The pheasant was excellent, though, and what ever was that delicate seasoning she used in the potatoes?" she asked, clearly to fill the gap in conversation.

Geoffrey Fitzroy snorted. "Delicate seasoning? You must be shamming us, Marigold. It's onions," growled the earl.

261

"Confounded stuff gives me gas." He took another swallow of port, then wiped his greasy lips on the crumpled linen napkin he'd stuffed under his chin. "Heard about that demonstration in Cork, Nolan?" He took another generous swallow of liquor.

"Yes." Nolan shook his head. "Tragic business. They say women and children were hurt in the scuffle."

"A little too fast with their bayonets," Dunstan complained. "When will the King learn he can't change these people by brute force?"

Ignoring his son's comment, the earl added, "They say Kinsale is next."

Looking aghast, Millicent blurted, "Oh, surely not, Father. The people here have always been—"

"They're ripe for it," her father cut off. "They pelted my landau with rotten vegetables just yesterday when I was returning from Somersets'." As if the others at the table were not sufficiently impressed, the rotund man repeated, "And rotten, mind you, not even the decency to use fresh. The stink of it. God's blood, it took that Samuel fellow a whole afternoon to scrub the leather seats."

At the other end of the table, Taggart gave his father-in-law a level stare. "Starving tenants can ill afford to waste fresh food on such a hopeless case."

The earl's jowls moved up and down in agitation. "I don't think I like your tone, sir. You may own this house, but my son and I are still in the peerage book and His Majesty's loyal subjects. As all here should be," he added, defying the other guest to say otherwise. "You best remember that if you hope to keep your thriving shipping business in the Colonies. I still have friends in London who would put a word in King George's ear if I requested it. All that wealth you enjoy in Virginia, mind you, results from that favor of King George. See that you stay on his good side. I can warn you from experience, crossed, His Majesty is a formidable enemy." The earl jabbed his finger toward the end of the table. "And George of Hanover doesn't have my forgiving nature. So be warned."

First left then right—Millicent saw the set expressions on her father and husband's faces. Even though it was proper for her to sit directly opposite her husband at the other end of the

262

table, by choice she sat at her husband's right. She'd asked Taggart not to embarrass her father by having him vacate his usual chair at the head of the table, and to her relief, he'd agreed, if reluctantly. But she read the warning signs when the coldness entered his brown eyes.

"I . . . I have often thought your experiences in America could teach us in Kinsale how to live with our Irish tenants," Lady Millicent tried. Her gray eyes pleaded with her husband. This small supper had been to celebrate Dunstan's return, and she did not want it to end in a political quarrel.

For a reason he could not explain, when Taggart read the entreaty on his wife's expressive face, he relented. "Well, many countries are represented in Virginia. Though practicing Catholics are still not welcomed by Puritans in New England, for the most part, in Virginia people have managed to carry on their daily activities without slitting each other's throats."

Grateful for his acquiescence, Millicent gave her husband a dazzling smile. "I do wish you could talk with some of the more moderate English and Irish representatives, like the Duke of Montrose and Liam Collins. Don't you think that would help, John?"

For a few seconds John Nolan looked ill prepared for her ladyship's question. Then he gave his hostess a condescending smile. "If you are present, I am sure men would not think of fighting, my lady."

"Thank you. How gallant you are, dear John. And Edna and Marigold could surely help, too."

Edna nodded her eager assent.

"Well," Marigold said, "if I am strong enough and it will not be too expensive, I might be able to assist."

The earl saluted his daughter with his third glass of port. "And this place needs to have dancing and music in it once more. Been too long since we had fun here—high time I'd say."

"Oh, yes." Millicent turned back toward her husband. He gave nothing away in his face. "Please Taggart, let us have a party. And we could have extra food so the tenants could share in the feast. Oh, do say yes, for I feel it would help ease the strain between Irish and English here. We could be a peaceful

263

example to Dublin and Cork. If the King hears of this, perhaps it will soften his resolve to send more troops to Ireland. Please, Taggart."

The Irishman thought for a few moments. It just might help to bring some of these more moderate Catholics and Protestants together at a festive occasion. Good food and wine, with lovely ladies. Who knows? he mused. "All right, we'll do it . . . oh, say three weeks from Saturday next. There," he added, enjoying the happy yet amazed looks of his wife and sister. "That should keep the pair of you out of mischief. You thought I'd say we had to wait until later this summer, not May, didn't you?" he teased, a boyish smile making the dimple in his chin more noticeable.

"And we'll have to start planning the menu and wine list right away," interjected the earl. "Nothing like a good English feast to stir the blood."

This last sentence took some of the merriment from O'Rahilly's expression. So, he thought, the earl intended it to be mostly English in flavor, did he? He envisioned the earl's version of the party, his own Irish friends relegated to a small corner of the room, while the earl played at still being the lord of the manor. He cleared his throat. "And, of course, now that Dunstan is recovered," we can have the *Bóthar* ceremony."

"Oh, no." Edna looked distressed. "Taggart, I'm sure Millie would not appreciate that."

"*Bóthar?*" Dunstan looked as puzzled as the others about the table.

Appearing pleased with himself, Taggart bade his sister, "Why don't you tell them, Edna?"

"Yes, do," encouraged Marigold Nolan. "Is it some ancient ritual? It sounds frightfully romantic. Do we all dress in bed gowns or something?"

Edna frowned. "It is an ancient custom not used these days. Years ago when an Irish lord was victorious in battle, it was the custom that the former male owner would present some token to the victor—a symbol of the passing of the property and power from one house to another."

A blue vein in the earl's temple became more visible. "You mean I'm supposed to give that upstart brother of yours a present in front of my English friends and those Irish vermin?"

"You've already signed the written paper making it legal," Taggart embellished in a smooth tone. "This is just a more public presentation, according to the Irish custom." His smile became roguish. "Of course, I am willing to forget the present. It's only meant to be a token."

"Are you implying I'm too poor to come up with a cursed gift for you? Bah, a bag of horse turds would suffice. Pining for your old job, are you?"

"Father, please." Dunstan shook his head. "You are ruining our meal with such language."

Geoffrey's bushy eyebrows rose. "Censured by my own son. Be gad, I never thought I'd see the day when my own flesh would take the side of an Irish rogue against his defenseless father."

Taggart clenched his right fingers about his fork but said nothing.

Millicent knew her father and husband were close to a full brawl. She interceded quickly with, "I am sure the embroidered waistcoat I have nearly completed might be acceptable for the ceremony, would it not, Taggart?"

Taggart's expression was magnanimous. "Why, that would be a grand gift. And you do have a special skill for that needlework," he added.

The earl folded his beefy arms across his chest with difficulty. "Well, I won't do it. If you want a Fitzroy to humiliate, you'll have to use that horse's ass, Dunstan."

"Father!"

"Really, my lord, that is hardly called for." John Nolan added his censure to Lady Millicent's.

"Well," grumbled the earl. "What's the matter with him?" he demanded to no one in particular. "At his age I'd fought two duels and fathered three bastards. And another thing," he added, picking up steam, "how can an English officer allow himself to get injured and lost in India? Following his men into the thick of it and on foot, so your superior, Colonel Shelby, wrote me." He gave his son a look of disparagement. "What the devil do you think the lower ranks are for? I didn't buy

265

your commission to have you toss it away getting yourself crippled."

Dunstan's gray eyes smoldered as he confronted his father. "You know I was there because you insisted all Fitzroy males serve in the military. Yes, I followed my men into battle. A viscount or a butcher's son, we all bleed and die the same, Father." In agitation, he groped for his cane, clearly struggling to leave the table. "I thank you all for your kindness in welcoming me home. It's late, and if you will excuse me, I will retire. Please do not get up," the Englishman added with stiff formality. He never looked at Edna.

"As to your ceremony," Dunstan commented as he got awkwardly to his feet. "Taggart, is it the custom for the person who has run the estate to hand the symbolic gift formally to the new owner in this *Bothar* business?"

"It is," O'Rahilly answered.

"Then it is Millicent who should do the honors, for Edna has told me it is my sister who handled the accounts, saw to the daily running of the grounds, including care of your own sister and the tenants on our—your land."

Things were not going as he'd planned. Taggart had no quarrel with his wife, and he did not wish her to participate in this Irish ceremony. The ball would allow Edna to meet more suitable Irish prospects for a husband, not this gentle yet penniless Englishman. "A woman has never participated in this ceremony. No, Millicent cannot be present. It would not be acceptable to the other Irishman. And your fellow Englishmen, you know, would not stand for it."

Leaning on his straight walking stick, Dunstan had to see the truth of Taggart's words. "Very well, then. I shall do it. But my father will also be present." He raised a hand cutting off his father's protest. "You will not have to speak or do anything, but it is a matter of Fitzroy honor that we face our . . . our difficult times as a united family."

It was the closest Millicent had seen of her brother ordering the earl. And she realized her father was impressed by his son's uncharacteristic show of strength.

Dunstan's unyielding stance seemed to placate Geoffrey Fitzroy. "Oh, very well," he muttered with a shrug.

Without another word, Dunstan turned and left the dining room.

Why, Millicent wondered, had her husband brought up this business about *Bothar?* It had only caused her father and brother to exchange harsh words. And didn't she have a right to be present? After all, Dunstan was correct—she'd run Fitzroy Manor single-handedly these last few years.

Chapter 19

Millicent stitched the green thread on the last leaf along the edging of the watered-silk cloth. The gold waistcoat would rival any from Paris or London, she thought, pleased the work had turned out so well. Of course, she'd never expected to have this gift presented so formally to her husband, and it was disappointing not to be allowed entrance into the Irish ceremony. She winced when the needle pricked her finger, a result of her sudden agitation. And all because the males of both families, except Dunstan, felt it was no place for a woman. "Stuff," she muttered before bending over her embroidery once more.

The last three weeks had been a flurry of activity at the Hall. New furniture, paintings, clothes, and food had been arriving steadily. Carpenters and cabinetmakers throughout Ireland were hired to make the place presentable for the ball.

And the replies tumbling in proved it was going to be a crowded affair. Perhaps the uproar over her wedding had died down a little. Sadly, she realized the Irish rebel activities were likely the cause. Estate owners had more pressing matters to think about. Just this afternoon on her rounds, she'd noticed the increase in British troops about the square. Kinsale was taking on the appearance of a fortified arsenal. Well, she thought, perhaps tomorrow would help alleviate some of the strain. There were to be no armed guards here at the party. On that point she agreed wholeheartedly with Taggart.

The May afternoon sun streamed through the windows of

the downstairs sitting room, and Millicent glanced up from her sewing to see Edna and her brother out in the rose garden. One would have to be blind not to read the love in their eyes, she mused with a smile. Their letters had sustained the relationship during their months apart and up until Dunstan's disappearance.

Millicent could not help wondering if she and Taggart would ever know this happiness. Taggart would be home soon from visiting Calvert Huntington. Would he see Garnet? Quickly she tried to dismiss these thoughts, for she wanted to trust him, and he'd told her there was no mistress. Yet, he'd not said one word about her moving back into their shared bedroom. Now that Dunstan was alive, there was no reason to spend a fourth evening alone. And in truth, she was eager to return to their room. The corners of her mouth turned upward as she came to a decision. This very night she would move back into their bedroom.

"Millie!" Edna cried out as she raced into the room, dragging a laughing Dunstan behind her. "We wanted—it is so wonderful!" So excited, she had to stop for breath.

"What my dearest Edna is trying to tell you is that she has consented to become my wife."

Millicent thrust aside her embroidery and rushed over to her brother and his future bride. "Oh, I am delighted at this news!" She embraced them both.

"Is Taggart back yet? Have to do this properly," Dunstan added, only half in jest.

Millicent caught the look of wariness in Edna's green eyes.

Edna was the first to speak. "Oh Dunstan," the shorter girl teased, "there is no hurry with the formalities." The dimples at the corner of her mouth were more pronounced when she smiled at her betrothed. "Isn't it romantic to let it be our little secret for a while longer?"

"Nonsense, we can announce it tomorrow evening at the party," countered the auburn-haired young man, He grasped his cane a little tighter, a gesture necessitated from the longer walk in the garden, but he seemed determined to keep things jovial. "I'm so smitten I want the whole world to know our good news."

"But, darling," Edna pressed, "I really think it would be better to wait."

The door opened and Taggart came into the room. The smile on his face turned to a sober expression when he saw the way his sister had her hands on Dunstan's linen coat sleeve. And the Irishman hadn't missed what she'd called him.

"Taggart." Dunstan colored, then moved away from Edna. The smile he gave his brother-in-law was a little strained. "I should like to speak with you in the study if you have a moment."

At first Millicent thought her perceptive husband was going to refuse. Then he nodded curtly and led them into the larger room to the right.

It didn't take long for the congenial male voices to turn to shouting. Millicent clutched her hands in her lap as she sat on the sofa next to Edna. Both women's eyes concentrated on the closed door of the library. In less than ten minutes the door flung open and Dunstan charged out of the room.

Never had the Englishwoman seen her oldest brother in such a state. His lean face was suffused with color and a muscle along his jaw worked as he fought to control his uncharacteristic feelings. Using his cane, he walked past them as quickly as he could manage with his bad leg. "Don't wait supper for me," he stated over his shoulder.

Before Millicent could comfort her friend, Edna made a tearful retreat out toward the hall, apparently heading back to the seclusion of her room.

Millicent chanced a look at her husband. It surprised her to see him walk calmly out of the—his library, she corrected. His expression was unfathomable. She watched as he made a pretext of adjusting his immaculate neckcloth. The silver buckles on his black shoes gleamed as he came to stand in front of her. She moved her gaze up his white stockings, brown knee breeches, and matching coat.

"I am sorry it has to be this way, Millie." He sat down next to her.

She gave him a level stare. "You speak as if you had no choice."

He appeared caught off guard. "What other choice is there?

270

You know I like Dunstan, but facts must be faced. He has no money, and he's totally English in his outlook, if not his blood—two qualities that hardly make him suita—I mean, the best prospect for my sister. Edna had enough poverty in childhood; I'll not shove her back into that life even if she cannot see the wisdom of my actions right now." He reached out to take his wife's hand in his own. "They're both young; they'll meet others. It has always been my hope that Edna might marry one of her own—well, someone like Dr. Collins perhaps."

Millicent snatched her hand away, then stood up, hardly able to believe her own ears. Hands on her hips, she demanded, 'I'm English and had no money, yet you married me."

"But that was different," countered the Irishman. He stood up to join his wife, unable to hide his amusement at her defensive stance. Yes, he thought, he did like the way she dressed and wore her hair these days. The flowered muslin gown suited her slender frame. "Sparrow, I know this is a disappointment to you, but I must do what I believe is right for my family. How can I allow my sister to marry a man who can't support her or answer for her future?"

"And he's a Fitzroy."

He grimaced. "Well, that name does little to recommend him to me as a future brother-in-law." Then he told her about Ben Abrams's findings that her father had presented the falsified evidence, which led to Taggart's father being hung for a treason he never committed.

She knew her father was not blameless in this matter, but to deliberately bring about a man's death? Was her father capable of such a horrendous act? But the implication of Taggart's half-spoken word kept echoing her mind, shutting out all other concerns. Her hands tightened into fists at her sides. "Suitable, that is the word you almost said. I'm a Fitzroy and had no money, but your sense of duty caused you to overlook my failings, isn't that it?"

"No, I never said that." The black-haired man's voice rose as his determination to remain congenial began to dissipate.

"Ah, but you do mean it. And the *Bothar* is just another way to humiliate the Fitzroys."

He shook his head adamantly. "You're wrong. The truth is I want that Irish ceremony so that your father and our guests will understand that I'm now legally the new owner of Fitzroy Hall."

"And the King knows of this?"

His smile was triumphant. "Yes. It was His Majesty's prime minister who advised me on using the Irish ceremony, along with the English legalities. If the Irish tenants and our English neighbors fail to grasp who is actually in charge here, I'll never be able to run the place." Anticipating her next argument, he added, "And it is true, Millie, no woman is ever present at these ceremonies. I must stay with the custom or the Irish will not accept me here."

So, she discovered, Taggart felt her brother wasn't good enough for Edna. Millicent couldn't hear all his explanations as he continued to speak. The implications of his actions today cut deeply. All during the time he'd been the Fitzroy groom she'd always tried to show a regard for his feelings, even if sometimes she'd made inadvertent mistakes. But never had she made him feel he was less than they were. Refusing to show how much he'd hurt her, she glared up at him.

"You have learned certain English ways very well, O'Rahilly. What an arrogant snob you've become." Her back straight, head held high, Millicent grabbed her skirts, turned, and left her scowling husband alone. After this insult, she thought, she certainly wasn't moving back into his bedroom tonight or any other night.

By the next afternoon, Taggart was frantic. Dressed in a formal suit of buff-colored breeches and coat, he adjusted the top of his dark-red waistcoat as he rushed into the servants' hall. "Has she been through here yet?"

Colleen Mulcahy shook her head for the third time, grabbed another onion, and began peeling it with a small knife. The room was hot from the cooking going on throughout the entire day. "You mind those pies," she shouted to the two younger kitchen maids assisting her. Then she looked sympathetically at her employer. "No one has seen her ladyship since yesterday."

None of the servants knew where she was. Dunstan and Edna had no idea. Of course, he realized all these people were so devoted to his wife if she'd asked them to tell Taggart the little people had taken her, they'd have readily done so. He began to swear aloud, then caught himself. But their guests would be arriving in less than two hours.

Having checked everywhere but the stables, Taggart put on a pair of leather riding gloves and decided to look in on the horses as a last resort. Was he in for another chase into the village for her?

With the identity of the persons who had sent Millicent and him those false notes still unknown, O'Rahilly was still uneasy about her habit of riding out alone. But, he mused to himself, he might as well talk to Buttercup for all the good it did to try and order Millicent to do anything. He knew he'd taken the only logical course open in refusing Dunstan's suit for his sister's hand. However, Millicent hadn't spoken to him or come near him since she'd left him outside the study yesterday. When he'd knocked at her door this morning, she had already left. Where the devil could she be this time? Damn it, was he going to have to bell her like a wayward calf to keep her from wandering off without telling anyone?

Samuel was obviously in another barn. Taggart bent his head and entered the larger stables where Laidir and Buttercup were kept. Unable to believe his eyes, he blinked at the picture in front of him.

His wife was dressed in those blasted breeches and shirt once more. The former Lady Fitzroy had a firm grip on a pitchfork as she mucked out Laidir's stall. Her auburn hair was pinned up and, he thought, she looked quite pleased with herself. "Just what in bloody hell do you think you are doing?"

Millicent stopped and glanced up. Still holding the pitchfork between her leather-gloved hands, she answered, "I should think it is quite obvious."

"Is the gown or jewelry not to your liking, then?" he asked, genuinely concerned that his choices had not pleased her.

"They are beautiful. Thank you," she added with appreciation.

Hands on either side of his waist, he grated, "Then pray explain this to me."

"As the Fitzroy financial circumstances have reversed from nine years ago, I am now taking over your old duties."

"Groom?" A loud laugh escaped before he realized his wife was quite serious. "*Leasu!*"

"There is no call to be vulgar," she pointed out, clearly understanding his Gaelic word.

"What new cork-brained notion is this? The party? You cannot expect me to allow you to stay here."

"I'm not coming to your party," she stated.

"The hell you're not. You are my wife and your place is—"

"Where I choose to be."

"*Breallog.*" He took a step closer to her.

"I am not an idiot. If my brother isn't good enough for the O'Rahillys, then neither am I."

"If you think I'll permit my wife to muck the stables like some barefoot peasant, it's sadly mistaken you are." He glowered at the stubborn young woman, wishing for once he was more than three inches taller than his wife, for she appeared anything but intimidated by him. "You take off when you damn well please without a word to anyone, you insult me in front of my friends, and now this. Well, by God, you'd be well advised to realize I will take no more of your stubborn ways. I must have been mad ever to suppose you were meek. The red in your hair is true all right. But you've met your match in O'Rahilly, brat. Now," he ordered with finality, "Let's have an end to this foolishness. As it is, Bridget will have to rush you through your bath and dressing. The duchess said she'd arrive early, and your proper place is by my side to greet our guests." He congratulated himself on his calm, yet commanding tone. And he'd managed from slipping completely into his brogue this time.

But at the mention of Garnet, Millicent's hands tightened on the pitchfork. "My presence will not be missed. No doubt you can persuade the blond rose to act as hostess for you."

He gave an ungallant sniff in her direction. "At least Garnet knows how to behave in polite society. A man appreciates a well-behaved, sweet-smelling rose."

His barb hit her vulnerable feelings, but this time she fought back. "Arrogant lout!" she shouted. "So you like roses, do you? Well, here's a bouquet for you." She hoisted the huge fresh contents of the pitchfork at him.

Lady Millicent could not hide the smirk when she saw the warm, oozy horse droppings cascade across Taggart's white ruffled shirt and neckcloth. Whatever was the matter with her? She wondered, then giggled out loud. Why, she felt absolutely marvelous, almost blessed. A pity she hadn't done this sooner.

Astonished, at first Taggart could only stare as the warm stuff made a malodorous trail down his red waistcoat, beige coat, and breeches.

"Manure suits you," she added, imitating his tone from the evening he'd complimented her gown. "It matches your eyes."

Amazement changed to something else, and her husband's dark eyes narrowed. If she'd been a man he would have called the fellow out for such an insult. The jeering face of her father came to mind, followed by Edwin and Garnet as they humiliated him in their filthy cellar. Automatically, he pulled off his gloves, tossed them to the hard ground, then stalked toward his wife, never taking his furious dark eyes off her. His wife, he derided himself, the Fitzroy he'd married, only to have her treat him in this degrading manner. "Damnation!" he bellowed with pure rage and reached out for her.

Millicent tried to back away as she held up the pitchfork, now using it like a weapon of defense. However, Taggart wrenched the offending tool out of her hands and tossed it as if it were a twig. It clamored to the dirt-and straw-covered floor on the other side of the stable. His strong hands grabbed both her wrists with such force, she thought the bones would break. "Taggart, we should talk this over. Don't do something you'll regret. Friend of King George or not, the magistrate would hang you if you murder me."

Unyielding, his laugh was dangerous. "I can always stuff your tall frame down the well and say you went on another of your charity calls to Fogarty's Pub, and a highwayman slit your throat." Yes, he wanted her to squirm a little. How many times has she caused him to worry about her or bite back his anger as he gave her time to get accustomed to their marriage? "No more," he vowed out loud.

Good God, he was going to strangle her right here in front of Buttercup, Millicent thought, glancing at her horse in an illogical hope of rescue. She tugged and pulled at Taggart's hands. "Release me at once, you overbearing oaf." His unyielding stance did nothing to calm her own rising temper at this latest treatment, and she kicked one of his stocking-covered shins forcefully with the sturdy toe of her right boot.

With a howl of pain, Taggart automatically let go of his virago of a wife.

The lady reasoned retreat seemed most prudent, and raced for freedom.

However, despite his throbbing leg, O'Rahilly bounded to the stable door just ahead of her. Roughly, he grabbed her wrists and dragged her over to the side of the stable.

"Laidir has better manners," she shouted, then aimed another kick but missed. "Why, you are nothing but an Irish hooligan."

"Irish hooligan, am I?" he grated over his shoulder. "Sure and I'll show you how 'tis the Irish way of tamin' a hellion of a wife." With an iron hold on his wife's hands, he sat down on one of the wooden benches along the wall and quickly tossed the struggling woman facedown across his ruined breeches. "You're my wife an you'll bloody well start acting like it."

Incensed by this new humiliating position, Millicent twisted her neck to glare up at him. "And you are my husband and you'll bloody well start acting like it, too." Before her husband could swing back his right hand to connect with the center of her breeches, she punched his already bruised shin with all the force she could muster.

"Damnation!" O'Rahilly bellowed in excruciating anguish. His brown eyes smarted as white-hot pain shot up to his knee. "Will ya cripple me?"

The time for dignity had passed, and his lady scrambled off his lap and began running, while the Irishman's hands comforted his injured leg.

She could hear the awkward movements of leather dress pumps pounding the earth floor behind her. Millicent turned about to sidestep the charging Irishman, but Taggart was too quick for her.

All traces of English manners departed when he lowered his broad shoulder to tackle his retreating spouse head-on.

Searing pain pulsed along the back of Millicent's whole body when she landed heavily on the hard stable floor. She bit her lower lip rather than show the man holding her how much she wanted to burst into tears. Instead, she forced herself to concentrate on getting free.

O'Rahilly could not believe her strength as they wrestled and tumbled about the ground. This was no milk and water miss, and it was taking all his muscle to ward off her flaying arms and legs. With a low Gaelic curse, he snapped his dark head back just in time to avoid a doubled fist on his unprotected nose. "Hellion" was all he could rasp out, barely able to catch his breath as each of them sought the advantage.

Her own chest heaving from outrage and lack of air, Millicent glowered up at the man unsuccessfully attempting to hold her still beneath him. During a brief lull, she pushed her upper body forward and stated, "Go to hell, O'Rahilly." But she couldn't hold back a whimper of pain when the black-haired demon shoved her right back, and her aching shoulders connected with the ground once more.

With the full weight of his body to keep her still, Taggart took her chin roughly in his right hand. "You will be dressed and downstairs to greet our guests in one hour, is that clear?" Her affirmation did not come as quickly as he desired, so he tighted his hold on her slender chin. "I said, is that understood?"

"Yeees," she snapped, for she felt too exhausted to go another round.

Her husband moved off her and stood up, then lifted her from the stable floor. When she tried to step back from him, his hands on her arms held her still.

Having spilled his rage, Taggart felt calmer as he eyed his wife. The sunlight through a small window in the wooden structure reflected the red in Millicent's tousled hair. In her struggle, the pins had tumbled to the floor, leaving him a pucture of her he'd not soon forget. Unlike nine years ago when she'd worn this outfit to rescue him or more recently in the darkness of Mistress Alice's establishment, Taggart now saw clearly how the white shirt and black breeches hugged her form. His eyes traveled to her breasts, clearly outlined against the soft fabic. He could see her hard pink nipples as her labored breathing caused them to strain against the too-confining material. And when she'd been running ahead of him, he hadn't missed the firm shape of her well-endowed buttocks against the tight-fitting black breeches. God, he thought, trying to control his urge to carry her over to the clean hay and make love to her, what the devil was this exasperating woman doing to him?

But when he saw the fury and pain in her gray eyes, he found less joy in his latest attempt to tame her. *"Gealbhan,* I—" He pulled his hand back when he saw the hatred in the steel of her expressive eyes and knew it was futile to attempt to repair things between them now. But he was quite sure she would be present to greet their guests this night. When he freed her arms, she stepped back from him quickly.

Never had anyone treated her in this manner. Did Taggart hate her so much? Millicent's chin lifted at that familiar angle. "Just remember that I will be downstairs this evening not because you are my husband and have decreed it. I will refrain from keeping my guests waiting because I know how to behave, for I am a lady and always have been . . . unlike a certain Irishman who merely makes an outward pretext at being a gentleman."

A long sigh of frustration made its way from his tightly held lips as he turned and walked out the stable door. But the price for her acquiescence had been dearer than he'd ever expected. If he did not love her, why was it painful to realize she hated him? He allowed no ready answer to enlighten him. He couldn't look back.

Having checked with the servants, Dunstan Fitzroy started walking toward the stables. Garnet and her husband were already here, and the host and hostess should be present. Taggart was strange, Dunstan concluded. He wouldn't let him marry Edna, but the Irishman insisted on providing him with a new wardrobe. Despite his protests, the clothes had been ordered. No wonder Millicent was at loggerheads with her husband. What could you do with a man like that?

Dressed in dark-green coat and breeches, Dunstan's smile widened as he took in his brother-in-law's appearance. So, he mused in growing amusement, Taggart finally realized that the usually quiet-natured Millicent could be roused to a full temper. Good for his little sister. The taller man sniffed pointedly when he got closer to his once fastidiously-tailored brother-in-law.

"Don't say a word," warned Taggart in a cold fury. "Not one bloody word."

Ever the gentleman, Dunstan complied. He was too busy trying to contain the open laughter that threatened, and it was almost a relief to have the Irishman move toward the Hall.

However, after Taggart left, still in the shadows, Dunstan saw the stable door open once more. This time he viewed the silhouette of his sister, dressed in boots, breeches, and wide-sleeved shirts. Her back was to him. All humor left his lean features when he saw her wipe her eyes on the arm of her shirt. Her sobs tore at him. When he saw her wince as she rubbed her shoulders and neck, Dunstan forced himself back farther from view where the shrubbery and trees were thicker. He knew his proud sister would be further embarrassed if she realized he was aware of her humiliation.

Something began to burn inside Dunstan as he watched his sister walk to the servants' entrance to reenter the house. She was the daughter of an earl, no less. Their ancestors had been confidants to England's kings and queens for centuries. Former friend or not, how dare that Irishman treat his sister in this manner!

As she entered the back door to the kitchen, Millicent tried to compose her features. Silently she prayed no one would notice her unusual entry.

"My word, Millicent, are you setting a new style?"

The English girl closed her eyes, wondering what she had ever done to deserve this further degradation. She smelled the familiar attar of roses, and heard the Duchess of Montrose's tinkling laughter. There was nothing to do but ride it out. She forced a smile "Hello, Garnet," she said refusing to call her "your grace" this time. "I was just . . . checking on one of the mares."

"At this hour?" giggled the blond-hair beauty dressed in a low-cut aqua silk gown. She studied the taller girl, then motioned Millicent over to a corner of the room. "I dislike saying anything in front of these servants, for you know they love to gossip, but . . . Poor Millicent, I never thought you would go to seed so quickly." She opened her lacy fan and ruffled it slowly across her pretty face. Her voice became a whisper. "You know I hate to see you hurt, my dear. When Calvert and I had dinner with some friends in London you should have heard the talk at table. They say that wealthy colonial only married you for the revenge against your father, and that the earl allowed it because your husband has the King's regard, and Fitzroys needed the money." Garnet's blue eyes looked ready to spill with tears. "But I defended you," she added, before brushing back a perfectly formed blond curl near her cheek. "I told them you married Taggart O'Rahilly to save poor Edwin from being butchered by that heathen."

"Thank you, Garnet." Millicent tried to keep the sarcasm from her modulated voice. "Everyone knows my husband did not marry for love, nor was he smitten by my looks. Now, if you will ex—"

"Oh, my dear, is that wicked Irish Stallion making you work in the stables now?" Not waiting for an answer, she went on in a rush of sympathy. "Now, if you ever need my help, you know you can count on me."

Millicent straightened to her full height. "How kind," she replied without warmth. "Wouldn't you be more comfortable in the front of the house with the other guests?" Was Garnet snooping, trying to get a morsel of gossip from their servants? Millicent wondered. The kitchen was an area Millicent was sure Garnet did not frequent at her own estate, in Ireland or London.

Garnet's laugh became a bit nervous. "With both host and hostess nowhere to be found, I thought it my duty to see if I could assist." She glanced about the large kitchen, ignoring Mrs. Mulcahy's unfriendly stare as the older woman put the finishing touches on a saddle of lamb.

Millicent knew Garnet might be a tad miffed that the O'Rahilly table this night would easily rival any elegant home in London. Hadn't she and Edna worked tirelessly to plan this? And Taggart had shown a keen interest in the renovations. Pigeons with peas, veal, ham with golden oatmeal crust, fresh salmon—yes, all would go well tonight, and Taggart would be proud of her.

Determined to be pleasant, Millicent apologized, "If you will excuse me, your grace, I must dress."

"Oh, yes. Of course. And do have that Irish maid of yours toss some scent in your bath water," Garnet chimed up the narrow wooden stairs after Millicent. Then there was that little-girl laugh once more.

Lady Millicent had just descended into her fragrant bath when the adjoining door to the large bedroom crashed open. With a squeak, she wiggled farther down the smooth sides of the brass tub, hoping the bubbles would hide most of her. But then she chided herself for showing such timidity in front of her husband. After all she had every right to be here.

Even with his head start, Taggart had bathed and changed in record time. He looked handsome in dark-gray with lacy cuffs and embroidered waistcoat. It angered her to feel so drawn to him—especially after the way he'd just treated her. "Sir," she protested, "this isn't a tavern. Kindly knock before galloping in here."

Ignoring her words, he stated his purpose briskly. "I've come for your clothes."

Clutching the large beige sponge in front of her breast, she showed no bewilderment. "So, all the gowns are to go back, is that it? A way to make me heel until I learn my place. You thought I was as self-centered as Gar—as other women of your acquaintance. How little you know me. It's what is inside of people that makes them a lady or gentleman, not the cut of

281

their clothes. Take the lot of them, and good riddance to you both. You'll have to let them out if you are planning to bestow them on the Duchess of Montrose."

"What are you going on about? I'm talking about those blasted pants and shirt."

Her eyes widened in disbelief. "No. They're mine. I won't let you—get away from that chest." Forgetting everything but saving these clothes, she stood up in the brass tub and hopped out with such speed she slipped on the wooden floor where the carpet had been pulled back. She would have fallen had Taggart not reached out to catch her.

"God's blood, madam." His tone was half scolding, but he chuckled, astonished at how he could laugh despite his earlier anger. "Will you leave me not one suit of evening clothes for tonight?"

His hands were cool on her warm skin and she looked across at the wet spots on his coat and breeches. "I . . . I'm sorry, but those breeches and shirt are special to me. It is important to me to keep them." How could she explain they symbolized her freedom?

His hands felt on fire as they stroked the wet skin of her shoulders. Without her glasses, her clean scented skin beckoned him. Before he could stop himself, he bent his head and pressed his lips to her soft cheek, then he found he wanted more and claimed her lips as his denied passion smoldered to the surface.

When he finally freed her lips, Millicent had to hold on to his broad shoulders to steady herself until the room stopped spinning. The Englishwoman shuddered as she was forced to discover she was still hopelessly in love with this man. And he merely played with her, for hadn't he confessed he did not love her?

He misread her reaction. His smile was gentle when he bent down to pick her up easily in his arms. "Ninnyhammer," he called her but not unkindly. "You'll catch cold." As if she were fragile and not the virago who'd tossed manure at him less than an hour earlier, Taggart lowered her into the warm, soapy water. He moved his head to whisper in her ear, "If I did not have to go downstairs to greet our guests, sparrow, I should

282

enjoy bathing you myself. Every delectable inch of you."

Color suffused her cheeks, but she couldn't think of a rejoinder. Why was he staring at her so? It was a few seconds before Millicent could take a tentative look up at the black-haired man bending over her. "Then you won't take them?"

"Wha—?" he'd been thinking about the way her small, firm breasts bobbed up and down in the scented water. He touched the indentation at his chin. Part of him almost gave in, but then the crashing reminder of her safety set his mind, and he stood up. He still hadn't found out who had sent those notes to them. And that outfit made it all too easy for her to go riding off when she pleased, and he didn't have time to keep her from cleaning out the stables at these odd hours. Besides, the way they fit her, showing every part of her—why some unscrupulous character might take advantage of her. This line of thinking wasn't going to help. Without a word, he stormed back to the wooden chest at the foot of her bed. He pawed through the few items quickly.

And the kiss had made little difference to him, she thought. Lady Millicent fumed when he held up the breeches and shirt. "You have no right to take my things." But before he went out the door, she couldn't help asking, "What are you going to do with them?"

He frowned. "Burn them, as I should have done long before today." The door rattled as he shut it behind him.

Garnet's offer of help came back to taunt her. "Irish Stallion, indeed," muttered the Englishwoman before she squeezed the sponge with a vengeance.

Millicent was silent all during the time she and Bridget worked on getting her ready for the party. She'd made sure her maid hadn't glimpsed certain regions when she'd bathed and dressed. Even after more than an hour, it was still painful to sit down, her back and shoulders felt so bruised. Irish barbarian, she fumed.

By trimming Millicent's auburn tresses, Bridget had gotten the hair to wave at the ends. It was pulled back high from her face, with some of the fiery strands gathered in soft ringlets that touched the back of her shoulders. "You, see, my lady, it does behave better with a good cutting. Oh, you look lovely," she exclaimed, after putting the finishing touches on Millicent's more flattering hair style.

For the first time that evening, her mistress smiled. "Thank you, Bridget. It is kind of you to stretch the truth." She adjusted the ruby earrings that Taggart had presented her days ago, along with this gown and necklace. How much further things had deteriorated between them since then.

"But I wouldn't bam you, ma'am." Bridget's blue eyes mirrored her earnest feelings. "Sure and I've always thought ya only needed a bit of help with your hair and choosin' your gowns. Oh," she put a hand to her mouth, clearly horrified that she'd dared criticize the employer. "I'll be beggin' yer pardon."

Millicent chuckled. "You're quite right, you know." With her mother dying when she was still a child and the problems running the estate, in addition to never being a beauty by the world's standards, Lady Millicent realized she'd never really taken the interest in such things. "I am grateful for all your patient assistance, Bridget. And," she addressed the younger girl, "you've even shown me that it doesn't have to take so long or be as uncomfortable in a ball gown as I'd imagined."

"Well, you're thinner so the stays don't have to be laced so tight."

This was her first ball, the English girl thought with a combination of excitement and uncertainty. With a mischievous wink at her maid, Millicent lowered the bodice of her red silk gown just a tad, before removing the handkerchief that covered the upper part of her bosom. After a moment's hesitation, she slipped off the spectacles and set them on her dressing table. True, things took on a hazy appearance, but when she looked into her mirror, she decided to chance it. Just for one night she wanted to be beautiful . . . well, at least passable. Her smile faded when she remembered Taggart didn't love her, but then she refused to give in to self-pity. Why shouldn't she enjoy her first ball?

"Oh, my lady, don't forget the master's vest."

Millicent looked down as the maid handed her the box

containing the vest Dunstan was to give Taggart during the ceremony naming him official new owner of Fitzroy Hall. Then a thought occurred to her, and her smile deepened. There was just enough time. Looking the picture of demureness, Lady Millicent said, "Thank you, Bridget. That will be all."

Alone, Millicent grabbed her glasses, rushed to her sewing box, and found her knitting needles. There would be another day to give her husband the waistcoat in private and to replace the roses on the blouse she was embroidering for Edna. Well, she vowed, O'Rahilly had a surprise coming if he thought he could bully her. The question of how would he take this forced its way into her mind. But only for a second. She went back furiously to her yarn work, then giggled out loud at how deliciously wicked she felt.

Chapter 20

"Good God!" Edwin Somerset almost dropped his quizzing glass when he caught sight of Millicent O'Rahilly descending the long marble staircase.

With the box in one hand and hand-painted fan in the other—her most prized gift from Taggart that he'd shipped to her so long ago, it seemed—Millicent smiled at her former betrothed. "Good evening, Edwin. I am glad you are looking so well." He was dressed in bright green and yellow stripes, yards of lace, with his full wig powdered in yellow to match the color of his hose. When he bent over her gloved fingers, she caught his overpowering jasmine scent. Dosing with strong perfume seemed a habit with the Somersets, she mused with undisguised merriment.

"I know you truly did not wish to wed me, Edwin," she whispered. "Can we not be friends?"

Edwin's rouged lips turned upward. "How could any man be cross with you tonight?" He offered her his arm and led her farther into the room.

Dunstan and Edna did not come over to greet her right away. It was difficult without her glasses, but it looked like Edna and the tall Englishman had been arguing.

"Doesn't she look smashing?" Nigel Somerset piped up to his wife.

"You do, my dear." Abigail Somerset looked a little uncomfortable, her round form laced into a pale-pink gown at least a size too small.

286

"About time you showed up," spouted her father. Wine-glass in hand, the Earl of Fitzroy unhooked one of the front buttons on his dark-blue coat and sighed with relief. "Time for that heathen ceremony. Damn fool nonsense. Probably have us all dancing Irish jigs. What's the fun in that without a wench, eh, John?"

Millicent thought Nolan's smile appeared strained. There was none of his easy affability with her father.

Glass midway to his mouth once more, Geoffrey Fitzroy's eyes bulged as he took in his daughter's appearance. "God's nightshirt, what did you do to yourself? Why, damn me, if you don't look pretty. Never saw you like this before. About time, too."

"My maid, Bridget, is a treasure." Not offended, Millicent smiled. "Thank you, Father. A daughter appreciates knowing her father won't run in terror at her appearance. Oh, Dunstan," she addressed her brother, not having missed the way Edna distanced herself from him, "here is the gift I promised you could give to O'Rahilly. Please make sure he realizes I alone am responsible for it."

He accepted the box, a look of sympathy on his lean face. "I know this isn't easy for you, Millie. And I still feel you're the one who deserves recognition after all you've done managing the estate."

"Well, let's not go into that now," she interjected. "Tonight should be a time for pleasant company and music. You'd best go now."

"Yes," Dunstan agreed. "Taggart and most of the others are already in the library waiting. But it shouldn't take long."

"No," she agreed with an impish twinkle in her gray eyes. "I dare say it won't."

Taggart looked about the polished wooden table that had been brought in here earlier just for the occasion. Calvert Huntington, Nigel and Edwin Somerset, a few of the earl's friends, along with John Nolan, Father Michael Collins, and five other O'Rahilly friends sat watching him. His eyes fell on Dr. Collins. Well, it had all gone very well, he thought, congratulating himself. Just the symbolic gift, then everyone could rejoin the ladies for a pleasant evening.

"Gentlemen," Taggart began graciously, "I do thank you for witnessing this occasion. It is my hope that we can all live together here in Kinsale without resorting to violence."

"Here, here," seconded John Nolan.

Taggart tried to ignore the look of disgust on the earl's wide face. He nodded to Dunstan, the prearranged signal.

Dunstan rose from his wooden chair. "Now that you have all witnessed the legal transfer of Fitzroy—I mean, O'Rahilly Hall, it—"

"I have not decided on the name yet, Dunstan." Taggart made his voice casual. "For now let us leave it by the name all are familiar with."

Dunstan couldn't tell if this was a concession on Taggart's part. He continued. "As is the Irish custom, a present is now presented to the new owner." He handed the box to his brother-in-law. "Lady Millicent asked me to tell you this comes from her alone."

Taggart looked down at the box containing the waistcoat she had embroidered with her own hands. He felt a twinge of remorse at having lost his temper with her only an hour earlier. Almost reverently he placed the unopened box down on the shiny table surface.

The earl looked quizzical. "What did she give you? Can't be worth much, for I sold the valuables long ago," he added, with a harsh laugh.

"This present from my wife is worth more than gold to me. If any of you wish, before you leave you may see the handsome gift my wife made with her own hands especially for me." Pride on his face, he passed the box to Nigel Somerset.

The vicar opened the lid and slipped the top under the box. Puzzlement edged across his face. Then his eyes grew large as he viewed the contents. He cleared his throat and passed the box to John Nolan, then Father Collins.

The priest read the attached note. Tongue in his cheek, it was clear he was maintaining his composure with great effort as he offered it to his brother, Liam.

Anticipating their admiration at such a fine waistcoat,

Taggart smiled with pride. "My wife has a skillful hand. I will tell her how pleased I am with her needlework, Dunstan. A man can never have too many of these."

"And I thought most of us just had one," shouted the Earl of Fitzroy with a boisterous laugh as he squinted at the contents. Then a few of the others burst into loud guffaws, obviously unable to contain their reverent expressions any longer.

Calvert wiped his eyes on his pocket handkerchief. "Who ever would have thought Lady Millicent would—? Why, she has so little to say for herself, always quiet." He chuckled again. "Extraordinary woman."

"The lady is full of surprises," John Nolan commented as he watched Taggart's confused expression.

"Chit's got more gumption than I credited her for," commented the lady's father.

Had they all taken leave of their senses? Taggart wondered. What the devil was so funny about a waistcoat? The last to admire it, Dunstan looked tentatively inside the box. Clearly, his brother-in-law had not expected whatever was in there. With a feeling of unease, the Irishman walked to the other side of the table. "No, he said, stopping Dunstan from replacing the lid. "I should like to see what has amused my guests far better than any French farce."

He took the box in his left hand and used the other to hold up the "gift." The cylindrical piece of open knitting was over a foot long. There were embroidered pink roses attached to the front of the oversized codpiece. He read her note, feeling the heat rise in his face with each impudent word:

I am positive the Irish Stallion will have little trouble filling this, especially if his anatomy matches the size of his conceit. Millicent Fitzroy O'Rahilly

"Damn me, I don't think I ever laughed so hard in my life," Geoffrey Fitzroy confessed. "Wait until they hear this at the club."

Clearly, the others saw their host did not appreciate the humor in his wife's present at this solemn Irish ceremony.

Calvert spoke first. "Well, gentlemen, let us join the ladies, shall we?"

Even the earl could easily read the storm warnings, for he got up and followed the others out.

Only Dunstan stayed behind. His face was drained of color as he clutched the handle of his cane and focused his gray eyes on his brother-in-law.

Taggart crushed the offending missive in his hand and tossed it back into the box, then roughly replaced the lid. "Damnation!" pounced out in clear, masculine anger. Why did she defy him at every turn? Only minutes ago he'd been berating himself for being so harsh with her. Hell, he thought, the blood pounding in his ears, that brawl in the barn hadn't cowed her at all. Look how she defied him, made him a laughingstock in front of these men?

"I . . . I'm sure my sister didn't mean—"

"Nothing from you, sir." He grabbed the box, shoved it under his arm, and headed toward the door.

"But, Liam, we've danced three times already." Millicent gave the doctor a beguiling smile.

He shook his head, but his gray eyes warmed when he tried to scold her. "Not only are you the loveliest woman at this party, but I am trying to save you from that furious husband of yours. You do know the difference between courage and foolhardy, do you not?"

"Why, of course." She curtsied as the minuet ended, and he led her back to the side of the room. "The latter is a trait men share with donkeys."

Though the floor was crowded with other couples, the doctor could not hold back his rich masculine laughter. "My lady, you are delightful."

"It must be this red dress, for I have always wished for one, but it is having a most peculiar effect on me," she countered. Not wishing to take all of the doctor's time after he'd been so sweet, she excused herself, saying she did have to find her husband. "Poor dear, he often forgets he has a wife." It was only half in jest because she had not seen him after he'd stormed out of her bedroom to burn her clothes. She greeted their English and Irish guests, moving gracefully among the elegantly dressed people.

Millicent spotted her husband off in one of the small rooms next to the large ballroom. The large number of guests necessitated the use of separate rooms for food and refreshments. True, she'd decided to make amends for her earlier joke, hoping he would accept her need for revenge after his uncivilized behavior this afternoon.

However, all words of greetings left her when she saw her handsome husband in the arms of the duke's wife. In a third change of clothes—black this time, with fresh white ruffled shirt—he and Garnet where alone in the smaller, dimly lit room. Millicent hadn't missed the way Garnet had entwined her arm about Taggart's neck. And he appeared to her in no rush to free himself—all he needed to do was stand up to his full height and the petite woman would be forced to let him go, or was she hoping to hang on for the ride? Millicent knew Taggart could not see her as he played in that . . . blond spider's web. Tears stung her eyes, and she turned and made a hasty retreat back to the ballroom.

The last thing she wanted was to cry in front of anyone, so she eased her way to the library, feeling the need for a few moments outside to collect herself.

After opening one of the double doors that led to the garden, Millicent breathed in the balmy May air. The night was filled with the heady scents of spring flowers. She walked the length of the stone terrace and finally came to lean against the high railing, where she could see the harbor in the distance as the moon danced along the calm water. The stone of the railing was cold on her gloved fingers, and the loveliness of the night seemed to mock her tortured feelings.

Is this what it would be like for years to come? she asked herself. This hurtful pain, the open wound that could never heal. Hadn't she forseen this? And why she'd refused his offer. Loving him, close to him, yet having no other choice but to watch him attend another woman, just like her mother had. "But I am not totally like my mother," she sobbed against the darkness.

"My lady?" called a familiar male voice behind her.

With a start, Millicent wiped the moisture from her eyes, before greeting, "Liam, I didn't hear you."

The doctor reached into the pocket of his silk coat. He handed her a very practical square of cambric. "Forgive me, but I saw you leave," he added with concern.

"Thank you." She dabbed at her eyes. "I'm making such a cake of myself. And I've always been so level-headed. Do you suppose I've caught some tropical disease? I mean Dunstan was in India, Taggart all over the globe, and I wondered—"

"No, I don't believe you have a disease," the taller man interrupted, his voice gentle. "I came out to rescue you from Taggart, but it appears I'm not needed. What did you say to placate the dark Irishman?" he teased.

Millicent knew Liam was trying to cheer her, but his words made her divulge the truth. "My husband cares little what I do; since we were children he's loved another. He only married me to repay a financial obligation—the O'Rahilly honor, you understand."

"My lady." Liam's gray eyes were warm with caring. "If you were my wife, I would not let you out of my sight, let alone allow any rascal of a doctor to converse alone with you in a dark garden on a spring evening."

She smiled and reached out a hand to touch his beige coat sleeve. "Thank you, dear Liam."

He placed his hand over hers, then bent his head lower.

Millicent moved her lips just in time so that his kiss was bestowed on her soft cheek.

Liam appeared disappointed that she changed the direction of his kiss, but he accepted it. "If I can help you, if you should ever have need of me, please feel free to—"

"Ask your husband for assistance."

"Taggart!" Millicent said, taken aback by her husband's sudden appearance from the shadows. "I never heard—"

"So it would seem," O'Rahilly stated. Having finally extracted himself from Garnet's clutches, this was the last thing he'd expected. Hadn't he purposely waited to seek his wife out so his temper wouldn't get the better of him? Only to find her in the arms of Liam Collins, that handsome—where were her spectacles? And that dress! Why, it hadn't looked so daring when he'd purchased it. He took a closer look at the area where the tops of her firm breast were exposed. "Your gown, madam, is—"

"It is lovely, isn't it?" Millicent finished, purposely misunderstanding the train of his thoughts.

His tone was an accusation. "You removed the handkerchief."

"Yes," she agreed sweetly. "As most of the ladies here have done. You may be experienced in choosing ladies' gowns in London, Taggart, but I dare say you have not kept up with the changes from Paris."

Inwardly, Lady Millicent was a jumble of confusion. Should she send Liam away and face her husband's wrath alone? Well, best get it over with. She turned to the doctor.

However, Liam whispered to her before she could speak. "Do you trust me not to hurt you or that hard-headed husband of yours?"

The lady did not miss the open friendship in the handsome doctor's expression. She nodded. "But I'll not see you harmed, either."

His smile was boyish. "We Irish know how to handle these things."

"I dare say," she quipped, wondering why even the part of her that was Irish hadn't fared too well in the stables this afternoon.

It took all of her control to keep her face impassive as the doctor led her back toward the French doors.

"Now, you did promise me the next dance, my lady. Oh," he added over his shoulder. "Nice to see you, Taggart. Don't catch a chill out here all by yourself."

Millicent shook her head as they rejoined the party. "You really are outrageous, Liam. Going past O'Rahilly like—well, I think Taggart's scowl matched his black evening attire."

"Do him good. Forgive my frankness, my lady, but your husband has found his conquests with women as easy as stealing apples similar to when we were boys. Now, let us have that dance."

"But, Liam," she protested, laughing as the doctor led her in the next minuet. She smiled at John Nolan as he and Marigold

293

made there way away from the two lines of dancers. "I do not play games with men. Directness has always been my way," she whispered when their hands touched as they came together, then stepped back in accurate step with the others. Men on one side, ladies on the other.

"It will do your husband little harm to realize others find his wife lovely." Then Liam stepped back with an impudent grin.

Millicent gave up trying to reason with her friend, though she felt this was a lost cause. Why, Taggart had made it quite clear he didn't care a fig for her. She searched the crowd, unable to find him. He was probably paying court to the Duchess of Montrose once more.

However, Taggart was standing behind her on the other side of the room. He was only half listening to what a few of his Irish friends were telling him.

"Best have a care during these times, lad," John Nolan warned. "Calvert caught one of his servants stealing a silver spoon last week. Can't trust anyone these days."

Taggart's dark eyes were focused on his wife. Never had he seen her look more animated and desirable, he thought. Her cheeks were flushed as she danced with the auburn-haired doctor, damn his eyes. He was tempted to charge over there and take the doctor's place. But he realized it would only make juicier tales for some of these people to tell in their clubs and the local pub.

As the evening progressed, Taggart found he was becoming more and more incensed with the attention these young bucks were paying his wife. And she seemed to enjoy it, he mused. Look at her, smiling at O'Hara's sons. And Edna, he scoffed inwardly. She politely declined their requests, refusing to dance with anyone but her Dunstan, while the viscount sat brooding on the other side of the room. There was irony for you. All the prospective husbands he'd invited here for his sister to look over were spending their time with his wife.

And he was even more irked when he couldn't get a dance with his own wife. One of those young puppies always beat him, and after the third try, he felt it was too humiliating to keep racing over to wherever one of the rascals deposited her—a different partner each time.

Millicent knew she was going to collapse if she didn't rest this next dance. Laughing and flirting with her latest partner as he led her over to the edge of the room to the cushioned chairs and benches, she sat down without thinking. Automatically, she winced as her bruised body made contact with the brocade-covered chair. She looked up to see the smirking face of her husband.

"Anything wrong, my dear?" asked the devil incarnate.

Blast his eyes, he hadn't missed a thing. She fanned her face with the hand-painted red fan, and countered, "Nothing the good doctor cannot take care of." His smirking countenance had sparked her flippant remark, but she did not understand why he was staring at her fan with such open vexation.

When Taggart glanced down to see Edna's gift in her hands, his raw feelings seemed to burst. "Where did you get that fan?"

"It is mine," she answered, standing up to her full height. In truth it hurt and angered her that he so easily forget the gift that meant so much to her. She held the fan more tightly in her gloved fingers.

His breathing was labored as he fought but lost the battle to keep the words inside. So, she had taken the prettier fan for herself. Had she also taken the money he'd sent Edna? His sister still had not explained where the money had disappeared. And he knew many English masters perused the packages sent to their mansions. But never, he thought in disgust, had he thought Millicent capable of it. "Yours, you say," he growled, ignoring the looks from the people around them. "I say you lie. You stole that from Edna O'Rahilly when she was your servant." Her earlier defiance incited him on to speak his mind.

Millicent looked aghast. Two spots of color strained her cheeks at his terrible allegation. And in front of all these people. He was treating her like a criminal. She hadn't missed the gasps from some of the men as well as their ladies. "You have made a mistake, sir. However, as it is clear you think me reprehensible in this matter, I shall gladly return this fan so that you may give it to your sister." Tears stung her eyes, but she fought them back. "I would rather die than possess anything that is not mine." She thrust the fan into his hands, then turned to her guests. "I do wish you all to stay and enjoy the rest of the evening's festivities. Pray excuse me for a moment," she added with a curtsy, then raced from the room.

Something stopped Taggart from going after his wife as he looked down at the closed fan in his fingers. Throughout all their differences, he'd always assumed Millicent was a woman of honor. Even after that night he had received the note stating where he could find his wife, he knew she would always honor her vows as his wife. But this? He could barely look back at the brightly colored ivory fan. How could she take it away from his sister? And the memory of her with Liam Collins did little to assuage his fury. "Play," he ordered the musicians along the side of the room. Instantly, a soothing piece by Handel floated across the large room.

Caleb came over to him a few moments later with a message on a silver plate. Taggart scanned it, then nodded. Devoid of expression, he quickly excused himself from his guests.

As Taggart entered the library, he saw John Nolan, the earl, and Dunstan standing about the long wooden table that had earlier been used for his *Bothar* . . . mistake, he conceded. The earl was the only one who looked pleased. "Well," he demanded, clearly in no mood for further encounters with the Fitzroys this night.

Holding something behind his back, Dunstan walked over to him. Without warning he raised a leather glove and struck Taggart forcefully across the face.

The narrowing of Taggart's brown eyes was the only indication of his reaction to this latest insult.

Dunstan did not flinch. "My father will act as my second. I assumed John Nolan would be your choice."

Taggart's eyes became almost black with fury. "What the devil are you blathering about?"

Dunstan's voice matched the other man's anger. "You have insulted my sister for the last time. To call her a thief in front of our friends—it is the last in a page of intolerable insults you have thrust upon her. Tonight has cancelled our friendship."

"Dunstan," he tried, realizing he did not want this. Millicent had no right to take Edna's possessions, and he'd lost his temper after one of the most regrettable days of his life. "Dunstan, surely we can settle this without such drastic measures."

"I always knew you were a coward, O'Rahilly." The earl gave the Irishman a contemptuous look. "Dunstan won't fight like Edwin, and you know it. A gentleman's fight is too good for you."

Taggart watched the three men standing in front of him. The earl's words changed his decision. "Give the time and place to John," he growled, then turned on his heel and left the room.

Chapter 21

Though Millicent almost choked with hurt and anger, she forced herself to return to her guests after bathing her face with cool water. She put a hand to her throbbing temple, for an instant wishing she had worn her glasses tonight. Those who had overheard the argument between husband and wife seemed too polite to mention it openly, though she saw Garnet giggle in her direction as she whispered something to John Nolan from behind her fan.

Then Lady Millicent spotted her husband only a short distance away. How suavely Taggart carried out his duties as host, smiling easily with his guests, complimenting an older woman's attire, joking with the young O'Hara brothers.

Well, she decided, smoothing down the front of her dark-red gown, she would show him she could do the same. She turned to answer when the vicar's wife asked her a question.

"Yes, I am fine, Abigail."

"But, dear child, you look frightfully ashen."

The taller woman tried to smile. "Merely a slight headache. Probably all the excitement of my first party."

"Perhaps these will help" came a masculine voice behind her.

She'd felt Taggart's presence even before he'd spoken. Slowly Millicent turned and accepted her spectacles from his outstretched hand. "Thank you," she responded with difficult politeness.

He hadn't missed her words to Abigail Somerset. So, she had

not been a part of the social scene here in Kinsale. Something touched him as the true vision of her life settled over him once more. His features softened. "I had Bridget fetch them from your room." When they had more privacy he added softly, "I should hate to have you ruin those lovely eyes by making them work too hard. Besides, I'd not like to take the chance of your mistaking some other man for your husband in a darkened rose garden."

As if she could ever fail to know Taggart's touch, his voice, everything about him was special to her. No one in the world could make her emotions fire and ice within the same moment. She looked down at her glasses, trying to think of a neutral comment. "Mrs. Halsey used to tell me how unattractive men find them on a woman."

"Mrs. Halsey was a bitter prune. It isn't like you to be so impractical," he said, gently touching her cheek with his fingers.

Lady Millicent moved her face away from his warm hand. "Pray, sir, do not paw me in front of our guests." She was rewarded to see him look chagrined before his hands fell to his sides. After his treatment in the stables, then calling her a thief in front of these people, did he have the audacity to try flirting with her now? Swoon in his arms, is that what he expected? These heated thoughts forced her to look away rather than show her true feelings. I am a lady born and bred, she recited her mother's teachings inwardly. A lady never creates a scene in front of her guests. However, Millicent's right hand itched to clout that rakish grin off her husband's face. Abruptly, she busied her shaking fingers by putting the glasses back on. Coldly, she stated, "I do view the world much more accurately with them. They assist me in discerning a gentleman from an ill-mannered clod."

He cleared his throat, beginning to despair that his attempts to show Millicent his regret for his lost temper were failing miserably. "And you are just as attractive with those spectacles on," he tried once more.

"You cannot be serious," his wife scoffed.

Taggart nodded and leaned closer. "So much so, my dear, I insist you always wear them from now on. They become you, sparrow." Then he looked lower to take in the tops of her firm breasts as they teased his eyes against the soft silk of her bodice. "As does that red gown."

Unmoved, her gray eyes took in his handsome form in black evening clothes. "A pity I cannot return your pretty speech, for I still believe manure suited your attire better."

His smile became a grimace as he strained to maintain a pleasant manner. "Will you dance with me?" he whispered.

Aware of their guests, Millicent smiled sweetly and quietly replied, "Roast your liver. I would sooner dance with your horse."

She was making it damnably hard to apologize, thought the repentant sinner. "Please," he coaxed again, "I would very much like to dance with you." He realized this might be the last time he could hold her soft form in his arms.

"If you will excuse me," the auburn-haired woman countered with cool politeness. "I see dear Liam again, and I choose to dance only with gentlemen."

Grinding his even white teeth until his jaw ached, O'Rahilly cut off her retreat with the loud request, "My dearest lady, will you not consent to dance even once with your unworthy husband?"

People around them smiled and applauded at the handsome Irishman's gallant words.

"How utterly romantic," Abigail Somerset gushed.

"Oh, do say you will dance with him," encouraged another guest before she giggled shyly behind her fan.

Trapped, Mrs. O'Rahilly turned to face her husband, ready to give him the dressing-down he deserved for this latest ploy. However, he was not smirking in triumph as she had expected. Indeed, she hadn't missed the uncertainty and pleading in his dark eyes as he waited for her answer.

There seemed little choice in front of all these people anyway. When he held out his arm to her, Millicent forced herself to smile and place her gloved fingers on the black material of his coat sleeve. It was a surprise to feel the nervous tension in the muscles of his arm.

"Thank you, my lady."

She was further perplexed at his genuine show of gratitude

over such a small concession.

As the music for the minuet began and other couples joined them, Millicent tried to remain calm, if mute.

Enchanted by her appearance, Taggart attempted to push aside his troubled thoughts and regrets. "Will you not let me hear your sweet voice?"

Silence.

He could not hold back the chuckle at her quelling look. "You really are a provocative leprechaun," he said before they moved to execute another intricate step.

"Nay, sir, I am too tall for any elf."

"I would have you as you are." Deviltry lurked in his dark eyes. "But I stand by my opinion that you are a mischievous imp."

"At times, O'Rahilly. When it suits me."

Only half in jest, he directed, "Then see that it suits you to confine anything beyond a verbal flirtation to your husband and not the family doctor."

It was impossible for him to be jealous of Liam, wasn't it? She moved her foot forward without missing the short step required. "I shall give your suggestion the slight consideration it warrants."

His brows rose as he acknowledged her challenge, but he waited until they came together before whispering, "Let me catch you in Collins's arms again, and that brawl in the barn will seem a trifle compared to what I will do to you . . . my lady," he added before slowly moving back gracefully to his correct position directly opposite her.

The color in her cheeks heightened at his blatant words. "While you are free to meet in unoccupied rooms with a duchess, is that not so?" she tossed. The words out, Millicent bit her lower lip at the failed attempt to guard her tongue. Would he now think she'd been spying on him?

So, she had viewed him when Garnet had followed him earlier. Unfortunately, his wife hadn't seen him extract himself from the blond-haired witch. Though he admitted being irritated at Liam's forwardness with his wife, he'd merely been having fun with their verbal sparring. Apparently, Millicent had taken his playful threat seriously just now. He continued their dance in silence while he pondered her last remark.

When the minuet allowed them the opportunity, he conceded, "Your point is well taken, Millie. But remember, I took the same vow of forsaking all others in front of Father Michael. Before that morning, I'll admit there had been other women, but I never deceived any of them with promises of marriage. And for all my black faults, and I've many, I am a Catholic, and that vow before the priest I intend to keep. Do you think me remiss to expect the same from my wife?"

"No," she answered in quick defense. "I will honor my vows as well."

Pleased by her answer, the Irishman moved closer to her once more. "Perhaps we both should learn to talk things over before allowing appearances to guide us in a rash direction," he said, thinking about the Chinese fan in his pocket. And when the dance ended, he stepped away from her and executed a graceful bow.

She felt it . . . he'd kissed her ear after he'd whispered these last words to her. His warm lips on her sensitive skin made her shiver. It was impossible to stop the racing of her heart. How could he be such a black-hearted demon? To buffet her feelings so completely . . . his livid rage in the barn, calling her a thief, now was he actually trying to seduce her? "I . . . I must see to our guests," she stammered before making an awkward curtsy.

As she walked away from him, it dawned on her that the roguish smile which deepened the dimple in his chin just now proved he knew how much his kiss had unsettled her.

It was after two in the morning before the last guest departed.

"Good night," Millicent called to John Nolan and Marigold. "Thank you for coming."

"Lovely party," Abigail Somerset commended as the vicar assisted with her cloak. "Nigel and I had a wonderful time," she added with a warm smile.

Though she wanted to confront Taggart about his horrible accusations concerning her fan, now that they were alone, Millicent couldn't look at him, for fear she'd see his mocking face after her reaction to his intimate kiss on the dance floor. Did he think she had no pride, that all he had to do was snap his fingers and she'd fall into his arms? With a toss of her head, she turned toward the stairs, positive he would not ask to speak with her.

And when her assumption proved correct, there was little choice but to trudge slowly up the long marble staircase ahead of him. What a day this had been, she mused. But the humiliating accusation tonight had been the worst. If ever she doubted it was over between them, tonight seemed to prove it.

Taggart's fingers tensed about the closed red fan. Despite the late hour he needed to find the truth of this right now. He tapped lightly on Edna's door.

"Taggart?" Edna had tossed a pink wrapper about her shoulders. There was none of her usual warmth when she opened the door for his entry.

"I am sorry to disturb you at such a late hour, Sister. But I need some answers." His expression was grim as he entered the redecorated room that had once belonged to his wife. "I came to return this to you. I believe your employer took it from you when you were her maid, along with many of the coins I sent you."

Edna accepted the fan and opened it. She blinked when she saw the familiar hand-painted flowers and birds; it was the beautiful Chinese fan she'd slipped to Millicent. Her green eyes studied the somber expression of her brother. "Millie never stole anything from me in her life. I used most of the money to keep Fitzroy Hall going so Dunstan would have something to come back to. I let Millie think her embroidery and shrewdness with accounts saved us from starving." She didn't flinch from her brother's look of amazement. "And I allowed Millie to think the prettier fan was your gift. The plainer one you meant for her, I kept on my own."

"But why?" The money meant nothing to him; it was the fan that plagued him. "I stated clearly this one was yours." Taggart could not hide his irritation as he was forced to realize he'd only used this gift as an excuse to vent his anger on his wife after finding her in Liam's arms. Jealousy was a new emotion for him, and he suddenly realized he'd not handled it well at all.

Her black curls bobbed up and down as she confronted her brother. "It was little enough in my mind, not that I think you deserve her. Sure and you always had her heart, but did you ever think to write her a line of friendship? She worked harder than any Irish tenant here. And it never stopped with just the estate. Just ask Dr. Collins, if you care to know the truth of it." Edna's eyes sparked green fire.

God, what had he done? Taggart's hands fell limply to his sides. But Edna had to be wrong about Millie's feelings for him. And it was clear Liam's attentions had pleased her, far better than he seemed able. Even during their dance tonight, he hadn't had a chance to make it up to her. When she walked upstairs in front of him just a minute ago, he hadn't missed the coldness in her gray eyes.

"I couldn't write her," he confessed aloud, "not while I plotted her father's ruin. Of all the things others may accuse me, a liar is not one of them."

She shook her head, and turned back toward her dressing table to reach for her lacy nightcap. "You've become just like the English you hated—and arrogant into the bargain." It was clear she was thinking of his refusal to allow her to marry Dunstan. "That pride of yours will strangle you one day, Taggart O'Rahilly."

"Tomorrow to be exact." He turned quietly to leave. "I should be obliged," he added softly over his shoulder, "if you would return the fan to Millicent tomorrow with my deepest apology for having so wrongly accused her of stealing it from you."

"You didn't come here at this hour just to return a fan." The petite woman's eyes became wary. Before he could leave, she was after him like a persistent terrier. She pulled on his black silk sleeve. "Why can't you return it?" At his tight-lipped silence, her voice became agitated. "Tell me, what have you done? I can see it in your eyes."

He shrugged his shoulders, realizing it was useless to try and hide the truth from his sister. When he turned back to look at her, there was a despairing sadness in his expression. Taking her hands in his, he explained about the fan and the result at being called out by Dunstan.

Edna's round face was a mask of disbelief. "But . . . surely you will not fight with him at dawn?"

"I have no choice. There were witnesses. Dunstan and the others would think I turned coward or pitied Dunstan because of his leg." The torment on his sister's face matched his own. "I still refuse to consent to your marriage with him, for I believe Dunstan is not the best husband for you, but . . ." He gave her cold cheek a reassuring pat. "You have my word I'll not fire at him."

The Irish girl wrenched her hands free. "Dolt, do you suppose a brother's death would be any less painful? Call off this madness. Please," she added, reaching up to stay her brother's arm.

Gently, he removed her hand and stepped back. "It's too late." Without another word he left his sister's room.

Still dressed in his black evening clothes, Taggart entered his own room. He tossed off his outer coat, poured himself a generous brandy, and sat down in the overstuffed wing chair near the fire. Sleep was the last thing he wanted. There would be eons after tomorrow for that deepest of slumbers. "To the corpse," he toasted, lifting the bulb-shaped glass to his lips.

His eyes never left the closed door leading to Millicent's adjoining room. He thought of his sleeping wife. He'd been mad to think they could make a happy marriage out of all this turmoil and tonight, he had again acted like the unpolished groom he'd once been.

He took another swallow of the strong liquor. At least he'd leave her a wealthy widow. The vision of her so close, only a few feet away, haunted him. Her auburn hair was probably ruffled across the white lacy pillow. Her straight nose, the kissable mouth, and silky skin. He put the glass down and stood up. When he came to stand in front of the marble fireplace, he gripped the edge with both hands. God, how had everything gone so wrong? Would she mourn him? he wondered. The vision of Liam holding his wife in the garden thrust its way into his mind.

After a few more images along this road, he reached for the lighted brace of candles from his dresser and moved silently toward the carved wooden door. He turned the brass knob and entered. Just one last time, he wanted to see her. This vision of her would have to sustain him forever.

With the eerie feeling that someone watched her, Lady Millicent came awake with a start. She craned her neck over her shoulder.

It was Taggart. The ruffled white shirt contrasted wickedly with his black coat and breeches. How handsome he looked came to mind before she could censure her thoughts. And the heavy candlestick he held illuminated his face, allowing her eyes to focus on the cleft of his chin, before moving higher. Just as she thought she could read it, he seemed to veil his expression, and her automatic warmth at his presence vanished.

For she remembered why she had reason to be angry with him and rolled over cautiously to sit up. When he placed the lighted candles next to her on the nightstand, she said, "It is late and I am tired. If you have come here to lecture me on the ruin of thieves, I should be much obliged if you wait until tomorrow."

Despite himself, he felt his lips quirk upward. "That haughty act won't work tonight, Millie, for I've learned you only use it when you feel backed into a corner. I didn't come to lecture you." He came to apologize, yet there was something else that captured his attention as he watched her, tousled and flushed against the bedding.

Her gray eyes became wary, and she backed farther into the downy pillows. When she saw him slowly begin to take off his dark waistcoat and white cravat, depositing them neatly on one of the wooden chairs, she began to feel alarm. Her initial giddiness at his proximity was also disconcerting. If he took her in his arms right now, it would confirm to them both that she was hopelessly in love with him. At least if they kept their distance, she could salvage some of her pride.

Determined to have this one last time with her, O'Rahilly pushed all else from his mind. And it wasn't difficult when he saw the tops of her pink breasts as her pale-apricot nightdress slipped off one shoulder. When he caught her glance move toward the lower drawer of her bed table, he chuckled, openly reading her thoughts. "I don't think the pistol will be necessary. I'll come quietly—well, at least not so loud as to wake the household," he added with a rakish wink in her direction.

But he became more serious when he sat down on the edge of the bed. Tonight he wanted her to desire him, ache for him, experience for once the hunger that had tormented him night after night these last weeks.

With deliberate slowness, he touched his fingers to the area just where her breasts separated, then moved lower. Through the soft material of her nightgown, he felt her nipples harden beneath the pads of his fingertips. When he bent his head to kiss her lavender-scented skin, his lips found the pulse of her throat. She was so soft and warm.

Millicent held her breath, trying to fight the urge she experienced to surrender to this man. He'd insulted her, called her a thief in front of her friends, acted like a bully, and— She gasped when he began kissing the sensitive skin at her earlobe, followed by his tongue back on her breasts once more. His touch branded her, seared her aching flesh to his.

No, she shouted at herself, she couldn't give in, not again. He didn't love her. It was almost impossible to sound bored but she forced, "Garnet busy this evening?"

He stopped and pulled away from her, not liking the discovery that her mind was not on his lovemaking. "No busier I imagine than Dr. Collins," he tossed back.

She grappled for the advantage with a sweet smile. "Liam is such a dedicated man, so kind and gentle. We are all lucky to have him as our physician."

"You mean you're lucky," he snapped, finding it impossible to ignore his earlier irate feelings. "I suppose you like those polished men with their light coloring and ready manners, as they easily spout flowery compliments."

"Yes, such a refreshing change from dark, brooding . . .

307

philandering louts. But I suppose Garnet can appreciate the Irish Stallion more. Given her undiscriminating tastes, I imagine any horse—or jackass in a storm would suit her. Now, be a good Irish Stallion and . . . bugger off," she stated, choosing a vernacular phrase she'd never uttered in her life.

Taggart found his voice only after he got over the shock at his lady's colorful language. "I loathe that nickname. Don't call me it again," he ordered. "And I'd advise you to curb your appalling impudence before I recall too well the 'gift' presented to me this evening."

"You're not fond of your name, Irish Stallion?" she dared, a brazen challenge sparking the gray in her eyes. "From what I hear it is quite appropriate, since you seem to live up to it with such religious fervor. Besides, it gave me the perfect idea for your *Bothar* ceremony. Did you like my gift? I made it myself. Of course, if it's too small I can always make you another. Pray, shall I sew pansies and butterflies on the next one . . . Irish Stallion?" she hurled with reckless abandon.

"English hellion," he snarled, and roughly grabbed her arms. With lightning speed he had her out from beneath the covers and on all fours, facing the headboard of the smaller bed. Never built for such abuse, the furniture creaked noisily in protest.

Fully aware that she'd gone too far, Millicent now admitted she'd let her hurt feelings unbridle her temper. His arm encircling the front of her waist felt like an unyielding tree limb. She struggled frantically.

Bending over her with his free hand he tore himself free from the buttons confining his manhood. "So, you think I'm an Irish Stallion, do you?" he taunted. He eyed her peach-covered bottom before leaning over her bent form. "Shall I take you the way a stallion takes a mare?" he growled near her ear.

She also struggled against her own feelings as she felt his heated body next to hers. He wasn't hurting her now, but she felt her pride demanded she fight. However, her exertions seemed only to increase his resolve. She felt his lips near her ear, and a shiver ran the length of her slender form.

"When I was your groom, I often had to protect a mare's neck with a large piece of leather before she was mounted. A stallion is apt to bite his lady's neck during the throes of arousal."

When Millicent felt Taggart nip the soft flesh at the sensitive area above her shoulder, she couldn't hold back the quiver of desire that assailed her.

He felt her response, and he couldn't hide his satisfied smile as his anger was replaced by something else. But he wanted to increase her desire, make her cry out, beg him to take her. Then she would finally understand the torment she'd been putting him through. His breath fanned her skin. "I want to taste every inch of you, feel your hot skin writhe under my hands and mouth." Her body wriggled against his, and he realized his words had caused her reaction, so he increased this mode of seduction after he kissed her shoulder, running his lips along the pink area that showed the slight marks from his teeth. "Oh, *Gealbhan*, I've ached for you. And what a naughty little firebrand you've become," he rasped against her ear once more. "Have you any idea how many nights you've kept me awake as I stared at that cursed door, wanting you to come back to our room?"

When Taggart felt her body become more pliant, he removed his arm from under her, for he realized she would not run away this time. He gently gathered her long hair in his hands and stroked it, moving it to her right shoulder before bending down to kiss the back of her neck. "You have such beautiful hair." He fondled and caressed the back of her, until his own control felt near to breaking him. Because he did not want to take her too soon, he forced himself to lean back against the heels of his black dress shoes. With a self-mocking grin, he realized this woman had his emotions in such a turmoil that he hadn't even removed his shoes before wrestling with her on this small bed. God, he was acting like the lout she'd called him, he mused with a chuckle as he changed his position to slip his shoes to the carpeted floor.

He reached out and began skimming the wispy material of her nightdress up over her legs and hips. "I thought you knew

309

how much I desired you," he said, liking the warm feel of her when he leaned her back against the front of him to allow easier access for pulling the gown over her head. "My lovely sparrow," he murmured aloud as he gently guided her back to her kneeling position.

However, his smile vanished when he viewed her back in the candlelight. He called himself every kind of a loathsome cur when he saw the bruised skin. Suddenly he was haunted by the vision of her wrist that time he'd helped her out of a tree. He'd forgotten how easily her tender skin bruised. His eyes stung with tears.

Never, O'Rahilly vowed, would he do this to her again. There would be no more rowdy brawls on stable floors for his wife. He'd find some other way to reason with her. Never this way, for it was far too painful for them both.

"Taggart?" Millicent asked in puzzlement, then alarm when she looked over her shoulder. "What is the—?"

He was off the bed before she'd even completed the sentence.

"Stay here. I'll be back."

The look on his face and his curt directive made her eyes fill with tears. She turned about and snuggled back under the covers. Was he rejecting her again because she was not to his liking now that he had seen her in a fully lighted room? Had he meant only to tease her, leave her this way when they both knew she desired him? Insecurities tore at her as she was forced to wonder if her love for him was stronger than her anger or her pride.

When Taggart returned, he found his wife had become a lump under the covers. "Sparrow?"

"Go away before I kick you in the shins again."

Grinning broadly, he bent over and scooped his naked wife up in his arms. "You know," he added, a wicked gleam in his eyes as he held her close against the open shirt that barely covered his chest, "inside you are really not as frail as I'd once thought. Though I seem to be the only one in Kinsale aware of it, there are times when you can be a regular spitfire. Can you see me without your glasses?" he asked, completely changing

310

the subject. "I shouldn't want you to miss anything."

"Of course I can see you," she bristled, but liked being in his arms too much to struggle more forcefully.

"Just as long as you know it's me kissing and caressing all those delectable parts of you." He bent his head to capture her warm, soft mouth. Then he pulled back, aware his self-control was on unsteady ground. He began walking toward the half-opened door. "We'll both be more comfortable in our own room." Still holding her in his arms, he kicked the door open the rest of the way with his boot.

"Taggart?" she asked after his change of footwear registered, so out of place with his formal evening clothes. "What are you doing in those old boots?"

He walked over to the bed and gently placed her in the center of the large mattress. "I had to go to the stables for a moment. Now roll over."

His brisk order was not what she expected after his gentle treatment just now. "Why? Don't tell me you're getting back at me for that gift by making me want you to distraction, then leaving me again."

His face clouded. "No, but I am very sorry I lost my temper in the barn this afternoon. If it's any consolation, I now feel I deserved every name, every punch, every kick, and all the mischievous pranks you've ever played on me. Edna told me the truth about your fan, darling. I'm sorry I so misjudged you."

"Well you should be." The lady made no effort to hide the hurt buffeting her feelings. "How could you ever believe I was capable of that after I'd given you my solemn promise to watch over Edna?"

He shook his head sadly. "'Tis the truth, I never feel totally comfortable in the role of gentleman no matter how hard I try. Too much of the rough Irish groom remains. Haven't I proved to us both I'm only a clumsy, uncultured man, certainly no gentleman. I failed miserably at that, and so many things," he added, almost to himself.

Millicent felt her heart warm at his humble declaration. He was allowing her to see his insecurities and genuine sorrow.

For the first time, she realized part of his Irish heart was as vulnerable as her own. "Oh, Taggart," she cried, holding her arms out to him, "please come here."

His own eyes were moist when he came over to take her in his arms. "My sweet, lovely sparrow," he murmured in her reddish-brown hair as he crushed her slender form to him.

She could not suppress a moan of pain when his fervent embrace made her suddenly remember her aching shoulders.

In anguish, Taggart quickly pulled his arm away from her. "God, darling, I'm so sorry."

Wanting to ease the torment in his earth-colored eyes, she tried to muster a reassuring smile. "I will heal . . . now," she added, thinking how much his words had helped. Then she kissed him softly on the mouth.

"Ya shame me with your kind nature," he rasped.

Her lips turned upward before a throaty chuckle escaped. "If it will make you feel more deserving of me, I'm willing to pound your shin a few more times, O'Rahilly."

He delighted in the return of her trust enough to make her impudent with him. "You have managed to turn it a vivid purple already, thank you very much." He grinned despite the truth of his words.

Now it was Millicent's turn to appear contrite. She watched as he reached for a white jar that was now on the night table next to their bed. "Oh, Taggart, I did not realize my own strength. I was so furious I just came at you."

His smile became rueful. "Who more than I understands how lost temper and jealousy can cause a person to strike out without thinking. Now, will ya roll over, there's a darlin'," he added, deliberately allowing the lilting tone to come into his voice. It was good, he thought, not to feel the need to hide himself from her.

"Oh," she exclaimed when the cool cream settled on the back of her leg. "That feels so much better. What is it?"

"I've used it many times on a horse when they get a cut or sore—numbs the flesh."

It was quickly taking the sting and puffiness from her skin.

She sighed with contentment when his skillful hands moved upward. But when she sniffed over her shoulder, she could not help wrinkling her slender nose. "It certainly doesn't smell very appealing." His fingers were slowly massaging the slippery cream across her shoulders and back. She buried her face into the pillow, trying hard to muffle the moans of pleasure his touch was causing. "I . . . I think you've got it all." Her voice was barely a croak. The mattress sprang back as Taggart got up to wipe his hands on a linen towel before he returned to sit on the edge of the bed.

"You must know I want you, especially tonight," he added, trying not to think of the duel he had to fight at dawn. "But if you wish me to go now, I will understand. I've hurt you enough, sparrow."

"Oh," she protested, turning about to face him. The contact this time caused her no discomfort. "Please, I do want you to love me." She bent over and pressed her body close to his, unable to hide the blush of her boldness when she felt the clear evidence of his desire through his tight breeches.

Pleased by her response, her husband wasted little time getting out of the rest of his clothes. "Will you trust me?" he asked when he joined her on the bed.

"With my life," she answered earnestly.

Again, he felt humbled by her open reaction. He reclined on his back and reached out for her, lifting her easily to sit across his bare legs.

"But this isn't like before," she said, briefly disappointed he wasn't going to take her as he'd so expertly done their first night together.

"This will be less discomforting for you. Trust me, there's a darling."

"But how can we do it this way?"

Using his hips and hands Taggart showed her how to please them both. "Just think of me as the docile pony who adores you," he teased. "That's right, lean forward. This way you can set our pace."

She bent over him, smiling as the rhythm of their actions pleasured her. "But, Taggart, this gooey ointment will get all

313

over you."

He ran his hands up along her hips. "As long as you keep that numbing stuff off the parts we want to feel, 'tis all right."

"You are an Irish scoundrel," she accused in mock reproof.

"At times, *Gealbhan*. Just as you are an impudent, adorable hellion." With her next forward thrust, he lifted his upper body to kiss her lips with a sweet fierceness. When he came back against the pillows, he reached in front to stroke her moist pink skin above where they joined. "Beloved sparrow," he murmured, his voice husky with arousal.

She was unable to hold back, and she increased the rocking movement of her hips against him. But then she gave him a saucy look and stopped her upward movements. It was clear from his breathing, along with the sweat breaking out on his forehead, he was certainly affected by her. This discovery showed her his desire, and she told herself to take joy in that for now, even if this was all he felt. "Docile pony?" she echoed innocently. "More like a randy black stallion would be more to the point." She kissed his strong nose, then heard him groan when she began running her tongue along the indentation at his chin, while she rubbed her small, firm breasts across his muscular chest.

"Sure and you're a fairy wench sent to taunt me," he moaned against her breasts as she moved closer, then backed away. Never could he remember feeling so aroused or helpless, yet he had no wish to escape. "You've bewitched me with both your English and Irish ways," he confessed. What had this auburn-haired woman done to him? But he knew he reveled in her touch and wanted her to lead them this time. "Will you have no pity, then, sweet sparrow? Sure and you're killing me making me want you so, then pulling back like the naughty, teasing elf ya are."

His words and touch stirred her, causing her body to ache with intense need for fulfillment. Her hands splayed across the coarse hairs of his hard chest as she quickened their pace. Her own face was pink with her efforts, and she was grateful when he reached out to hold her long mane of straight hair back from her damp face. "I . . . I shall let you live," she added with impudence, "so that sometime in the future you will take me as you almost did tonight . . . the way a stallion takes a mare."

Her lurid words caused all sorts of erotic images to cascade against his heated thoughts. *"Gealbhan,"* he cried out, both in ecstasy and torment, for he knew this would be their last night together.

Chapter 22

Dunstan stared at Edna in disbelief. "You should not be here," he admonished, grabbing for the dressing gown at the foot of his bed.

Still dressed in the pink nightdress and matching wrapper, Edna O'Rahilly turned around while the Englishman covered himself hastily with his brown robe. She felt him next to her, smelled the citric scent of his soap. When she turned to see the concern in his serious gray eyes, she swallowed, knowing full well she had to see this through.

"I want you to leave now," Dunstan ordered, forcing a coldness in his tone he did not feel. "There is nothing more to say. We cannot marry and that is an end to it."

For days prior to the party tonight she'd pleaded, cajoled, and argued with him. Why wouldn't he take her away so they could be married secretly? She saw the stubborn set of his lean jaw again, then took a deep breath. "Very well, then I'll state my other reason for being here. It's to beg you not to fight my brother in the morning?"

"How did you know?"

"I know, that's all that matters." His over six foot frame appeared even taller to her when she saw him straighten and back away.

"It's too late. Your brother has insulted my sister for the last time. I'll not let my family become the doormat for Taggart O'Rahilly—boyhood friend or not."

"You'll kill each other over a silly fan?" the young

316

Irishwoman almost shrieked. Then she attempted to modulate her voice while she explained the misunderstanding about the Chinese gift.

His expression did not change, but Dunstan conceded, "It is regrettable your brother failed to make a quiet inquiry first. However, it is only one of many incidences where he has deliberately sought to destroy the Fitzroys. Father told me about them tonight. God knows my family is not perfect, but it is still an honorable English name. I am the last of my House in Ireland, the only one remaining in a position to defend it."

Why did he suddenly seem like such a stranger? Edna searched his face but could not find the kind, soft-spoken man who had touched her heart with his endearing letters and visits home. Had this last campaign in India hardened him, the wounds going far deeper than the gash on his leg? Clutching her hands in front of her, she tried to think of a way to reach him. Would he respond to a gentler coaxing? Her brother would keep his word and not fire at Dunstan. But she couldn't stand by and see Taggart killed, either.

"Oh, Dunstan." It came out as a breathless sob, then the petite Irishwoman leaned closer to his tall frame. She had to crane her neck to look up into his eyes, for he stood with such restraint she almost expected a military salute. Silently she hoped his reflexes were as quick as before, else she'd probably crack her skull. She thrust her arms out in supplication as she swayed forward.

Dunstan automatically reached out to catch her. "Oh, my darling" tore from him. All traces of cool reserve vanished. He placed his left arm under her legs to lift her small form easily against his chest. "Edna," he said in alarm when he looked down to see her pale face dangling over his right arm. Despite his scarred leg, he managed to get them both over to the curved brown settee against the wall. After he deposited his precious cargo on the cushioned furniture, he hobbled to the edge of his bed and grabbed his cane. It made the walk to his shaving stand less difficult.

From lowered lashes Edna watched the auburn-haired man retrieve a clean square of linen from his chest of drawers, then dip it in the poured water of a white basin. She made sure her eyes were closed before he bent over her. But his worried expression caused her a twinge of guilt about the deception, but, she pushed it aside, for this was her last hope.

Awkwardly, the towering Englishman made it to his knees. "Beloved," he whispered as he tenderly dabbed her face. When he felt her wrist, relief etched across his face with each steady vibration against his fingers.

Edna moaned, then slowly fluttered her green eyes open. "Oh my, is that you, Father?" She touched the masculine face, secretly reveling in the feel of his recently shaved cheek, then over the nose too long to be called handsome but straight and strong, like the line of his jaw. "Whe—where am I?" She asked, adding a pathetic mew of alarm as she backed away from the person she thought the dearest, sweetest man in the world.

Good Lord, she was delirious, Dunstan thought. Bracing his hands on the wooden cane, he hauled himself off his knees in record time.

He returned with a glass of cognac and before sitting down, nudged a wooden chair over to the sofa with his bare foot. "Don't be afraid, darling Edna. Give yourself a moment and it will come back to you. You fainted, my love. Can you sit up?"

With surprising agility, Edna came to a sitting position.

"Here, sip this, there's my good girl."

The raven-haired beauty accepted the bulb-shaped glass. "Oh, yes. It is coming back to me—Dunstan," she added with just the right touch of hesitation, then a beguiling smile popped out as she stretched her slippered feet out on his sofa. She took a sip of amber liquid. Handing the glass back to him, she assured, "That is better. Thank you."

After he set the glass down on the table next to the brocade-covered sofa, he took one of her small hands between his larger ones, chaffing it gently to bring her back to health. As he leaned over her, the Englishman was captivated by the innocent expression on her adorable face. Despite his intentions, he kissed the dimple at the corner of her soft mouth. "Oh, my love, if I cannot have you for my wife, I shall die of grief," he confessed, a tormented sob in his cultured voice. When his code of ethics nudged him and he attempted to pull away, it surprised him to feel Edna's strength as she

318

maneuvered his head back down to her face once more.

Aware of the effect she was having on her Englishman, Edna pressed herself closer against him. She kissed the area below his throat, where the vee of his robe left his chest vulnerable. She delighted in the feel of the faint wisps of reddish-brown hair across the muscles of his bare chest. When he made a token movement to back from her once more, she clung to him like the ivy along the stones of Fitzroy Hall. "Love me," she dared. "I don't want to wait. With or without my brother's consent, you must know I've always been yours."

Edna reveled in the hard feel of his shoulders through the material of his robe. These last few weeks of care and better food had caused Dunstan to regain more strength. His determination to work with the horses had speeded a partial return of his former muscular physique.

Dunstan felt the moisture on his forehead, well aware of the tightening between his legs as Edna continued her kisses and caresses. God, how he wanted her. Hadn't the dreams of her in his arms kept him alive in India? For a moment he lost himself in the Irish green of her eyes, the sweet scent of her midnight hair, and the warm feel of her small round body as she pressed into him.

Before he knew it, he was joining her on the sofa. He gathered her in his arms with an urgency he'd never allowed to surface until now. Her ruffled nightcap came off easily in his hands, then he buried his face in her thick black curls. Bending her upper body across his arms, he claimed her lips with a dominance he'd never unbridled before.

On and on the torrid kiss went, until Edna thought she was actually going to swoon. This was an unleashed Dunstan, and she was breathless with the discovery that his passion did indeed match her own. Like his sister, Dunstan's cool reserve hid the smoldering fire that existed deep within.

Edna surrendered to him. It was not only the original intent of keeping him from fighting her brother in the morning, but now there was something else which demanded he finish what he'd so expertly started. "Oh, Dunstan," she gasped when she was forced to pull away for air. Her body throbbed and burned where he touched her. "I never realized how wonderful you are."

He chuckled in open amusement at her confession, so like his little Edna—direct and fiery. However, the moment gave the self-disciplined part of his makeup a chance to surface. What the devil was he doing? he shouted at himself. He looked down to see that he'd roughly torn the pink ribbons on her wrapper, clearly in order to gain unrestricted access to her voluptuous breasts. He pushed air into his heated lungs, suddenly shocked to realize he'd been on the verge of taking her virginity right here in his room, without a show of responsibility for her reputation or her future. He told himself only a despicable bastard would take such advantage of a helpless woman after she'd swooned in his arms. And he loved this beautiful Irishwoman. In self-condemnation, he shoved himself back, grabbed the familiar cane, and got up so abruptly, he stubbed his bare toes against the leg of the chair he'd recently vacated. "Devil take it," he growled, then fumbled with his robe, pulling the cloth sash tighter about his waist than necessary. He turned his back ot Edna in order to spare her maidenly blushes if she saw his condition. Hell, he was the eldest in this room; why was he acting so irresponsibly? "Edna," he grated, attempting to recapture a normalcy to his voice. "It is better if you return to your room now. I shall look out first to be sure none of the servants are in the hall." Without another word he walked stiffly to the door and peered out. Despite the feeling of throbbing discomfort, part of him was relieved to find his body had returned to a healthy masculine reaction. After his severe injuries, he'd not exactly been plagued by unrestrained lust.

When he poked his head back in, Edna was standing just behind him. "It is safe for you to leave," he said over his shoulder.

However, Dunstan was not prepared when she shook her head stubbornly and closed the door herself.

"You mean, you don't want me?" she demanded. This thought of open rejection hadn't occurred to her, for she'd assumed the Englishman loved and desired her. Then a horrifying thought made her eyes turn to green saucers. "Oh,

Dunstan, I'm so sorry. You mean your injury ... you can't—"

"Damn it, Miss O'Rahilly," he swore as heat turned his compexion ruddy. "One of my legs is permanently damaged, not what lies between them." The strain was evident on his lean face. His auburn hair was about his shoulders now, and he pushed a few strands back with an impatient hand. "I desire you so much I shall be lucky to be able to walk in the morning, let alone sit a horse. Now," he snapped, "will you kindly leave here before I do something we will both regret in the morning."

Never had Dunstan spoken this way to her. "Well," she sniffled, thrusting her small nose up at him, "'tis obvious you do not wish my company this night. Never let it be said we O'Rahillys lack the subtlety to know when we are not wanted." She gathered her nightdress about her as if it were a regal ball gown. "A good night to you, sir." She tugged the torn wrapper up farther on her bare shoulder.

He hadn't missed the hurt in her emerald eyes, despite her attempts at a dignified retreat. It was clear she had no idea what hell it was to send her back to her room. When she would have brushed past him, Dunstan held her still with one hand. "No, don't struggle, Edna, for you must hear my reasons before you leave."

After he felt her relax, the viscount let go of her arm. "There is nothing on earth I'd rather do than make love to you right now." His hand tightened on the gold handle of his cane. "But I want you honorably as my wife. Nothing less," he added, the unyielding hardness back in the steel of his eyes. "I will not be like my father in this. Don't you think I've known for years how he used the Irish girls on this estate?" Dunstan made no effort to hide his disgust. "My father paraded them through this house as if they were flowers he had every right to pluck. In London before my mother died, it was the same with English girls, most off the street or from the taverns he frequented. No," he stated emphatically, holding up a hand to silence her when he saw her open her mouth to protest. "I will go back to raising my horses. Calvert Huntington has already consented to make me a loan to get me started. When I have enough money, I'll approach your brother again." If I'm still alive, the Englishman thought with sober reality, for he realized he did not want to be the instrument of O'Rahilly's demise.

As Edna stared up at Dunstan, she was forced to admit her plan had failed on both counts. He would not marry her without her brother's consent as the head of the O'Rahillys, nor would he back down from meeting him in a duel of honor—to the death. She walked unsteadily to the door as the silent tears almost blinded her.

Alone in the hallway, Edna buried her face in her hands, wondering why God had abandoned her and Millie.

Lady Millicent watched her husband. How endearingly boyish he appeared. The sleeping black wolf, she thought. With a soft smile, she felt the warm thoughts envelop her. The darkness in the room hid her color as she remembered how expertly he'd painted such arousing pictures of her with his Gaelic words and expert lovemaking, taking her for a second time during the night.

"Millie?"

Millicent heard Edna's small voice. She looked down to see that Taggart was fast asleep. Silently, she slipped out of bed and went to the door.

"Oh, Millie, please come to my room. We must talk!"

Edna appeared so distressed, Millicent wasted little time grabbing for her robe and slippers.

When they reached Edna's rooms, the shorter girl told her all about the duel, which was to take place in only a few hours.

"God's teeth," Millicent cried as she collapsed next to Edna on the side of her bed. And Taggart had breathed nothing of this to her. "You are right, Edna, neither one of these two mules will back down." Deep in concentration, Lady Millicent got up to pace back and forth along the new Oriental carpet. From Edna's report of failed attempts, Millicent knew she'd only waste precious time trying to reason with either man. Despite everything, she did understand why her dear brother had felt compelled to defend her honor. Hadn't she wanted to strangle the O'Rahilly herself when he'd accused her in front of everyone?

Hands behind her as she walked back and forth, Millicent stopped as a strategy began to form in her mind. But blast it, Taggart had burned her comfortable breeches. And she didn't dare chance going back to their rooms for clothes, lest her husband awaken, and Edna's clothes would all be too small. "Well," she said aloud, "I'll have to toss my old red cloak over this. It's on a peg downstairs. Come on, there's no time to waste." She headed for the door. "Delay Dunstan in the morning as long as you can. He'll expect hysterics and you can always swoon again. That would be good for another half hour, for I know my brother is smitten with you," she quipped, feeling a trifle lightheaded at this new danger. "Taggart will assume I've come back to my own room, and he'll be relieved at the chance to slip away."

"But, Millie," Edna said in alarm as she clutched her hands together in agitation. "I . . . I thought you'd, you know . . . use your feminine wiles to convince my brother to call it off."

"Stuff," Millicent scoffed with a toss of her head. "In the first place, I don't have that many wiles to use. And in the second place, if I tried that approach your randy brother would make love to me until dawn, then go right out and do exactly what he damn well pleased anyway."

"Millie!" Edna could not hide her shock at her friend's blatant comments.

"It is the truth and you know it."

"But, Millie, where are you going?"

Over her shoulder, Millicent answered, "To make certain my husband never reaches Temar Road at dawn."

"But, your ladyship," Fergus Mulcahy complained, "I don't like this. What if we should meet some of King George's men? A patrol might come by here. No, I don't like it at all."

"We're not here to enjoy it. All we have to do is seize and rob him." Millicent pulled her red hood closer to her face. Riding sidesaddle was not as comfortable as breeches astride Buttercup. She shifted her form, trying to fight the queasiness

323

in her stomach. Probably nerves, she told herself. "Believe me," she addressed the six other men. "If there had been any other way I would take it." She looked at Fogarty, the pub owner. "We should have little trouble at this hour," she encouraged, purposely smiling at the five other young, strong Irishmen. "And I'm sure Fergus told you all how eternally grateful I shall be for you assistance. You helped my husband kidnap me almost two months ago. This should be child's play for you. Nevertheless, I still wish you would allow me to pay you for your time."

"We wouldn't hear of it, me lady." Fergus looked at his companions, who nodded readily in agreement. "The lads wouldn't take a thing for helpin' Taggart abduct ya. Sure and we'll be takin' the same for robbin' yer husband. In addition to which, we'll keep our gobs shut about this. And may the saints watch over ya," he told the cloaked woman, "for if ye were my wife and I found out ya'd deliberately had highwaymen waylay me, why I'd strangle ya with me bare hands, that I would."

The Englishwoman knew it was the strain of danger that made the men laugh nervously. "Please," she warned, alarmed at their loudness.

Immediately they were silent.

Millicent strained to hear. Yes, there it was again, the muffled sound of a horse and rider approaching. "Wait until I give the signal. And remember, he'll not be armed," she added, remembering that Edna said John Nolan was to bring the dueling pistols in his carriage. "All you need do is get him at gunpoint, take his purse, and keep him here until later in the morning. Have you the rope, Fogarty?"

"Yes, my lady." The older man held it up.

"All right, put your masks on, and I'll wave when I'm certain it's Taggart." She turned Buttercup and headed up to the high ridge as look out. The fog was thick as the sun barely began to light the horizon. Pushing her spectacles up, she squinted and saw the unmistakable silhouette of her husband astride Laidir. She looked down at her friends, their faces hidden behind hastily cut black cloth masks. Her slender arm rose, giving them the agreed upon signal.

The men were on Taggart, knocking him off the black

324

stallion before he knew what had happened. One of the disguised Irishmen pointed the unloaded pistol Millicent had lent him for this purpose. Without speaking, he motioned with the gun for Taggart to stand to the right of the other "highwaymen."

Watching unobserved, Millicent could almost feel Taggart's fury as he came to his full height, brushed off his dark clothes, then slowly obeyed.

In truth, Taggart was cursing his decision right now to have John Nolan bring the brace of pistols in his carriage. Accosted like a defenseless maid, he thought, feeling humiliated for being caught without so much as a sword for defense. "It would seem" he grated, "you gentlemen, and I use the term loosely, have me at a disadvantage." Then, without warning, he was at them with his fists.

None of Millicent's comrades had obviously anticipated his fighting ability, and when O'Rahilly sprang to action, he easily knocked the pistol out of his assailant's hand. With horrified eyes, Millicent saw that their friends were hard pressed to subdue the strong Irishman.

"Bloody hooligans," she heard Taggart shout. Then there was a stream of Gaelic metaphors, followed by more blows from his fists. Feeling things were not going as planned, Millicent put her knees to Buttercup's flanks and raced down the embankment.

Three of the young men were down on the hard ground nursing an assortment of bloody noses, black eyes, and wrenched bones. When she saw the youngest lad in the group scramble for the fallen pistol and raise the silver butt cap over Taggart's skull, she shouted in protest.

But it was too late.

Her husband landed with a loud thud just a few feet from her. She jumped off her horse and was at his side immediately. "Taggart," she cried. "I said no violence," she snapped at her companions. She breathed a sigh of relief when she heard the strong beating of his heart near her ear as she bent over him, cradling his upper body in her arms.

"No violence?" countered the young man who had struck Taggart unconscious. "Beggin' your pardon, me lady, but me and the boys will be carryin' a few bruises for days after this." Similar to the others, he now removed his mask, stuffing it into his coat pocket.

She looked about the sea of cut and bleeding men and had to agree. These good men didn't deserve to be beaten to a pulp, either. "Yes, you did what was necessary. I'm sorry I yelled at you."

She reached into her cloak and pulled out an embroidered pocket handkerchief and wiped the blood from her husband's head. There was a large lump beginning to form on the back of his skull, but nothing felt seriously broken, thank God.

"Now what are we going to do?" Fergus complained. "We were only supposed to keep him here at gunpoint for a few hours. How are we going to get him back to the Hall without being seen?"

Millicent drew in her breath when she heard the sound of an approaching carriage. Her fears were for her friends. If these were soldiers and not John Nolan, they wouldn't hesitate to bring in a group of Irish highwaymen. "Help me pull Taggart away from the center of the road."

Without hesitation, three of the men gently lifted O'Rahilly and set him down in the soft green earth.

Millicent came back to the circle of worried-looking males. "I want you to hide in those trees past the ridge until we leave. Do you know the spot?"

"Yes, but we can't leave ya both here alone, me lady," Fergus protested. And the other men echoed his concern.

She looked down at her faithful servant, then up at his companions. Old Fogarty still held the now useless rope in his hands. "Please leave. I shall be fine. Remember, I'm English, they will not harm me. And Taggart is an American, with the King of England for a friend. Go, for I would never forgive myself if you came to harm."

Grumbling, the men did as bidden.

Alone, she stood protectively in front of her husband as the coach approached. A ragged breath escaped when she saw it was John Nolan's carriage. However, her surprise was further confounded when Garnet peeked out from the open window. She pulled her long cloak closer about her and looked down at the tops of her ruined slippers. This would not be easy.

"Why, Millicent, a little early for your rounds to the tenants, is it not?" Dressed charmingly in blue velvet, Garnet's smile did not quite reach the blue of her eyes. Her feathered bonnet was worn at a delectable angle, and the light of dawn danced off her blond curls.

Hating to ask but realizing there was no other choice, Millicent walked over to Nolan's coach. "Please, Taggart has been injured. Would you take us back to the Hall?

Instantly, Garnet shouted an order back to John's footman. After the young man assisted her down, she came over to the taller woman. She peered around to see the man prostrate on the dewy ground. "How did it happen?"

"We . . . were riding and Buttercup ran off after being frightened by a stonechat. As the morning sun warmed her face, Millicent pushed back her red hood. "Two highwaymen ambushed us on our morning ride. Taggart tried to stop them from robbing us, but they hit him on the head. Your timely approach must have scared them off."

"Thomas," Garnet called up to the driver. "You and William lift Mr. O'Rahilly into the carriage."

Millicent helped the two servants with her husband. However, when she realized Garnet had not driven here alone, she stepped back, allowing the servants to ease her husband on the other unoccupied seat.

She nodded at John Nolan, then saw the wooden box he held across his lap. But why was Garnet with him?

"Now," Garnet said with a sly smile, "you know that ridiculous story about a bird scaring Buttercup is not true. And Taggart would not risk his life for a few coins. Why, I've heard he could buy Fitzroy Hall five times over and still be one of the wealthiest men in London." She eyed Millicent up and down. "Although I know until recently you were quite hopeless in the fashion arena, even you must know boots and a bed gown under a frayed cloak are hardly appropriate garments for a morning canter. A fastidiously tailored man like Taggart would never allow his wife to go out dressed in such a manner."

Trapped, Millicent blustered to the offensive. "I could ask you why you are here, and with John Nolan."

"Very good," Garnet came back. "It appears we both have a desire for anonymity this morning. But I will not help you unless you tell me the truth." The hardness was back in her blue eyes.

The lady knew there was no choice. Then quickly she told Garnet about her efforts to keep him from dueling with her brother.

Garnet laughed outright. "Lud, you do get into the most scandalous predicaments. Poor Taggart," she mewed in mock sympathy.

"Then you won't tell my husband, your grace?" she pressed, knowing full well Taggart would view this in the same light as if she'd murdered his sister. Her proud husband would never forgive her treachery if he found out. "Please, Garnet, I will do anything you ask, but please, take my injured husband home. Tell his servant Caleb you found him in the road after he'd been set upon by robbers."

Garnet seemed to weigh the sides carefully as she tapped her gloved hand on her ruby lips. "All right, I shall keep silent on this, for I would not like poor Calvert to be bothered by finding out I came here, merely to see that your husband was not harmed, you understand."

Millicent bristled at the implication but held her tongue. "Thank you, Garnet, I will not forget your favor to me this day."

"No, I shall see that you do not," her blond adversary stated.

Garnet gathered her skirts and allowed Nolan to assist her to reenter the coach. She sat next to the handsome man dressed in dark gray, then looked across at the unconscious Irishman.

Placing a familiar hand on John's linen-covered arm, Garnet whispered something to him.

Frowning, John protested, "But what are we—I mean," he amended, with a scowl at Lady Millicent who stood just outside the coach. "My lady, what am I to tell your brother and father? They are waiting in the clearing right now." He looked down at the wooden box on his lap. "Your husband asked me to be his second and bring the weapons with me this morning."

Millicent bit her lip, then made a decision. She leaned near

328

the carriage window. "If you give me the pistols, I shall ride my horse to the edge of Temar Road and explain the situation."

"You said Buttercup had run off."

Millicent refused the bait. "She came back." Then she eyed Nolan again. "Will you allow me to explain the situation?" she pleaded.

"As you know it," countered Garnet's tight-lipped companion.

Her chin lifted at the older man's tone. "As I know it." Then she heard Taggart moan and feared he might come around at any moment. "Please," she added in desperation. "You know I can talk my way out of a difficult situation." Surely John would remember her acting ability that night she'd saved Taggart from a beating when he'd taken the earl's favorite horse.

"Devil take it, John, give her the wretched pistols. I'm getting cold in this morning air."

"But," Nolan protested. "What if she fires?"

"There will be no duel today," Garnet interjected emphatically. "No, do as I say," she added, her usual softness around men dissipating for a moment.

Reluctantly, Nolan handed Millicent the wooden box.

As Millicent accepted the box, she couldn't help looking down at Taggart once more. His face was pale and drawn. She almost sobbed outright when she spotted his vest where his coat had opened. He had worn the gold embroidered waistcoat she had made for him and given to him the morning of Dr. Collins's last visit. It touched her that he had chosen to wear it on this of all days.

As the carriage drove off, Millicent forced back her tears and raced back up the bank to get Buttercup. She tied the wooden box to her saddle, thinking of the way John and Garnet looked at each other. Well, she had more important things on her mind than the relationship between the Duchess of Montrose and John Nolan. She cursed the sidesaddle that seemed to slow her pace. "Faster," she cried to her horse, pushing the filly to the limit.

"God's nightshirt, it's Millicent!" Geoffrey Fitzroy waddled over to his daughter. "Dunstan, don't help her down. Last thing we need is having her spout one of her logical sermons at us." He eyed his wayward daughter. "This is no place for you, chit. How the devil did you find out about it?"

Despite his father, Dunstan assisted his sister from her horse. But he admitted, "Father is right, Millie. You shouldn't be here. Edna told you, didn't she?"

Ignoring his correct insight, she blurted, "Taggart has been injured by highwaymen." In a rush, she told them how she asked John Nolan to take the injured man home in his carriage. She never mentioned Garnet's presence.

"What humbug. Knew the man was a coward," the earl derided.

But before she could defend her husband, she saw John Nolan racing toward them on foot.

Millicent thought he looked relieved to reach them.

"I . . . I sent my footman with your husband, my lady," John Nolan explained, then gave Millicent a knowing look as he complied with her deception. "I was concerned for your safety alone on these roads. What if the highwaymen returned? Thank heavens you are unharmed. Here," he directed, taking the box of pistols from her. "I'll relieve you of this burden."

"So, your story was true, girl. Damn disappointing," complained the earl. "Well, we'll just have to schedule it when that Irishman is well. Not too hurt, is he, Millie?"

Assuming this would be the end to this dueling nonsense, Millicent could not hide her shock. "Father, there is no longer any need for a duel."

"Poppycock, that upstart O'Rahilly insulted us."

"Dunstan?" she pleaded. "Surely you are going to let this matter rest. Edna explained to you about the fan. It was all a mistake, a stupid, bloody mistake."

"You watch your language, my girl," the earl admonished.

"Her ladyship is overwrought," John Nolan added in a placating manner. "Come, we should take her home."

She wrenched off Nolan's arm and hauled the wooden box out of his hands. "All right, confound you. We'll fight the duel as planned." She opened the box of dueling pistols. "John, give

330

my brother the first choice."

"Millie, you can't be serious." Her brother looked aghast.

"I am in deadly earnest," she stated in cold fury. "I'm an O'Rahilly, and I shall stand in my husband's absence."

"This is insane," John Nolan protested, still refusing to take the box Lady Millicent was thrusting under his nose.

She whirled about to face Nolan and her father. "No less deranged than two grown men willing to die over that bloody fan. Yes, Father, I said it again. And their bloody pride." Motioning Nolan away from the others, she shoved the opened pistol box at him once more. "You'd best do as I say and offer Dunstan the first choice of weapons," she hissed for his ears alone. "Else I'll tell Marigold her husband has taken the Duke of Montrose's wife for a—what would you call the relationship, sir?"

Nolan's hazel eyes darkened. His handsome face contorted in a furious scowl. He seemed to read her threat as a serious impediment, for he no longer tried to stop her.

Coldly she nodded and walked over to stand a few feet from her taller brother.

"Millie, you're daft if you think I'll go through with this folly. You're my sister and a woman for heaven's sake. Stop spewing such nonsense." He looked at Nolan, who now held the box open in front of him.

The early-morning breeze ruffled Millicent's straight hair about her face when she adjusted her cloak to free her arms. "I'll have an end to this right here and now, Dunstan," she shouted. "In front of witness, this business is to stop here, for I'm the one who was supposed to have received the insult, and I am an O'Rahilly now." She knew she would have to press harder to get her protective brother to face her. "Or are you afraid I'll best you, now that you're a cripple with only one good leg?" she taunted, regretting the cruel remark but finding it necessary.

Dunstan's gray eyes sparked at her barb. Angrily he hurled his cane to the ground and grabbed the nearest pistol Nolan offered him. With expert ease, he held the weapon up in his right hand.

His sister could not look at John Nolan. She kept her eyes on

331

the dark flintlock pistol nested in the green felt interior. She needed both hands to raise it out in front of her.

As if her father suddenly felt the farce had gone on long enough, he shouted, "You've made your point, girl, now lower the blasted gun before it goes off and kills us all."

Unflinching, she kept her stance, waiting for her brother's next move. A new look of admiration and understanding suddenly passed between brother and sister.

Dunstan raised his pistol, aimed to the side of her, and fired. He smiled across at her and stood waiting.

She nodded and lowered the long barrel of the gun farther away from her target than he had, for she knew she lacked his skill with a gun and would never chance endangering him. She squeezed the trigger with two fingers. There was a metal sound, but nothing happened.

Used to firearms, Dunstan's eyebrows rose with his suspicions. When he saw his sister try to squeeze the trigger once more, he shouted, "No, Millicent! Drop it and move away!" He raced to her, despite his limp.

At her brother's warning, she tossed the gun out of her hands, but the force with which it exploded knocked her backward on the hard ground. The ball missed her chest by a hairs breadth, but her hands felt scorched.

John Nolan was at her side first. His face was ashen as he bent over her. "My lady," he cried in alarm.

All three men helped her rise. She swayed, leaning heavily against her brother. Millicent felt the powder burns on her hands. What had happened?

"You might have been killed," John said in a distraught voice. "Those guns haven't been used in years, but I told my man to test them. I'd never have forgiven myself if you had been injured."

"It can happen," Dunstan said. "It wasn't your fault. But thank God I recognized the signs."

The earl added, "I've seen a man's face blown off from a misfired pistol, and—"

"Father, please," the viscount directed when he saw his sister's pallor.

Millicent felt her stomach heave and clamped a hand over

her mouth, willing her body to obey her mind. She allowed the three men to help her to Buttercup.

"Here, John can ride your horse," Dunstan directed, as he supported his sister against his chest. "You'll ride in front of me on my horse, Millie, for you look ready to drop."

When she felt more comfortable on her brother's horse in front of him, she twisted her head and asked, "And does this mean you and Taggart will not fight any more duels?"

"I swear," Dunstan promised, raising his hand and voice so the others could witness. Then he smiled at his sister and gave her a quick hug before they began the ride back to the Hall. "And I am just beginning to sympathize with my poor brother-in-law," he admitted. "You are a handful. Thank heaven you're now his problem and not mine."

She aimed a playful jab to his ribs. But later as they neared Fitzroy Hall, she couldn't help shuddering as she realized she might have been killed by this morning's accident.

Chapter 23

From her vantage point on the chair a few feet from their bed, Millicent watched as Dr. Liam Collins examined her husband's head. She could tell Taggart was more restless today with his role as invalid. Last evening had been the first night in which the sleeping powder had not been necessary to quell his excruciating headaches. Oh, she thought guiltily, if only that lad hadn't panicked and hit Taggart with the handle of her pistol.

"Well, now that I see it today, I'd say it doesn't appear as serious as I'd first thought," Liam reassured. "However, you've still got a nasty lump and there's a cut above it." After the doctor bathed the wound, he reached into his medical case for a packet.

"Now," he directed to Millicent. "Here is more of that powder to mix with tea if he complains of pain again. A day or two more of bed rest and he'll be as good as new." He handed Millicent the packet. "With the authorities so concerned over this rebel business, they haven't the manpower to protect decent citizens from highwaymen. Place will be swarming with every bandit imaginable," complained the doctor. "Lucky Nolan found him and scared off those scalawags."

Feeling testy from three days of confinement, along with the frustration of being so close to his wife yet unable to do anything about it in his present condition, the patient glared at the young doctor. "Liam," he snapped, "you needn't talk as if I weren't in the room."

334

When both parties seemed to take little notice of his comment, he became more disgruntled. "And where did you get this blasted nightshirt?" he demanded from his spouse, holding up his hands to show the elaborately ruffled cuffs. "'Tis the nightwear for a fop. Caleb knows I never wear them."

With a tolerant look at her husband, Lady Millicent answered. "I asked Dunstan to lend it to you. It appears he no longer wears them, either. He said his former Army life instigated the change. I dare say you've both become rather uncivilized these last few years." She couldn't hide her blush, despite her flippant tone. But she quickly added, "I thought it would render a more modest countenance in front of your physician." She didn't tell him it also helped in her efforts to nurse him with a detached manner.

"Oh," Liam added with a grin at Lady Millicent, while he clearly ignored Taggart's scowl. "If your patient should prove ill-tempered later on, that powder will also put him to sleep."

"Thank you, Liam. How perceptive of you." Millicent gave the good doctor one of her sweetest smiles, then adjusted her wire frames. "But we must all bear our little crosses," she continued, in a tone of mock suffering. "And I appreciate the salve for my hands," she added, looking down at the white cloth wrapped about the palms of both hands.

"The viscount told me about that wretched accident. You're a very lucky woman, my lady."

"Yes," her husband echoed. "You might have been killed. As it is I was frantic when I heard of it." He glanced at the doctor, realizing this conversation was better left until he and his wife were alone.

Millicent hadn't missed the concern on her husband's face. "Well, at least you and Dunstan have reconciled your disagreement. Don't you realize I could not bear knowing I was the cause of either of your being injured or killed?"

When O'Rahilly saw the torment in her eyes, he could not help being moved. "I understand it now, sparrow. And despite my ranting at you when I learned you'd taken matters into your own hands after those rowdies jumped me, I'm grateful you got Dunstan and me to see the foolishness of our ways."

Her gray eyes warmed at his admission.

Liam cleared his throat as he looped the brown leather strap of his medical box over one shoulder. "Since you're both on the mend," he added with a chuckle, "I'll be leaving."

After the doctor left, Millicent walked over to her husband. "Would you like some tea now?" she offered, fluffing up the pillows behind his back a little awkwardly because of her bandaged palms.

The black-haired man inhaled the sweet scent of her hair as she went about her nursing duties. His earlier irritation vanished, and he reached out for her, silencing her squeak of surprise with a kiss that demanded more.

Her actions were only halfhearted as she tried to wriggle free. At first she returned his ardent kiss and pressed her slender form closer, while wrapping her bandaged hands about his neck. But just as quickly she recalled Liam's advice on quiet bed rest. When he relaxed his hold, she pulled back. Flushed, she made a pretext at adjusting the wrappings wound about the center of her hand. "Taggart, the doctor wanted you to rest. Such activity will surely make your head ache again."

"I have another ache to dispel right now, wife. And I'll have a care of your hands, sweet elf. As you are learning, there are many ways to wrestle the snake of Ireland." With an audacious leer in her direction, he reached for her once more, but she was too quick this time.

She scampered off the bed, just as Caleb knocked at the door with his master's lunch. Trying to compose her features, she held the door open for his servant.

The tall black man entered carrying the tray of steaming food.

"Good," Taggart said with appreciation as the silver cover was lifted from the full plate of food. "I'm starving. At least this pleasure isn't to be denied me."

A look passed between husband and wife, and Taggart chuckled as he watched Millicent's skin take on scarlet hue. After Caleb left, he admitted, "I really shouldn't tease you so, gentle sparrow." He wondered if he dared tell her that he was captivated with the outward English lady and the fiery woman of passion she kept hidden.

Unable to join in her husband's amusement, Millicent's

stomach heaved at the smell and view of ham and gravy potatoes. "Well," she said over her shoulder as moisture broke out above her upper lip, "I'll leave you to your lunch." With more haste than usual, she rushed to her adjoining room.

After losing her scant breakfast in a nearby basin, the Englishwoman washed her face, then reclined on her bed for a few moments, trying to will her head and stomach to quiet down.

However, Millicent sat up quickly when a thought occurred to her. Hadn't she helped Liam enough on his rounds to know the signs? And things had been so hectic of late, there had been little time to pay attention to the normal activity of her body. Mentally she counted. Yes, she thought as the realization hit her, it was weeks past the usual start of her flux. Amazing, but it had to be the result of their first night together after the wedding. Leave it to that Irish Stallion, she mused with a smile, despite having just been ill. In a few days when Taggart was feeling better she would tell him the glorious news—they were going to have a child.

When Taggart came down for supper two days later, Millicent decided this would be the night for her good news. She would wait until he was in bed, then put on her prettiest negligee and enter their room. He was fully recovered, she was sure, so that if he wanted to make passionate love to her to show his appreciation, she was more than ready to assist him. The happy emotions bubbled up inside her, and she almost blurted her delightful news over the poached salmon.

Taggart studied his wife for a moment. The candlelight made her hair glow with a fiery burnish. Behind her glasses, he saw that her gray eyes sparkled with an intensity he hadn't seen since their glorious night together after the party. "You no longer need the bandages," he commented, looking across at her slender hands as she reached for her wineglass. "When I first came awake upstairs, I feared the damage was permanent."

Quickly she sought to reassure him. "No scars or pain. None at all."

His smile broadened as he continued to watch her. Despite the rest of the family at table he said, "You look inordinately pleased with yourself. Solving the world's problems agrees with you." Deviltry flickered from his earth-colored eyes. "If you can also find a way to get these Irish and English fanatics to stop hurting their countrymen with their violent demonstrations, you will let me know." When she didn't take up his challenge, he pressed, "Just what shenanigans have you been up to while I've been confined to a sickbed?" He was only half in jest. "Though I honor your determination to help those less fortunate, if you've been at Fogarty's or a certain house outside of Kinsale, I'll—"

"No, I've been a perfect saint," the bespectacled woman defended, suppressed laughter in her voice. She pulled herself away from her romantic anticipations about later this evening when she felt the bewildered stares of her father, brother, and Edna, in addition to her handsome husband. Lowering her gaze to her fruit-and-cream dessert, she recited, "You are my husband and master. It is my duty to refrain from making a fool of you."

"Quite so," Taggart replied, not taken in by her show of docility for a second. "See that you remember it in private also."

"Of course," she added so the others could hear, "but you've always managed so well in that department without my assistance."

"English brat," he whispered under his breath, but he couldn't help grinning at her sauciness.

"I dare say" was all she would concede. She smiled when she saw the top of his waistcoat, just above where his coat buttoned. Her gift did indeed seem to please him.

The Irishman quickly wished they were alone, for he was sorely tempted to come around to her chair, lift her in his arms, and—his hungry eyes took in her cream-and-lilac muslin gown. That was the way he thought of her, surrounded by spring flowers. He was forced to busy his hands refolding his white linen napkin rather than embarrass his proper wife by giving in to the irrisistible urge to slowly remove her spectacles and smother her impudent face with kisses.

338

Taggart glanced at his father-in-law who still sat at the other end of the table, consuming a second helping of dessert with undisguised relish. "My lord," he addressed, trying to be civil, "you really should curtail those late-night carousings until this conflict has died down. The Duke of Montrose told me the King has ordered more hangings. It will only cause these hotheads to seek their own revenge. The more fanatical ones are out for blood. Why not wait a few weeks, then things will certainly have died down."

"Harumph," the earl scoffed, then wiped his mouth on his already spotted napkin. "Irish hooligans, I call them. So they want revenge do they, just like you, no doubt? A knife in my back, a ball through the heart, or perhaps you favor slitting my gizzard. That's your game, is it? Well, you can put your advice where the monkey put the nuts, O'Rahilly."

Taggart's lips became a grim line as he forced himself to swallow his heated retort, for he wanted no more squabbling in his household. Wasn't it bad enough to have the strain between Millicent and him, along with his sister pining away for a man who could not make her a suitable husband? And the time was fast approaching when he had to return to Williamsburg. He'd stayed away too long. The letters from Ben Abrams urged him to come home to attend to his shipping business. And the house on the James River was now ready for occupancy. But how could he leave when things were so unsettled?

At his worried silence, Taggart saw the others resume their meal. However, he was concerned that his sister was not eating again. She gave the appearance of moving the food about the china plate, but he hadn't missed how little she'd eaten during these last few days. There was a listlessness in her manner, something he'd never seen in the rambunctious girl. Dunstan sat across from her, appearing silent and detached.

The Irishman cleared his throat. "Dunstan, you do not have to go to Calvert for a loan. I . . . I have given the matter some thought, and I should appreciate it if you would take over the administration of the stables, expand the number and quality of our horses. Calvert tells me you're an expert with them, possessing a knowledge about breeding them he's never encountered before."

Dunstan's surprise was evident. He spoke tentatively, but it was clear he was pleased by his brother-in-law's comments. "Before I left for the Army, it was my hope to return and expand these stables. We could make them pay quite handsomely with the right breeds and men to run them. Hunting, carriage, racing—these horses are in demand here and throughout the Continent. I know of at least ten families who would eagerly buy our horses, for they've been complaining for years about the lack of good mounts in England."

When he saw Dunstan's open enthusiasm, Taggart felt he had done the right thing to make his offer. Somehow, it didn't sit well that his wife's brother felt forced to go outside the family for assistance. He owed the man that much. But could he let this man marry Edna? He still had no means to support her.

He shook his head, trying to sort out the present problems. It might take years before Dunstan's business showed a profit. Look how long it had taken him to build up Williamsburg Shipping? But, he thought, he'd been lucky to have help through Millicent's unselfish gift and Ben Abrams's investment. Yes, he did owe Dunstan the chance to form his horse-breeding stables. However, he also had to think what was best for his sister, and that meant she would be better off marrying a wealthier man, like one of the O'Hara brothers.

When he read the gratitude in Millicent's eyes for his offer, Taggart raised his wineglass to her. "To Dunstan's success with . . . Fitzroy Stables."

Edna's face became more animated. "To Dunstan," she added in a breathless whisper.

Even the earl exhibited unusual restraint in raising his glass without a cutting remark.

"Thank you," Dunstan added after he'd taken a sip of the reserve burgundy. "And I swear I'll pay you back every shilling—and then some," he added, a boyish grin suddenly appearing on his lean face.

Taggart nodded, but a part of him felt a stab of embarrassment. For some time now he'd secretly observed

Dunstan as he went about taking care of the horses on the estate. Though the Irishman had been an efficient head groom, he realized Dunstan outmatched him because he clearly loved these horses. And it was now evident to Taggart that his brother-in-law wasn't afraid of hard work—he currycombed, fed, and exercised the horses right along with the stable hands. And Calvert told him Dunstan had been over to study every book the duke had on equestrian bloodlines.

Yes, Taggart mused silently, this was the life Dunstan was born to live. Man and beast were easy with each other, a mutual affection and respect between them. The money and horses meant less to him than they obviously meant to Dunstan. But the one person his brother-in-law wanted—Edna—Taggart knew he couldn't bend that far. Something else had come with his financial success. Responsibility was a heavy burden, he thought as he stared at the contents of his crystal goblet. "Well, when I return home to Williamsburg shortly, I'll need someone I can trust to look after things here. Give it some thought, will you, Dunstan?"

Millicent couldn't comment on her husband's casual offer or Dunstan's open pleasure at this news. Only one thing registered in her mind. Taggart was planning to leave Kinsale. And he'd made no mention that she would be going with him.

Feeling the need for privacy while he tried to sort his troubled thoughts, Taggart quietly excused himself while the others went into the music room after dinner. He didn't miss the brief disappointment in Millicent's gray eyes when he'd taken his leave. Perhaps there was hope she would return to his bed, he thought. But why did she continue to go to her sitting room? Didn't she realize a man appreciated knowing his wife wanted his attentions? He didn't always want to be the one who demanded she return to his bed. No, he'd just have to cool his heels until she came around. But God, he hoped it would be soon—this monk's life of abstinence was not to his taste at all.

After increasing Laidir's pace, he made his way through the tall grass to the old O'Rahilly cottage. The balmy spring air and soft darkness appealed to his mood. The Irishman dismounted and walked the rest of the way. There was a full moon, but he scowled when he looked up to see the outline of the earl galloping past him alone in the distance. "Jackass," he muttered. He might have saved his breath attempting to warn the earl from tramping off the estate alone after dark during these restless times.

The new door was not locked, and he bent his head and entered. Moonlight came through the one window in the small cottage. He looked about the place, spied the flint, and lighted the candle he found on a small entry stand. As he held up the candle, his brown eyes widened at the change in his former home.

He walked about the one-room structure. Wood planks and a cream-and-black Oriental carpet now covered what had formerly been a dirt floor. There was a beige sofa, overstuffed brocade-covered chair, a small round table. Two rural landscapes by George Lambert hung on the plastered walls. Placing the brass candlestick down on the table, Taggart slumped into the wing chair. The earl would never have fixed the cottage up. Who would—? He caught sight of the colorful doily where his candle now rested. A white embroideried swan glided across a blue-and-green lake. The rich red and yellow threads of the wildflowers along the riverbank made him think of Millicent. So, he mused, again she had managed to outwit her father, moving these things to the cottage before he'd sold them to pay his debts. But she could have hidden them anywhere. Why here?

He stretched out his legs in front of him. Yes, she knew how much this cottage meant to the O'Rahillys, especially Edna. Her kindness touched him, making him feel ashamed at how he'd bullied her before. As he sat gazing at the colorful needlework, he thought about her and all their encounters with each other. A slow, warm smile lighted his handsome face as it came to him in the inviting tranquility of this room—he loved Millicent. And he had the distinct impression he'd felt this way for a very long time, only his pride and desire for revenge had blinded him to the truth. Her unselfish actions could have showed him how to love years ago if he'd only had eyes to see. "Sparrow, I never realized—not until now," he murmured out loud.

For hours, Taggart sat in the dimly lighted cottage, savoring his discovery. Memories of the past and plans for the future intermingled. And for the first time in years, he felt a relaxing peace wash over him as he came to terms with both.

Unable to sleep, Millicent straightened her frilly nightcap and slowly walked to the door to the adjoining room. After knocking, she entered, but it gave her a start to realize the large bed had not been slept in. But it had to be close to three in the morning. Where was Taggart? Garnet and Calvert had now returned to spend the summer here rather than in the dusty heat of London. Her spirits plummeted as the inner pain cut at her once more. She felt her stomach, disappointed at not feeling the child's movements yet, though by now she was certain of her pregnancy. But instead of coming awake in her husband's arms after sharing this dearest of news with him as planned, she stood alone in her nightgown, staring at their large empty bed.

After quietly checking a few rooms downstairs, Millicent was forced to concede Taggart was nowhere in the house. Had he ridden out tonight to secretly meet Garnet now that she was back in Kinsale for the summer? She recalled his warning to her father at the dinning table. How could he disregard his own safety this way, riding out alone?

She refused to give way to tears. After going back to her room, she quickly put on one of her more serviceable nightgowns, then tossed Taggart's latest gift, a new wool cloak in her favorite red, over her shoulders. Grabbing her boots, in record time she crept down the dark backstairs and headed for the barn.

After checking the stables and finding Laidir gone, Mrs. O'Rahilly decided to plunk down on a bench outside the structure.

Crossing her arms in front of her, she prepared to wait for her husband's return. Without emotion, she was determined to have it out with him. Never would she be a spineless mouse, looking the other way if he chose to take his pleasure elsewhere. She would hear him out, but O'Rahilly would have to choose—either Garnet or Millicent, never both. And she would not tell him about their baby. His choice had to be a free one. She swiped at the betraying drop of moisture as it escaped from behind her glasses. If it were a contest of intelligence, or wit, or even physical strength, she would have felt more than equal to the task. However, she thought, clutching the soft material of the new red cloak about her, despite the warmth of the evening, in this one area where beauty seemed the major weapon, she'd never felt totally secure. She couldn't help recalling how Garnet had touched her husband in Nolan's coach that day, running her slender fingers along the waistcoat Millicent had embroidered. Had Garnet already won?

Less than an hour later, she heard a horse approach in the distance. Taggart was sauntering back very slowly, she mused, with a spark of temper. He probably thought there was no longer any need for haste or secrecy. Hands clenced at her sides, she stood up to wait.

But with a start she realized the horse approaching was not Taggart's black stallion. It was her father's mount, a light-brown gelding, thicker in the shanks than Laidir. Sighing, she realized the earl was probably foxed again.

However, when she observed that her father was slumped forward, one arm dangling down the horse's neck, Millicent quickened her steps.

"Father?" she called out to him as she reached for the horse's bridle. Her breath came back in a gasp when she saw the blood across his clothes, the saddle, even the horse's neck. The earl's throat had been cut from ear to ear. His body was tied to the horse's saddle. "Oh, God, no," she cried, almost unable to take in the grisly scene. Her fingers shook as she forced herself to untie the single knot of leather that held the corpse to the saddle. Unable to think about getting help, she only knew she had to free his body from this grotesque binding. But she screamed when her father's heavy body pitched to the side at her. Before she could get out of the way, the gray-tinged corpse hit her, and she toppled to the ground next to it.

On her knees, Millicent rolled her father's body over, trying not to look at his throat. After gently closing the bulging, terrified eyes, she tried to concentrate on searching for some clue as to who might be responsible for this monstrous act. True, she knew her father did not love her but felt it her duty to see that the perpetrator of this foul deed was brought to justice.

She pushed a tangled strand of auburn hair away from her face as she rested on the back of her legs. Instantly, she crouched back down on her knees as she saw a piece of cloth clutched in her father's right fist. It was difficult, but she finally managed to pry the material out from his stiff, cold fingers.

With mounting horror, she looked down at the unmistakable silver-and-gold embroidery and recognized it as a piece of silk material from the vest she had made her husband. "Taggart?" she breathed. Thoughts she tried to bury fought their way into her consciousness. She knew how much Taggart hated her father and blamed him for his own father's death, but surely he wasn't capable of murder. But the vision of his cold ruthlessness as he held Edwin Somerset to the ground with his sword came crashing to her. He'd looked more than ready to kill that day, and hadn't she felt his own fury on at least one occasion? Frantically, she rubbed her fingers along her throbbing right temple, forcing herself to think. But it couldn't be Taggart, not the man who had held her in his arms, kissed her and—no, she could not think of that now. He went out tonight, and there was the cloth in her hands condemning him.

She stood up, realizing she had to summon help. The magistrate was a friend of her father's. He would surely insist on an investigation into the earl's death. She went back to her father's body, ready to replace the cloth so that the authorities could handle this and see that justice was done. However, something stopped her. Tears came to her eyes.

Millicent then stuffed the incriminating evidence deep in the pocket of her red cloak, before she opened the door of the stable to awaken Samuel.

After falling into a peaceful sleep, Taggart came slowly awake. It amazed him to see that the sun was already up. Standing, he stretched his arms over his head, feeling invigorated more by the serious thinking he'd done the evening before. He touched the roughness of his face. First he'd wash and shave, then it would be time to awaken his adorable wife to share his news with her.

He began humming an old Irish ballad as he headed back toward Fitzroy Hall. It had proved useful coming back here, for he had finally made some decisions. Things would work out for all of them, he mused. He took a deep breath, inhaling the welcoming scents of dew-covered flowers and green grass. Strange, how he'd forgotten how lovely the countryside appeared in spring.

However, when Taggart arrived at the Hall, it was to find the manor in an uproar. Sir Jeremy was there with six of His Majesty's redcoats.

If Sir Jeremy Cartgrove, Chief Magistrate of Kinsale, thought Lady Millicent's husband looked oddly rumpled, he said nothing as he explained what had occurred during the night.

Taggart's countenance gave nothing away as he took in the startling news. However, he wasn't a hypocrite and couldn't pretend sorrow upon learning the earl was dead. It was a gruesome business, though.

He went instantly to his wife. When the Irishman took Millicent's cold fingers in his hands and looked at her drawn expression, he heartily regretted that she'd been the one first on the scene. It was no picture a gentle-natured lady should ever have to witness.

Millicent could not help drawing her fingers away from the warm hands that tried to comfort her. She attempted to read his expression, but it was closed to her. Had Taggart killed her father? The questions refused to stay buried. No ready answer came to her.

"Well," finished Sir Jeremy an hour later. "I'll leave a couple of my men stationed here if you like, my lady?" His gray wig didn't fit properly and he kept moving it forward on his head. "Can't say we have any leads, but it is my belief it was probably some of those Irish madmen we've been having such trouble with lately. We'll get them, you mark my word," the short man in his fifties reassured her. "And they will have a fine hanging, I promise."

Millicent paled at the older man's remarks. Though it was obvious he'd hoped to console her, the Englishman's words had the opposite effect. "It . . . it will not be necessary to station your men here, Sir Jeremy. Both my husband and brother, along with our servants, are more than adequate for protection. Besides," she added, attempting a smile, "I know how shorthanded you must be."

"Quite so, bless you, my lady." Shooting Taggart an unfriendly look, Sir Jeremy addressed Dunstan. "Is that agreeable to you, my lord?"

It was evident to Millicent that Sir Jeremy felt Dunstan was the rightful head of Fitzroy Hall.

"Yes, that will be fine," the new Earl of Fitzroy answered.

Millicent looked at her brother. His somber face was pale as he leaned on his wooden cane. The servants had offered their condolences but she knew they were not overcome with grief. Edna placed a comforting hand on her arm.

"'Tis rest you'll be needin' now, Millie. I'll send for your maid."

Millicent hardly heard what her sister-in-law was saying as she permitted herself to be led upstairs, while Taggart and her brother continued speaking with Sir Jeremy. The one thought that kept clamoring at her was, how could she allow innocent men to be killed when she suspected her own husband had been the murderer? Then she heard Sir Jeremy's voice.

"Mr. O'Rahilly," the magistrate demanded in an unfriendly tone, "a few of your servants overheard you threaten your father-in-law when Lady Millicent had ridden out to Mistress Alice's."

"Oh, God!" she cried. The blood drained from her face, forcing her to clutch the cold pink marble of the banister for support.

"Taggart!" Edna shouted over her shoulders.

Instantly the tall Irishman bounded up the stairs toward the two women. A quick glance at his wife told him what was needed.

Millicent felt herself being lifted upward as a strong arm encircled her waist and the backs of her knees. "Nooo. Not

347

you," she cried, and began to struggle.

"'Tis reaction from the news," Taggart told his sister. "Shhh," he soothed at the woman he held close to his chest. Silently he cursed himself for having fallen asleep in his old cottage. He could have prevented her from viewing such a grisly sight. "Put it out of your mind, sparrow. You're safe now. Don't you realize I'd never let anything harm you?"

Her gray eyes became larger behind her spectacles. The horrible irony of his statement struck her and she stopped pushing against the brown linen of his coat. How easily honeyed words came to him, she thought. Whether he'd done the despicable deed or not, she wasn't sure. But she would find out, she vowed. The piece of bloodstained embroidery hidden in her red cloak upstairs stood between them. And she knew she had to solve this mystery alone. Then she thought of her own secret, the child she carried within her. What ever would she do if her investigation lead to Taggart as her father's murderer? "Oh, God," she moaned once more. "What can I do?"

At the top of the stairs Taggart headed automatically to their large bedroom.

"No," she protested, ignoring the way Edna looked at her. "Please, I would rather sleep in my own room, if you do not mind," she added for her husband's sake in front of his sister, though the bile rose in her throat.

"As you wish," he conceded, but it was clear he did not like the situation.

"Everything will be all right, Edna." Taggart gave his sister a reassuring smile. He realized she didn't catch his meaning about her future also, but this was hardly the time to go into it. "Thank you, but I'll see to Millie now."

Edna nodded and left.

Millicent forced herself to appear in control. "I can manage on my own," she hinted, hoping he would leave.

"Nonsense. I'm not adverse to playing ladies' maid. I gave Bridget the rest of the day off, for the poor child was hysterical. She and Colleen were mumbling some nonsense about curses and reciting old Irish chants to ward off evil." When she didn't smile at his light banter, he began talking to her about the cottage and how she'd pleased him by it, all the while hoping the sound of his voice would calm her. When he reached out to unlace the back of her gown, he was struck at how tense her body felt under his fingers.

She tried to pull away. "I'm quite capable of tending to myself. Really, Taggart, I'm not a child."

"Then stop squirming like a rambunctious brat and hold still."

Clamping her lips together, she did as bidden.

"There, that's the last hook." With irritating efficiency, he got her out of her petticoat, corset, and chemise. He certainly knew his way about a lady's intimate apparel, she mused with a touch of asperity. And his patient forbearance was a surprising irritant at this moment.

"Now," he added pleasantly, after he pulled out a fresh white nightgown for her, the one with maidenly ruffles up to her slender neck. "This will do nicely." After he had her in the nightdress, he said, "Hop into bed, there's a good girl."

Her reproachful silence seemed only to amuse him. In less than fifteen minutes he was back in her room with a steaming cup of hot chocolate. She shook her head. "Thank you, but I want nothing."

Knowing she needed to rest but appearing too overwrought for natural sleep to overtake her, Taggart had put one of the doctor's small packets of laudanum in the steaming liquid before returning to her. "Please drink it down for me."

Despite his polite gentleness, she hadn't missed the determination in his eyes. "This is not the deck of one of your ships," she pointed out, "and I'm not a member of your crew. I appreciate the chocolate, but I do not wish any. What I do desire is for you to leave at once."

His bark of laughter was the last reaction she expected. And her father not even buried, she thought, appearing quite scandalized.

"Be thankful you're not on my ship, for sure and I might be tempted to toss you over the side to improve your manners." He set the steaming cup down on the night table next to her bed. The small piece of furniture sagged as he came down to sit next to her. "And in the same measure, you would be well advised to remember that I'm your husband, not some bumbling servant to be dismissed at your will. Now," he repeated with a mocking grin, "drink your chocolate before I forget all the English manners I tried so hard to learn at William and Mary."

"I dare say," she stated as her chin made that automatic rise. "And haven't you already proven what an uncivilized brute you can lapse into on occasion?" Right now he appeared quite capable of having killed her father and probably smiled as he did the wicked deed.

Taggart assumed she was thinking about their confrontation in the stables. He was just about to reassure her that he'd already promised himself never to do it again, but something stopped him as he studied the look in her censuring gray eyes. Her safety was vital to him, and her uncertainty in this area might make her more receptive to his suggestions along this line in future.

Purposely, he forced a severity into his expression. "Uncivilized brute, am I? Then, madam, you must know just how easily I could persuade you to drink it." He gave her a few seconds to consider his words.

"The chocolate," he reminded, offering her the cup once more.

There appeared little choice, and Millicent thought it seemed illogical to force an issue over such a trifling matter. Silently, she accepted the cup and drank the entire contents. Though she wouldn't admit it to her husband now, the chocolate was soothing, though it was slightly more bitter than she usually preferred. In her present condition, she only hoped it would stay down, at least until this forceful man left. Being ill in front of him would only be a further embarrassment right now.

Taggart took the empty cup out of her hand and placed it on her table.

She snuggled deeper into the mattress, suddenly surprised at how drowsy she felt. And she didn't even protest when her husband tucked the covers about her. "You really are a scoundrel," she murmured, then yawned, not quite understanding why she felt so exhausted. "It's a totally reprehensible habit, going about fighting women."

"Yes, I know. I'm an unscrupulous blackguard," he agreed. Her eyes were closed so she couldn't see the amusement on his face.

"I can't think how you'll end up," she chattered on in a sleepy voice. "I'm trying to help you, but I can't work miracles."

Silently, Taggart stayed by her until he knew she was asleep. Bending over her, he gently slipped off her spectacles and placed them near the empty china cup. She had worked miracles, he thought as he brushed a strand of long hair away from her cheek. For hadn't she taught him how to love and let go of those dark feelings he'd harbored inside his heart for too long? Because he wanted her to rest, he forced himself to leave her room rather than stay, for he knew where that would lead him. Soon, he promised himself.

But once outside the door, his thoughts sobered. The mystery of those notes they'd each received was still unsolved, partly from his own inclination until now to put them down as someone's prank to cause trouble between husband and wife. Then he thought of Dunstan's information about how the pistol had misfired. But hadn't it been meant for Taggart's use? Or was it for Dunstan? And now the earl's murder.

With a purposeful stride, the Irishman headed for his own room to change into his riding clothes. If Sir Jeremy couldn't get to the bottom of this, it was time he did some secret investigating on his own.

Chapter 24

Her father's funeral took place the next day. Due to the nature of the Earl of Fitzroy's death and the fear of further violence during these dangerous times, Vicar Somerset held a short service for the immediate family and close friends only.

Dressed in a black bombazine dress and matching cape, Millicent surveyed the tiny group of mourners at the gravesight, a spot she had picked out herself as the most appropriate place on the estate. Would she be buried here, too? she couldn't help wondering. It was clear to her now Taggart would probably not ask her to come with him to Williamsburg.

The Duke of Montrose stood somberly looking down at the deep, wide hole. "Geoffrey will be the first Fitzroy to be buried here in Ireland, not in his family's crypt in England," he commented softly.

Garnet appeared bored, and Millicent hadn't missed the glances that passed between the blond-haired beauty and John Nolan.

John's thin wife, Marigold, dabbed at her eyes, lost in her own thoughts. "He was such a sweet man. A paragon of English virtue. How we shall all miss him," she sniffled.

Millicent saw Taggart's dark brows rise in astonished disagreement at such praise for the recently departed. But thankfully he said nothing.

Dunstan appeared older than his four and twenty years as he read a short passage from the *Book of Common Prayer*, then sprinkled the first cup of earth over his father's cloth-covered body. On the other side of the grave, Taggart stood with his arm protectively about Edna's shoulders. Almost, Millicent thought, as though he purposely wished to set the two of them apart from the English who had come to mourn one of their own.

Millicent had to admit her husband's virile handsomeness could not be disguised even in his black mourning clothes. But at the least, she thought, he might have offered the merest condolence for her father's death. Yes, she knew the men were far from friends, but still, a small word would have been appropriate.

"My lady, I am sorry." Dr. Collins bowed, took her black-gloved hand in his, and kissed her fingers. His gray eyes clearly hadn't missed her drawn expression. "Tell your husband he should take better care of you," he stated in a lowered tone.

"Is that your professional advice, Collins?"

With a start, Lady Millicent turned her head to see her husband standing right behind her. He did move like a black wolf, she mused with a kind of irritation. Saying nothing, she turned back to Liam, giving the doctor a look of appreciation for his concern.

The lighter-haired Irishman appeared unruffled by Taggart's question. "It is a clinical recommendation as well as friendly advice. Your lady is not as strong as she'd have others believe."

"I know how to take care of my wife, sir."

"If you did, I would not feel compelled to mention it," the handsome doctor countered, then took his leave.

"Interfering popinjay," Taggart muttered under his breath. When Millicent moved away from him once more, he found it difficult to hide his frustration. For days even before her father's death, he'd tried to get close to her, to coax her back into their room where he could speak his heart to her. Yet, today, like all the others, she put him off. Politely, yes, but with that cool English wall about her once more. Why? he shouted at himself, tormented because he could find no answer.

Horrified, Millicent put down her embroidery. "Edna, you

353

cannot go through with this."

"I've given the matter a lot of thought and 'tis really the only way. So you can see why I cannot go on the rounds with you this afternoon."

The last few days following her father's burial had passed slowly. Taggart had ceased trying to talk with her, yet she now wondered if this was exactly how she wanted things between them. He rode out early in the morning, overseeing repairs to the estate. Then in the evening he locked himself in his study to go over the accounts and correspondence from Virginia, he said.

However, her present concern was for her sister-in-law and her rashness. "But, Edna, your plan is dangerous. Sean Kelly is not a man to dally with. He's had his eyes on you for years, and I don't think this will work. Dunstan is such a soft-spoken, gentle man. Good Lord, what if he does nothing?"

Edna's dimples were vivid as she grinned across at her friend. "Then it looks like I'll have ta marry Kelly."

"God's teeth," Millicent sputtered, "do not joke about such a disaster."

Edna's expression became forlorn. "I'm desperate, Millie. As long as Taggart refuses us permission to wed, your brother won't even consider running away to be married." Tears filled her green eyes when she confessed, "I even went to his room and offered myself to him. He . . . he sent me away. Sometimes I really don't think he does love me. Taggart didn't let anyone stop him from marrying you," she pointed out.

Millicent moved closer to her friend on the sofa and put her arm around Edna's shoulder. Sadness filled her, for both their plights. "Oh, Edna, things aren't always what they seem. Your brother only married me out of duty because I gave him money years ago." She couldn't bring herself to confess to Edna that his first choice had been Garnet but she was already wed by the time he returned to Kinsale.

Pulling back from the black-haired girl, Millicent stated, "I don't approve of your plan . . . but I will do as you ask."

"Thank you, Millie. Now, be sure to wait until Taggart and Dunstan come back from buying those horses."

"Is that where he went?"

"Of course," Edna answered. "Surely your husband must have told ... I see," she finished, reading Millicent's expression.

Not wanting to speak of her own troubles, Millicent encouraged Edna to finish her instructions.

"Well," Edna went on, excitement showing in her green eyes, "I've left the note on Taggart's dresser so he'll see it when he returns to change for dinner. Now, don't fret, Millie. Haven't you proved successful in all the times you've taken off?"

"But those two times were different. I was forced to defend people I cared about—Dunstan and Annie Kelly."

"Well, I'm forced to get Dunstan to marry me. If he weren't so lily-livered I wouldn't be in this mess."

Millicent caught the angry spark in her friend's words. "Dunstan isn't a milksop and you know it."

"Well," Edna conceded. "Sure and he's shown courage in battle and finally standing up to his father, the old lecher, may he rest in peace," she amended, crossing herself. "But your brother certainly has some queer notions about honor. Probably his English blood."

Millicent was tempted to tell Edna that a part of Dunstan was Irish, but, she knew she dared not risk it. "But you have no idea how Sean will react." she pointed out.

Edna's cocky grin returned, reminding Millicent of Taggart just before he did something outrageous.

"Sean and his brother are now working at Nolan's place. Of course, I know he doesn't care a fig about my mind. He's going to pick me up at three to go riding, and he said he'd let me step in to Fogarty's to see where his brother was bested by you. By that time Dunstan should arrive, take me in his arms, and beg me not to run away with Sean. I'll ask Sean to forgive me and thank him for his proposal of marriage, then I'll swoon, and Dunstan will beg me to marry him in front of Fogarty and the whole brood of Kinsale men. I'll accept, then your brother will carry me out of the pub in his arms, and we'll ride slowly back to the Hall on his horse. His kisses, I'm sure, will revive me."

Millicent held her head in her hands and groaned. "Edna, this is not a fairy story. What you propose is not a certainty.

355

Please don't do this. Good God, if you've caught these romantic posturings from me, I'll never forgive myself."

"I've thought of this on my own," the petite Irishwoman shot back. "And my mind is made up. With or without your help, I have to see this through. Else I'll die an old maid. I want to marry your brother," she added, a sob in her lilting voice.

Millicent's heart went out to her friend, and she did understand what love caused a woman to do. "But please tread carefully. I do not trust Sean Kelly. He can be treacherous, like his brother."

"But this is my last hope."

Millicent turned her face away, sadly realizing it probably was, for she could think of nothing further to do to solve this dilemma. "Men. For all their supposed intelligence, they can certainly be the most illogical mules." She looked up when she heard her door close as Edna left to put in motion her final plan to win Dunstan Fitzroy as her husband.

Lady Millicent's hands were shaking so hard, she was forced to stop her needlework. Clenching her slender fingers in her lap, she listened to the sounds in the next room. There was the usual thumping about, then silence as Taggart obviously found Edna's letter.

Then, without so much as a knock on her door, Taggart thundered into her smaller room. She forced herself to look up with a puzzled expression. "Why, whatever is the matter? Couldn't you get a fair price for those horses?"

"Devil take the horses," the towering Irishman growled. He waved the parchment in front of her nose. "My sister has run off with that lowlife, Sean Kelly!"

Within minutes Taggart had Dunstan and Millicent downstairs in his library.

Millicent felt guilty when she saw the frantic worry on both men's faces.

"I can hardly believe that sweet child would—"

Taggart's harsh laugh cut Dunstan's words off. "Want to

know what that 'sweet child' wrote?" he demanded shaking the missive like a rat he'd captured. He looked down and read a passage from the neatly written letter:

> And as Dunstan is too much a coward to go against your wishes, it is now clear he will never marry me. Since Sean Kelly has favored me for years, I have decided to accept his proposal of marriage.

"Whaaat?" Dunstan roared with an unexpected show of emotion. "She dares call me a coward." The taller Englishman snatched the letter out of his brother-in-law's hands.

Millicent was shocked to see the change in her usually affable brother as he scanned Edna's note.

Dunstan crushed the parchment in his right hand and tossed the wadded ball into the fireplace. "I'd not take those insulting words from any man, let alone your gypsy of a sister, no matter how much I love her."

"Yes, and she ended it by calling you a milksop," the Irishman added with exasperating relish. "And I'm beginning to think she's right, Fitzroy, for you've certainly made a fine mess of things."

"Me?" Dunstan's reddish-brown eyebrows shot up to his hairline. "After you refused to give your permission, what in bloody hell was I supposed to do, roll her in the stables as if she were some dockside whore?" he thundered. "I want Edna for my wife, with no slinking about."

"Well, she's certainly slinking about now," Taggart stated. He looked down at Millicent, who seemed struck speechless by her brother's coarse language. Then he turned back to Dunstan. "And if you hadn't been spineless enough and refused your father's directive that you go gallivanting about as a soldier, both our sisters wouldn't have grown up like wild Indians."

"Just one bloody minute," the taller man shouted. "If you hadn't been so all fired up to build an empire in the Colonies, you'd have stayed here and raised Edna yourself. And for all your outward polish, you still have not learned how a gentleman treats a lady, like my sister. No one ever laid an angry hand on her in her life until you married her."

"That's more than evident," the O'Rahilly snapped, hands on either side of his waist. "For all her outward gentility, Millie can be a rag-mannered hoyden on occasion."

Taking the same stance as his brother-in-law, Dunstan countered, "No worse than your sister, I'll wager."

Millicent's eyes grew large behind her spectacles. She'd never seen her brother so angry. Both men looked like rivals at a cockfight. Good Lord, she thought in desperation. There wasn't time for a brawl here, for she had to get Edna's rescue started or all would be ruined.

However, her husband's low laughter was the last reaction she expected right now.

"'Tis the truth," the O'Rahilly confessed, then laughed again. "They're both like unbridled colts, and we've only ourselves to blame."

Millicent was relieved and surprised to see that her husband, for once, was the first to cool his temper. "I . . . I received a note from Edna also," she ventured timidly, trying to remember her sister-in-law was counting on her.

Prepared for both males' rapt attention, she proceeded. "Edna told me to burn it after I read it and not tell a soul," she lied. "Oh, I can't betray her trust," Millicent added, with just the hint of a wrenching sob. "But I'm so worried about her." This was the truth, for it was getting late, and Dunstan was supposed to have departed on the rescue by now.

Dunstan was at her side first. She could tell he controlled his strong emotions with difficulty. "Now, darling, you must tell us all you know."

"Yes, of course." She sniffed.

"Here." Taggart walked over to her chair and impatiently handed her his large cambric pocket handkerchief.

"Thank you." She removed her wire frames and dabbed at the imaginary moisture near her eyes as she'd seen Garnet do on many occasions. "Edna said after they went for a ride, they were going to make a brief stop at Fogarty's to tell the others their good news." She put her spectacles back on. "Oh, yes, Edna wanted to see the spot where I . . . ah . . . I spoke with Patrick Kelly about Annie. Then they were supposed to head for Cork."

When both men raced for the stables, Millicent had no choice but to follow.

Dunstan even saddled his own horse, while she stood nervously looking up at both men. What now? Edna didn't want her brother along on this romantic escapade.

After adjusting his right leg in the stirrup he'd had made to accommodate his scarred leg more comfortably, the new Earl of Fitzroy raised his hand in protest. "Edna is now my responsibility, Taggart. I'll go alone."

Millicent caught the new determination in her brother's lean face. Had there been other changes in him during these last few weeks? It amazed her when Taggart nodded his approval after a few seconds. He dismounted from Laidir and came to stand next to her.

"But, Taggart, shouldn't you go with—"

"No," the Irishman cut off. "Dunstan is right," he said, looking up at his brother-in-law. "And my sister will be lucky to have you as a husband. You're a fine man, Fitzroy," he stated openly.

A look passed between both men, and Millicent was moved by the respect and affection she read in their glance. With his hand about her shoulders, Taggart was holding her back protectively away from Dunstan's feisty stallion, but her total attention was on her brother.

"You will be careful," she called out. "Ever since that time he nearly raped Edna in the cottage before I made her come to live at the Hall, I've never trusted him." Her even white teeth snapped together as it dawned that she's spilled something neither she nor Edna ever meant their men to know.

"And she consented to go off with a man like that?" Dunstan bellowed. His fingers tightened on the leather straps in his hands.

"Don't you want to take a pistol or sword?"

Dunstan shook his head adamantly at his younger sister. "No, I'll fare all right on my own this time. I've learned to deal with these Irish on their own terms."

Millicent shivered. She made a move to go after him as he

raced his horse out of the stables, but Taggart held her back.

"He knows what he's doing. Here, you're cold as ice," he scolded softly, then took off his frock coat and wrapped it about her slender shoulders.

As Taggart led her back to the house, Millicent couldn't help observing, "You and my brother seemed to have resolved your differences."

Taggart smiled across at his wife. "Yes, we had a long talk this afternoon." There was regret in his tone. "I gave Dunstan my permission to marry Edna. We were racing home to tell you both the good news, but then I found her note."

Millicent continued to put one slipper in front of the other, all the while her emotions in a torrent. None of Edna's scheme had been necessary. My God, what if Sean harmed Edna or Dunstan?

"Well, Edna. I guess we'd best be goin' while it's still light." Sean Kelly looked across at the pretty dark-haired lass, who just matched his height. "And a pub is no place for my woman," he pointed out.

Edna tried to smile at the pug-nosed, freckle-faced man. Time was running out, as were her methods to stall their departure. Where was Dunstan? "Of course, Sean, but shouldn't we have a toast first?"

"That ya should," Fogarty piped up. "Drinks are on the house."

When the pints were filled all around, the other Irishmen lifted their mugs in salute. "Ta the happy couple" reverberated about the small pub.

But then the door crashed open.

Dunstan Fitzroy bent his head and entered the Irish pub. Despite his limp, he moved with surprising speed. Without cane, gloves, or tricorn hat, it was clear he'd ridden here with haste. He brushed back a strand of reddish-brown hair that had worked free from the once neatly tied ribbon at the back of his neck.

About time, Edna thought, breathing a sigh of relief. However, she was confused when she looked up to see her

360

love's expression. There was something about his countenance, or was it the look in his eyes she could not fathom? He
dwarfed everyone in the room. But instead of declaring his
undying love, he ordered a whiskey from old Fogarty.

"Sure ya don't want milk?" Sean Kelly demanded with a
raucous laugh at his friends.

Appearing the gentleman, Dunstan offered, "Would you
like to join me?"

"Don't mind if I do. Make that my usual glass," Sean stated.

"Same size for you, my lord?" The solid, squat man used
Dunstan's new inherited title, but the challenge was clear.

Dunstan looked down his aquiline nose at the belligerent
Irishman. "Yes, the same."

All this time he hadn't said one word to Edna, nor she to
him. The petite Irishwoman stood next to Sean, suddenly
beginning to feel uneasy. What about her plan? Her green eyes
took in the large tumblers of whiskey that Fogarty placed on
top of the wooden bar. Even as a commissioned officer on
furloughs home, her quiet Englishman only drank an
occasional glass of Maderia. If he drank that, she thought in
exasperation, he'd be too drunk to carry her off into the
sunset, let alone be able to talk intelligently about why he
worshiped her. "Ah, Duns—I mean your lordship," she
amended in front of the others, "our Irish whiskey takes a
certain . . . ah . . . practice to enjoy properly." She gave an
encouraging smile to Sean. "I'm sure my betrothed will
understand if you have a mug of ale instead."

"That I would, my lord." With a smirk, Sean grabbed his
glass first. He drank half the glass before stopping to wipe his
mouth on the back of his coarse linen coat sleeve. "Edna is
right," he said louder than necessary. "Ya English don't have
the constitution for our Irish whiskey." Then he finished the
rest of the glass and placed it back on the rough bar. There was
applause all around.

Dunstan's expression was unreadable as he took the large
glass in his right hand. He studied the dark contents for a
second. "You both are clearly under one misconception. Edna
O'Rahilly is not your betrothed, Mr. Kelly."

Sean snickered. "Well, I never really said I'd marry her.

This is just a sort of wedding night, don't ya understand?" He gave the other man a worldly wink. "Ya know how it is."

Edna's bonnet almost came off with the force she turned to glare at the youngest Kelly brother. Her strong reaction caused her to forget much of the polished speech Millicent had so painstakingly taught her through the years. "Ya just wanted a little slap and tickle is that it, ya little wart?"

Kelly looked defensive. "Ya didn't seem to protest too much when I gave ya a squeeze when we were walkin' our horses along the harbor earlier."

"Well," she huffed, "that was because I believed your intentions were honorable." Edna felt Dunstan's gaze, but she couldn't look at him right now. It was partly Dunstan's own fault for this predicament. Her small head bobbed up in irritation. "Sure and it was clear there were no other prospects, so I took the last dregs from the barrel, since I'm not about ta be an old maid."

"Last dregs, am I?" Sean Kelly echoed, his displeasure now focusing on the pretty woman next to him. "And here I kept me intentions honorable even after ya swooned before I could kiss ya."

"Oh, Kelly, don't be such an ass. I can faint at the drop of a hat; it was just a—" Instantly, she clamped her less than prudent mouth shut. From the quick look at Dunstan she knew he was remembering the time she'd fainted in his room. It was exasperating that right now things had gone so contrary to her plans. All attention in the pub focused on the three of them. Edna made a pretext at removing her straw bonnet. "It does seem a trifle warm in here, does it not?" she inquired to no one in particular, as she attempted to regain control of the situation.

Dunstan glared down at the top of Edna's black-curly head. "I believe I do need this," he stated with barely controlled fury. Still holding his beaker of whiskey, Dunstan raised it to his lips and began to drink.

Her eyes became green saucers as she watched the tall Englishman down the entire contents in one uninterrupted swallow.

"He didn't even stop at the halfway mark," one of the

patrons piped up.

With a steady hand, Dunstan replaced the empty glass on the rough counter. He smiled and nodded his acceptance of the other men's shouts of admiration. Then he turned back to the couple in front of him. It was clear Sean didn't like being bested. "Well, then," the Englishman stated in an affable manner, "shall I send for Father Collins so the wedding can take place before your honeymoon?"

"But I don't want ta marry her," Sean Kelly blustered.

"Hear now, Sean Kelly," Fogarty admonished from his position on the other side of the bar. "That's no way ta be addressing his lordship or ta be actin' with O'Rahilly's sister." The gray-haired man then turned to Dunstan. "I give ya me word, me lord, we all thought Kelly meant to wed the maid."

Edna's face flamed at this humiliation in front of her countrymen. It appeared no one wanted to marry her. Dunstan was saying nothing on her behalf. In truth, he'd practically given her to the unappreciative Kelly.

"Well," Dunstan drawled in the guise of one bored, "I suppose I could marry her myself, just to take her off your hands, Kelly."

"Don't be doin' me any favors," Edna snapped, her mortification giving way to a more heated emotion. Hands on her hips, she demanded, "Sure and I'll be askin' what holy miracle changed yer mind? You," she scoffed, "who practically asked me brother's permission before you'd so much as piss."

"Young lady, you will watch your language," Dunstan warned, tossing off his pretended calm. Something dangerous glinted in his gray eyes when he looked down at her.

"Why? 'Tis appropriate for the surroundings . . . and the company," she shot back.

"Take a good look around, Edna, for this is the last time you'll ever enter a pub, or come in twenty feet of Sean Kelly."

Such was the tone of Dunstan's voice that Edna's arms dropped to her sides. She could hardly believe the change in the man. Was she actually just a tad frightened of this new, masterful Fitzroy?

"Here, now," Sean Kelly protested, the strong whiskey

363

clearly affecting him. He attempted to move closer to the man towering over Edna, but he staggered to the right and had to hold on to the curved front of the bar. "You'll not be takin' away my pleasure for the—"

"Shut up, Kelly. You're drunk," Fogarty cut off.

Dunstan took Edna's elbow without his usual gentleness and began dragging her behind him toward the door.

"Run off, that's right," Sean jeered. "There'd be little triumph for me bestin' a cripple anyway. Besides, I don't have the chief magistrate in my pocket like you Fitzroys do."

Edna plowed into Dunstan's back when he abruptly stopped walking. His hand left her arm.

Sean grabbed the half-filled whiskey bottle off the counter and smashed it against the bar. The strong-smelling liquor ran down the front of the rough wood. He smirked as he held up the dark jagged glass by the narrow neck of the bottle. "Come on, or are ya too much a gentleman coward to have a real fight? Afraid to dirty yer nice English clothes?"

When Edna saw Dunstan's military posture become even straighter when he moved away from her and began unbuttoning his frock coat, she knew things had gotten completely out of hand. "Sean," she spoke up, moving to stand toe to toe with the inebriated Kelly. "I apologize if you feel insulted by my . . . my foolishness tonight. The fault is mine, not his lordship's, so please . . ." A squeal popped out of her when she felt Dunstan's arm go about her waist from behind.

She was unceremoniously deposited on the hard wooden bar. Blushing, Edna was forced to tug down the hem of her gray traveling skirt to cover the tops of her serviceable black leather shoes. It irked her to realize she was too short to get off the bar with any sort of dignity without assistance—a fact she was positive Dunstan realized. What ever was the matter with him to act so ungentlemanly?

"Yes, your actions tonight were foolish, Edna O'Rahilly, and I'll get to you later," Dunstan promised. "For now, don't venture from that spot. Mr. Fogarty," the earl directed, "see that she does as she's told for once."

"That I will, me lord."

Edna craned her neck behind her and realized Fogarty was

ready to hold her there if she should dare move. With fear for her beloved, she watched Dunstan toss his coat next to her on the bar. It was followed by his discarded white neckcloth. He rolled up the sleeves of his pristine lawn shirt, and she was taken aback to see the tanned muscles of his arms. It was now clear he'd been spending long hours working outside during these last strained weeks when they'd seen so little of each other. However, she was positive this gentleman was no match for Kelly's sly tactics.

Still waving the dark-green bottle in front of him, Sean moved on the taller man. "How do I know ya won't have me arrested after I beat ya to a pulp?"

Dunstan walked slowly over to his adversary. "You have my word before witness that I'll not press any charges."

"Hell, I'm goin' ta enjoy this. You Fitzroys have had this comin' for years."

His confidence clearly high, Sean smirked at the men who had moved to a safer vantage point at the back of the room. He wasn't prepared when the earl came down with his fist and knocked the jagged bottle out of his hand. The thick glass rolled along the wooden planks toward the back of the room.

With a loud Irish curse, Sean landed a punch to Dunstan's midsection. The blow was so forceful it knocked the tall man to the right. His face contorted with pain as his right leg connected with the hard front wall. But just as quickly he recovered and landed a punch on the pugnacious Irishman's jaw.

With horrified eyes, Edna watched the raucous proceedings. Chairs were overturned as the men continued the match. There were even some encouraging shouts for Dunstan coming from the back of the room, but she could see no cause for revelry. The blows and scuffling came so rapidly she couldn't tell who was winning.

With the loud sound of a fist connecting with a jaw, Dunstan sent Kelly reeling into the crowd of Irishmen gawking from the back of the room. He stalked closer, his booted feet apart, as he waited for the unconscious man to get up once again. His chest moved in and out with his labored breathing. With the back of a bruised hand he swiped at the perspiration and blood on his face.

"He'll be out for hours," one of the young men commented as he and a companion lifted Kelly and placed him across two tables. "You've won, Englishman. And ya gave Kelly more than a fair fight."

"Aye," piped up another. "For Kelly's bested many the man with twice his lordship's muscle, and him with a bad leg and all. Beggin' yer pardon, me lord."

Ignoring the rest of their congratulations, Dunstan turned and stalked back to the bar.

His open shirt was spattered with Sean's blood and his own sweat. Edna saw the dark bruise on Dunstan's cheek. He went to his coat and pulled out a white cloth from the front pocket and wiped the blood off the corner of his mouth where another well-placed punch from Sean had landed. He shrugged back into his outer coat and stuffed his neckcloth into the pocket.

"You men and your ladies are invited to our wedding in two months time," the new earl stated with a smile.

"Will ya be havin' another spot of whiskey, me lord, before the ride home?"

"Thank you, Mr. Fogarty, but Miss O'Rahilly and I will be leaving now. After giving us permission to wed today, Taggart will be worried about his sister."

"Permission?" Edna returned as the implications of his words hit her. "And you frightened me near to dyin' just now, lettin' me think ya were handin' me over to Kelly like a bowl of mush." The reaction after her terror for his safety caused the green fire to rekindle in her eyes. "Sure and I might of known ya'd not have the courage to marry me on yer own. Well, I'm not so sure I'll be acceptin' your proposal after all."

Hands on either side of her legs, the Earl of Fitzroy leaned against the bar. "You'll marry me in two months, Miss O'Rahilly, that is a fact." And instead of assisting his intended off the bar, the new Earl of Fitzroy bent down and hoisted her over his right shoulder. His left hand held her ankles to his waist. "Good night, gentlemen," he said in his well-modulated voice. With his free hand he reached in his pocket, pulled out a handful of gold coins, and deposited them on the bar. "Please raise a few pints for us. And, Mr. Fogarty, here's something extra for any damage to your establishment."

"Put me down!" Edna shouted. She lifted her head to see the grinning faces of the Irishmen who were returning eagerly to the bar.

"Well, that's more than kind of your lordship," Fogarty commented. Many others added their appreciation. "And there's more than one here who enjoyed seein' the Kelly get bested for once, isn't that so lads?"

Others affirmed the truth of Fogarty's words as they grasped their pints of ale. "To his lordship," they toasted, their pewter tankards high in the air. "To the future bride and groom."

During this time, Edna kept squirming and shouting to be put down. All to no avail. Injured leg or not, it didn't seem to influence Dunstan's determination or his hidden strength. He walked out of Fogarty's with Edna's upper body dangling down his back. The wind was knocked out of her with the force with which he hoisted her facedown across the front of his leather saddle. Then he mounted behind, before nudging his horse to a slow trot.

To Edna's further humiliation, when she looked up from the earth below, it was to see that some of the patrons had followed them out of the pub to watch the continuation of the entertainment. "Dunstan," she hissed, "let me up at once." It was still light out and the streets of Kinsale were teaming with people. "I'll never forgive you for this, you English cur."

Dunstan glanced down at her back. "Such language," he admonished with a click of his tongue. "Though I love you the way you are, my black-haired gypsy, you'll not twist me around your little finger so easily as before. This will be an equal partnership."

"I'm getting dizzy," she whimpered from her mortifying position. She moved her body upward, only to feel Dunstan's strong hand push her back down.

"It will do you little harm," he stated. "Be thankful I'm not giving you the hiding you so richly deserve." However, he did readjust her form to a more comfortable position across his thighs. But he took his time trotting through the center of town.

To Edna's further consternation, he greeted English and

Irish friends alike, as if he were out on a Sunday afternoon canter. All the while, she was wriggling and sputtering to be freed from her facedown position.

When the Duke and Duchess of Montrose stopped in their carriage, Edna prayed the earth would open to hide her.

"Does this mean what I think it does, Dunstan?" The laughter was evident in Calvert's raspy voice. Garnet giggled beside her husband.

"Yes," Dunstan answered with a grin. "Edna and I are to be married in two months time. I hope your graces will attend the nuptials."

"Splendid," the man replied as he leaned farther out the open window of his elaborate carriage. "Congratulations to you, too, Edna."

Edna said nothing but increased her wriggling to be free.

"His grace is speaking to you, my dear," Dunstan pressed. "Edna often needs a subtle reminder about her manners. We are waiting," he said to the woman still draped across his legs.

"Thank you, your grace," Edna bit out, lifting her head to see the barely controlled laughter from the Duke of Montrose.

The rest of the ride through the center of town was equally eventful. At least four other times Dunstan forced her through this humiliating ritual. When they were out of town, he finally placed her upright in front of him. She could have shot him herself when he laughed openly at her expression.

"You see," he whispered in her ear as his arms tightened around her when he increased their pace, "it did you little harm. And I know I thoroughly enjoyed it."

Edna was tempted to call him a name disparaging to his lineage, but when she saw the warning look in his gray eyes, she thought better of it. This was a new side of Dunstan Fitzroy she'd never seen or felt before.

Chapter 25

Even though Millicent was overjoyed that her brother and Edna were to be married soon, she was more concerned right now with the turn of events concerning the investigation into her father's murder. Taggart had shown little amazement when the English authorities rode out this morning to tell them they had two Irishmen in custody for the murder.

But she was almost certain the O'Hara brothers weren't capable of such an act. Why had her husband said nothing? The painful questions haunted her.

Millicent made her way up the back stairs toward their room. She knew this would be her best chance to enter unobserved. After opening Taggart's wardrobe, she began searching through his neatly arranged clothes. Shirts on one side, breeches on the other. Then she pulled out one of the wooden drawers and spotted the stack of waistcoats.

Close to the bottom, she found it and pulled the piece of cloth out of her apron pocket as she held up the torn waistcoat—the one she'd embroidered for him as a gift. The small scrap of material matched the right corner perfectly. There was no indication that he'd attempted to have the vest repaired. Her last hope that it might not be the same vest vanished. And her father had been clutching this incriminating evidence when he died.

She sucked in her breath when she heard the tread of boots outside the door. Quickly, Millicent returned the waistcoat to its former place and stuffed the piece of cloth back in her apron. Aware the door was going to open any second, she rushed to a chair next to the bed, grabbed the book from his night table, and sat down.

If Taggart was surprised to see his wife here engrossed in a book, he did not show it. A warm look came into his eyes. "Good morning," he greeted affably. He began taking off his outer coat. "I had to come back for a lighter one. It reminds me of Williamsburg today. A fine warm morning."

She looked up at him, unable to see any hint in his handsome face that he was a murderer. Wouldn't it show in the depths of his midnight eyes? Yet, the evidence seemed to burn her hand when her fingers touched the scrap of cloth in her apron pocket.

Taggart studied her serious expression. Perhaps Liam was right. She did look tired this morning. Even behind her frames he noted the puffiness around her gray eyes. He tossed the heavier coat on the bed and walked over to her, easily taking the book from her. He held out his hand to her. "Come here, Millie."

New suspicions about his true nature caused her to hesitate. However, after a few seconds she found herself placing her hand in his, and he drew her up to stand in front of him. Just as quickly, he sat in the overstuffed chair and brought her down easily to sit on his lap.

She appeared so sad, he mused. Was she grieving for her father? It surprised him, for he hadn't thought the earl could have inspired her to such depths. "You look like a forlorn kitten this morning," he said to the top of the ruffled pinner and green bow that held her hair away from her face. "Miss prim and proper, yet I find you engrossed in my book on horse breeding," he teased against the softness of her ear.

His warm breath fanned the auburn hair near her ear and neck. She squirmed at this close contact of her soft curves against the hard muscles of his legs. When she made a move to get up, his gentle yet firm hands held her down.

"You fly from me too often, sparrow. Do I please you so little?"

"Oh no, I usually enjoy being with you." She looked at the open question in his eyes and colored at the desire she read in their brown depths. His face was coming closer as he smiled that roguish way, almost as if he could read her thoughts, guess just how much she wanted him. His fingers stroked the back of her slender neck, and the spicy scent of his cologne assailed her once more. Her large eyes scanned his handsome face, then stopped at the indentation at his chin. Was this what loving a man did to you? she couldn't help wondering. How many women throughout the centuries had walked into a love they knew would only destroy them? This man seducing her so expertly may have murdered her father and had the duke's wife for a mistress. Yet, when he touched her she melted, and her mind and body, everything inside her cried out for him to do more.

Taggart felt her response. He caressed her lips with his mouth, slowly at first, then moved to the slim line of her jaw, up across her smooth cheek. "I burn, *Gaelbhan.*" How long will you keep us apart like this?" he rasped close to her lips once more. "That's right," he confirmed, "I do want to undress you and lay your enticing naked body on those cool sheets over there. He watched the heat suffuse her face, but he took her chin in his fingers and made her confront his gaze. "Why do you deny us? You turn away from me, yet I see the fire in those gray eyes of yours." Without waiting for her reply, he slowly drew off her spectacles and placed them on the night table. "Kiss me back this time," he commanded, his right arm bending her upper body. "Please," he added in his coaxing Irish lilt. "'Tis not half so pleasurable unless you're with me, sparrow."

There was sadness in Millicent's half smile when she turned her face away. "You are a devil come to torment me, Taggart O'Rahilly. I do want you," she confessed. "But unlike a certain duchess I've never wanted to learn those games to entice a man." Tears misted her eyes. She loved him but instantly knew if she gave in to him once more he would only break her heart—whether meaning to or not, it now seemed inevitable. Then she reached up and slipped her hand under the gathered hair at the back of his neck. "You are a rascal. Taggart O'Rahilly. If I say no, would you force me?"

His face became serious at her words. "No, that I would not, for I've come to realize I want more from you, Millie. I want you to be mine of your own free will." He thought he saw her withdrawal, and with a hard sigh of disappointment, he lifted her off his lap to stand in front of him. So, he thought soberly, she did not want to make love with him. He'd hoped to coax her back, but this morning proved something to him. He stood up and grabbed the lighter coat from the wardrobe.

She blurted out the words before she lost her nerve. "Taggart, I saw the torn waistcoat in your wardrobe."

He colored, appearing ill at ease. "I . . . I was embarrassed at not having taken better care of your gift. It must have happened when I was set upon by those highwaymen." When she made no response, he left, for he felt there was nothing further to say.

Millicent stood in the middle of the room, staring after him. In the hazy light, she finally allowed the tears to escape. Why didn't she call him back, beg him to make love to her as they both wanted? But how could she love a man who killed her father, a man who did not love her? she demanded. For hadn't she seen the waistcoat in Nolan's carriage as Taggart lay unconscious. There was no tear then. It had not happened with the scuffle to waylay him. Holding her arms close to her chest, she paced the length of the room. The pain was physical it hurt so deeply.

After a few moments, the Englishwoman came to a halt. It was clear her logical mind would not accept Taggart as a true husband until she found the answer to her father's murder. One way or the other this stood between them. She realized she would have to use her English contacts to ferret out the truth on her own. How could she stand by and see innocent men hung for a murder she was positive they'd not committed?

Millicent touched the front of her stomach. She could have sworn she felt the faintest of movements. However, her joy was muted, for she had still not been able to tell her husband that she was almost two months pregnant with their child. And, of course, he didn't suspect a thing, for she spent her lonely nights in the adjoining room, and he never saw her these days without a roomy gown or apron to cover the slight increase in her stomach.

In exasperation she decided this train of thought would lead nowhere. She went back to her own room and pulled out a green riding habit. It was time she did a little inquiring on her own.

Instead of spending her mornings at home, for the next few weeks Lady Millicent began riding out daily to visit the English families in the area. A comment here, a dropped word there, and she was able to connect this with her afternoon rounds to the Irish families. She managed to call on Garnet and her husband.

Garnet seemed the perfect hostess as she poured tea into the dainty blue cups. She gave her elderly husband a beguiling smile as she offered him the plate of small teacakes. Millicent politely declined food. She sipped her tea, occasionally studying the dissimilar couple. It was a warm day, but Calvert sat dressed in wool coat and breeches of an older fashion, with a full-bottomed powdered gray wig, and scarflike cravat about his scrawny neck. His adoring eyes hardly left his wife.

"This is the first summer I will be spending totally in Kinsale," Garnet remarked to her guest. "Daddy used to allow me to visit my aunt in London for most of the season. The heat never bothered me. Of course," she added, a hint of complaint in her childlike voice, "dear Calvert says he cannot bear to have me out of his sight for even a week. Tell me, Millicent, is it always so du—quiet here in the country?"

Lady Millicent knew Garnet loathed Ireland as much as the deceased Earl of Fitzroy. "Yes, and to some it is a heaven with its pretty harbor and lovely green countryside."

"Quite," the duchess replied with an unneeded pat to her bouncy blond curls. "John Nolan tells me you're up early visiting the various English estates. Of course, your husband's friendship with the King almost assures you both a ready acceptance in society. Seeing to your social obligations at last? Taggart will be so pleased."

How did Garnet know what would please Taggart? Forcing down her pique, Millicent set her teacup back down on the round wooden table. A mistress was privy to these intimate details, was she not? Using her practiced discipline, Lady Millicent folded her slender hands across the green velvet of her riding skirt. "Actually," she dared, "I've been trying to find out more information about my father's murder."

Calvert frowned. "Wretched business," he grumbled. "But that investigation is no job for a woman. You leave that to the magistrate, my dear. Sir Jeremy tells me the O'Hara boys are to be tried next week. Young hotheads, and the oldest was to go to France to study next year. Old O'Hara is quite distraught. Imagine after joining the Church of England, working all his life as a successful merchant, then to have his sons turn out to be members of that fanatic group. Shocking."

Garnet yawned behind a dainty white hand. "Well," she apologized, getting up. "I must get ready for my daily canter. Please stay and visit with Calvert awhile. I know he always enjoys seeing you, Millicent. He says you are one of the few females who can converse intelligently. So you see, my dear, you do have something to offer," she added in a condescending tone. With a swish of her yellow dress over her hooped petticoat, the Duchess of Montrose left the room.

After a few silent moments, Millicent spoke first. "Your grace, I'm convinced the O'Hara brothers didn't kill my father. I've known those boys and their family for the last nine years. It's my belief someone has submitted misleading evidence against them."

Her words caused the Duke of Montrose to sit up. "That's a bold statement, my dear. It reminds me of what young Taggart said—well, that was years ago."

Millicent moved forward in her chair. "Please continue, your grace. You cannot know how important this is to me."

The man of seventy became silent as he clearly thought for a few moments. "It was the warmest summer I can recall. You and Dunstan had been here almost two years by then. There was a bonfire; and Irish rabble burned George II in effigy. Taxes were too high, and the Catholics said they couldn't pay the tithes. Your father was convinced Shamus O'Rahilly was the ringleader."

Astonished by the duke's analogy of the two deaths, Millicent encouraged, "Was there any one else who might have supplied the documents to my father?"

"No, your father brought them to the court himself to submit the condemning evidence. Nolan drove him in every day alone. Your father never used his attorney for this case, I'm positive." The duke ran a bony hand along his concave cheek. "No, you'll find no answers there."

"But what proof is there that the O'Haras killed my father?"

Calvert shrugged. "I do not know; you would have to check with Sir Jeremy, for he was the one who told me about their arrest."

Realizing this was a dead end, Millicent thanked the duke for his hospitality and left.

Fifteen minutes later, Lady Millicent was on her way home. However, she held Buttercup still when she heard the sound of horses approaching through the thick grove of trees. The riders were in a hurry, if she was any judge of the pace.

She sucked in her breath when she saw the approaching riders were Garnet Huntington and John Nolan. They stopped far enough ahead of her to prevent discovery. Millicent saw John laugh up to the blondhaired beauty before he lifted her from her sidesaddle. The duchess's descent to the ground was slower than necesssary as the squire moved her small body along his in a far from proper manner. Then they kissed, and Nolan pulled off Garnet's riding hat, impatiently tossing it to the ground.

Millicent turned away when she realized they were obviously intent on more than conversation. She didn't need much imagination to realize what would follow. Well, one thing was clear, Nolan wasn't going to be home this afternoon. The Fitzroy estate was the largest in the county; no doubt Nolan felt safe to use his old friend's property in this manner. With a firm set to her lips, Millicent turned Buttercup around and headed in the direction of town.

She would see Sir Jeremy Cartgrove, the chief magistrate. Perhaps he would shed some light on this case, and she might even ask him a casual question about Taggart's father, Shamus. After all, Jeremy might have only been an assistant at the time, but perhaps he could remember something useful about that older case. Calvert had pricked her interest, for until now she'd never considered the remotest chance that the death of Taggart's father and her own might be connected in some way. Was it possible?

Trying to keep the box of expensive chocolates out of direct sunlight Taggart gingerly held the redribboned container in both hands as he walked close to the edge of the shops. Who ever heard of a man courting his wife? he asked himself, then laughed openly at his impulsive purchase. There had to be five pounds of assorted nuts, bonbons, and other confectionary delights in the huge box. Well, he admitted, he really hadn't courted Millicent properly. Something inside today made him realize he didn't want to let this strain between them continue. He missed her, not just as a bed partner, but also as a friend with whom he could talk openly.

When the Irishman turned the corner to head back to Laidir, he almost bumped into Garnet Huntington. She was coming out of Dr. Collins's office. When she spotted him, her whole countenance changed.

"Why, Taggart," she greeted enthusiastically. "One hardly sees you in town these days."

He managed a smile, but before he could move on, he felt her dainty gloved hand on the light material of his beige sleeve. "Sweets?" she teased, eyeing the large red box he held in his hands so carefully. Her pink mouth turned upward and her blue eyes became more provocative. "My, you have become the gallant. A secret lover, perhaps?"

"My wife," he answered without hesitation, discovering just how protective he did feel about Millicent.

"Really?" Garnet's wheat-colored brows rose in disbelief. She moved closer to him and tilted her face up to his before whispering, "I can hardly believe the Irish Stallion prefers water when he can have more potent abrosia."

To save the present for his wife, the Irishman was forced to hold it in just one hand. He felt Garnet's full-blown breasts press against the front of his unbuttoned coat. He took in the heady scent of roses. Thank God no one was about, for he liked old Calvert and was determined not to hurt him. No, someone else would have to tell him about his wife's scandalous behavior. He pulled back so quickly, Garnet almost lost her balance as she was pitched forward without support. With a smirk, he regained his dual hold on the box of candy.

The lady's blue eyes turned to ice at his obvious rejection. However, just as quicky Taggart saw her expression return to the practiced sweetness.

"Well, I really must be going, Mr. O'Rahilly. No, don't beg me. I cannot allow you to take up any more of my time."

"Yes," he countered evenly, "And I must be getting home with this surprise for my wife."

"The surprise may be for you, Taggart, for your wife hasn't been home all day."

Wary, O'Rahilly did not take her bait right away. "So you say, madam, but I have learned just how much to trust your words."

"Then trust your eyes, for your sainted wife has been spending the last few hours with the chief magistrate, obtaining information about her father's death from him— probably not even averse to using her feminine charms, as limited as they might be, to get what she wants."

"I warn you, Garnet, I will not tolerate your lies about my wife."

Clearly unafraid, Garnet's expression challenged him. "For over a week now, your wife has been going about Kinsale visiting the most prominent English families in the county. My friends tell me she is pumping them for information about her father's death. If you don't believe me, ask my husband, for this very morning she sat in our drawing room sipping tea and asking us to shed more light on the murder. It wouldn't amaze me to learn she was gathering other information for Sir Jeremy Cartgrove. How else do you suppose he was able to arrest the O'Haras with proof so quickly? She wouldn't be the first woman to act as spy for her fellow Englishmen. Wait here and see if she does not come out of Cartgrove's office. Or are you

377

afraid of the truth?"

Stunned by this news, Taggart watched Garnet step around him and cross the street to her landau. He saw her smile at him over her shoulder as she allowed the young footman to assist her in stepping up into the open carriage.

Part of him wanted to leave after she drove away, but there was something that taunted him, making him stay to prove the blond-haired woman wrong.

For half an hour he stood in the back of the corner shop, never taking his brown eyes from the office across the street. At first, he laughed at himself for standing in the shadows like some dockside thief. Finally, the door opened. He held his breath.

No, it couldn't be her, not his Millicent. He blinked, only to have his worst fears confirmed when he saw his wife being escorted out the door. She was smiling down at the older man as they turned the corner. A few moments later he saw her ride sidesaddle across Buttercup as she raced out of Kinsale toward Fitzroy Hall.

The past came to haunt him. If she was capable of spying for the English, would she turn over his friends as easily as her father had done years ago?

The answer mocked him. In fury and sadness, he shoved the ruffled box of candy at the first passerby. "Give it to your wife," he growled.

Astonished, the scruffy-looking Irishman nodded in delightful appreciation. "Sure and that's a grand gift. Thank ya, sir. 'Tis a fine Englishman, ya are."

Alone, the man's words echoed at Taggart. Dressed as he was and with his practiced speech, he'd certainly succeeded in masking his Irish roots. It was a bitter laugh that escaped O'Rahilly's lips. But he felt the salty moisture in his eyes. Had Millicent indeed made good her promise for revenge because he'd forced her to marry him? And all these days—was this why she'd kept him at arms length? She'd bided her time and chose to act when the opportunity presented itself. "Bitch," he muttered under his breath as he walked back to his horse, thinking that her visit to the chief magistrate was proof of her spying. She'd obviously gone there to give the English authorities information about the Irish freedom fighters. "Curse you," tore from him. He had to grip Laidir's saddle until his knuckles shone white to keep from crying out more of his pain. Millicent was worse than Garnet for this.

The talk with Sir Jeremy had proven useful. It was still too soon to confront anyone, for she needed more concrete proof, but Millicent was sure she was on the right track.

The day's activities had exhausted her, though, and when she returned she bathed her face and told Bridget she would lie down for a few moments.

In less than an hour she was rudely awakened by her husband.

"Asleep like an angel."

His words were an accusation. Without her spectacles, Millicent took a few seconds to clear the fuzziness from her eyes. Suddenly, she recoiled at the look of cold fury on Taggart's face. Then she smelled the scent of roses—Garnet's perfume on his coat, along with strong whiskey. "If you have something to discuss with me, kindly wait until you are sober." She attempted to pull back from the punishing hands on her arms but to no avail.

"I haven't been drinking nearly enough," he snapped. "What a fool you played me for. To think I was getting ready to court you like a simpering swain," he confessed. "Your gentle nature," he spat, his hands tightening on her slender arms. "Until now, the thought never hit me that you resented your Irish blood. Ya told the heartrending story about your ancestors so convincingly I'd believed you. What other favors do ya give for the right information?"

"I don't know what you are talking about. Pray leave my room until—ouch," she cried at his touch on her skin. "You are hurting me."

"Think of it as part of the perils of being a spy. Sure and we Irish are a curious lot, aren't we, my dear?" His brogue was thicker in his emotional state. "We don't take kindly to betrayal from our women."

"I haven't the foggiest notion what you are talking—" Her

379

words were cut off when he gave her a violent shake that snapped her head back. Her straight auburn hair came loose from the pins and billowed about her face like a red cloud.

"Don't try to deny it, for I saw you leave Cartgrove's office this afternoon. And I've learned this isn't the first time you've been goin' about to those aristocratic families needling them for information. Did you plan to have my sister hung as well? What about Father Mike? Do you know he still continues the hedge schools at night, teaching Catholic children to read and write, along with their catechism? I'm sure Cartgrove would pay much for that proof, for he'd love to get the Jesuit hung for treason."

Millicent was truly afraid when she saw the wild look in Taggart's eyes. But she couldn't tell him her suspicions, for it was too soon, and she knew he'd never allow her to see her strategy to the end if he even suspected it. "I still do not understand what you are upset about. Calling on Sir Jeremy and a number of English families was merely to fulfill my social obligations now that I am your wife. Really, Taggart, you must learn to trust me."

With a dangerous growl, he shoved her roughly back against the pillows. "I'd as soon trust an adder," he said in disgust. He spoke half to himself. "Years ago I should have been warned but like a blind fool I failed to see it. Didn't the lies trip off your tongue easily to yer father that night near the bogs? You're just like the duchess, only," he said, deliberately wanting to be cruel, "she's much prettier."

Those last words changed everything for Millicent. Any explanation or pleading died in her throat. It took all her self-mastery to hide how deeply those words slashed her. He accused her of being a liar. And she'd be the first to admit she was not a beauty, but to have the man she thought she loved, the man who had seen her naked, had held her and had kissed every inch of her—to have Taggart now confess these three words . . . The pain was a mortal blow against her heart.

The Irishman almost went to her when he saw her try to hide the wounded look in her large gray eyes. "Do you denounce being a spy, then?" he asked, suddenly wanting to believe her. "For God's sake, you're part Irish, how could you spy on your own?" Her silence unnerved him. "Do you deny it?" he pressed again. If she refused it now, he'd accept it and show her he hadn't meant those last words.

She felt the skin on her hands cut as she dug her nails into the palms to keep her voice steady. "You've already called me a liar. Now you would not believe me no matter what I said."

He read the stubborn set to her chin. So, she was a spy for the English after all. His stomach churned as the truth of her treachery hit him. He looked about the room. It seemed as if the walls were closing in one him, leaving him no air to breathe.

He vaulted from her room and entered his large bedroom, only to feel the same way when he saw the bed they had shared all too briefly. This house would always be English. He could change the furniture, refurbish it to his own tastes, but it would always be Fitzroy Hall, always taunting him as an outsider who had once been a groom here and would never belong as its master.

He couldn't stay under this roof another day, he realized. As he charged to his wardrobe and began tossing a few clothes onto the bed, he almost thought he heard the dead earl's jarring laughter.

Chapter 26

Edna was busy with a fitting for her wedding gown, and therefore Millicent had gone on her rounds alone this afternoon. And though Taggart had made her promise never to ride out alone after dark and she agreed to the wisdom of this directive, she saw no reason for such caution in the middle of the afternoon. Besides, today she had felt the need for the solitary ride.

Low in the sky, the sun seemed to mock her feelings as she rode through the meadow towards the Hall. Though she tried not to think of it again, it came back at her. Taggart had moved out of Fitzroy Hall to the old O'Rahilly cottage on the estate.

Even though Annie Kelly and the others said nothing about it on her rounds this afternoon, Millicent didn't miss their sympathetic glances when they thought she wasn't looking. Such news traveled quickly in the small town.

As she rode through the grove of trees, Millicent tried to think about the future. So far, she was the only one who knew about her condition. Used to her mistress waiting on herself, Bridget seemed to accept her wishes for assistance only after she'd dressed herself in her petticoats.

However, Lady Millicent knew she could not hide her condition much longer. But she didn't want Taggart to return to their bedroom merely because she was carrying their child. Too many times duty had compelled him to act in a manner she assumed was contrary to what he actually wanted. Edna and Dunstan were kind, but they were immersed in their upcoming wedding plans and Dunstan's work to form his own horse breeding business. Of one thing she was certain. She didn't want pity from anyone, and that included herself. Besides, she continued in a practical vein, once she found the proof to back up her suspicions as to both their fathers' deaths, she hoped Taggart would forgive her need for secrecy. But how could he even suspect her of providing the information that led to the O'Hara brothers being arrested for her father's murder when she was positive they were innocent?

She clasped the red cloak about her as she quickened her pace. The sun would soon be setting, and she chided herself for running so late today. Whether it was her pregnancy or hurt over Taggart, but lately she had begun to tire more easily. If only she had the courage to stop at the O'Rahilly cottage— even just to rest for a few moments. Would it be harder to face her husband if he were there . . . or to realize he was out, perhaps completing a romantic evening with his mistress? Garnet did have a talent for organization, Millicent had to give her that. To keep John Nolan, Taggart, and Garnet's own husband from finding out about the other seemed no small task.

So lost in her thoughts, she hadn't spotted the group of strangers coming out on foot from the thick grove of elm trees. She brought Buttercup up with practiced skill, but when she attempted to go around them, three other men stopped her by grabing her horse's reins.

Their faces were hidden behind crudely made masks of dark cloth. Despite the balmy spring evening, she felt a shiver of fear run through her. "If you intend to rob me, you will be disappointed." She reached into the inner pocket of her cloak and tossed the small purse of coins she carried at the group of men who stood in her path. "This is all I have. Take it and leave me in peace." Moving her hand down toward the leather satchel looped across the pummel of her saddle, she made a motion to get her hands on the unloaded pistol she always carried.

"Stop right there," ordered the tall man. He turned to his shorter partner. "Take it before she pulls one of her tricks on us again."

The shorter one grabbed the pouch and tossed it to the ground. As yet the two in front of her had made no effort to retrieve the tiny cloth purse that had landed near their feet. One of the other men finally let go of her horse to pick it up. She saw him stuff it into the frayed pocket of his coat. The shortest man folded his arms across the stained gray shirt covering his chest. "Well now, Lady Millicent, finishin' your good deeds a little late tonight? Me and the lads thought ya wasn't comin'."

"Yeah," his larger companion responded. "It would of been real disappointin'." The other men laughed outright.

She peered down at the six men who blocked her escape. "Then if you know my schedule, you must know I'm sympathetic to the Irish cause. However, you'll also know I deplore violence as a means to any end."

"Hah. It didn't stop ya from threatening to shoot—" The shorter man seemed to catch himself. "Get down off yer horse."

Millicent swallowed but tried to keep the terror from her voice. "Please let me pass. I wish you no harm, and I am not your enemy."

Even before she could cry out, Millicent was forcibly plucked from Buttercup's back. She landed hard on the wet grass. Pairs of hands pulled her roughly to her feet, only to drag her forward. "Let me go! You are making a mistake." Someone shoved her, obviously to move her along faster.

"I've waited a long time for this moment, me lady. But ya won't die right away."

Instantly, Millicent recognized the jeering voice. She shivered despite the warmth of the evening. Now she knew the identity of two of the six men. In spite of her frantic struggles, Millicent felt her arms yanked forward as Patrick and Sean Kelly tied her hands to one of the smaller trees.

"Here, now," piped up a younger male voice. "We never agreed—me and the boys don't hold with killin' women."

"Shut yer gobs and do as you're told," Sean Kelly told the others. "You're bein' well paid; that's all that counts."

"Why are you doing this to me?" She could already feel the soreness in her arms and legs from their brutal treatment.

"Did ya hear that?" Sean Kelly demanded of his brother. "Sure and she's got a mighty short memory. As if you and I don't have a list of things against anyone by the name of Fitzroy or O'Rahilly."

The circulation in her wrists was constricted by the tight leather thongs holding her upper body taut against the gnarled tree. Her struggles were useless, as the bleeding skin along her wrists proved. "Please let me go." Then her tactic changed as she turned her face to the right to glare up at the brutal men. "My husband will kill you for this."

Harsh laughter barreled out of Patrick Kelly. "From what I hear, he'll thank us for gettin' rid of an unwanted wife."

"Why, talk in town is that he don't even stay under the same roof with ya," Sean hissed near her ear. "Always thought ya were too English ta warm a man's bed. But here in the woods I'll make sure ye're more obligin'. Already promised the others they could watch us. Me and me brother have an old score to settle. And this should make sure ya stop snoopin' about the magistrate's office. Let Cartgrove do his job with the O'Hara brothers."

"But . . . if the O'Haras are in jail, who will be blamed for my death?" Millicent couldn't help asking.

"We'll find someone," Patrick Kelly whispered, then glanced quickly at the four other unsuspecting men. "No more of your words, yer ladyship," he finished in a taunting voice. Patrick Kelly stepped aside and nodded to his younger brother.

Sean pulled a lethal-looking knife from his tattered coat.

"No, please," Millicent cried when she felt her cloak and dress being brutally cut away from the back of her body.

"Ya owe me the pleasures I would a taken from O'Rahilly's sister that night ya interrupted me," Sean stated.

She wasn't brave, she thought. But there was no one to help her. Silently she prayed that the baby wouldn't be harmed. The night air felt cold on her warm flesh.

Sean moved closer behind her and rubbed his hand on her back. She whimpered when he reached around to pinch her right breast cruelly.

"Will ya stop pawin' her tits and mount her," Patrick Kelly complained. "We ain't got all night."

385

Over and over, Millicent repeated Taggart's name like a talisman for strength against the terror of what was about to happen. "Please find me. Taggart!" she sobbed, then heard a loud ringing in her ears, but the noise stopped as her body slumped lower.

Taggart had been writing a letter to Ben Abrams making arrangements for his return to Williamsburg. He stopped when he thought he heard Millie's voice. After putting down the quill pen, he moved the brass candlestick to the right. He touched his temple, then peered about the room. Had he heard her scream? God, what the devil was the matter with him? He didn't believe in all that superstitious nonsense that Edna and Colleen still adhered to.

He got up from the small round table and walked about the carpeted floor, no longer able to concentrate on his letter.

Then he smiled at himself. He was changing, for he'd spent the last few days working hard on the legalities to turn Fitzroy Hall back over to the new Earl of Fitzroy. It would be his wedding present to Edna and Dunstan. Strange, but he felt freer knowing he would no longer own the manor. If only he'd been able to shed more light on the earl's murder with equal success. It would not be easy to get Sir Jeremy to confide in him, for the magistrate, Taggart knew, looked upon him as a usurper at Fitzroy Hall. And he still hadn't located that bunch of hooligans who had robbed him that morning on his way to fight a duel with Dunstan. However, he now admitted, though he was still furious at the humiliation of being overtaken by a bunch of rowdies, he owed those men a debt of thanks. It just might have saved his life, for he'd never intended to fire a shot at Dunstan. But he now realized some of his former friends did not trust him in the same manner as the old days. They gave the briefest information, and he knew they were not telling all. And could he blame them? he challenged. For he'd been away nine years, and he was more American now than Irish. He'd return soon, he promised himself, even if he had to go alone, without his wife.

There it was again. Was he going mad to hear her voice when

there was no one in the room? He felt restless. Pehaps a ride might clear his head.

O'Rahilly had only gone about a mile on Fitzroy lands when he spotted the group of men beyond the clearing. Without hesitation he reached for the pistol he carried in his saddlebag and fired over his head. He knew he was too far away to hit anything in this dim light, but he hoped the sound would frighten whoever they were. "Chief Magistrate!" the Irishman bellowed, using an old trick that had saved his hide on more than one occasion, "bring your men over here." He knew his voice carried, and hoped the trespassers up to no good would be too scared to wait for confirmation of his bluff.

As he suspected, the commotion through the trees increased as the scared men sought to escape before His Majesty's troops overtook them. They ran like hares through the thicker part of the forest. He heard a few Gaelic expletives.

It was their way, he thought grimly. If they suspected one of their own had turned informer against a fellow Irishman, the more dangerous rebels would pay a call on the unfortunate sod and see he was duly punished. Had they been on Fitzroy land before? Could this be where they met and so successfully eluded capture until now?

However, his train of thought quickly turned to horror when he spied the crumpled heap against one of the trees. He slowed Laidir, not sure at first if it was human or animal. He dismounted a few feet away but lengthened his stride when he saw the human outline on the damp grass.

"Millie!" he cried, bending down to untie the slender arms still chaining her to the young tree. "My God, what have they done to you?" At first he was terrified that she might be dead, but a ragged breath escaped his lips when he felt the faint pulse at her soft white throat. "Can you hear me? Beloved," he whispered, the word coming out in a sob of pain.

Her reddish-brown lashes fluttered open. "Taggart?" she whimpered through cracked and bleeding lips.

He tried to soothe her with his voice. "Sure and who else would it be but himself chasin' after ya again ta fetch ya

387

home?" His reassuring tone almost slipped, forcing him to stop for a second. "I'll try not to hurt you, darling . . . but I've got to lift you."

"Oh, I prayed you would find me before Sean could . . ." A sharp, wrenching pain in her lower abdomen caused her to cry out. She clutched her stomach.

"Noooo!"

It was then that O'Rahilly glanced lower. Her green skirt and light petticoats were stained with a mixture of water and blood.

"Please, God, no!" Millicent cried. "It's too soon," she sobbed, in more agony than from her rough treatment by the Kelly brothers. "My baby. Not the baby."

Taggart forced his body to act, lifting his wife carefully in his arms. All the while her words lashed at his mind and his heart.

Dr. Liam Collins looked grave. "There—there are some things I must do to help Mil—her ladyship. If you do not wish—most men don't like to witness these things. This is the time for you to leave."

Taggart shook his dark head. "No, I'm staying. Just tell me what I can do to help."

"Your rescue came in time to prevent her from being raped, but, I'm sorry, Taggart, I can't save the baby."

When the O'Rahilly answered, he felt the smarting moisture near his eyes. "I . . . I knew it after I found her still tied to that cursed tree." He turned away from the doctor for a minute, clearly attempting to master his emotions. The cruel irony almost unmanned him. Those Irish scum had nearly killed her. His wife's lineage echoed through his tormented brain. Those bastards had harmed one of their own.

"Taggart?"

O'Rahilly turned to face the doctor, his haggard face looking far older than his years, but the control was back in his voice when he spoke. "I'm ready, Liam."

Without squeamishness, Taggart stayed and helped the doctor with Millicent.

As they tended her, it was Liam's professional mastery that slipped. "God, I'd like to kill those Kelly brothers. You'll have to see the magistrate. Does Dunstan know?"

"He and Edna haven't returned from Somerset's yet. I'll tell them in the morning." The doctor's remark got him thinking about the Kelly brothers. But he would need proof. He winced when Millie moaned, but he continued to place the herbal-soaked cloths on her torn flesh. If his suspicions proved true, he vowed, the Kelly brothers will wish they'd never been born.

The next few days passed in a blur for Millicent. She remembered sleeping intermittently, then something bitter tasting was given to her, and she fell back into a drug-filled sleep. All during those days and nights she heard Taggart's low, gentle voice near her. He talked to her about Williamsburg and the past when he had sailed to China and the South Seas. In English and Gaelic, he soothed her with his words. She could hear him and feel his presence when he turned her or bathed her, but she was far too weak to even open her eyes.

On the fourth day, she came slowly awake. Her throat felt dry, and she could hardly speak. She looked about their master bedroom. The room had been recently cleaned, for she could smell the rosemary on the white sheets. However, when she saw the man sprawled on the setee just a few feet from her, she was shocked. At first she hardly knew him. Even without her spectacles, she could see Taggart had at least three days' growth on his face. His black hair hung limp and lank as it touched the collar of a far from crisp shirt. In only open shirt, black breeches, and stained hose, he looked worse than she'd ever seen him. "Taggart, what ever has happened to you?" she croaked, her voice sounding strange to her.

He came awake with a start. His bloodshot eyes focused on her as she raised her naked upper torso. She held herself up with her slender arms.

Taggart came over to her immediately and sat on the edge of the bed. He reached out and brushed some of the auburn strands from her drawn face, poured her a cool glass of water, then helped support her as she drank it thirstily.

"Thank you," she said automatically. "Taggart, have you been ill, too? You look positively awful."

He couldn't hold back a sad smile. "I'm selfish I guess, for I wanted no one else to tend you."

Memory flooded at her when she tried to lean against the pillows. The cuts on her back showed her it was not a dream.

He dreaded this moment, but Taggart knew it had to be faced. Millie would settle for nothing less than the truth. "Darling," he whispered, taking her hand in his, "we lost the baby."

She knew, yet the words seemed to make the awful truth more painful. She bit her lip, pulled her fingers from his hand, and turned back to the pillow, pressing her face hard into the downy cushion. When she turned back to look over her shoulder, she couldn't read Taggart's expression.

He wanted to hold her, tell her of his grief at the news. Yet he felt awkward, not knowing what she wanted now. Before this had happened, that morning in this room, she had rejected him. Did she hate him? "You should never have interfered in these political matters, sparrow."

His words only added to her sorrow and the guilt she felt. He must blame her for the loss of the baby, she thought.

"Why didn't you tell me you were carrying our child?" he demanded, hurt and anger in his tone.

"I tried many times, but always . . ." She sat up, ignoring the pain this time as she pressed her tender back against the pillows and looked across at him. "You must admit things have remained strained between us for weeks. I thought it would only—complicate matters."

"Damn it, woman, you try my patience." He bounded off the bed, his voice becoming more audible. "If I were some nitwit with a broken leg, penniless orphan, or elderly curmudgeon, you'd confide in me. But since I'm who I am and you can never forgive me for forcing you to marry me, you'll ruin both our lives over your stiff-necked pride. And you'll risk your own life and our child's to spy for the English, who won't shed one tear over the death of another unwanted Irish brat. I thought once that we could have a true marriage." He sighed bitterly. "But I see that it is too late. Under the same roof, we only wound each other. It will be best if I leave Ireland."

His words of resignation cut at her. He did blame her for their baby's death. And part of her felt he was right, but she couldn't beg him to forgive her. And right now he sounded as if he did want them to live apart. Hadn't he just said it would be for the best—best for him, not her. But there it was. Tonight was one more thing that pulled them apart. "Perhaps it is for the best, all of it," she told him. "A child of mine would have only been one more encumbrance for you."

Encumbrance? He could hardly believe his ears as he stared down at her. Why, she sounded as if he wouldn't have welcomed the baby. He knew he shouldn't have yelled at her just now, but he blamed himself for not being there when she needed him. What kind of husband was he to let her go traipsing about alone? And it was only the grace of God that caused him to find her, for he didn't even live in the same house with her. "I'll send Bridget to you, then. It appears we'll only quarrel if I stay."

Without another word he left the room. Millicent whispered his name as she buried her face in the pillow and wept—for the loss of the baby and the only man she had ever loved.

Two days later, Millicent awoke to find a hastily written note next to her pillow:

My Lady, when you read this I will be on a ship for London. From there I'll be returning to Virginia where I belong. Dunstan and Edna already have my wedding present of Fitzroy Hall and a large sum to get them started. Your brother will not find Edna's dowry small, either. I have arranged with my solicitor to have all the money you desire at your disposal. Your brother has already told me he wishes you to remain at the manor. However, I believe it would be best for you to go abroad to Italy or France. I shall have Ben Abrams contact you shortly to make the arrangements. For the reasons we both know, you will be safer there than in Ireland.

It is no doubt difficult for you to believe, but I never meant to hurt you. I do wish you a happy life. My absence will more than likely insure it.

I shall always remain your friend.,

Taggart

Hardly able to finish the letter, Millicent's shock quickly
gave way to sorrow, then outrage. How dare he arrange her life
without even consulting her. And he hadn't bothered to see
that the Kelly brothers were brought to justice before he ran
off. She may have given the impression of spineless
acquiescence as a child, but she was a woman now and would
make her own decisions. If he did not love her, she would still
go on living. And she'd damn well choose her own future.

With a new determination she made up her mind to go to the
magistrate and have the Kellys arrested and then pursue her
leads about the death of both their fathers. Then she would
plan her future—and it would be her decision alone.

Dunstan and Edna were married with all the pomp and
ceremony of a formal English wedding. Though Dunstan was
reluctant, Edna had insisted on the Anglican ceremony, wisely
knowing her husband's position necessitated her outward
acceptance as a member of the Church of England.

Millicent agreed with Edna's choice. Privately, Edna could
practice her Catholic faith as Millicent did. It was the reason
she'd never told Dunstan of his Irish blood. His sense of honor
would certainly cause him to declare his Catholic heritage,
thus opening himself up to losing all his rights to Fitzroy lands,
as well as his influence to help those Catholic tenants on his
estate. Unlike Taggart, who was an American with King
George's close favor and had no plans to live in Ireland,
Dunstan could own the Fitzroy lands here only if his religion
was Anglican.

"What a pity Taggart could not be present."

Across from the banquet table, Millicent was calm as she
faced the white-faced woman. "My husband had neglected his
shipping business for too long. But his generous presence is
felt," she explained, thinking of his gifts to the newlyweds.

"Yet," Marigold went on, "I hear they are not even taking a

honeymoon. Perhaps they are becoming wiser with the use of their money. I am against waste."

"My brother and his bride wish to stay here in their new home. But I shall be traveling to London soon," Millicent added, trying to be polite. "They tell me David Garrick is opening in a new play, now that he's manager of Drury Lane Theater." Even though still not fully recovered, Millicent felt Dunstan and his new bride should have a time alone to enjoy their first days of marriage.

"Yes, quite," Marigold answered, then she darted a glance at the couple. "The new earl does look handsome."

Lady Millicent smiled when she looked down to the center of the long table to see her brother and sister-in-law. No two people were more suited to each other; their love showed clearly each time they glanced at each other. Edna's green eyes and deep dimples shouted her happiness. And Dunstan's persistent exercises had paid off, for he had not needed the cane for the wedding ceremony. Though he would still need its use occasionally, his limp was becoming less noticeable. Millicent was proud of her brother's maturity and inner strength. And she knew Taggart felt the same way. If only— well, it would do no good to dwell in the past.

"We are so glad you have recovered, my lady," John said on her right. "But why not come and stay with Marigold and me for a few days? You can always go to London much later. She still looks a little peaked about the cheeks, don't you think, my dear?"

"Yes, John." Marigold agreed. "Faith, you almost appear as fragile as myself. Do say you'll come."

At first Millicent was going to refuse, but the prospect of a longer trip did not appeal to her as yet. She still tired easily which was why she hadn't seen the magistrate yet about the Kellys.

"Thank you for your kind invitation. Yes, I should like to visit you very much." And perhaps she might find the proof she needed directly in the fox's den. She had little to lose now, she told herself.

"Splendid." John grinned broadly. "It's settled then. You can have your maid pack a bag and return with us tonight."

"Shan't I need to bring Bridget along?"

"Why, no, my dear, we have scads of servants," the Squire answered. "They'll be just you, Marigold, and myself to wait on. A cozy group, what?"

By the second night, Millicent felt she could no longer keep up the charade. So far, the squire and his wife had given her little oportunity to investigate. When he rode out each afternoon, Millicent could hardly maintain her polite smile, for she knew he went to meet the Duchess of Montrose. And Marigold, she realized, suspected nothing, as she chatted away and dragged Millicent along with her to visit friends who only conversed about their ailments.

It was just after the squire left and Marigold excused herself with one of her sick headaches that Millicent thought would be her only chance to slip into John's study.

Cautiously, Lady Millicent made sure none of the servants were about. They were a closed-mouthed lot, efficient but lacking the easy way of Millicent's servants who spoke readily with her. There was something eerie about the house—everything was far too orderly and quiet—John and Marigold ran it more like a mausoleum than a home.

When she tried the knob and it opened, she slipped inside and closed the door. She had not expected to see the shutters closed at this time of day. It left the room dark. Not sure what she hoped to find, she went over to one of the windows and opened a shutter halfway. The afternoon sun streamed through the window. Books lined the shelves, a large wooden desk and chair to the right. Leather chairs, plain homespun mat on the floor. For all their years in Kinsale, she hadn't remembered the Nolans ever having a party here. Indeed, she had never been in this house until now. Why did the Nolans live so reclusively? True, the furnishings were sturdy, yet . . . It appeared the Nolans did not hold for waste. No hints of gold or silver, few indications that this was a wealthy man's home. But she knew the squire was doing well—at least that was what she and other aristocratic families nearby believed.

After arriving at the desk, she was disappointed to find

nothing out of the ordinary. Her determination overcame her temerity, and she opened the middle drawer. Bills, a business letter, a deed, and ... She stopped and pulled out the document once more. It was a document stating that Fitzroy Hall and all its lands would now belong to John Nolan. It was dated months ago but there were no signatures on the document. Staring at it, Millicent began wondering why John Nolan would have—?

"So, I see you have found it at last," Nolan's voice came from the doorway.

The extent of her astonishment at the discovery had made her unaware until now that John had quietly entered the room and shut the door once more. Dressed in his earlier coat, it was clear today he'd intended no tryst with Garnet Huntington. Without flinching Millicent stood up from the plain wooden desk. Her gray eyes challenged him. She took the offensive. "Sir Jeremy tells me at the time of Shamus O'Rahilly's conviction you were the only one my father spoke with. And there is no one who remembers you pleading his case to any judge or lawyer." Her chin lifted. "In fact, I have now come to the conclusion it was you who falsified those documents against Taggart's father." She held up the expertly forged legal documents. "Another skill you've acquired over the years, I see. All you did was hand them to my father each morning when you drove him into court. He never suspected you'd forged those documents, did he?"

John walked closer into the room. "No, Geoffrey Fitzroy was never a complicated man. And he disliked Shamus as much as he loathed his arrogant son. However, your father could also be a stubborn old fool."

John opened his coat, giving Millicent a clear view of the lethal-looking sword that hung on his left hip. However, his words were almost congenial. "I've always thought you had a clever mind, my lady." John's hazel eyes were amused but cool. "What a pity you were born female. Dunstan will be more easily duped. I never counted on you being such a determined little snoop, dredging up old cases. And the townspeople love you so, not to mention that old fool, Calvert Huntington. No, I shall have to be careful how I dispose of you this time. If those two Kelly oafs hadn't bungled the job I paid them for, I wouldn't be in this tiresome predicament."

"Just like you handled my father's death."

John's smile was triumphant. "Quite so. The Englishman fingered the hilt of his sword. "I'd lent the ton of lard a fortune during the last two years, all with the understanding that I'd be repaid when you married that weakling, Edwin. I could easily have gotten Edwin and your father to sell both estates. They were both so unlucky at cards and investing. But then your father cheated me by letting you marry that . . . colonial. He said he got a higher offer from the damned Irishman. You see, your father never expected to have such a generous allowance and all his old debts settled. That had never been part of our bargain. I couldn't afford to best the offer, and your greedy father knew it."

"So you murdered him one night when you and he were out drinking together."

"Yes. No one crosses me, and I couldn't afford the financial loss. Your husband thinks nothing of tossing away a fortune. I, on the other hand, have not had his luck with investing.

"But Taggart started out with less than you."

Something sparkled in the handsome man's eyes. "But unlike your husband, I married a woman who controlled the purse strings. Marigold, you see, is a dried-up old miser. She only gives me a small allowance. The rest I must—well, let us say I have to seek my own comforts elsewhere."

Despite the danger, Millicent gave the man in front of her a level stare. "How tiresome Taggart and I must have proven to you."

"On the contrary, my dear. Because of your brother's sense of honor, that duel gave me an unexpected opportunity. If Dunstan failed to kill your husband, the pistol was set up to do the job when the Irishman fired it. What a pity you had to interfere. Imagine my worry when you insisted on firing the thing? But you made up for it when you pleaded with Garnet to see Taggart home."

John laughed outright as if he shared some private joke. "It was dear Garnet who thought of planting the piece from Taggart's waistcoat on Fitzroy's body. She's so handy with a

396

knife, cut the edge right off and made it look like a rough tear. However," he added, losing some of his congeniality, "again I hadn't counted on your blind loyalty to that husband of yours. A pity the gun hadn't killed you."

Millicent blanched when she realized the pistol's misfiring had not been an accident. Stepping away from the desk, she looked about the room, trying to plan a new strategy.

"There is no escape, my lady. I will arrange it to look like a suicide. I made certain you would have entry to this room and my desk. The grieving wife, distraught over losing your child, being abandoned by her husband. One of my servants will find you with a dagger in your heart, and I shall be distraught with grief that it should happen here—where my loving wife and I sought only to comfort you. I will tell Sir Jeremy how concerned we were over your despondency. Oh, it will be touching."

He had planned it well, Millicent realized. If she died now, all the secrets died with her, for she was the only one who knew the truth. She faced her murderer. "You will answer to God one day for your crimes, John Nolan. And see if I don't rouse your servants with my shouts."

Nolan appeared amused by her spirited response. "Go right ahead, my dear. However, I should warn you they've become used to the screams of tenants in this house. I've trained them well to mind their own business. And Marigold is probably fast asleep upstairs. No, we are all alone, my lady."

The brass knob of the study door turned and it rattled open. Frantic dark eyes scanned the room quickly. "Not quite alone, Nolan." Sword in his right hand, the black-haired O'Rahilly deftly moved into the room.

John Nolan looked as astounded as Millicent. "You were— my man saw you board that ship himself!"

Taggart locked the door and deposited the key in his waistcoat pocket before he answered. "I made certain he would," he answered smoothly. "I needed time to investigate on my own." He turned to his white-faced wife. "I'm sorry I had to deceive you, sparrow, but it was necessary."

Her husband's composure slipped. "But God in heaven, I aged ten years when I returned tonight and the newlyweds blithely informed me you were the guest of John and his wife. Christ, you do flirt with danger."

His hard eyes turned back to John. "I'll offer you a choice, Nolan. We fight it out here, or I'll take you into the magistrate for trial. I owe you that much, for we'd once been friends."

Nolan shrugged out of his coat, clearly making his decision. "You must know I'd never allow myself to be hung by the neck. I've always insisted on living like an English gentleman."

Terrified, Millicent could not believe her husband was going to fight a duel. It was too dangerous. "Taggart, please, don't do this."

"No, Millie, you will not interfere in this." Taggart's black eyes were hard stones. "Not even God himself could stop me." He removed his outer coat, waistcoat, and neckcloth, and placed them on top of Nolan's desk. "Take the key from my pocket and leave," he ordered.

"No, I cannot go. Please, my love, don't sent me away."

Taggart touched her cheek. "I've been such a blind fool, Millie. No matter what happens, will you remember that I loved you, even when my pride and stupidity kept me from seeing it?"

She read the open feelings in his face, and knew he spoke the truth. Tears misted her eyes. She nodded, then came into his open arms.

"A touching scene," John Nolan mocked from the other side of the room. "I shall almost regret having to kill you both."

Taggart moved his lady behind him, motioning her to a chair at the other side.

"By all means," John said, "have a seat, my lady, for I want you both to hear what I have to say before I kill you." When she was seated on the smooth wooden chair against the opposite wall, Nolan spoke again. "O'Rahilly, your father never told you I was responsible for his arrest because he knew I'd kill you if you even suspected the truth."

Standing only a few feet from John, Taggart reminded himself that Nolan was trying to bait him. He forced a sardonic smile on his lips as he casually held his sword in his right hand. "You play both sides against the other with the ease of an expert chessman. You've everything to gain if the English continue to control Ireland—wealth, power, and lands. Yet, you secretly stir the Irish rebels into more violence, knowing full well it will keep His Majesty more determined than ever to control them."

John's returning smile was taunting as he slashed the air almost playfully with his foil. "When your father found out I was working for the English, he threatened to tell his Irish friends I spied against my own. My own," the Irishman scoffed. "As if I had anything in common with those dirty, ignorant rabble."

Taggart gave him a level stare. "It's over, John. I now realize you forged that note to make Millicent believe her brother needed to see her in secret. If I'd played the outraged husband and abandoned her, you would have convinced Edwin to marry her after I'd gone back to Virginia. You and your accomplice have failed."

"Accomplice?" Millicent echoed, almost rising from her chair.

Chapter 27

Without looking at his wife, Taggart answered. "The duke's wife, Garnet, was so very . . . accommodating with information about us, my dear. And if my solicitor, Ben Abrams, is correct, she also earns a tidy sum for feeding Nolan's information on rebel activities to the very devoted Captain Bembridge."

Before she could stop herself the words were out. "But she was your mistress. Why would Garnet betray you?"

Taggart's black eyebrows rose in amazement, but it was John who spoke first, after he gave way to a harsh laugh at his opponent.

"Garnet, O'Rahilly's mistress? My lady, you must be mad? Why, Garnet hated your husband. It seems their mutual dislike goes back many years." His eyes mocked Taggart. John appeared to enjoy this encounter even more. A look of anticipation of the outcome showed clearly from his well-disciplined features.

"Oh, yes," John continued with obvious relish, "Garnet kept nothing from me. She told me how she enjoyed watching your frustration as she pranced in front of you. You see," he answered simply, "Garnet has always confided in me. I do believe she loves me, poor thing. Even thinks I'm going to divorce Marigold to marry her. The lovely duchess has spies everywhere. How do you think I knew about the Kelly brothers' hatred of you and your wife? It was she who proved so useful, having Sean toss that rock with her hand-written

400

message through your window."

Attar of roses, Taggart thought. That had been the faint scent he'd inhaled from the note just before he'd burned it. And John was responsible for the death of their baby. "Any compunction I had against dueling with you is gone forever, Nolan."

"Ah, there's that O'Rahilly temper. Yes," John encouraged, "let it out."

His words had the opposite effect on the black-haired man, for it served as a reminder. "In just a few moments Sir Jeremy and the Duke of Montrose will be arriving with redcoats to arrest you. I have learned to make contingency plans, you see."

For the first time, it was Taggart who looked self-satisfied. "I believe I neglected to tell you that the Kelly brothers have already confessed, John. It didn't take me long to convince them it was to their advantage," he added, a menacing gleam darkening the brown of his eyes. "They spilled their guts to the chief magistrate, with Calvert and myself as witnesses."

It was clear John had never expected this startling news. "I paid those two a king's ransom for their silence. I should have known I couldn't trust any Irish scum."

Taggart noticed the man now perspired more profusely through his lacy shirt. "I saw Garnet's carriage not far from here," he pushed. "No doubt she will be getting impatient for you to join her. You did have gall to meet on Fitzroy property. I wonder how she will explain herself when her husband finds her after the soldiers leave here? Of course, I regret having to hurt Calvert and your wife, but the truth will come out."

A fevered spark shone from Nolan's hazel eyes. "Not if you and that wife of yours are dead," he yelled lunging for the younger man.

"Taggart!" Millicent screamed. Forgetting all his commands, she began rushing to her husband's defense, for she read the increased danger in John's expression.

Taggart just managed to parry the other man's attack, then moved to the side. "Stay back!" he ordered his wife in a harsh tone that brooked no argument.

"But I love you. I always have."

401

In the briefest second, Taggart's dark eyes softened at Millicent as he held the sword firmly in his right hand. "Thank you for giving me that . . . my beautiful wife."

She saw the gratitude and joy in his warm brown eyes. Please, God, don't let him die, she prayed. Not now, when they'd finally recognized the truth about their feelings for each other.

The echoing sound of steel hitting steel reverberated throughout the sparsely furnished room. Millicent watched the equally matched males. In his late thirties, John Nolan was in excellent physical condition.

At first they appeared to be testing each other's skill. However, when his opponent's blade just missed Taggart's face, she bit her lower lip to keep from crying out.

Nolan lunged once more, this time pricking Taggart's arm through his white lawn shirt. But her husband pushed back against the other man so that their bodies locked. Nose to nose, each man tried to smash the other's face with his sword hilt.

"I'll enjoy killing you, O'Rahilly. Perhaps I'll even sample your wife's pleasures before I slit her throat."

Only the narrowing of Taggart's eyes gave evidence of the strong reaction he felt toward the other man's threat. "You'll never get the chance. You've harmed those I love for the last time." Abruptly, he backed away from his enemy.

When John came at him more vicously the next time, Taggart was ready. He knew John's type now, the way he aimed low then thrust upward to confuse his opponent.

The black-haired man moved his body to the right, while thrusting down and up. *"Fealltoir,"* he growled, then shoved the point of his sword deep into the other man's chest.

Millicent shivered at the coldness in her husband's voice when he'd hurled the word "traitor" at John.

Blood spurted from Nolan's chest and spattered Taggart's linen shirt. When the squire staggered back, his own sword clattered to the floor. A look of disbelief contorted the other man's face, as if he could not comprehend that Taggart had bested him. He gripped the sword, almost in an effort to pull it out, to change the destiny that awaited him.

Millicent rushed to her husband. She turned her face back to the dying man, but Taggart reached out an arm and moved her away from the grizzly scene. She saw the grim expression on his face and knew he'd little choice just now. John would surely have killed them both if Taggart hadn't stopped him.

She shuddered when she heard the low rattling sound from John's throat before he crashed to the wooden floor. His brown wig came off with his crumpled descent, exposing his shaved head. It lay next to him in a bloody pool.

"It's over now, thank God," Taggart whispered. "Can you ever forgive me for all the pain I caused you?"

She looked up into his tormented eyes. "I now realize I hurt you, too. You see, until now, I didn't know you loved me."

His dark eyes misted with tears. "I've loved you for years, but I was too blind to see it, too caught up in my desire to avenge my father's death. And because I always remember my rough beginnings, I never feel totally secure in the role of gentleman. I wronged you in so many ways, darling. Attributing Garnet's treacherous ways to you was the most unfair of all."

They heard the tread of boots and Sir Jeremy's voice outside the locked door. Marigold's high-pitched yell rose over the din as she pounded on the library door, demanding entry.

For a few seconds Millicent and Taggart stood in the center of the room holding each other, both giving and accepting strength for what they still had to face. But they would be together, she thought.

Millicent buried her face in her husband's black coat as they rode toward the Fitzroy lands, where Garnet would be waiting in her carriage. Having seen the way his blood-soaked shirt affected her, Taggart had insisted on tearing the thing off. The day was sunny and warm, he insisted.

"You do look like a pirate with just a frock coat covering your upper body." She studied him once more. In black boots and breeches, his dark chest hairs gleamed in the sun where his coat opened. "I shall always find you handsome. I suppose I'm romantic beyond redemption."

The indentation at his chin broadened when he smiled down

at his wife. "Just as I'll always find you beautiful, sweet sparrow."

"Oh, Taggart," she said, tears misting her eyes once more. "I . . . I do believe you now. It took me so long to finally accept that you truly love me." Too overcome, she buried her face into the edge of his coat once more.

"If Calvert and these redcoats weren't here . . ." he whispered, then let his words trail off. "Have you ever made love on a bed of wildflowers in a summer meadow?"

Their pace was unhurried, and the others were far enough behind to make their words private. She smiled up at him. "You know perfectly well I have not, since you have been the only man in my life. Of course, if I said yes, would your reaction be more interesting?"

He watched her saucy expression, reveling in its return. "I know you'll always be faithful to me—that is my pride and my delight, just as you are the only woman in my life." Then deviltry shone from his midnight eyes. "However, I anticipate making passionate love to you often to ensure you do not forget me."

"As if I ever could," she answered, enjoying the way he tightened his arm about her waist.

"God, I must get you home soon, else I'll shock the King's finest by taking my wife in the middle of this field."

She chuckled openly at his blatant admission.

"For shame," he teased. "Not even a ploy at appearing horrified at my suggestion?"

Not the least fooled by his censuring tone, his wife's smile became more impertinent. "You must remember, sir, until recently I received such words so rarely. In truth, I'm too happy at the discovery you feel so wonderfully lustful about me," she added without guile. "It does ever so much to restore my self-confidence."

"You know, my love," he murmured against her ear. "You are an impudent little hellion."

"Yes, I dare say." Millicent strained upward to place a warm kiss on his cheek. Then her expression became more serious. "I've missed you so much. I don't ever want to spend a night without you again."

Love and desire showed clearly on his face.

But just as quickly a frown etched across his features when they came upon Garnet's carriage. Hidden in a secluded area of trees and green shrubs, Taggart slowly led Calvert, the magistrate, and soldiers to the spot. The young male driver quickly descended from the top of the carriage. He looked wary and ready to defend his mistress to the death. Taggart suspected Garnet had probably bribed the boy into loyal silence . . . and perhaps not just with gold coins.

"We mean you no harm, lad," Taggart shouted from the distance. "We're here to speak to your mistress."

Taggart dismounted and gently lifted Millicent from his horse.

Millicent glanced at Calvert, who dismounted his horse without assitance. For a man of seventy, Calvert was showing a surprising degree of stamina. But then he'd always shown more strength than his physical appearance indicated. "Taggart, why did the duke insist we all return here with him? Surely, this is a painful confrontation, better suited to privacy between husband and wife?"

In a low tone, Taggart answered her. "He still loves his wife, darling. If she confesses to being tricked by Nolan in front of Sir Jeremy, there will be no need to involve her in a trial. I told Calvert that if you agree, we will not bring formal charges against her."

Millicent searched her heart. "Though I shall never be able to forget what she did to us and the sorrow she caused, I . . . I do not seek Garnet's death. It would not bring back our baby." She was forced to remain silent for a few seconds while she attempted to compose herself. Then she nodded. "I agree; let God judge her. I'll not be the instrument for having more blood spilled."

Irish and English—Taggart knew he loved both parts of his wife. He raised her hand to his lips, his eyes promising that he would say and do more later.

When Calvert came to stand next to her, Millicent looked down at him with sympathy. It was clear the news of his wife's

405

unfaithfulness and treachery was an unexpected blow.

"Millicent agrees, Calvert." It was not a sign of disrespect to refrain from using his title. Taggart felt they'd gone beyond formalities this day.

"I . . . I am deeply grateful to you both," Calvert said in a low rasp. "And I give you my word Garnet will never hurt either one of you again."

"I'll not give her the chance," Taggart vowed as he continued to keep a supporting arm around his wife's shoulders. "If my wife agrees, I wish to take her back home to Williamsburg to live. I've learned I'm an American now, and Ireland is no longer a place where both of us can live in peace."

"Oh, yes," Millicent cried, "I will go with you."

The Irishman studied his wife's expressive face. "You'll not mind leaving your home, for I know how fond you are of Ireland? It had your heart long before I did."

Tears misted her eyes as she moved closer to him. "I'm sure there will be times I'll miss the green hills and the people I love here, but . . . I'll always feel I'm home if we're together."

"My dearest love," Taggart said in a husky voice. He squeezed her hand gently, almost forgetting they were not alone. "I shall try to make you happy."

"You are a very lucky man," the duke stated, emotion cracking his gravelly voice. "Would that my wife were half as honorable as yours—let's get this business over with."

The magistrate and his men stayed a respectful distance, so they would not hear the private conversation between the four people. Calvert, Millicent, and Taggart walked slowly over to the coach.

Calvert winced when he saw the familiar ornate seal of Huntington on the coach. Apparently, his wife now felt so sure of her ability to deceive him, she saw no reason to refrain from using their own carriage on these outings.

But before he could clutch the shining brass coach handle, the door opened from the inside.

Garnet stepped out, dressed beautifully in aqua satin, matching gloves, and straw hat decorated with blue flowers.

Millicent almost felt sorry for her. It was clear she had no idea what had happened.

"Why, Calvert, what a surprise. Thank heavens you've come. We had a little trouble with one of the wheels. Perhaps one of these gallant gentlemen will help—"

"Stop it, Garnet," Calvert cut off with uncharacteristic severity. "The charade is finished. I've been a blind fool. But no more." He took in a deep breath, his lined face looking paler than usual. "I've come to tell you that your lover, John Nolan, is dead."

Garnet's high tinkling laughter carried to the men in the distance, who stood at attention near the chief magistrate. "Why, what ever are you talking about? For shame, husband, playing a joke in front of those young, impressionable soldiers. And what will Lady Millicent think, living the life of a nun? Why, to even jest that I have a lover—how mean of you." The high-pitched giggle followed.

Millicent felt ill as she watched Garnet's pathetic efforts to trick her way out of the situation. She gave Taggart a grateful look when he took one of her cold hands in his.

Calvert appeared dispassionate as he studied his flirtatious wife, almost for the first time. He then looked down indifferently at a spattering of mud on the white stocking covering one of his spindly legs. "There is no joke here, except if it is the old man who thought he could happily wed a young, beautiful wife." His wig-covered head snapped back up. "I thought you chaste," he accused, losing some of his control. "My young white rose. But you have proven yourself false, lying, and scheming to get what you want—wealth, a title, a misguided revenge on these two fine people. You are a stranger to me, madam. I do not know you, and I am now convinced I never wish to partake of that privilege. But for good or ill we are tied together for life," he added grimly. "I will not allow the Huntington name to be tarnished any more than you have seen fit to do so until today."

All trace of coquettishness vanished from Garnet's petite features. "It . . . it is true, then. John Nolan is . . . dead? How could such a thing happen?"

Blunt and to the point Calver answered. "John drew his

sword first. Taggart O'Rahilly had little choice but to defend himself and his lady wife."

A wild look came into the blond woman's eyes, and she screamed, a bloodcurdling sound of an animal in pain. "Noo, he can't be dead! Oh, John, I can't live without you." She buried her face in her gloved hands as she vented her painful rage at this terrible news."

"Come, you mustn't carry on so in front . . ." Calvert's voice trailed off.

Instantly, the duchess dropped her hands to her side as she glared at her husband. "You old fool, what do you know of love? John was a real man of flesh and blood." Her voice spewed venom. "I'd have played the whore for him any time or any place. Do you know he made love to me one night while you slept upstairs?" The wild look came back into her icy blue eyes. "He took me on the carpeted floor like a common strumpet, and I begged him for it. Yes," she taunted, "in all the ways I could never love you. You're not a man. The only thing you're good for is a title and money. My one consolation is that you'll die soon and then I can begin to really live again."

Millicent knew the woman was distraught over John's death, but Garnet's revelations made her ill. "Please, Taggart, can't we leave here?"

"Soon, my darling." He knew Millicent was physically shaken by this scene. "Let us see if we can't hurry this confrontation.

"Your husband has asked us to be present so that a formal inquiry in court can be avoided." In a lower tone, Taggart warned, "I'd advise you to cooperate, Garnet. If you tell him John coerced you into helping him, it will go easier for you. I know you wrote the note telling me where to find my wife that night. But I also know what it is to love, for if you taught me anything it was to make me realize how different my wife is from you, thank God. Though you deserve punishment, you have my gentle wife to thank for our restraint, for it is she who urges us to let you go and have a quick end to this sordid business."

At the mention of Millicent, Garnet's lips compressed.

"Your sainted wife," she scoffed. "Are you here to bring the lamb down, too?"

Millicent looked down at the beautiful woman and suddenly realized there was nothing about Garnet she envied. Taggart loved her and though, to the world, she knew she was not a beauty, in her husband's eyes she was the woman she'd always romanticized about becoming. She was lucky, indeed. "I have no wish for anything but to go home with my husband. We will never be friends, your grace, but I will not seek your death."

Hatred sparked from Garnet's cornflower-blue eyes. "Spare me your platitudes. So, you love your husband, do you? I wonder. How loyal would your husband be if he knew you played the highwayman that early morning he was on his way to fight a duel of honor?"

Millicent shut her eyes against the anguish she experienced from Garnet's attack. Completely unprepared, she shivered when she could finally take in her husband's shocked expression. She'd forgotten this awful secret that Garnet had sworn never to reveal. When she felt Taggart let go of her hand, she wanted to beg him to forgive her, but she forced herself to stay calm. The old Fitzroy reserve in the face of adversity was a difficult habit to break.

A muscle worked at Taggart's jaw as he wrestled with his anger. Until now, he'd always attributed the assault and robbery to a band of starving Irish hooligans, which was mainly why he'd not pressed Sir Jeremy to find them, though the honest servant of the King had promised to find the culprits and bring them to justice. This new information stunned him beyond words and just as quickly he felt a mounting fury that his slip of a wife had dared commit such an outrage against her own husband. *"Leasu."*

Millicent knew he had every reason to be furious, well, upset, yet she hoped they could talk about this later in private. Reconciliation was so recent between them, she felt heartsick that this information had to come out now.

Garnet looked pleased with herself. "Given the punishment for highwaymen during these difficult times in Ireland, I am sure my dear Sir Jeremy will know what to do with you, Millicent."

God, Taggart thought, he had no intention of seeing his wife or their Irish friends turned over to the English authorities. And he tried to remember Millie had acted to save both him and her brother. How was he going to get them out of this new predicament?

The Irishman cleared his throat. "Though it injures my pride a bit to learn my wife had arranged to have me miss my dueling appointment, I know love for her brother and me forced her to such action. I will press no charges against her. Therefore, it appears we all have reason for silence on these matters." He addressed the duke. "Calvert, Millicent and I will not press charges against your wife for deliberately forging that note which led Millie into danger at Mistress Alice's." His dark eyes narrowed. "Had she been seriously injured in that brothel, Garnet, not even the magistrate could stop me from killing you myself. Now, is it agreed that we will all remain silent?"

Calvert and Millicent gave their assent quickly.

"Garnet?" O'Rahilly pressed.

"If you wish to remain as the Duchess of Montrose," Calvert warned his wife, "with the wealth and status of that position, I should advise you to comply. Even your father would disown you if he found out about your scandalous conduct. Do you agree to be silent?" he demanded.

Clearly Garnet could see there was little choice right now. "Oh, very well then. I will not speak on this matter."

Taggart's body seemed to lose some of its tenseness. "And now, I am taking my wife home. He shook Calvert's hand. "You, Dunstan, and Millicent have showed me I was wrong to hate all English."

"Yes," Garnet spoke up, clearly trying to gain the advantage again. "When you get to know more Englishwomen better, you'll find they can be very agreeable." She wet her pink lips, and her blue eyes devoured his muscular, bare chest.

Taggart hardly looked at her, but he placed a protective hand on Millicent's arm. "Since my wife is the only Englishwoman I shall be close enough to judge, I will certainly never be in the position to test your theory."

At that moment Milicent realized Garnet still desired Taggart. She almost felt sorry for her. And she knew Taggart had spoken the truth. He wanted nothing ever to do with Garnet.

Calvert cleared his throat. "Do not look so pleased with yourself, madam," he said to his wife. "Since you are clearly under some misapprehension about imminent widowhood, let me clarify something. My doctors tell me I am in excellent health and should live at least as long as my father and grandfather." His eyes were clear and cool as he watched his wife's changed expression. There was a certain grim satisfaction as he stated, "All the Huntington men lived to well in their nineties. So you see, my devoted wife," he bit out, "we have at least twenty or so more years of marital bliss ahead of us. And I can assure you, I shall keep a closer watch on you from now on."

Well, Milicent thought, as she allowed Taggart to lead her away, it appeared Garnet was not coming out of this unscathed. She'd lost John Nolan, whom it was clear she really loved, and her husband, Calvert, was going to hold her on a tighter leash from now on.

As Taggart toweled his wife's long reddish-brown hair, he spoke of his love again.

Milicent reveled in this new intimacy between them. He raced them here on his horse, barely saying two words to the servants before he hustled her upstairs to their rooms. Dunstan and Edna were obviously pursuing a similar evening, as Caleb had informed them that the earl and his new bride had already retired for the night.

Her skin still tingled where Taggart had touched and kissed her. Sitting on a brocade-covered bench before the fire, she sighed happily as the man standing over her gently dried her straight hair. "You would make a skilled ladies' maid, Taggart, though I fear my petticoats are ruined beyond mending."

He tossed the towel to the floor and drew her up to stand

411

before him. "In truth I could not wait another second without taking you." He grinned as he remembered the fierceness with which he'd loved her and her passionate response. When she'd modestly protested she needed a bath first, he showed her just how much he needed her right then and could not wait, as the bath surely would.

"Dunstan's old breeches and shirt were easier to get out of," she commented wistfully.

"If I give them back to you, sweet elf, do you promise only to wear them for me in the privacy of our bedroom?"

"What! You did not burn them?" Her gray eyes sparked with surprised happiness.

He shook his head. "I meant to, but the arousing memory of the way they hugged every delectable curve of your healthy body stopped me. Right now your precious clothes are hidden at the bottom of the chest at the foot of our bed." He laughed when she made a motion in that direction. "Later. Besides, you haven't given me your promise as to their use."

"I promise," she said. Delighting in his body, Millicent buried her face in the glistening dark hairs across his chest. "You smell deliciously of my lavender soap." She giggled as she pressed her naked breasts closer. "Thank you for making love to me so expertly."

He chuckled at the polite tone that came so naturally to her, no matter the circumstances. "You're quite welcome, my lady. It is my intention to do this often, especially during our voyage to America."

"And after we reach Williamsburg, too, I hope." She kissed the area of his chin where his dimple beckoned her. "I love you."

His eyes misted as he studied her endearing face. Without her glasses, her eyes took on a smoky hue. He loved the feel of her alabaster skin as he ran his fingers down her back.

The lady realized what he was about, and a faint smile played at the corners of her mouth. Stepping back from her handsome husband, she eyed him up and down. Hands on her hips, she walked about him. "Yes, you are a magnificent Irish Stallion. The name does suit you, you know?"

Rich laughter rumbled from his chest. He grabbed her and scooped her up in his arms. "As long as you're the only one to call me that—and in the privacy of our bedroom, I shall do my best to live up to the name." Walking back over to their large bed, he placed her in the center before joining her.

The Irishman leaned over and claimed her lips in a long, fiery kiss. His tongue caressed hers with the promise of more delights.

Running her hands through the thick black hair that just touched his shoulders, Millicent remembered something. "Taggart, ah, we still haven't—I mean, the time you were going to love me a certain way, you know, we never did finish it in that manner."

He couldn't help smiling when Millicent blushed as she tried again to ask for what she wanted. "Are you hungry? Would you like me to have Bridget bring you some mutton or cheese?" he asked solicitously, a look of innocence on his clean-shaven face.

"No, thank you, it isn't food I want." She felt embarrassed that he didn't comprehend what she was requesting. Raised a certain way, it wasn't easy to say the bold words outright. Only infrequent losses of temper had ever freed her to say those type of words. This was different.

Finally he took pity on her. The Irishman kissed her heated cheek. "I should not tease you so, sweet sparrow, but you have the most endearing ways about you. So," he whispered close to her ear, "you wish to complete our game of stallion and mare, is that it?" He ran his tongue along her delicate earlobe.

"Yes, oh yes," she answered, relieved and delighted he understood. "I want that very much. At different times during the last few weeks, I've dreamt about it, then came awake only to find myself alone in the next room." The tender love showing from his eyes gave her more courage. "I felt like crying when I stared at the door, knowing you were only a few feet away from me, yet I didn't know then that you loved me."

"I understand," he soothed, moved by her words, "for I felt the same way. We must never let pride separate us again, darling. I need you too much."

413

Then Taggart O'Rahilly took his passionate wife a second time in this new, exciting way.

If the servants heard anything amiss from the two couples enjoying connubial bliss upstairs, they were far too polite to comment directly. Though Fergus Mulcahy was seen nudging and winking at his wife as he stared at the four happy young people having a scandalously late breakfast the next morning.

Now you can get more of HEARTFIRE right at home and $ave.

<u>FREE</u> Preview Each Month and $ave

Zebra has made arrangements for you to preview 4 brand new HEARTFIRE novels each month...FREE for 10 days. You'll get them as soon as they are published. If you are not delighted with any of them, just return them with no questions asked. But if you decide these are everything we said they are, you'll pay just $3.25 each— a total of $13.00 (a $15.00 value). **That's a $2.00 saving each month off the regular price.** Plus there is NO shipping or handling charge. These are delivered right to your door absolutely free! There is no obligation and there is no minimum number of books to buy.

TO GET YOUR FIRST MONTH'S PREVIEW... Mail the Coupon Below!